Also by Mia Sheridan

AVAILABLE FROM BLOOM BOOKS

Travis

Kyland

Stinger

Grayson's Vow

Becoming Calder

Finding Eden

Stinger

MIA SHERIDAN

Bloom books

Published by Bloom Books, an imprint of Sourcebooks
P.O. Box 4410, Naperville, Illinois 60567-4410
(630) 961-3900
sourcebooks.com

Originally self-published in 2013 by Mia Sheridan.

Printed and bound in the United States of America.
KP 10 9 8 7 6 5 4 3 2

This book is dedicated to my daughter, Lila Anne. Always listen to your heart, break the rules once in a while, and know you are loved. Life is wild, baby girl, just as it should be.

♏

THE SCORPIO LEGEND

Scorpio is the only sign that has three different animal symbols, each of which represents a different stage of the Scorpio transformation. First, the scorpion, symbolizing the raw energy of the sign. The scorpion's sting is defensive and reactionary, and often, because of its selfish nature, it is completely unaware of its own power and impact. As the scorpion learns to control its sting and hold its instincts at bay, it becomes the eagle. The eagle, though still cold, has more perspective; it flies high above the ground, using its power deliberately and purposefully. Finally, the eagle becomes the dove. The dove is a tranquil creature, recognized as a bringer of peace and worthy of leadership. The dove becomes the dove only after it gets what it wants most in the world. Scorpios, above all others, have the ability to transform selfish poison into universal love.

PART 1

CHAPTER 1
Grace

Las Vegas, Nevada

As I walked into the luxurious Bellagio Resort and Casino, tired and rumpled from my flight, I saw two signs directing guests to the conferences being held that weekend. There was the one I was in town to attend, the International Law Students Association Conference, and then there was another one, the Adult Entertainment Expo. Well. *I guess that's Vegas for you,* I thought. *Where you can see everything from law students and tourists, to porn stars, and perhaps even aliens from distant planets. It hadn't taken me long to realize—just walking through the airport actually—that* when it came to the City of Sin, shock value was practically nonexistent.

If I didn't figure that out from the pantless man the cops were chasing through the airport upon my arrival, then I definitely got it from the G-stringed Elvis impersonator who flew by me on roller skates as I stepped from my shuttle in front of the hotel. "You're not in Kansas anymore, honey," the driver had said, laughing as my head swiveled to watch the rolling, half-dressed Elvis glide away.

Apparently not.

As I walked farther into the lobby, my mouth dropped open and I halted as my head fell back. The ceiling was filled with the most stunning glass blossoms—hundreds of them in every color imaginable. I moved in a circle, my breath halted, unable to look away from the gorgeous, overhead art. *Wow.*

When I finally tore my eyes away from the ceiling, I realized there was beauty everywhere. I was so completely awestruck by the stone pillars and gallery of fresh flowers and floating hot-air balloons behind the check-in that I almost didn't hear the woman desk clerk call out to me. I wheeled my small suitcase up to the counter and smiled brightly at her. "Grace Hamilton. I have a reservation."

The desk clerk smiled back. "Okay, let me just look you up… Okay, here we go. You're here for the law student conference starting tomorrow?"

"Yes."

"What school do you go to?" she asked as she took my credit card and swiped it quickly.

"Georgetown," I said, returning the card to my wallet.

"Great school! Well, have a good time. You're on the twenty-sixth floor, checked in until Monday. Checkout time is noon. Here's a folder for those attending the law student conference. You'll find a schedule, a name tag, and some other information you might find handy for this weekend."

"Thanks," I said, taking the folder and then grabbing my suitcase handle before turning to walk toward the elevators. As I rounded the corner, I ran smack-dab into a hard, male chest. "Oh, gosh! I'm so sorry!" I exclaimed.

"No, I'm sorry—" he started to say at the same time.

Our eyes met and we both fell silent, me blinking as he steadied me with both hands on my upper arms.

He was about my age, twenty-three or so, with sandy-colored hair that was just a little too long and curling up at the ends, and one of those handsome faces that manages to be both manly and boyish at the same time. Simultaneously rugged and pretty. *Double wow.* His hazel eyes were fringed with thick, dark lashes, and his full lips were curved into a half-smile.

I cleared my throat, pulling myself together as I managed to quickly take in his frame. He was lean but muscled, clad in dark jeans and a conservative, button-down, white shirt, sleeves rolled up.

He stared at me for a couple beats and something in his expression seemed to soften as my eyes moved back to his and his smile grew bigger, revealing a small dimple to the left of his bottom lip. He bent to pick up the key card I had dropped when we collided.

As I watched him scoop up my card, the strangest feeling washed over me, almost like déjà vu, like we had met before. I frowned, confused by the odd sensation, wondering if he was a law student that I had seen in passing at school, here for the same conference. Yes, that had to be it.

He straightened, holding the key card out to me, and I caught sight of the name tag clipped to his shirt. "Oh, you *are* here for the conference," I exclaimed. "I thought I might—" And that's when I read it: *Carson Stinger, Straight Male Performer, Adult Entertainment Expo.*

I stared at the words for a couple beats, re-arranging them, *digesting* them, and then meeting his eyes once more. He was smirking now and his eyes no longer held that softness I had seen just a minute before.

I pulled my shoulders back. "Well, then, I'm sorry again for the...uh, not watching where I was..." I let out a small, uncomfortable laugh, beginning again. "Well, have a good time...er, a nice time, um, enjoy"—I gestured toward his name tag—"the show. Or rather, not the show, but the... well, enjoy the weekend."

What the hell was wrong with me? I was never flustered like this! I was going into law because I was good at finding the right words under pressure. And here a good-looking, *straight-male,* porn star rattled me so much, I could barely form a coherent sentence?

And that's when he burst out laughing, deepening that tiny dimple by his mouth. "I will, buttercup. And you enjoy your weekend too. Let me make a wild guess, law student conference?"

I had started to walk around him but stopped when I heard the clearly condescending nickname and the amusement in his voice. "Yes, actually. Is there something wrong with that?"

"No, not at all. Looks like we're both here to hone our skills when it comes to *getting people off.*"

My brows snapped down. *Ah, a double entendre. How clever.* "Well that's...that's a disgusting way to put it."

He moved closer to me until I was forced to step back. "Why? Getting people off is such a rush, buttercup. Don't be ashamed of wanting to do it well."

I coughed and narrowed my eyes. *Eww.*

I tapped his nametag with my index finger. "I do a lot of things well, *Carson,* none of which I'm ashamed of," I said, leaning into him so that he knew I wasn't going to be intimidated by his blatant, juvenile, sexual innuendos.

He stared at me for a beat, that amused glint still in his

eyes, and then grinned, slow and sexy as his eyes dipped to my cleavage. "I bet." He took that full bottom lip between his teeth and looked back up at me.

I gawked at him for a second because I felt my nipples get hard under my white blouse and I did not appreciate that. Not one bit. I was going to have a talk with my body later and lay down the law. There was absolutely no getting turned on by porn stars purposefully trying to shock and intimidate for no apparent reason. Porn stars! People who had all kinds of sex in front of cameras! It was indecent. The fact that any small part of him turned me on pissed me the hell off. I saw his eyes travel downward again, this time to my puckered nipples showing easily through the thin material of my blouse, and his smirk got bigger. I flushed in irate humiliation.

I made a frustrated, angry sound in my throat and marched away from Carson Stinger, Straight Male Performer.

A cool shower helped me calm down from my lobby run-in. When I felt levelheaded again, I toweled off and then changed into my brand-new black bikini and white crochet cover-up, before heading out to the pool. My conference didn't officially start until the next morning, so I planned on spending several hours lying in the sun, reading and relaxing. The life of a law student didn't leave a lot of room for R & R and so I was going to take advantage of it while I could.

It took me about twenty minutes to simply walk through the pool area and decide where I wanted to sit. There were five pool courtyards, luxurious cabanas, umbrellas over plush seating, and rows of lounges, all with the same Mediterranean design. It was breathtaking and I tried my best not to walk through with my mouth hanging open at all the opulence.

My dad was a police officer and a single parent, who raised me and my two sisters on his own after he and my mom divorced. We never wanted for anything, but we certainly didn't have the money to vacation. In fact, until I left for college, I had never been out of Dayton, Ohio, where I grew up.

After stopping at the bar for an oversized virgin daquiri, I parked myself on a lounger with some shade and started lathering my pale skin with sunscreen. I had been holed up in libraries and classrooms for months, not to mention the desert sun was no joke.

I had just read a couple pages of my book when my phone rang. *Abby* came up on my screen.

"If you saw where I was right now, you'd be so jealous," I said in greeting.

She laughed. "Well, hello. If you saw where *I* was, you so *wouldn't* be jealous. I won't make you guess—I'm still an itchy, calamine-spotted vision of loveliness, splayed out on the couch." I groaned on her behalf. Poor Abby had gotten poison ivy while hiking with her boyfriend, Brian. "But back to you," she went on. "Let me see... I swear I smell coconut and hear the gentle lapping of water—poolside with a drink in hand?"

I laughed. "Bingo."

"But wait, what is that? What is that I see? A textbook in your hands instead of a steamy romance? The horror. Please tell me I'm wrong."

I looked down at the large textbook sitting open in my lap, *Concepts & Insights Series: Administrative Law.* "Oh stop, you know that I have to study this weekend if I'm going to ace this summer course. Anyway, this place, Abs, it's outrageous. Truly. We have to come back here and stay for longer than a weekend. And I'll promise not to bring my textbooks, okay?"

"Hmmm. The reality of getting you away for a weekend that doesn't involve textbooks? I'm skeptical. But a girl can dream. What happens in Vegas stays in Vegas, right? The debauchery sky's the limit—I'm in."

I laughed again. Abby and I had met on a roommate search site when I had first moved to DC and not only hit it off as roommates but had become best friends as well. She was funny and sweet and just slightly outrageous when she wanted to be. She was good for me. I considered her my third sister.

"I'm sure you are," I said. "Speaking of which, there's another conference at this hotel. You'll never guess what it's for."

"What? Do tell."

I looked around quickly to make sure no one was listening in on my call and then mentally shook my head at myself. This was Vegas; no one was going to blink when I said the word *porn*. Still, I whispered, "A porn convention."

Abby let out a loud guffaw. "Oh my God, Grace, you've gotta get me some autographs. Please!"

"What? Whose autograph do you want exactly?"

"No one in particular. I just want to be able to say a porn star wrote a note to me."

I let out a short laugh. "Actually, I ran into one in the hotel lobby. Literally. He was a total ass."

"Why? What'd he say to you?"

"Ugh. Just made some disgusting suggestive comments and then gave me a look that made me want to take a shower." *A cold shower.* But she didn't need to know that, and I was trying to forget.

Abby laughed. "Was he a greasy-looking Ron Jeremy type?"

I paused. "Actually, no, he was a jerk, for sure, but, well"—I lowered my voice to a whisper—"he was hot. I actually didn't know porn stars *were* hot. I guess I figured if you were doing a job like that... I don't even know what I thought. But he is not what I pictured a porn star to look like."

"Why, Grace, I do believe you're blushing."

"Oh, shut up, you can't even see me."

"I know you, girl, you're blushing. Now get off this phone and go find you some hot porn star. I bet he could teach you some new tricks up in your hotel room tonight."

I groaned. "Oh God, no, Abby. I wouldn't touch a porn star with a borrowed body. Especially one as cocky as him."

"You're no fun."

"When it comes to porn stars, no, I'm not." I laughed. "Seriously, you doing okay?"

"Yeah, I'm fine. Brian's coming over in a little bit and we're gonna see how sexy we can get using nothing except our privates and our feet—the only places I'm not covered in rash."

I laughed out loud. "Oh God, did I need that visual? Okay, have fun. I'll see you Sunday, okay?"

I heard the grin in her voice as she said, "Okay, babe, talk tomorrow."

"Bye, Abs," I said, still smiling as I hung up the phone.

———

I spent a couple hours at the pool, finishing my studying and taking notes so that I could review them on the plane home. Even though I was doing schoolwork, just sitting out in this gorgeous location, sipping a frozen cocktail, felt decadent. I never did things like this. I had been pushing myself like crazy for the last five years and I barely had time to breathe, much less sit by a pool for an afternoon. First, I had had my head in a book for four years through college, pushing myself to graduate magna cum laude and earn a scholarship to one of the top law schools on my list. Once that was accomplished and I had started at Georgetown, I began pushing myself yet again—only this time it was because my goal was to graduate in two years, take and pass the bar on my first try, and be recruited into a top law firm in Washington, DC. It was The Plan. I'd always had a plan, and I never strayed from it. Never. And once I achieved one, I moved on to the next.

As I lounged, my damn mind drifted to Carson Stinger, Straight Male Performer, several times. It still irked and confused me that he had frazzled me so much. And in only about two minutes! What was that about anyway? No one frazzled me. I was un-frazzle-able. I was frazzle-less. I prided myself on being cool, calm, and collected. And suddenly, a porn star who looked at me lasciviously had me stuttering and stammering and running for safety? It was beyond irritating. And the further fact that he had turned me on was completely maddening. *Seriously, Grace, is that how desperate you are? That a good-looking porn star whispers a few allusive sentences to you and your panties are wet? God!* I lay back on my lounge chair, crossing my arms, frowning and squinting up into the blue Nevada sky. After minute, I shoved my sunglasses on my face, and closed my eyes, forcing my mind to go over the material I'd studied.

After a little bit, I got up and started to gather my things, and pulled my sundress on over my suit. My shoulders had a definite pink tinge and I needed to get inside and start thinking about dinner plans.

As I walked past the entrance to the lounge, the cool quiet called to me. I hesitated. A visit to the bar hadn't been on my personal itinerary, but the air conditioning inside felt wonderful, and now that my studying was done, a margarita with an actual shot of tequila sounded like just the thing.

I took a seat at the elegant bar and glanced around. It wasn't very crowded for a late Friday afternoon, but presumably, people were probably still out by the pool or getting ready for dinner. "What can I get for you?" The bartender asked with a smile, placing a napkin down in front of me.

"A margarita, please. On the rocks. No salt." The bartender turned away with a nod and I took a deep breath and joined my hands in front of me on the bar, smiling a contented smile. This was definitely more my speed than the whizzing, dinging, atmosphere in the casino just beyond.

"No salt?" a voice from my left said. "Who orders a margarita with no salt?"

My smile evaporated and I swiveled my head, leaning around the gentleman a couple stools down and staring at the one just past him. *Seriously?* "Why, if it isn't Carson Stinger, Straight Male Performer," I said. I groaned inwardly. *No, no, this is good, Grace. You've been given another chance to heal your wounded pride. Come out of this exchange on top—so to speak. Gah. Everything was a porn pun now.*

He was staring at me strangely, waiting for me to say something, a look on his face that was amused yet watchful.

I raised an eyebrow. "If you're considering telling me you've got something for me that's nice and salty, please restrain yourself. Predictability bores me." I turned as the bartender placed my drink in front of me and I took a long sip.

Carson chuckled. "I doubt it."

He doubted it? He doubted what? That predictability bored me? I opened my mouth to say something but snapped it shut. He was right. I loved predictability. I lived for it, actually. Before I'd come up with a response, he was moving down the bar with his beer in hand to take the stool right next to me. I turned to glare at him.

"What I was actually going to say, buttercup, was that you're really missing out ordering a margarita without the salt. It's all about licking the salt off the rim and then sucking the sweet liquid through the straw. The contrast of sweet and salty on your tongue is so, so good." He leaned closer to me as he lowered his voice. "Try it once, just once. You'll never want it any other way."

Okay, now he was just trying to get a rise out of me. And why? What exactly had I done to this man? I seethed, even angrier at the fact that his words were turning me on—again. My traitorous body liked his damn, deep, sugary voice and purposefully titillating words. And the way he smelled, that was nice too. *Stupid body!*

"Let me buy you one," he offered, his lips curving. "Seriously. Just one drink my way. You can do a taste test and see who's right. We can get to know each other a little better."

I rotated my body, facing him fully and taking a deep breath before smiling sweetly. What I was going to give him was the plain, unadulterated truth. And it was going to work beautifully. "I'm going to lay it out straight for you here, Carson. And the reason I'm going to do that is because I have every confidence it will scare you off badly enough that I can then finish my drink in peace, and we can part as mere acquaintances who simply have nothing in common."

He looked at me dubiously as I joined my hands in my lap, tilting my head as I continued. "I'm the kind of girl who wants to get married in a big, white dress, wearing my grandma's pearls. I want a husband who loves me faithfully. I want him to come home to me every night, and I don't want to have to worry about whether he has his secretary bent over a desk because he's the kind of man who has too much honor for that kind of disloyalty. I want to wait a year and then start trying for the two kids that we'll eventually have, a girl and a boy. And when we have those kids, I do not want, one day, to have to look in their little faces and explain why their daddy is on the internet *having relations* with everyone from college honeys to cougars gone wild for cash. I want to throw a cartoon-themed birthday party at a jump house for my six-year-old, not mark the occasion by explaining what a 'money shot' is. I have a feeling your life goals are somewhat different than mine. And by 'somewhat,' I mean utterly and completely. Does that explain why it would be a waste of time for both of us to continue being in each other's company?"

He appeared thoughtful for a minute, turning back to the bar and taking a drink of his beer. Finally, he faced me again. "How did we make those two kids?"

I pulled my head back. "Uh, you might want to rethink your career choice if you don't know—"

"What I mean is, what *position* did we make our two kids in? Doggy-style? Reverse cowgirl? The Garfield? Flying circus? Butterfly? Table lotus? Bended knee—"

"Stop!" I put my hand up and then dropped it just as quickly, giving myself a shake. "Okay, first of all, I have no idea what some of those are, nor do I want to know. But secondly, what does that have to do with anything?"

"Oh, believe me, you want to know. Why it matters is because someday when Princess is screaming at three in the morning with a loaded diaper, or Junior gets expelled from preschool for punching his classmate, I want to be able to think back to the moment that we created them, and I want to smile and remember why it was the best fuck of my life and why whatever shit—literal and figurative—I have to deal with later on is worth it."

My mouth dropped open against my will. "You're disgusting."

"You're the one who had my baby. Twice."

"I did not, nor will I *ever* have your baby. That was my point."

"So you're just going to abandon Princess and Junior? Nice mom."

I stood up, throwing a twenty-dollar bill on the bar. "Done. You enjoy your drink, Carson Stinger. I look forward to seeing you again, um, never." And with that, I grabbed my purse, turned tail, and started walking away as Carson called out, "Also, babe, you play hot secretary for me when I get home at the end of the day, and I'll have no need to do my real one."

I raised my arm and flipped him off. His throaty chuckle followed me out the door.

Carson

I heard the slap of her flip-flops fade away and took another swig of my beer. Uptight, little brat. *Hot*, uptight, little brat but a brat nonetheless. I knew her type. She could get all indignant, stick that haughty little chin in the air, tell me why she was better than me, and walk away, but I saw the way her body reacted. She wanted me. Most women did, if I was going to be honest. Everyone was given one gift or another—mine was a smile women creamed their panties over and a body to match. Why be humble about it? It's not like I could take any credit—I just knew how to use my God-given assets. The girl though, Grace Hamilton—I'd seen it on her luggage tag—she'd never let herself indulge, not knowing what I did for a living anyway. But just the fact that her body responded should have been enough for me. So why didn't that thought make me happy? It usually did. I folded my napkin in half and then folded it again. What was different here? I downed the last of my beer and frowned at the display of bottles behind the bar, trying to solve the riddle.

It had been the strangest thing. I'd been walking to the front desk to leave a message for my agent, who was flying in from LA the next morning, and I had crashed into someone, her blond head colliding into my chest, just under my chin, and I was able to smell her clean, flowery-scented hair, gathered up in one of those twists.

As she'd looked up at me, flustered and breathless, my own breath had caught in my throat at the beauty of the heart-shaped face gazing back. She had the biggest, blue eyes I had ever seen, a cute little nose, and the prettiest damn mouth—full, light pink lips with a pretty bow shape on top. So... sure, she was pretty, beautiful even. But I saw pretty girls all day long. Why did one glance at this one have me staring, trying to memorize her face like a lovesick schoolboy? I had no damn clue. We had both paused before moving back from each other, and I'd taken in her slim body in a fitted, black skirt and a silky, white blouse. I loved that

14

look. *Hot schoolteacher.* I had looked into her face and I could see a slightly confused warmth shining from her crystal-clear eyes. In that gaze, I had almost forgotten who I was. *Almost.* And that never happened.

But then her eyes had moved down to that stupid name tag, and I saw the disappointment and judgment fill her expression. And so I had purposefully made her uncomfortable, and I had *enjoyed* the look of disgust and then anger that filled her pretty face. I had enjoyed the way she stomped away from me, shaking her sweet, little ass. I had just done it again in the bar for the same reason. It meant I had won, so why didn't I feel like a winner? Why was I still sitting here actively thinking about it? About *her*? It was completely pissing me off. I should probably go and find some willing female to come back up to my room with me for an hour or two so I could distract myself from whatever that feeling was. Yeah, that sounded like a plan.

My phone rang as I was placing money on my tab on the bar and I looked at the screen. "Hey, Courtney," I greeted my agent as I walked out.

"Hey, Carson, love, you all set for Monday morning? I have the address of the shoot and some details. I'm gonna send them to your email. Can you pull it up on your phone?"

"Yeah, that's fine. I'll let you know when I get it."

"Okay, good. It's at the Four Seasons in Beverly Hills. A balcony shoot, followed by a shower scene."

I groaned. "Shit, Courtney, This'll only be my fifth film, and already my second shower scene? I told you I hated the first one."

"Oh please. Am I supposed to feel badly for you that you get to do Bambi Bennett in a shower? Poor thing." I could hear the sarcasm dripping from her voice.

15

"Shit, it's awkward—there are two cameramen and a mic in that tiny space. From where I'm standing, it's not hot. Also, *Bambi Bennett*? Christ. Am I fucking a deer?"

"I know. It's a stupid name. She's new to the site. Look her up. She's all kinds of gorgeous. Lucky you. Kisses! Text me when you get the info." And with that she hung up.

Courtney owned the site I had recently signed a contract with—ArtLove.com. It was supposed to appeal mostly to women, the largest growing porn-watching demographic. Most of the shoots were in exotic locations and we were encouraged to look like we were really into each other—different than the *wham, bam, thank you ma'am* type of porn that men tended to like. The first shoot I had done was in Belize, in an outdoor shower, and despite what it might have seemed like to the viewer, I was just hoping I could stay hard through it. A film crew of sweaty dudes all up in your business wasn't exactly a wet dream come true, no matter how gorgeous the girl was.

Apparently, though, after only a couple films, I had a small fan following. And so my agent had all but insisted I show up this weekend to make an appearance. I had stayed at the meet-and-greet bullshit for as long as I could stomach, and then I'd snuck out and run straight into Miss High-and-Mighty. It wasn't that I didn't appreciate my fans…but rather, I guess I tried not to think about my fans too much because let's be honest, they admired me for reasons that made me think it was better that I not shake their hands.

I started toward the elevators that would take me up to my room where I could get ready for the pool. It was the easiest place to pick up a girl, one who didn't care to know who I was or what I did—and the feeling would be mutual.

"Whoa, hold the elevator," I called. I flashed my room

key to the security guard standing at the front of the alcove as I jogged toward the elevator I'd spotted going up, doors just beginning to close.

The doors bounced back open as an old woman stuck her purse out, and I stepped inside. "Thank you so much."

"You're welcome, honey," the old woman said with a smile, both of us facing the closed door as the elevator began its ascent.

"The Lord is testing me," I heard a quiet voice whisper under her breath. I glanced to my left and two people over to see who had muttered those words, and there stood Grace "White Wedding" Hamilton. Go figure. I chuckled softly to myself at her tight expression.

I leaned forward and grinned at her. I could tell that she saw me in her peripheral vision by the way her spine straightened, but she continued to stare straight ahead at the door in front of us. *What a total brat.*

The old woman standing next to Grace leaned around her and grinned back at me, waving a flirty, little wave. It was cute and so I laughed and waved back. Grace's head swiveled to me and her eyes widened as we made eye contact, me still smiling. Then just as quickly, she turned to look straight ahead again, tension so thick you could cut it with a knife.

The elevator stopped at several floors and began to empty out, and pretty soon, it was just me and Grace and the old woman. We all stood quietly, staring straight ahead.

At the next floor, the old woman moved to the front and Grace and I both automatically stepped backward to let her pass. As the old woman stepped through the open doors, she turned and winked at me and then shot Grace a wink too. When I looked over at Grace, her head was tilted, and she wore a small smile on her pretty, pink lips.

The doors slid closed and then she glanced at me, the smile morphing into a frown.

"So we meet..." I trailed off as the lights in the elevator flashed, and then stepped forward when the car gave a huge jolt. "Holy shit!" I exclaimed as Grace let out a high-pitched squeak.

The elevator slammed to a stop, groaning loudly, and the lights flickered. I looked across the small space into wide, terrified eyes. We were stuck.

CHAPTER 2
Grace

As the elevator groaned to a stop and the lights flickered one more time, fear trickled through me like acid. I didn't like small spaces. Not at all. *Dark. Tight. No air.* I sucked in a deep breath and practically threw myself at the phone cubby, yanking open the small metal door and pulling the handle of the phone. I pressed zero and as it rang, my eyes darted to Carson who was standing in the corner, leaned against the wall, watching me carefully.

"Maintenance," a gruff voice answered.

"Hi, hi! Yes, hi, this is Grace Hamilton. I'm a guest here this weekend." I pulled in another breath. The air was starting to feel *thin.* "We're stuck in an elevator. It just stopped suddenly and…" The phone crackled and then died. *No, no, no!* "Hello? Hello?" I made a panicked sound in my throat, dropping the phone, and then taking three big steps over to my large purse, abandoned in the corner. I pulled out my cell phone and looked at the bars at the top of the screen. No service. *Shit!*

Breathe. Breathe.

No room. No air. It'd be gone soon. All of it.

Carson was still staring at me, unmoving, just watching me with an unreadable expression on his face. He was useless!

"Don't just stand there! We're trapped! Do something!" My breath hitched in my throat and I could feel my heart beating out of my chest. I lifted my fingers to my throat and felt my pulse racing wildly. I attempted to take a deep breath, but my throat suddenly felt as if it were swelling shut. *I can't breathe. Oh God, I can't breathe. No air. No air.*

I stumbled back against the wall, making eye contact with Carson, who now had his brow furrowed as he moved toward me. I gripped the bar on the wall behind me, knowing I was about to die of asphyxiation, here in this elevator, the last eyes I saw those of Carson Stinger, Straight Male Performer. *Oh no, no, no, no. Not like this.*

"Hey, calm down, buttercup," he said smoothly, wrapping his hands around my upper arms just like he did when we collided in the hotel lobby. "Deep breath, take a deep breath. You're okay. They're going to get us out of here, all right? Just take a deep breath. Keep your eyes on me."

I blinked rapidly as his face swam before me, my breath now coming out in raspy exhales as I fought to take in oxygen. The walls were closing in. I wanted to cry but there wasn't enough oxygen in my lungs for that.

"Shit, buttercup, come on, you're not going to pass out on me in this elevator. Deep breath."

For several minutes we both stared into each other's eyes, the worry in his deepening as he watched me struggle and begin to flail.

Oh God, Oh God, air, air!

The wall of the elevator met my back and Carson

stepped away and started looking around the elevator, eyes wide, panicked now, searching for what, I didn't know. He flew over to the phone and lifted it and listened for a second, and then slammed it back in its small box and kicked the door shut. "Shit!"

I'm dying. Oh God, please, air.

He turned back to me, and my eyes were tearing up in my effort to take in what little oxygen was making it down the tiny passageway that was now the inside of my throat. I was sure I was turning blue.

"Sister Christian, oh the time has come!" Carson suddenly belted out.

Even in the midst of my panic attack, I startled. *What the—*

"And you know that you're the only one to say, okay."

He took a step back as my eyes followed him, my breath still sticking in my swollen throat as I struggled to draw in air.

He pointed at me. "Where you going, what you looking for?"

What the hell is he doing? What the HELL is he doing? Oh! A little air. That's good, that's good, Grace.

"You know those boys don't want to play no more with you. It's true." At the last two words of the stanza, he lowered his chin and gazed into my eyes.

Better, better. More air, better. Okay, okay. I'm okay. Why is he singing while I'm almost dying here? He actually has a really nice voice—deep and slightly throaty. Figures he'd have a really nice voice. Figures he'd have a SEXY voice. Ah, air. Okay, I'm okay.

My arms lowered, my splayed hands coming away from the base of my throat. My breathing slowed marginally and I realized that the instrumental of "Sister Christian" was playing over the sound system. Carson was singing along to the elevator music. And doing it well. *To distract me from my panic attack.* And it was working.

I took in a large inhale, my vision clearing as I now watched him. He was in the middle of the elevator and as what would have been the drum solo came up, he started playing the air drums furiously, closing his eyes and bobbing his head to the beat, biting his lower lip. This couldn't be real. I had passed out and was having some strange out-of-body experience.

"You're motoring! What's your price for flight? In finding Mr. Right? You'll be all right, tonight."

I couldn't help it, I let out a very small laugh. When he heard it, his eyes snapped open and he looked up at me, and relief washed over his features before he grinned. It was the same grin that had almost knocked me on my ass when he gave it to the old woman. It was real. And maybe my mind was still oxygen deprived, but in that moment, something told me that even though he smiled an awful lot, a genuine one from Carson Stinger was rare.

His expression turned serious and he walked toward me singing slowly, "Babe, you know you're growing up so fast. And Mama's worrying that you won't last to say, let's play."

As he finished the last few words, he held his fist up to his lips, pretending it was a microphone and then he thrust it in front of my mouth.

I blinked momentarily, but now adrenaline was racing through my body at the sweet relief of air flowing freely into my lungs, and so I did something I'd never, under ordinary circumstances do: I grabbed his fist and sang into it, "Sister Christian, there's so much in life. Don't you give it up before your time is due, it's true." Then he leaned in and we were both singing together, "It's true, yeah!" He jumped back and played more air drums before jumping forward again and singing into his fist with me. "Motoring! What's your price for flight? You've got him in your sight. And driving through the night."

Our faces were mere inches apart now, and I could smell his minty breath as he sang with me: "Motoring! What's your price for flight? In finding Mr. Right? You'll be all right tonight."

He stepped away from me again and, this time, mimicked the electric guitar solo, moving his hips forward with every pretend riff, swiveling them to the chords as I watched, laughing out loud now at his ridiculous antics, and the fact that he was actually good, and we were singing at the top of our lungs in an elevator wedged between floors in a luxury hotel on the Vegas strip.

He grinned at me as he continued singing the chorus a couple times over. Then as the song slowed, he started walking slowly to me again singing, "Sister Christian, oh the time has come. And you know that you're the only one to say, okay. But you're motoring. You're motoring, yeah." He trailed off as we both stood staring at each other, his breathing harsher than mine now from all the furious air playing. I was breathing steady even as his chest quickly rose and fell. The bizarre nature of the situation rolled over me again and I burst out laughing, and then so did he. As our laughter faded, he tilted his head to the side and said, "If you wanted to hear me sing, buttercup, you could have just asked."

I let out another short laugh, but it quickly faded. I looked at him seriously for several moments. "Thank you for that. Who knew Night Ranger could cure a panic attack? But it worked. Thank you." I took a big, deep breath. "Thank you, Carson."

He smiled and then did a slow bow that was interrupted by the sudden ringing of the phone.

––––––––––

"Hello!" Carson said after he'd grabbed the receiver from its box. I stared, my hands pressed together in the prayer position. After listening for a minute, he groaned. "That long?" he asked. My hands dropped. *Damn.* "Isn't there anything that can be done to get that part here more quickly?" He listened for another minute. "Yeah, okay. Keep us updated, all right?"

"What'd they say?" I demanded after he'd hung up.

"Well, the good news is that they know we're in here, they know the problem, and the part to fix it is on its way. The bad news is that it's two hours away."

"Two hours?" I screeched. I took a deep breath. "Two hours?" I said, more calmly. "We have to sit in here together for two hours?"

"Afraid so," he answered, walking to the wall and sliding down it to sit on the floor with his feet drawn up and his forearms resting on his knees.

I stared at him for a minute and then walked to my side of the elevator. I sat down on the floor as well, bending my knees to the side, glancing over at him and pulling my sundress down over my legs, all the way to my ankles. When I glanced up at Carson, his eyes lifted from my legs to my eyes. I saw the small frown on his face right before his expression went blank and he raised his eyebrows, smiling suggestively. "A lot of things to do in two hours, buttercup. Any ideas?"

And he was back. Carson Stinger, Straight Male Performer. I cocked my head to the side, looking at him through narrowed eyes. "Why do you do that?" I asked.

He pulled his teeth over his lower lip, looking bored. "Do what exactly?"

"Pull that 'sex in your face'...*mask* on?"

He stared at me thoughtfully for a minute. "Mask? A mask would imply that I'm hiding something beneath it. What would that be exactly?"

I looked away and shrugged. "The guy who just made a crazy fool of himself singing 'Sister Christian' to me to help me cope with a bad situation?"

He chuckled. "I just did what was necessary so that you didn't die on me. If I'm gonna be stuck in an elevator, better that it's not with a corpse. I'm into a lot of crazy shit, but necrophilia isn't one of them."

I made a gagging sound. "God, you're really..." I chewed on my lip for a moment, thinking. "No, you know what? I'm not buying it. I call your bluff, Carson Stinger. You're a phony."

He laughed, looking truly amused. "Well, who exactly do you think you are, buttercup? You know me so well after being with me for what"—he looked down at the watch on his wrist—"fifteen minutes?"

I sighed. "You're right. I don't know anything about you. Just that you're a phony, that's all. Call it a gut feeling."

He put a hand under his jaw and moved it back and forth for a second. Then he slid his long, muscular legs down and crossed them at the ankles as he continued to stare at me. "What I think is that you're into me. And you're trying to make me the good, sensitive guy that I'm *not*, so that when you slide across this elevator and climb onto my lap, you'll be able to justify it to yourself."

I choked on my own laugh and sat up on my knees to glare at him. "You arrogant asshole! The only way I would

25

crawl *anywhere* for you is if my very life depended on it."
I glared at him for a minute and then fell back onto my
haunches. I pointed at him. "Wait. You did it to me again.
See, that's the mask. You made me angry so that I'd forget
my point. Which is…you're a phony."

He laughed. "Still on that, Dr. Phil? Okay, then, what
about you, Miss Perfect Princess? What are you hiding
behind that hair pulled back so tightly it's about to strangle
you and that high-and-mighty attitude?"

"High-and-mighty?" I scoffed. "I'm hardly high-and-
mighty. And I'm hardly perfect either."

"Oh, I don't know. I think that's exactly what you
are—perfect. Why? Why do you need to be so damn
perfect? What has you strung so tight that as soon as you
lost control, you couldn't even breathe? What's under
your mask?"

I laughed loudly, overdoing it to show him how ridiculous he was. "*My* mask? Please. Now you're just making stuff
up to distract me. What you see is what you get here, *Carson*.
I hardly wear a mask. Now you…" I brought my hand up
and studied my nails.

"All right, buttercup," he said after a moment. "I've got
a proposition for you. How'd you like to play a little game?
It's called, Sink One for a Secret. It's not like we've got much
else to do. Especially if you planting yourself on my lap is off
the table."

"It was never *on* the table. What exactly does this Sink
One for a Secret game entail?"

He sat up. "Do you have anything in your purse like a
cup or a bowl or something?"

I gave him a look. "No. That's not exactly the type of
stuff I carry around in my purse." I opened my large bag and

26

looked inside. "Wait—what about the top of my hairspray?" I pulled it off. It was plastic and roughly the size of a Dixie cup. I held it out to Carson.

"That'll work," he said, snatching it out of my hand. He reached in his back pocket and pulled out a dime and held it up to me. Then he placed the hairspray cap in one corner of the elevator and went and stood in the opposite corner. "The rules are, if one person sinks the dime into the cap, the other person has to reveal a secret about themselves. No lying. No making something up. A genuine secret—something they've never told anyone else before."

I crossed my arms, looking from the cap in one corner to Carson in the other. "That's an impossible shot. The distance and the size of the cap—it can't be done."

He raised his brows. "Are you in or not?"

I exhaled. "Fine. Whatever. Go."

He paused. "Wait. Do you agree to the rules?"

"Yes, yes, a basket for a secret. I'm in." I knew it was impossible, and so why not? I'd play his dumb game.

He held the dime up, lining up his shot, moving to the right slightly, a look of pure concentration on his face as he tossed the dime overhand. It went straight in the cup, didn't even bounce. A solid swish. *What. The. Hell?*

I gasped. "You cheated! That's not even possible!"

"I *cheated?* How in the hell did I cheat? No way. Don't try to get out of this. You owe me a secret, buttercup. Let's hear it." He leaned his shoulder against the elevator wall, crossed his arms, and tilted his chin down, looking at me expectantly.

I glared at him. "I mean, it's not as easy as that! I don't have any secrets." I raised both arms up and let them drop.

He kept staring at me, not saying a word, expressionless now. "Tell me why you're so perfect, buttercup."

I made a disgusted gurgle in the back of my throat and crossed my arms again, looking away from him. I thought about what he was asking me. Did I really come across like that? *Perfect?* I felt the furthest away from perfect as a person could get. I was always trying not to rock the boat...trying to be *enough*...trying to make up for...

"My dad has had enough disappointment in his life. I'm just trying not to let him down anymore," I blurted out.

Carson tilted his head, his eyes filling with...*something*.

I looked away. "Anyway, that's all. My dad's had a hard time of it. He's a great guy. A great dad and I just want him to be proud of me. Is that so weird?"

"What disappointment has your dad had?" he asked quietly.

I stared at the wall for a minute, suddenly, *inexplicably*, wanting to say what came next. "When I was eleven, my little brother died of non-Hodgkin's lymphoma. He was the only boy. I have two sisters." I looked down at my feet. "My dad is a cop...a real guy's guy. I guess me and my sisters always felt like maybe...like maybe..."

"Like maybe one of *you* were expendable because there were backups?" Carson asked quietly.

My eyes snapped up to his and I just stared at him for several seconds. I had never thought about it in those terms but... "Maybe. Yes."

He nodded, still looking into my eyes. Then he walked over to the cap in the corner, plucked the dime out, and held it up to me. "Your turn."

Carson

My throat had gone dry and I felt a strange itchiness just under my skin when Grace told me about her brother and her dad. I didn't really stop and think about the feeling. I had never really talked about *emotions* with anyone other than my granny. But she had passed away when I was seventeen, and since then, I didn't go there much. I had initially suggested this game to take Grace off balance. I could throw a dime into a cup from farther away than across an elevator. I'd had hours and hours of practice. It's what I had done to distract my mind while waiting for my mom to get off set.

But then Grace had actually shared with me and just like that, *I* was the one off balance.

I handed her the dime and stood back as she glanced at me and took her place in the opposite corner from the small cap and lined up her shot, underhand.

I studied her as she focused. Damn, she really was a beautiful girl. Sexy but with a classic beauty that made me want to stare at the perfection of her features. She was slim but had curves in all the right spots. Just exactly what I liked. I could tell she would be just as pretty stepping straight out of a shower in the morning, without a stitch of makeup on. I twitched in my pants at the image. *Shit, this I did not need.* I bit my own tongue to distract myself from thoughts of Grace stepping out of a shower, just as she let the dime fly. My head turned to watch it land with a *plunk* straight in the cap.

I laughed out loud as she whooped and threw her arms in the air in a victory pose. Wait, shit, this was *not* funny. Only, the look of pure excitement on her face made me want to scoop her up and hug her. Until I remembered that I didn't hug. Anyone. Ever.

I sighed and tried to look as bored as possible. "All right. What is it you want to know about me?"

She tilted her head, narrowed her eyes, and scraped her teeth up her full bottom lip in a way that had me biting my own tongue again.

She walked back to her side of the elevator and slid down to the floor, pulling her legs up and covering them with her sundress like she had done before. I waited.

"A secret that you've never told anyone else, right?"

I nodded.

"Okay, why do you do porn?"

I gave her a suggestive smirk. "The answer to that question isn't exactly a secret. It's fun and it pays great."

She furrowed her delicate brows and stared at me for a minute. "Why do you *really* do porn, Carson?"

I chuckled, but it came off as uncomfortable as I suddenly felt. "Not everyone who does porn has some screwed-up childhood and dark past. The industry is a lot different than it used to be. There are all kinds of safety measures in place..."

She continued looking up at me silently, as though she wasn't buying what I was selling, even though what I'd said was true. But maybe not the whole truth. After a few moments, I sighed and slid down to the floor. Was I really even considering going there with this stranger? This princess? I sat staring straight at the wall for a minute or two and then almost against my own will, I started talking, "My mom was a porn star in the nineties. From what I know, it doesn't happen often, but when it does, it's taken care of pretty quickly—she got pregnant. She decided not to have it taken care of. I'm the bastard of any one of a hundred hired dicks. How do you like that fairy tale, buttercup?"

Her eyes widened and her lips formed a silent O. We stared at each other for a quiet minute. "That doesn't explain why you do it now too."

"I was practically born to do it, babe. Created in lust and sin. Destined to do the same."

"It's not your fault how you were—" And fuck me if those big, blue eyes weren't filled with pity. I felt something inside me squeeze in a way that I didn't fucking like at all.

"No, and it's not your fault you have a pretty little mouth, but maybe if you crawl over here, we can both use our God-given assets to make the next few hours go by a little faster."

She stared at me, her cheeks flushing. "That's why you do that. You pull that sex-on-a-stick, asshole mask on to hide the fact that you're ashamed of who you are."

Her words hit me like a punch. I wanted to flinch but I didn't. I *never* flinched and I wouldn't now. Not for her or anyone. "There's my little Dr. Phil again. Tell me, where did you get your clinical psychology degree from? Oh, that's right. The University of Bullshit. Tell me this, buttercup, are you as good at diagnosing yourself? Do you realize that that perfect-princess gig you have going on is all an attempt to make up for the fact that you believe *you* should have been the one to die instead of your brother? But guess what? Your brother did die. And all the perfect-princess crap in the world won't change that."

She sucked in a loud gasp, her eyes filling with hurt. I immediately felt like shit. "You *bastard!*" she hissed, getting up on her knees and "walking" on them toward me, anger almost instantly replacing the hurt I had first seen flash in her eyes.

31

I got up on my knees too, the bastard comment making my chest tight. She had used my own word against me and I didn't like the way that felt. "Prude," I hissed back.

"Man-whore!"

"Oh, real inventive, ice queen!"

The air in the small space had suddenly turned red. We met in the middle of the elevator, both on our knees, her neck bent to stare up at me, rage etched across her features. I knew my expression said the same thing.

"Piece of ass!"

"Sellout."

She balled her fists up and straightened both of her arms at her side, making a frustrated, angry, growling sound. I leaned in slightly, daring her to hit me. *Do it.* I *wanted* her to hit me. Why, I didn't know, but I did.

And suddenly we were kissing. Hardcore, angry kissing, our hands everywhere, groping and grabbing. And damn it if she didn't taste like sunshine and everything sweet and fresh this world had to offer.

CHAPTER 3
Grace

We groped at each other's bodies, moaning and panting and practically crazed with anger and lust. Or was it just anger? No, no, anger didn't feel this good. My body was on fire, every nerve ending zinging with the need to be touched by Carson. *Oh God, I am being touched by Carson Stinger, Straight Male Performer! No! Yes! Yes! Yes!* Three yeses to one no. Majority rules! God, he tasted so good. He tasted minty and like something that was just him. After one small taste, I was already craving more, sweeping my tongue around his mouth trying to get as much of it as I could, desperate with hunger for it. For *him*. He seemed just as desperate to taste me as his tongue tangled with mine, and his hands grabbed my ass and pulled me up hard against his erection. Oh God, he was big. Really big. And I was rubbing on him like some crazed cat in heat. A crazed cat in heat that had gotten ahold of some crack. Or catnip...or whatever notched up the level of a crazed cat in heat. That was me.

Meow!

I almost laughed at the way my mind was melting when I suddenly realized Carson was pulling me up to a standing position. I followed him willingly, our lips never once breaking contact. He walked us backward to the wall, and when my back hit solid surface, he pressed up against me, a growl coming up his chest. He let go of me and I heard both of his hands hit the wall on either side of my head as he caged me in. He kept working my mouth, licking and sucking my tongue as he pressed into me again, groaning once more. The sounds he was making and the feel of the wall behind me, anchoring me, cleared the lust fog just a little. Oh my God, this was crazy. What was I doing? A couple minutes before, we had both been tearing each other apart emotionally. How did this happen? Sure, he was great at what he was doing with his mouth and his body, but that was because he was a professional! *Oh my God! He's a professional! He's good at this because he does it* a lot. *As in* a lot, *a lot*. Again, what in the *hell* was I doing?

I opened my eyes and seeing his face millimeters from mine, his eyes closed and his long lashes fanned over his cheeks, brought me fully back to reality. I made a strangled sound in my throat and tore my mouth off of his, turning my head and putting both my hands against his chest, pushing him away from me. He staggered back, looking dazed, and we both stared at each other, shocked, panting.

"Shit, I'm sorry," he finally said, giving his head a shake.

"For what?" I asked angrily. "The insults or the kissing?"

"The insults. Not sorry for the kissing."

Oh.

He took a deep breath and ran a hand though his messy hair. Had I done that?

I blew out a breath. And damn it if, even though I was

still a little angry—more so at myself now—a part of me wanted to dive right back in to the kissing part.

I shook my head, clearing away the last of the fog. *We're in an elevator. He's a porn star. We just told each other a secret, and then viciously threw it right back.*

I laughed a small, humorless laugh and looked up at the ceiling, pulling in a long breath and letting it out again.

When I looked back at Carson, he was staring at me, a look of confusion on his face. "What's funny?" he asked.

I turned and sat down, banging the back of my head against the wall lightly. He came over and sat against the back wall of the elevator, directly to my right, drawing his knees up and resting his forearms on them again.

I groaned. "Us. We're awful people. We each shared a secret, and then used it against each other within five minutes flat." I shook my head and looked over at him. "I'm sorry too."

He took a deep breath and looked down for a minute before bringing those beautiful hazel eyes back to me. "No, that was me. I made the rules and then I attacked you instead of playing by them graciously. I was a sore loser."

I tilted my head, surprised at his response. "That game had high stakes." I paused. "How about if we just talk for a little bit?"

A grin spread over his face, that little dimple showing itself, and the true beauty of him momentarily stunned me.

I studied him for a moment. "Why aren't you a model or an actor or something? You have the looks for it."

He chuckled. "I know."

"Modest too, aren't ya?"

"I don't need to be modest. I didn't do anything to earn this face. It just is what it is."

35

I snorted. "Just when I was kinda starting to like you again."

"Does you liking me translate into more kissing?" He grinned again, shooting me that devastating smile.

"No. Now tell me why you don't model instead of... what you're doing."

"Let people primp me and put makeup on me for hours and then pose in front of them? God, that sounds a thousand times worse than porn. Shit."

"Worse than porn? So you *don't* like doing it then?"

He stared at me for a minute and I could see his wheels turning. Finally he said, "Truthfully, no, I don't like doing porn."

"Why?" I asked quietly.

"Because I like to fuck the way I want to fuck. I don't like being told what to do or moved around like a chess piece in bed. Part of the high of sex for a man is the chase. There's no chase in porn. And before you get mad, I'm not trying to push your buttons with that wording. I'm just being honest. I don't find it enjoyable. I mean beyond—"

"Right," I interrupted, "sex is like pizza and all that." I studied him for a minute. "How'd you get into it?" I finally asked.

He sighed. "Well, like I said, I kinda grew up in the business. My mom used to bring me on set with her. Not that I watched. I stayed in the dressing room, but I knew what she was doing out there, and it sucked. Pun intended." He grinned, but I didn't. I just felt sad.

He stared at me for a minute, his eyes narrowing briefly. I thought he might not continue, but then he began speaking again, "Anyway, my mom had always had a little bit of a drug problem, and when I was fourteen, it got pretty bad.

I went to live with my grandma in Massachusetts until my mom got clean, and then I came back to Los Angeles."

"That's where you're from?"

"Yeah. The City of Angels." He raised his eyebrows, looking away thoughtfully for a second before continuing. "Once I turned eighteen, several of the producers I knew started asking me to make a film. They said it'd get big-time attention. The son of one of the biggest stars of porn, now doing films himself. I said no for a while. I wasn't interested. When my granny died, she left me a little bit of money. Not a lot, but enough to travel around Europe for a couple years. When I came back, I worked at some menial jobs for a while—doing nothing, partying. Finally, six months ago, I was contacted by one of those same producers who now worked for a company that's a little more softcore. I figured, why the fuck not? What was the big difference between that and what I was doing with women I didn't know on the weekends?"

I grimaced. It all sounded so...empty. When I looked up at him, he had his head resting against the back of the elevator and he was studying me. "You a virgin, buttercup?"

I laughed. I was just about to tell him it was none of his business, but I realized that he had just offered up intimate details of his life. It would be like me slapping him in the face to say something like that now. Truthfully, it *wasn't* any of his business. But what he had just shared with me wasn't my business either, and yet he had given it to me regardless. "No. I've been with one person. My college boyfriend. I plan on being with one more before I get married."

"You plan on being with one more before...okay, *what?*"

"Well, wait, it makes sense and I'll tell you why. I still have to finish law school. And then I have to get hired by a top law firm and work for at least a year. I don't plan on

37

getting married until I'm twenty-eight and no one wants to marry a twenty-eight-year-old virgin. He'd wonder what was wrong with me. So I figure, I should be with two men before I meet my husband. One to take my virginity, *check*, and one to practice on so I can be good in bed." I smiled, impressed with my own reasoning.

He stared at me for a beat and then burst out laughing. "Shit, that might be even *less* romantic than *my* story. And that's a feat."

I frowned. "What's not romantic about that? I'm setting things up perfectly for the man that I'll spend forever with. I'm already thinking of him, and we haven't even met yet."

"What about the poor schmuck who you pick out to be sex partner number two? Destined to be kicked to the curb before you've even met him."

I scoffed. "Please. Like guys aren't okay with a couple months of sex before they're set free to move on to the next one?"

He smiled. "Well, true. Still, what happens if you end up falling for him? What happens to your plan then?"

"Falling for him? Well, no. That won't happen because it's not *part* of my plan. Certainly there will have to be an attraction, but—"

"I might have the perfect candidate, buttercup." He raised an eyebrow and then shot me that devastating grin.

I lgaped. "You?" I shook my head. "That's impossible, Carson. First of all, we don't even live in the same city. And listen, how would I ever tell my future husband that I had been with a porn star? No offense. Really. But that—"

"Why would you have to give him any details? Men don't want details about their women's past sexual experience."

"I guess not. But still... Wait! Are we seriously discussing this? That guy is still years away in the plan. I can't forget everything he teaches me before I meet the One. Sorry. Timing doesn't work." I shrugged. I figured he was messing with me anyway, but it was true enough.

"So you don't plan on having any more sex for the next, what? *Four* years or so? How old are you?"

"Twenty-three. So yes, he's about four years away in the plan."

"You're going to wait four years to have sex again because of some stupid plan?"

"It's not a stupid plan! I've always had one. It keeps me focused." I felt my face fall. Now that I had explained my entire plan out loud, it was beginning to sound less rational than it always had in my mind. "Anyway," I went on, "it's going to help me achieve my dreams."

"*Your* dreams? You sure about that?"

I snorted. "Now who's pretending to be Dr. Phil?"

He watched me. "Okay, fair enough. Let's get back to the sex then. You're planning *purposefully* on a four-year dry spell? Didn't you like it the first time?"

I felt my cheeks heat as I looked down. "Sure, it was fine."

"*Fine?* Uh-oh. Any man who gets a 'fine' from a woman on *any* topic is in serious trouble."

I took a deep breath. "Listen. It *was* fine, okay? Not spectacular. Not terrible. Just fine."

He studied me for a minute. "So he didn't make you come, buttercup?"

"God! I can't believe we're discussing this. No, he didn't make me come, okay? For all I know, I *can't* come with another person in the room. All right? Why don't you give me your email and I'll let you know in four years if

39

things have changed! Dear Carson, I work! Love, Grace. You'll remember me, won't you? You'll celebrate on my behalf?" I banged the back of my head on the elevator wall behind me. I felt embarrassed by this line of conversation, especially considering whom I was talking to. Actually, I was feeling kind of stripped down in a lot of ways. And he was making me question things I *never* questioned. How had this happened exactly? With this person? I started laughing and shaking my head.

"What?" he asked.

I groaned. "I don't know. This whole situation is just...*funny.*"

He nodded like he knew exactly what I meant. "Yeah, I guess it kinda is. All the same though, my offer stands. We could make a weekend of it at least. I think your future husband might be *really* happy you said yes to me." He shot me a practiced wink.

"You're serious, aren't you? Why? What's in it for you exactly?"

He just raised his eyebrows, remaining silent.

I shook my head and let out a sound of exasperation. "I mean, don't you get enough random sex as it is?"

"Listen, consider it a challenge for me, okay? I think I could give you something no one has before and that's a hell of a turn-on for me. See, we'd both get something out of it and then part ways as Buttercup and Schmuck Number Two."

I opened my mouth to answer and was interrupted by the shrill ringing of the elevator phone. Saved by the bell once again.

———

Carson

The phone rang a second time, and I realized that I had been holding my breath waiting for her answer. I was lying to her about my reason for asking to be Schmuck Number Two. Not about thinking I could make her come. I was pretty sure I'd be successful at that. And that *was* a turn-on. The thought of seeing an expression of pleasure wash over her beautiful face had me swelling in my jeans. But the real reason I was holding my breath for her answer was because I hadn't wanted anything in a really long time, longer than I could remember, and I *wanted* her. Not just her body but *her*. I wanted to see her reaction to my touch. I wanted to hear some more funny shit come out of her pretty mouth. I wanted to hear her try to justify her stupid plan. *I liked her*. And fuck me, I hadn't liked a woman in a really long time. It felt good to want something. And that shocked the hell out of me. I couldn't have her in any real sense, and it's not like I wanted that anyway. But a day or two of Grace Hamilton in a hotel room? Yeah, I wanted that. I wanted that a lot.

I got up and answered the phone. "Hello?"

"Hey, it's Rich in maintenance, just wanted to update you and make sure you're okay. We got the part we were waiting for and now it just needs to be installed. Shouldn't be longer than an hour."

"Okay, man. Yeah, we're fine. Thanks for the update." I hung up and turned to Grace.

"Seems you're stuck with me for at least another hour."

"At least?"

"Yeah, at least. Longer if you agree to spend the weekend

together." I hoped she couldn't tell that this meant something to me. If she turned me down, it was going to sting.

Her eyes widened slightly and her mouth opened as if to answer, but then she closed it again, looking confused. That's when my stomach growled. Loudly.

Grace grinned and tilted her head. "Hungry?" Before I could answer, she reached for her bag and dug around in it for a couple seconds and pulled out a granola bar. "Dinner, sir? Hold on. I think I have something here to wash it down with too." She dug around for another second and then pulled out a bottle of water.

I sat down on the floor next to her. "You're a goddess. Hand that over." I had just realized that I hadn't eaten lunch and it was about dinnertime. I was starving. She handed me the granola bar, and I tore it open with my teeth and then broke the bar in half and handed her one piece. But she shook her head.

"You have it. I'm not really hungry. Plus, you're a growing boy." She shot me the same exaggerated wink I'd given her a few minutes before.

I grinned. "Only when I look at you, baby." She laughed, smacking me lightly on the shoulder. I tossed the granola bar back, and when she handed me the water after taking a drink herself, I drank from it too.

"We better finish the water in this bottle. If nature calls, this bottle is what we're going to have to use."

She made a face. "I think I'll be okay for an hour. I stopped in the ladies' room right after I left the bar."

"I think I'll last too."

After a minute, I said, "Okay, another game—this one's called Quick Draw Favorites. I ask a question and you answer it with the first thing that comes to mind. Then you can do the same to me."

She looked at me suspiciously. "Is this another trick game that's going to have us kissing in the middle of the elevator again?"

"God, I hope so." I laughed. "But no, just for fun to pass the time. You in?"

She nodded. "Okay."

"Okay. Favorite movie."

"*Titanic.*"

"No. Pick again."

She choked on a laugh. "No? Um, I thought these were *my* answers."

"They are, but I can't let you pick a movie as craptastic as *Titanic* without intervening."

She turned fully toward me. "How is *Titanic* craptastic? It's an epic love story! It's beautiful! It's timeless! What problem do you have with *Titanic*?"

I sighed. "Grace, there was plenty of room on that floating door at the end of the movie. Are you going to tell me you weren't pissed off after they went through everything they did to survive and then she couldn't scoot over an inch so he could get up on that piece of wood too, a piece of wood that was plenty big for both of them? She let him die, Grace. I'm sad for you that you think that's romance."

She burst out laughing. "Wait, this is brilliant. You actually don't like *Titanic* because it isn't romantic *enough* for you. That's sweet." She batted her eyelashes at me.

My brows snapped down. "No, I don't believe that's what I said. What I said was that I like some realism in my movies. That was a cop-out because the writer thought Jack Dawson should sink to the bottom of the ocean."

She burst out laughing again.

"Are you done?"

She made a poor attempt to wipe the smirk off her face. "Yes. Next question."

"Favorite color."

"Cerulean blue."

I screwed up my face and glanced to the side and then back at her. "I'm going to let that one slide. Favorite season."

"Fall."

"Favorite dessert."

"Crème brûlée."

"Favorite sex position."

She paused and a pink color crept up her cheeks. "Um, missionary?"

I stared at her for a minute. "So not only did that college boyfriend not make you come, but he didn't try any other positions with you, did he? What kind of jackass did you hook up with anyway?"

"Stop! He was a nice guy. Very, um, sweet and, uh, considerate."

"I bet. Okay, you're depressing me. Your turn."

"You're such an asshole." But she said it with a small smile on her face. "Favorite movie."

"*Fight Club*."

"Never saw it."

"You never saw *Fight Club*? That's a crime."

She laughed softly. "Favorite color."

"Blue."

"What shade of blue?"

"Just fucking blue."

"That's not a shade."

"Yeah it is."

She shot me a smile. "Okay. So we *might* share the same favorite color."

"Maybe. If I knew what cerulean was."

She laughed. "Favorite season."

"Fall."

"We *do* have a few things in common! It's a miracle!"

"Who would have guessed?"

"Not me. Favorite dessert."

"Bananas Foster—my granny used to make it for me."

She smiled and then looked straight ahead. "Well, that was fun."

"Wait, you didn't ask me the last one."

"No, I didn't. I don't want to know. Really. I'm sure it's something I've never even heard of before. You can keep that one to yourself."

"Chicken."

She grinned over at me, and I was momentarily taken off balance by the beauty of her smile. I loved her teeth. I loved everything about her mouth. I wanted to taste it again. I stretched my legs out. My pants suddenly felt a little too tight.

We were both quiet for a minute. I was thinking about how things had seemed to shift between Grace and me. There was almost a...comfort level between us as we sat there listening to the quiet elevator music and sipping on her bottle of water. I was also thinking about how I had told her things about my history that I had never told anyone else before. There were people that knew because they were there. But I had never willingly shared my upbringing with anyone who didn't already know for one reason or another. But the fact of it was, no other woman had ever asked me to talk. And maybe it was as simple as that. I couldn't recall another woman who had wanted to hang out with me for my scintillating conversational skills. Maybe it was because I didn't have any. Or maybe it was because no one had ever been interested in finding out whether I did or whether I didn't.

We were both sitting there together, comfortable and at ease, but it definitely hadn't started that way.

"Tell me why you had a panic attack when you first realized we were trapped, Grace," I said softly, glancing over at her.

Her eyes flew to mine. She took another drink of water, clearly stalling and deciding whether she was going to answer me. After a minute she said softly, "My brother got diagnosed when he was eight. I was a year older than him. He fought for two years, but when the doctors finally told my parents he was terminal, my mom kind of lost it, and my dad took on the burden of planning his funeral without her. She was literally emotionally incapable."

She paused for a long time and I wondered if she'd continue, but finally she did. "My dad had to take us girls to the funeral home with him a couple times because my mom couldn't even watch us. One time me and my sisters wandered off while my dad was talking to the funeral home director, and I climbed into one of the caskets while my sisters were looking at something else. I think I just wanted to escape for a little while, you know? But I shut the lid and it latched into place and I couldn't open it. I panicked and started hyperventilating. I kept thinking something was touching my leg—a ghoul or the undead." She laughed a small laugh, shaking her head. But it faded very quickly. "But the place was so damn quiet, I was afraid to scream and make the noise it would have taken to get someone to open it for me. I didn't want to embarrass my dad. He was already barely holding on... And so

46

I stayed in there until someone finally opened it on their own, looking for me."

"God, Grace. That must have been terrifying," I said quietly.

"Honestly, I hadn't thought about it in years. But I don't know, being stuck in a small space again…I guess it just triggered that same feeling."

"Makes sense." I studied her pretty, serious face for a minute and then I smiled. "Plus, this time you had the added horror of knowing for sure that you were trapped with a demonic ghoul." I widened my eyes and did my best crazed-killer grimace.

She burst out laughing and I grinned at her, happy to see that faraway look of pain clear out of her expression.

After a minute, she raised her eyebrows. "I do believe you just got another secret out of me without having to sink a basket."

I smiled. "True. Okay, fair is fair—you get a freebie now too."

"Why do you call me buttercup?" she asked.

I turned my head in her direction and when she turned hers in mine, our faces were only inches apart. I looked into her eyes. I had told her a lot of personal stuff about myself, but for some reason, I felt like I needed to hold back now. "Maybe it's your hair," I said, glancing up at her blondness. "Will you take it down for me?"

"My hair?" she whispered. "You want me to take it down for you?"

I nodded. "Yeah."

She hesitated for a minute but then her hand slid up to the back of her head and before I knew it, a mass of silky sunshine was cascading over her shoulders.

"Jesus, buttercup. You're like an angel." I took a lock between my fingers. It felt as soft as it looked.

She smiled. "I..." Her voice trailed off as I leaned toward her. Her eyes widened, but she didn't move away, and just as our lips were about to touch, the elevator jolted and began to rise. We both pulled away from each other, her gasping in surprise. It was fixed. We were about to be set free. The only thing I could feel was disappointment.

CHAPTER 4
Grace

The jolt of the elevator brought me back to reality, and I realized we were about to be set free. "Oh, thank God!" burst out of me as I stood up and grabbed my bag and stood at the doors, ready to jump out the minute they opened. As it began a smooth descent, I looked back at Carson, and he was still sitting on the floor, unmoving, watching me with a small frown on his face.

"Hey," I started, "didn't get enough time in here? Planning on staying?" I tilted my head and smiled.

He sighed and began to stand, just as the doors opened.

I stepped through them, breathing deeply. "Ah, fresh air! Freedom!" I exclaimed.

A man in a dark blue suit came toward me. "Are you okay, Miss? I'm the manager, Mr. Savard. We want to apologize for the inconvenience that our elevator malfunction caused you. If you'll come with me to the front desk, I'd like to comp your room for the weekend."

"Oh, ah, I'm okay. But a comped room? Okay..." I said

as he took my elbow and led me away. I glanced back and another man in a suit was talking to Carson, most likely apologizing to him as well and offering him a comped room too. I'd see him at the front desk.

Mr. Savard led me to the check-in counter, and it only took a couple minutes for him to find my reservation and comp it on the computer. He also handed me a gift certificate to Picasso, a restaurant inside the hotel. He apologized profusely again, and I assured him we were fine and that it hadn't been that bad. *We.* Now where was the other half of that *we*? I stopped and looked around. He was nowhere to be seen at the front desk. I glanced around the lobby area and didn't see him there either. Did he refuse the comped room? If so, why would he just leave without even saying goodbye? My heart sped up. He had asked me to spend the weekend with him and I hadn't answered. I hadn't known what to say. I mean, it was just too crazy.

I *had* ended up liking him though, as unbelievable as that was. My shoulders dropped, and I stood there contemplating the time I'd spent with Carson Stinger. Yes, I'd judged him incorrectly and been pleasantly surprised. I would take that with me and consider the last couple of hours a good lesson about why not to judge a book by its cover. I took a deep breath and walked back to the elevators.

I chewed at my thumbnail as the elevator doors closed and rose to my floor, feeling troubled and out-of-sorts. *Of course you do. You were just stuck on an elevator. A harrowing experience, regardless of coming to like the company.*

I let myself into my room and dropped down on the bed, gazing up at the ceiling. It would be insane to even *consider* spending the weekend with Carson, right? It was so far outside my neat, tidy life that the very *thought* of it was

50

ridiculous...*wasn't it?* I forced out a laugh. It sounded as unconvincing as it felt.

Was I considering a weekend with Carson? Was I really even entertaining the idea? Did I want that? I thought about it for a few minutes, picturing his smiling face, his honed body. All right, fine, yes, I wanted it. *There, I said it.* I liked him, I had already admitted it. *I like Carson Stinger, Straight Male Performer.* It was nuts. Bonkers. Cuckoo. But admitting my attraction for him was one thing. Following through? That was quite another. Just because I wanted something, didn't mean I should do it.

It was only a weekend, though. How many other twenty-three-year-old girls meet a cute guy and spend a great weekend with them and then move on with their life? Him being in the business he was in didn't have to be a negative. In fact, maybe it made things that much more perfect—it wasn't like we could go anywhere beyond a weekend in Vegas. He knew that and I knew that. Maybe he was right—maybe it *was* within the realms of my plan. Why couldn't he be Guy Number Two? Why not? Couldn't I be crazy and outrageous just once in my life? *Just once?*

As I lay there debating, I pictured the proverbial angel and devil whispering into either ear. How had this happened exactly? I *never* gave in to temptation, and here I was strongly leaning toward spending a couple days with Carson Stinger in his Vegas hotel room, letting him teach me *things*? I brought one hand to my mouth, stifling a shocked giggle. *Oh my God. Who am I?* Two hours in an elevator with the man and I was unrecognizable to myself. And why did that thought not scare the living hell out of me? Why did I sort of... like it? I sat up quickly, giving myself a head rush. The head rush joined with a whole slew of excited nerves tingling all over my body, causing a noise to emerge from my throat that was half groan and half giggle.

Then another thought occurred to me. Maybe he had changed his mind. Maybe that's why he disappeared so quickly. I sighed, flopping back down on my bed. Maybe this was all a moot point anyway. I had no idea what his room number was and I was sure they didn't give out that information at the front desk. I let out a big sigh and then sat up again. The head rush was less this time. Maybe I'd give it a try though. And if I couldn't find him, I'd just have to resign myself to the long weekend of law presentations stretched out in front of me, just as I had planned.

Carson

I closed the door to my hotel room and dropped down on my bed, lying back and bringing my hands up to scrub down my face. *Shit.* Watching her walk away had sucked. But she had never agreed to stay with me and she had been so damn excited to get off the elevator, I knew that if I asked again, her answer would be no. She hadn't even turned to say goodbye. I wasn't going to make it more uncomfortable for her and I wasn't going to beg. Women begged me, I didn't beg them. End of story.

Still, I had thought we connected in a way that I never connected with women. Especially women I found attractive. God, I was such a fucking idiot—*you felt a connection, Carson. She didn't.* And this time, double fucking whammy, she didn't even want to enjoy my best assets. Not even that?

There were plenty who did though. I wasn't going to

lie around like a lovesick girl and write in my diary with my pink glitter pen all night.

I lay on the bed for a while longer before I stood up and stripped off my clothes and walked to the shower. As I was stepping out, I thought I heard a small knock at my room door. I stilled and listened but didn't hear it again. I wrapped the towel around my hips, and as I was walking out to grab some clothes, I heard some scuffling sounds right outside my door. My heart jumped, and I walked quickly to the door and flung it open.

Grace Hamilton was just turning away.

She jerked back around and let out a small screech as the door banged against the wall. I felt a huge grin about to spread across my face, but I forcefully stifled it, and leaned my towel-clad hip against the doorframe, crossed my arms, and raised an eyebrow. She was going to have to tell me she wanted this.

She took a deep breath and I could see that she was battling herself. I remained quiet, waiting. Hoping. Finally, after about a million years, she exhaled out all on one breath, "You asked if I'd spend the weekend with you."

I nodded. "Yes. I did." I continued to look at her expectantly.

Her eyes darted one way and then the other. "Are you still… I mean, do you still want to…"

"Yes, Grace. I do."

She let out another breath, but then bit her lip, shifting from one foot to the other. "Me too," she finally said, "I want that too."

I grinned, feeling something soar inside. "That's all I needed to hear, buttercup." I held the door open to let her cross through.

Grace

My heart slowed down when he swung the door open and gestured for me to walk inside the hotel room that looked pretty much just like mine. I had been shaking when I knocked on his room door, but then when he didn't answer, the disappointment that filled me was stronger than the nerves. I had been turned from his door and was rooting in my purse for some paper and a pen, not even knowing what I'd write yet, when he swung the door open and stood there in nothing more than a towel around his narrow hips. I had swallowed hard in order not to start drooling all over the hallway rug. He was lean but had defined muscles, and his skin was smooth and golden. He stood there looking completely comfortable in his skin. And why shouldn't he? He was used to disrobing for others' eyes. I pushed that thought aside, though, and told him why I was there. The look of happiness that spread over his face made me relax a little.

Not completely. But a little.

I walked inside and sat down on the bed, my nerves starting to buzz again when it hit me what I was doing. I looked around and realized I was bouncing my knee. I crossed my legs and looked up at Carson, uncertain what to do. What was the protocol here? He was watching me, an amused expression on his face. "I'm gonna go put some clothes on. I'll be right back."

"Oh, okay," I said, confused. Wasn't the point of this to take our clothes *off*? *God, what the hell am I doing?* I swallowed hard and considered bolting. *Maybe I haven't really thought this through.*

It had sounded like a decent idea in my room—exciting even, thrilling!—but now the reality of it had me feeling jittery and brittle.

Carson suddenly emerged from the bathroom wearing a pair of worn jeans and a Boston Red Sox T-shirt. Boston? Oh, right! "Your granny's team?" I asked, gesturing to his shirt.

He looked surprised. "Yeah. You remembered."

"You told me your granny was from Massachusetts an hour ago, Carson."

He chuckled as he started pulling on his socks. "Has it only been an hour?"

Not even an hour. But I knew what he meant. Time felt funny all of a sudden—passing in bursts of rapid heartbeats, and then stretching strangely, like nerves being pulled tight. We were both silent as he pulled on his shoes.

"So how'd you get my room number anyway?" he asked.

I scratched my neck. "Well, I went back down to the front desk and spun a tale of romantic elevator love for Mr. Savard. I told him that I had lost you in the mix and needed to tell you that I couldn't live without you. Turns out, he's a romantic who was willing to bend the rules."

He grinned. "I'll be forever in Mr. Savard's debt." He stood up. "Ready?" he asked, holding out his hand to me.

"Where are we going?"

"We're stopping by your hotel room so you can change and then I'm taking you to dinner."

Dinner. "Oh. Um, okay."

"You are hungry, right?"

I thought about it. *No, I feel like I'm going to throw up.* "Yes, I'm hungry."

"Okay, then, let's go."

I took his hand and stood up, and then followed him out of his room on legs that still felt rubbery.

We stepped on the elevator and as it began its descent, we both looked at each other and laughed. "It would be like getting struck by lightning, right?" I asked, not able to hide the slight tremble in my voice.

He smiled again as the elevator came to a stop at my floor. "Absolutely. And no one gets struck by lightning twice."

We stepped into the hallway, and when we got to my room, I took out my key card. Carson was suddenly right behind me and he put his hands on the door next to each side of my head. I stilled, the key card still inches from the key slot. My breath hitched in my throat as his smell surrounded me—clean soap and Carson, that delicious, unidentifiable scent that had me wanting to rub against him like a cat in heat again. I closed my eyes, my heart leaping, as I felt his breath against my ear. He nuzzled me with his nose and his lips for long moments, my nerves catching fire before he whispered, "I'm glad you said yes."

Oh. God, I was so turned on I was shaking, a steady throb beginning in my core and spreading down my limbs. I nodded jerkily and barely made the key card into the slot. I needed a cold shower if I was going to make it through dinner. I'd been attracted to men before, but I'd easily ignored it in order to fully focus on my studies. But this? This I couldn't ignore. I had never felt this level of lust, ever, and I didn't know whether I liked it or not. It made me feel out of control, cloudy, desperate. The feeling was scary, unfamiliar. I wasn't going to be able to push it aside. At least not easily.

I grabbed some clothes and glanced back at Carson as I went into the bathroom, and he looked cool, calm, and collected. He had fallen back on the bed and was flipping through the channels on the television. Meanwhile, I was about to go up in flames from a few whispered words and some PG nuzzling. *Oh, God.* Should I stop this before it got worse for me? I spun around and came back out of the bathroom. Carson looked up at me questioningly. I cleared my throat, my mind racing, that angel and that devil going at it from opposite shoulders. I opened my mouth and then closed it again. "Be out in a few minutes," I finally said.

The corners of his mouth shook. He was obviously holding back a smile. "Take your time."

I closed the door behind me. It was already eight thirty and when I took a few minutes to suck in deep, calming breaths, I realized I *was* actually hungry. So I showered quickly and started blowing my hair dry. I remembered Carson asking me to take it down in the elevator and so instead of putting it up like I usually did, I put some mousse in it and blew it partially dry so that it fell down my back in long waves.

I put on a little bit of makeup and spritzed some perfume on. Taking a cue from what Carson was wearing, I had pulled out a pair of dark gray shorts and a loose, black, tunic-type top. It was casual but I still felt like I looked nice for a date. I paused. Was this a date? Or was this just pre-sex dinner between practical strangers? My hormones had simmered down under the cool spray of the shower, but now I was feeling nervous again. Maybe I just needed to stop trying to define things and go with it. God, I was so bad at that. I craved structure and definitions and control. And here I was throwing all of that to the wind. For sex. With a porn star. I put my hands over my mouth to stifle a hysterical giggle as I met my own wide, blue eyes in the mirror in front of me. How was I going to feel after this was all said and done? Was I really going to be able to dismiss this as a weekend romp and easily leave it behind? I mean, technically, it *was* my plan. Only, this wasn't anywhere near how I pictured it going down. Was I capable of this? My decision in my room had been too quick. I needed time to make a pro and con list. I needed a few minutes to—

A knock came at the bathroom door. "You in there talking yourself out of this, buttercup?" Carson asked.

I pulled the bathroom door open and was met with Carson's beautiful face. He was smiling knowingly, and before I knew it, he had taken my face in his hands and was kissing my lips in a way that distracted me from all my bathroom musings. It was quick, but it was what I needed. It was what I was here for, right? And I'd needed the reminder. This didn't have to be complicated. My shoulders dropped and I relaxed my tight muscles.

He leaned back and raised a brow. I laughed a small laugh and shook my head at him, remembering that he had asked me a question. "No, I'm not talking myself out of this. Let's go."

CHAPTER 5
Carson

I grabbed Grace's hand as we walked out of the hotel. She looked over at me with a surprised expression on her face but didn't pull away. I was having a hard time keeping my eyes from drifting to her legs in those shorts and heels. From what I could tell, Grace's body was exceptional everywhere, but those legs… Christ, I never knew what a leg man I was until I got a glimpse of hers.

Her expression, however, still looked tense. I realized that I felt a little nervous too, but mine was with anticipation not worry. She looked downright worried, if not just a little panicked. That brain of hers was still working on this a mile a minute. I had known that that was what she was doing in the bathroom too by the way all the sounds stopped, and there was silence coming from the other side of the door. In my mind's eye, I could see her standing there talking herself out of this weekend and I felt a bolt of fear shoot down my spine. I had her where I wanted her to be—I'd be damned if I was going to let her walk away. Not yet anyway.

Her feet slowed as her eyes darted around nervously. "Carson, I—" But I didn't let her finish that thought. I knew she was trying to back out again.

I pulled her hand, leading her to the wall of the lobby, rather than toward the doors where we had been heading.

"Come here a minute," I said, stopping and turning to face her fully. She stared up at me expectantly and I took hold of both her hands. "Grace, this is different for me too." I looked into her eyes, hoping she'd understand what I was saying. "I know you're still questioning this and I don't want you to. If you want to leave, I obviously won't stop you. But I really hope you'll stay, and I really hope you'll let yourself enjoy our time together. Because the simple fact is that, for me, two hours wasn't nearly enough. Please tell me it wasn't enough for you either."

She searched my face for several moments, apparently finding something that relaxed her because she squeezed my hands and finally smiled up at me. "Not nearly enough," she said quietly.

I exhaled. "Okay, good. Can we focus on that then?"

She nodded, still gazing up at me. "It's just...things seemed to change so quickly between us. I kinda hated you and now I'm spending the weekend with you." She laughed quietly. "I'm having a hard time catching up with myself."

I knew exactly what she meant. I was feeling the same thing. But I was okay with it. I wasn't adjusting any plan. I was flying by the seat of my pants, just as I'd always done. This was unexpected but far from unpleasant. I was living in the moment, ready to soak up something I really, really wanted. I suddenly realized that Grace wanted to do that too. She just didn't know how. I could teach her a few things about physical pleasure, just like I'd said. My confidence in that arena was plenty high. But I realized in that moment that I could also teach her a little something about enjoying life as it came, about breaking the rules once in a while. "Yeah, life can change on a dime." I grinned. "Wild, isn't it?"

I leaned in and whispered close to her ear, "Lose control, baby. Just for a weekend. Let me take charge. I'll take good care of you, I promise."

She shivered and I saw her shoulders visibly relax. I kissed her forehead and looked down at her. She nodded, the expression on her face calm now.

"Thank you. Now man need food to have energy to drag woman by hair."

She laughed. "Well then, by all means, let's get man sustenance."

I took her hand again and we walked out the front doors, this time both of us smiling.

Grace

Carson led me out the door and toward the Strip. I was feeling relaxed now—he had somehow known that I was tense and said the words that I needed to hear to stop my wheels from turning. I wasn't sure how he'd known, but I was glad. I wanted to be with him; I just wanted to be able to enjoy it. And I hadn't known how to "go with the flow" until he asked me to give him the control. It was what I needed—someone to offer to take it from me so that I could relinquish it temporarily. I had never given up control before. Once I really thought about it, I realized that my whole life was based on control. I had never tried it any other way. So why was I willing to give it up to this virtual stranger for an entire two days? I wasn't exactly sure. I just was, and I was going to go with that. Final answer.

I grinned up at Carson and he looked at me with a quirk of his lips. "What?"

"Nothing. How tall are you anyway?"

"Six one. How tall are you, shorty?"

"Five three. And speaking of stats, I haven't asked how old you are. Am I robbing the cradle this weekend?" He looked about my age but looks could be deceiving.

"I'm twenty-three also."

"What month?"

"November."

"Oh, I'm September. So I am robbing the cradle. I'm two months older."

He laughed. "Good. I'm into older women."

"Ha-ha."

I looked around as we turned onto the Strip, walking hand in hand, my head swiveling everywhere. "It's incredible," I breathed out. "The lights…" I looked up at the names of the hotels all around us, glancing into the casinos as we walked by.

"First time in Vegas?" he asked.

"Yeah."

"On our way back, we can stop at the fountain. They do shows every fifteen minutes or so. I think you'll like it."

"Shows? What kind of shows?"

"Just wait and see."

Wait and see. "Okay."

We walked in silence for a little bit as I marveled at all of the sights and sounds around me. I couldn't help noticing all the women whose eyes lingered on Carson as we walked past them. I gripped his hand tighter as we crossed the street amongst the throngs of people.

"Where are you taking me anyway?"

"I'm not telling you because you can't judge until you get there and try it for yourself. I thought we deserved some greasy goodness after our ordeal today." He stopped walking. "Wait, shit, you do eat meat, right? You're not a vegetarian?"

"No, I'm not a vegetarian. But now I'm scared." I suddenly realized that I was starving though and I wasn't going to be picky.

He laughed and started walking again. "Don't be scared. You'll love it. I thought we could do something a little more upscale tomorrow night."

"The hotel gave me a gift certificate to Picasso. We could go there."

"It's a plan."

"Good. You know how I like a good plan." I shot him a grin.

"Oh, I know," he said, dropping my hand and putting his arm around my shoulders, pulling me into him as we walked. It felt nice and surprisingly natural. I could do this. I could *enjoy* this.

"Hey, speaking of my gift certificate, didn't they offer you a comped room too?"

"Yeah, they did, but I thought you were giving me the brush-off when you practically ran off the elevator, and I just figured I'd go on up to my room and not make things awkward up at the front desk."

I frowned. "I thought I'd see you there. I wasn't trying to give you the brush-off."

He smiled. "Yeah, I figured that out when you showed

up at my hotel room, begging me to take you in for the weekend."

I elbowed him. "Watch it, Stinger. I could still change my mind."

He laughed and squeezed me to him teasingly as he directed me to the door of a restaurant. I looked up at the sign. "Hot dogs?" I asked.

"Yup. World-famous hot dogs. Your eyes are going to roll into the back of your head. Promise."

"You did promise me that, didn't you? I didn't realize you meant hot dogs."

His eyes heated. "I promise all kinds of eye rolling, buttercup. This is just first up on the itinerary."

I snorted. "We'll see…" I was having fun joking around with him. But the eye-rolling talk had me nervous too and made me remember the supposed purpose of our weekend. Carson had already blurred the lines a little bit with a dinner date first and the reassuring words in the Bellagio lobby. *Go with it, Grace. Deep breath.*

The hostess seated us, and within a few minutes, we had each ordered a beer and a hot dog. Carson ordered some god-awful sounding concoction of bacon and sausage and nacho cheese with a side of onion rings. I ordered a chili cheese dog. I hadn't had one of those in forever and was surprised at how good it sounded.

As the waitress took our order, I noticed her trying to catch Carson's eye. He politely ignored her, smiling over at me after ordering.

Our beers were set down in front of us a few minutes later and Carson lifted his beer to mine. "To malfunctioning elevators," he said, grinning.

I laughed, clinking his bottle. I couldn't believe I was

cheersing to that. If someone had told me that about four hours ago, I'd have thought they were insane. "To malfunctioning elevators," I repeated. *God, I hope I'm still thankful to malfunctioning elevators by the end of this weekend.* I took a long sip of beer.

The waitress brought our hot dogs and I made faces at Carson as he laughed at me for trying unsuccessfully to eat mine in a ladylike manner. Finally, I just gave up and dug in like he was doing.

His eyes danced with amusement as he said around a big bite, "If you're not messy afterward, baby, you didn't do it right."

I rolled my eyes. "Ugh. You just get worse and worse, don't you?" But I couldn't help the smile that quirked the corner of my lips. I had accused him of doing his sex-on-a-stick act as a way to hide, but this was different. Those first couple times, he had used his sexual innuendos *against* me, using them to make me feel uncomfortable and then angry at my reaction to him. He knew the power he held. And he used that—in ways good *and* bad, I suspected. But he wasn't trying to do that now—at least I didn't think so. He was just trying to make me laugh. He was trying to help me let my guard down. And I had to admit, it was working.

I also had to admit that that hot dog was probably the most delicious thing I had ever eaten.

He used his napkin to wipe some chili off the side of my mouth and as his eyes lingered on my lips, I felt that throbbing start again. "Ready to get back?" he asked, his heated eyes lifting to mine.

Yes. No. I think so. Maybe. I just nodded.

He paid the bill and then we were back out on the Strip,

hand in hand, only this time not walking with as much leisure as we had on the way to dinner.

We crossed the street and walked in silence back to the Bellagio fountain. My heart was racing now. I knew where this was leading, and as much as I wanted it now, this was going to change everything.

There was already a small group of people waiting in front of the still water. Carson scooted me to the stone railing at the front, and as I stood silently, waiting for the show to begin, he wrapped his arms around my waist and held me. I leaned my head back against him and enjoyed the feeling of his big body wrapped around me.

After a minute or two, music started playing and the water burst up into the air. I sucked in a breath as I realized that the water was "dancing" to the music. "Oh my God!" I exhaled. "It's stunning!"

I felt the vibration of Carson's chuckle. "Pretty, isn't it?"

"It's amazing. How do they do it?" I couldn't look away.

"I don't really know. They play all kinds of different songs though. They're all choreographed."

"Wow." I suddenly realized what song was on and I giggled. "Listen to what's playing." I looked back at Carson and grinned as "My Heart Will Go On," the theme from *Titanic*, burst through the loud speakers.

He leaned down into me and in a mocking voice said, "Jack, Jack, don't ever let go… Well, that is, unless I try *once* to pull you up on this two-person raft and can't do it. Then, Godspeed, human popsicle. It was fun while it lasted."

I laughed. "You really are bitter about that, aren't you? You should try to let it go. There are professionals who might be able to help."

"I might look into that." He gave me a teasing grin and then pulled me back harder against him.

We watched the show for a couple minutes in silence, and when I took his hands in mine from the front, he leaned down and nuzzled into my hair, his scent intoxicating me again. I dropped my head back onto his shoulder, giving him better access. He took me up on my offer, kissing the sensitive skin of my neck, his warm breath tickling my ear. That now-familiar throbbing was starting and I wanted him to kiss me again. I wanted him all over me.

"Let's take this inside, buttercup," he whispered, his voice sounding strained.

"Why do you call me buttercup?" I asked softly.

"Hmm…maybe it's because you smell like a flower," he said. And then he grabbed my hand and we started walking toward the hotel as he grinned that heart-stopping grin at me.

CHAPTER 6
Carson

I led her as fast as possible to the hotel. As we made our way through the lobby, her shorter legs speed-walked to keep up with me. It wasn't very chivalrous, I knew, but I was a desperate man. I didn't think I'd been in this bad a shape since…well, since ever. After standing at the fountain watching her eyes light up with excitement at the water display and then holding her in my arms, drinking in the feel of her, the smell of her, my blood was pumping hot and fast with need. And not just a general need—a need for *her*, a need that was clawing its way through my body, demanding to be satisfied. I barely knew her, and yet everything about Grace Hamilton went straight to my head, like a strong shot of whiskey, making my brain spin.

But I had promised her I'd take care of her, take control. I needed to keep ahold of mine if I was going to put her at ease and make her feel safe enough to give herself to me fully. I knew that instinctively.

Give herself to me fully? I slammed the mental brakes. No, not fully. It was sex and it was a good time—just for the weekend. It was all I had to offer. And it was all she wanted to take. Still, I wanted this to be a satisfying experience for both of us—in as many ways as possible.

As we walked through the casino toward the elevators, I saw a group of people I recognized from the business, here for the expo, standing off to the side, talking and laughing loudly. I put my arm around Grace and nuzzled into her, trying to make sure none of them recognized me and called out my name. I didn't typically socialize with any of them, but they'd probably know who I was. The last thing I wanted was to remind Grace what I did or get sidetracked for even a minute from our destination—the privacy of my hotel room.

We stepped onto the elevator and I asked, "Do you need to stop at your room for anything?"

"Yes. If you don't mind," she said quietly, her eyes lingering on mine for a couple beats before they dropped to my mouth. My dick throbbed in my jeans. You could cut the sexual tension in the air with a butter knife. I turned to the panel of numbers and pushed her floor number with my thumb again and again, as if that would speed the elevator up.

We rode up silently and made our way to her room. She let us in and I stood by the door while she quickly gathered a few of her things. Then we got back on the elevator and rode a couple floors up to my room. I didn't feel the need to ask her what she was thinking. Her facial expression told me that she was steady, her eyes reflecting back the desire I was feeling.

It took me three tries to unlock the door and once inside, I threw my wallet and key card on the desk and turned to Grace. She was standing behind me, just having placed her travel bag on the floor, and I took the few steps to bring myself inches from her. Electricity sparked between us. We both knew exactly what was about to happen. We stood silently, staring at each other, the pulse at the base of her neck jumping and a faint color rising in her cheeks. As I watched her, holding myself back from touching her, I felt like I was going to burst out of my skin.

"You want this too, Grace." I needed to hear her say it again.

She nodded, her eyes twin pools of want. *For me.* "Yes," she whispered.

Yes. The best word in the English language.

I closed the small distance between us and took her face in my hands. She was watching me so carefully. I brought my lips to hers, taking a gentle taste of her lush mouth. Our first kiss had been angry, harsh, lustful, unplanned. The second one had been quick, almost chaste. This one was slow and deep, our tongues meeting and tangling, tasting. Each stroke of her tongue on mine sent an electric current straight to my cock. She tasted like fucking heaven. I was vibrating like a tuning fork. But I was going to take this slow. Now that we were here, now that we had both made it clear that we wanted each other, there was no rush. It was just her and me and the long night that stretched out before us. I couldn't help the deep moan that rose from my chest at the thought. My cock surged forward.

She brought her arms around me and pressed her body closer, a small moan emerging from her throat too. I felt that moan in every cell of my body.

After several minutes—or weeks, I couldn't be sure—I broke from her mouth and we both took in deep breaths of air, our eyes meeting again. Hers were heavy-lidded and shining with desire—I was sure mine were too.

I brought my lips to her ear, letting my teeth graze over her lobe, and asked her quietly, "How do you want to come the first time, Grace?" I heard her breath hitch as I continued. "Against my mouth? Around my cock? How, buttercup? It won't be just once, so I want to know how you want it the first time."

"Your mouth, Carson," she breathed out, more color rising in her cheeks. I could see her body trembling slightly.

I practically growled as I grabbed the hem of her shirt and brought it up as she lifted her arms so that I could remove it. I brought it over her head and tossed it to the side. Then I turned back to her and drank her in, standing before me in her shorts and a black lace bra, her creamy breasts spilling out of the cups. She still looked a little uncertain, watching me closely, waiting to see what I was going to do next. This girl, who had planned out her whole life, step by step, was looking to me for instruction. The thought made me dizzy with something I couldn't identify in that moment. Honor came to mind, but that seemed like a very serious word for a weekend of casual fun. But maybe it wasn't. I didn't know. I couldn't think straight.

What I was sure of, was that I wanted to watch her eyes as I touched her for the first time, but the sight of my hands on her skin had me mesmerized, and I couldn't look away as I traced the outline of her bra cups with one finger, her chest rising and falling in quick, shallow breaths. She drew in a gulp of air and pressed her breasts toward me, offering me more of her. I met her eyes as I released the front clasp of her bra and then looked down as it fell aside to reveal the perfect breasts beneath, pink, pearly nipples already hardened and begging for my mouth. I traced the underside of them, watching the twin buds pucker even

71

more. "You're beautiful," I said. And the way she was looking at me... with sexual need, yes, but also with trust. No one had ever looked at me that way. Not just in bed, but in general. It made my heart skip a beat. It made me feel suddenly unsure in a way I couldn't describe. *Are you trustworthy?*

Get it together. She's counting on you to keep control.

As I lowered my head and licked one nipple lightly, tasting it and flicking it with my tongue, Grace let out a long moan and let her head fall back. I cupped the underside of each breast, feeling the perfect weight of them in my hands. Then I brought my mouth to the other nipple as she raised her hands and ran them through my hair. "Ah!" she cried out. "Carson."

My name on her lips. Oh, God I liked that.

I lifted my head. "What is it, buttercup?"

"No! Don't stop. Please. It's so good. I feel like I could come just from that alone. God."

I smiled as I moved back slightly and unbuttoned her shorts and let them fall to the floor. She kicked her heels off and kicked her shorts aside. I sucked in a breath. "Jesus, you weren't wearing panties?"

She shrugged. "Panty lines..."

My eyes moved down her body, taking in her flat stomach and the section of bare skin between her thighs. She was breathtaking, her skin creamy and smooth. I couldn't wait to show her all the things she'd been missing out on.

I lowered my head back to her breast, the taste of her making my excitement rage out of control, my cock pulsating.

"You taste so good," I sighed out as I brought my mouth up to her neck, tasting her there too. She moaned again and ground her core against mine. "Carson," she whispered, "I want to see you too."

"Anything you want, buttercup," I said as I moved back slightly and pulled my T-shirt over my head. I quickly kicked off my shoes and bent to pull my socks off so that I could pull my jeans and boxers down my legs.

For a few beats, her gaze traveled down my body, pausing at my erection, her eyes widening slightly. "You're perfect, Carson," she whispered as her eyes met mine again.

I knew how I affected women. It was what I did, who I was. I had been told more times than I could count how much women appreciated my body. It's what women wanted from me. But for some reason, when Grace told me that she liked what she saw, something inside me soared in happiness. Maybe it was because I had an inkling that a girl like Grace wouldn't be here just for my body, despite what she might be telling herself. There was something that felt more all-encompassing about her compliment. It was a strange thought, really, and I didn't know what made it skate through my mind. But there it was. I liked it, but it made a small tremble move through me too, and so I pushed it away.

A thank-you to her compliment didn't seem like it was necessary. I stepped closer again and now our naked bodies were right against each other, my throbbing erection just touching the smooth skin of her stomach. Just that small contact made me hiss in a breath. I enclosed her in an embrace, pressing into her with more pressure and feeling every inch of her skin against mine. I began kissing her again as I walked her backward, and when the back of her knees hit the bed, she fell onto the comforter and I followed her down.

73

Grace

My back hit the bed and Carson was on top of me before I could even draw in a full breath. His hard, naked body touched mine everywhere and a thrill went down my spine when I felt his big shaft press into my belly. He was big, but I didn't think I needed to worry about that—my core was slick with desire, my vaginal muscles convulsing, begging to receive him into my body. As his mouth came down on mine again, his tongue delving deep, I ground up against him. I was desperate now. He had me so worked up, I was sure that all he'd have to do was touch me once and I'd fall apart. I needed it. I was willing to beg. Any nervousness I'd felt had burned to ash in the raging inferno of desperation for the release that I knew was right within reach.

Carson broke our kiss and moved down my body, flicking each of my nipples once with his tongue before kissing down my stomach. My breath hitched as I realized what he was about to do. I had asked him for it, but suddenly, I felt unsure. No one had ever done that for me before—what if I didn't like it? What if I couldn't come that way? What if he didn't like the way I tasted down there? "Carson, I don't know..."

His head came up as he scooted off the bed to the floor, on his knees in front of me. "Shh. Trust me." He reached out for my hands and pulled me up and to the edge of the bed until I was sitting up with my core right at his face. "Lean back on your hands and watch me," he ordered. I bit my lip but did as he said.

He pushed my knees apart farther until I was open and completely exposed to him. His gaze fell to my naked, wet flesh and then he leaned in and inhaled deeply. "Perfect," he murmured, right before his head lowered between my legs. My heart skipped a beat and more wet heat rushed downward.

I cried out in ecstasy as I felt his warm tongue lap all the way up me once and then circle my swollen nub. *Oh God, that felt incredible.* I opened my legs farther to give him more access and my head unconsciously fell back on a moan. "Eyes, Grace, watch me," Carson growled, his head coming up from between my legs.

"Yes, yes, eyes," I panted out. I'd do anything if he'd put his tongue back on me. I'd never imagined something could feel this good. My heavy lids opened half-mast and I gazed down at him. He lowered his head again and his tongue flicked my tender flesh, eliciting another moan. Fireworks were detonating under my skin, the glitter raining through my veins and a furious pulsing of pleasure was swelling and receding right where his tongue was now lapping at me.

Don't stop. Don't stop. Don't stop.

His eyes met mine as his tongue worked my pink nub, sucking it and kissing it. The room spun, that pulsing growing stronger. I gasped loudly as he put one finger inside me, never letting up what he was doing with his mouth. He moved his finger in and out of me, and I could hear the slick sounds of my arousal as he used one finger for a minute, and then two.

His tongue licking at me rhythmically was delicious bliss, and the addition of his fingers moving in and out of me was ecstasy, but the sight of his head between my legs was my undoing. The look of my thighs stretched out around his silky hair, as his head bobbed and worked between my legs, was so erotic that within less than a minute, the pulsing in my core rose to a fever pitch. I screamed as I shattered around him, waves and waves of pure bliss exploding through my body.

When I opened my eyes, I had fallen back on the bed and Carson was over me. I was still trying to catch my breath, the throbs of pleasure slowly fading. "Good, baby?" he asked.

I couldn't help the laughter that erupted out of me. He had told me he could make me come, and God, had he delivered. I might never recover. "God yes" was all I could manage.

He leaned down and kissed me and I tasted myself on his mouth. There was something even more personal about the fact that I was sharing that with him, and it was a reminder of where he'd just been. Another surge of heat raced down my spine at the memory of that picture and I shivered. Already, my body was greedy for more of what he had just given me.

As Carson swept his tongue inside my mouth, he rubbed his chest on my nipples and I moaned. He pulled away and whispered, "You want me inside you, don't you, buttercup?" His voice sounded deep and raspy.

"Yes, yes, please." I couldn't believe he had just given me the most mind-blowing orgasm of my life and less than five minutes later, I was begging him for more. There was still a steady throb deep inside me that I knew would only be quenched by him pushing into my body and filling me.

He stood up and walked over to the desk where he had thrown his wallet and pulled a condom out of it. "Scoot back, Grace," he said, as he started climbing back over me. He wasn't smiling anymore, and neither was I. I was mesmerized, watching his beautiful, naked body flex as he moved away from me and then back again, so powerful and perfectly male. I watched as he tore the condom wrapper open with his teeth and rolled it on. His erection looked

almost painfully engorged, red and standing straight at attention. *That's going to be inside me in a minute,* I thought. As I
looked up and my eyes met his, something flared between us.
A look crossed over his face, something I couldn't identify. It
made him look momentarily... younger, maybe even slightly
vulnerable. Or maybe my brain was just misfiring.

I scooted up the bed and waited for him to join me.
"Pull the sheets back, buttercup. I don't want you to get a
chill." It was a funny thing to say, considering that I still felt
like I was on fire. But I guess the air conditioner was on
high. Or maybe he just intended on taking his time with
me. A thrill shot through me and my stomach clenched.
I lay back, wondering what he was going to do. I realized
that for the first time I could ever remember, my mind
was empty—at least to anything except the sensations that
Carson was bringing me. I relished it. To let someone else
make the calls, to give someone else control, at least temporarily, it made me want to weep with relief. I didn't ponder
it very long; I just enjoyed it.

I pulled the sheet back and scooted under it, and then
Carson climbed under it too and leaned back over me, his
eyes heavy with heat. "I'm going to take you hard, Grace.
Tell me if it's too much, okay?"

"Yes, yes, I want that," I moaned, more wetness pooling
between my thighs.

I *wanted* it hard. I wanted him to pound into me. I'd
never had it that way. My inner muscles clenched in delicious
anticipation and a thrill shot down my spine, that furious
pulsing picking up strength and speed again.

He moved between my legs and I brought my knees up
and let my legs fall to the side, offering myself to him.

He took my wrists in his hands and brought them over

my head and held them against the pillow. He climbed on top of me and brought his lips to mine again, thrusting his tongue into my mouth seconds before he thrust into me from below. I moaned out in pleasure and he tore his mouth from mine. "Oh, fuck, Grace, baby, you feel good."

"Please," I panted out. What I was begging for, I wasn't sure, but he seemed to know.

He let out a quick exhale and started pumping into me. At first he went slow and deep, his movement controlled, rubbing a spot inside of me that I didn't even know existed. I panted out in pleasure, "Oh God, oh God, right there, yessss," and his eyes watched me, gauging my reaction and moving his body in response to my cues. When I started panting and pushing up against him, he started moving hard and fast, thrusting into me relentlessly, his eyes growing heavy, his mouth falling open. God, he was so beautiful it was heart-stopping.

As he slammed into me over and over, the pleasure spiraled higher and higher until there was nowhere to go but over the edge. I shuddered and screamed out beneath him as the orgasm exploded through my body. This one was just as intense as the first, but it was different, starting from deep inside, my internal muscles rippling and clenching deliciously. *Holy hell.*

As I came down, I watched his face tense and I knew he was coming. "Oh God," he choked out as his thrusts grew jerky and goose bumps erupted on his skin.

He moved his mouth to mine and moaned out the rest of his orgasm against my lips. As he kissed me slowly and deeply, he moved in and out of me leisurely, milking his own climax before his hips came to a stop, and he let go of my hands. "You're incredible, buttercup," he said breathlessly, moving his head to my shoulder to bite it playfully.

He pulled out of me and rolled off, standing up and heading to the bathroom, to get rid of the condom, I assumed. He was back in a flash, climbing back under the sheet and pulling me into his arms.

"You're very quiet over there," he said after a minute. "Tell me what you're thinking."

"I was thinking, so *that's* what sex is supposed to be like." I sighed, shock and awe still clouding my orgasm-fogged brain.

He let out a breath, pulling me closer.

"My future husband is going to make a shrine in your honor," I said.

He was quiet for a beat, then two before he finally said, "Hmmm. Remind me to give you an autographed picture before you leave so you can hang it directly above."

I smiled into his chest, kissing the smooth skin.

I used my pointer finger to trace his nipple and watched as it hardened. I brought my leg up over his and felt him twitch against me. "Grace..." he moaned out.

My head came up. "Really? You could go again so soon?"

"I guess I haven't gotten enough of you yet."

I laughed. "Well, good thing you have me all weekend. But I think I need at least a couple hours of recovery time. My bones feel like water."

"Okay, as long as you don't mind being woken up in the middle of the night."

"Hmm-mm. Not if you do that to me again."

I felt his grin against my forehead as he leaned down and kissed me. "Go to sleep, buttercup."

"Why do you call me buttercup?" I whispered sleepily. I'd keep trying until he gave me a real answer. He had to run out of silly ones eventually.

"Maybe because your skin is as creamy as butter," he said, and I could hear the smile in his voice.

"Hmmm." I closed my eyes and was asleep within minutes.

———————

Carson made good on his promise to wake me up in the middle of the night as he pushed inside of me and thrust lazily until we both tipped over the edge, the pleasure making us both moan into each other's mouths.

When I woke up to his delicious scent all around me in the early hours of the morning, I felt something hot and hard twitching against my ass and so I took his thick, hard length in my hand and stroked him until I saw the goose bumps erupt on his skin and he moaned out in release.

"You're gonna kill me, buttercup," he choked out, his voice thick with sleep. "But oh well, we all have to go sometime."

I grinned against his skin.

We fell back to sleep as a small sliver of sunlight showed itself at the edge of the blackout curtains and didn't wake up again until my stomach was growling with hunger and I'd missed the beginning of my conference.

CHAPTER 7
Carson

I slipped out of bed and pulled on my clothes. I watched Grace as I zipped and buttoned my jeans. She was asleep on her stomach, the sheet just barely covering her ass, her hair a mass of blond waves, going in every direction. She looked like a goddess. I had been inside her twice last night and this morning, and had three orgasms, and yet I still wanted to roll her over and sink inside her again. I couldn't get enough. The thought worried me a little because it was unfamiliar. I was usually halfway out the door before the woman even realized I was leaving. Not that I wasn't up front about what my hookups were about, and the women I chose were ones who indicated to me that that was fine by them. Whether they were lying or not wasn't really my concern. Not that I could have a normal relationship anyway—even if I wanted one. Girls who weren't in the business tended to have a big problem dating a guy who made porn films. I didn't blame them. And no way I could date a woman in the business. I knew better than anyone that sex on set was just work.

But to potentially develop feelings for a woman who fucked other dudes? No, thanks. So if I wasn't working, I stayed away from the whole crowd.

But here was this beautiful woman lying in my bed, tangled in the sheets that we had just fucked in—again and again—and I practically wanted to tie her down so that she didn't leave. Only, she *would* leave—Monday morning. And I'd be wise to get my fill of her and not forget that I'd be sending her on her way—just after a little more time than the others. In the end, I guess it was all the same.

So why didn't it *feel* the same? Why did the thought depress me so damn much? Why did it feel like this weekend was already going far too fast? I shrugged it off as best as I could. Whether I liked it or not, it was reality that my time with Grace was limited.

I made my way to the restaurant downstairs and ordered two coffees and a couple pastries to go. I jumped back on the elevator and headed back to my room to feed my sleeping goddess who for now anyway, was waiting for me. I couldn't help the smile that spread across my face. I could have ordered room service, but I didn't want anyone wheeling a cart into the room and seeing Grace naked, wrapped in a sheet. My smile faltered. It was an interesting thought considering I'd never had much of a problem with modesty. Or rather, lack thereof. I just... I knew Grace would and so I'd saved her the possible embarrassment. Yes, that was it.

I opened the room door, balancing the coffees in one hand and the bag of pastries in the other, making sure the "do not disturb" sign was still on the door handle.

I closed the door quietly and set the food on the desk. Grace was in the exact same position she had been in when I left which caused me to smile as I walked over to the bed and moved her hair aside. I leaned in close and whispered, "Hey, sleeping buttercup."

She wriggled and opened one eye as she gave me a sleepy smile. "Hey yourself," she said, sitting up and bringing the sheet up over her breasts. She glanced at the clock and looked back at me, startled. "Oh God. I missed the beginning of my conference."

"Yeah, I guess we didn't really talk about that, did we? You gonna be in trouble?"

She shook her head, but her eyes drifted to the side. "It wasn't mandatory or anything. No one will know whether I was there or not. I've just never blown something off..." She paused for a minute, seeming to perk up. "You know what? It's okay. But there is one presentation that I want to go to tomorrow afternoon, the one I really came for, but I'm okay skipping the rest." She looked almost surprised before she turned her face to me and gave me a bigger smile. "Is that coffee I smell?"

"Yup." I grabbed her cup and brought it to her. "Pastries too if you want one?"

"I'd love one. That was nice of you to get me food."

"Babe, your stomach was growling so loud I thought it was a plane flying overhead. I couldn't exactly sleep through that racket."

She laughed, putting a hand over her mouth so that she didn't spew the sip of coffee she had just taken. "It was not!" Her laugh dwindled. "Was it?"

"Okay, maybe not that loud, but my buttercup clearly needed food."

She smiled over the lid of her coffee cup and took another sip. "So, what about you? Are you going to be in trouble for skipping your show? I mean... you know, assuming you are?" She looked suddenly uncertain. We hadn't really made plans about how much of the weekend we were going to spend together.

"I am skipping," I told her. I wanted to spend as much time with her as possible. Night *and* day. And I was ecstatic that she apparently did too. "As far as whether I'll get flack for it? Probably. I don't know. I haven't turned my phone on since you showed up at my door. My agent has probably been calling me nonstop."

She stared at me silently for a couple beats. "Carson...if this weekend isn't a good idea for your...career, I don't want to cause trouble for you."

"Grace, I'm not exactly broken up about spending time with a beautiful, sexy buttercup, rather than throngs of porn fans." Why did I hate talking about anything that reminded her what I did? It was part of the reason she was here—my experience. And yet I found myself steering the conversation away from my job whenever possible.

She laughed a little uncomfortably and then got a stricken look on her face. "Last night...in the middle of the night, did you..." She looked around and her eyes landed on the empty condom wrapper on the bedside table. She breathed a sigh of relief. "Oh, okay."

I paused. That sinking feeling again before I specifically addressed what she was obviously—rightly—concerned about. "We have to get tested every month," I told her. "I just got a clean bill of health a week ago. You're probably safer with me than some random guy you might pick up at the pool."

She shifted the sheet over her chest with the hand not holding her coffee. "Well, that's...good. Still, I'm not on birth control. I guess we should have talked about that." Another shift of the sheet. "I'm usually more..."

"Responsible?"

Her eyes met mine and I couldn't read exactly what was in them. "Yes."

"We'll be really careful, okay?"

She nodded, taking another sip of her coffee.

"So, what do you want to do today? The city is our oyster."

"The first thing I want to do is take a shower. I'm a mess." She used one hand to smooth her wild hair.

"You're beautiful. But how about you finish your breakfast and I jump in for five minutes, and then you take one after me. Is that all right?"

"Yes, sounds good."

"Okay." I smiled and leaned in and kissed her lips. "Out in five."

Grace

Carson handed me the bag of pastries and some napkins and I sat in bed drinking my coffee and nibbling on the sweets, considering the situation at hand. I felt sort of stricken and sort of blissful. I choked down the giggles rising up my throat. I didn't know if they were giggles of hilarity or hysteria. Or both. I was eating in bed—which I never did—*sweets*—which I never ate—after letting a gorgeous porn star give me multiple orgasms through the night. And now I was blowing off my conference—unheard of—so that I could spend more time with him. And hopefully later he'd give me more mind-blowing orgasms. Who was I? And why exactly wasn't I heading for the hills? *Because you like him*, a small voice said.

I took a bite of pastry, chewing thoughtfully. Yes, I liked him. But that was good, right? I had always planned on liking my Guy Number Two. Yes, it could be argued—pretty well, most likely—that what I was doing was ill-advised on a few levels. But if I didn't even like the guy, it wouldn't make sense to deviate from my plan so drastically. You couldn't have fun with a person you didn't like. And as it turned out, Carson was very likable. He was funny—I never knew exactly what was going to come out of his mouth. And there was a sweetness to him that I didn't think he showed very many people. And he was sexy as hell and the things he could do with his mouth and his...

"What are you daydreaming about?" Carson asked. I blinked, startled to see him standing in the bathroom doorway wearing nothing more than a towel.

Mmm. You, as a matter of fact. "Oh, just, you know, stuff..." I said, standing up and stretching. Carson watched me, a slow smile stretching across his face. I liked that smile—*a lot*. But there was time for more of *that* later, and I really did need a shower. I scooted past him and closed the bathroom door, standing still for a moment. God, I was really out of my element here. It kept hitting me. *Get it together, Grace. He said he'd take charge. Just relax and let him. Stop thinking so damn much. It seemed to work out just fine last night.* Heat rushed through me as the slideshow of our night raced through my brain. My breathing evened and my nerves evaporated, at least for now, and I went about the business of brushing my teeth and showering.

When I emerged from the bathroom with a towel around me and my hair still damp, Carson was sitting up against the headboard, scrolling through his phone, still clad in nothing but his towel.

He glanced up from his phone, his gaze raking down my body. "Come here." An excited flush prickled my skin. I'd thought about there being time for more sex later, but this *was* later. Wasn't it? Sure was.

I approached him slowly and sat down on his lap, my back facing his chest, and then I pulled my legs up over his and stretched them out. Carson wrapped his arms around me and then swept my hair to the side and leaned down and nuzzled my neck, tracing my ear with his nose. I sighed, my nipples hardening and heat swirling through my belly at his simplest of touches.

I felt him swell and lengthen beneath me, a heady reminder that he was affected by me too. The knowledge made me bolder and I rotated my ass slowly over his growing erection. He moaned. "God, Grace, that feels so good."

He opened my towel and palmed my breasts, squeezing them gently and then rubbing his thumbs on my hardened nipples. He seemed to not only know exactly where to touch me, but in what combination…what pressure to use, how fast to stroke. I'd heard the phrase, "he played me like a fiddle," before, and now I knew exactly what it meant. It made me smile.

"What's funny?" he asked, obviously having heard my mouth move, or maybe he felt it against his cheek.

"This," I said. "Not funny though, *good*." His thumbs flicked my nipples again and I moaned and was rewarded by the feel of his cock jumping beneath me. My sounds of pleasure turned him on. I loved that. I loved everything about this—the way he touched me, the way he reacted to my pleasure, his scent, his sexy voice, the feel of his body under mine. I moaned again when he pinched my nipples gently and then pressed upwards against my ass.

He played with my breasts for a few more minutes as he kissed my neck from behind and I rubbed my ass against him. We were both breathing hard now, the humming sound of the air conditioner and our gasps and moans the only things filling the room. It felt like electricity was running through my veins, sending hot bolts between my legs.

He reached his hand down and ran a finger between my folds. "Jesus, you're wet, baby. Is all that for me? So I can slide right in? Tell me, Grace." His voice was thick, raspy.

One finger hit my spot and started circling slowly.

"Yes," I breathed out. "For you. Ahhh. Don't stop."

"For who, buttercup?"

"For you, Carson, for you." I was panting unabashedly now, aching for him.

"That's good." He pressed his swollen length against my ass. "Is this what you want, Grace?"

"Yes, yes," I panted. I grabbed the towel and yanked it out from underneath me so that I could get closer to him.

He chuckled. "You'll get it. I'm gonna give it to you, baby, but first you have to do something for me."

He continued fingering my clit with one hand and flicking my nipple with the other.

"What? Yes. I'll do it. What do you want me to do?" I'd do anything if he'd relieve me, if he'd fill the terrible, achy void.

I felt his grin against my shoulder as his finger sped up. "I want you to promise me you'll say my name when you come. I want to hear you scream it. Will you do that?"

"Yes, okay, yes." I was delirious with need now. I'd scream out anything he asked me to. I didn't know why he wanted that, and in that moment, I didn't care.

"Okay, good." He removed his hands from me and I

made a gasping sound of loss. "Shhh. I gotta keep you safe, Grace." He reached into the bedside table drawer, where he apparently threw some condoms at some point, and grabbed one. Then he tore it open with his teeth. "Turn around," he said gently, and as I did, he slid the condom down his length.

I stared at his stiff cock jutting straight up and licked my lips in anticipation. He sat up a little bit straighter against the pillows in front of the headboard and said, "Come down on top of me." His voice was strained and his eyes were unfocused. "If you don't like it this way, we can do something else."

My breath released. But I wasn't scared. I was so turned on, I was willing to try just about anything. I leaned up and then sunk down on him, taking just the tip inside of me. We both gasped in pleasure. Our eyes met and for a moment we simply stared at each other, something that felt hot and heavy moving between us. Our shared arousal, maybe, but it felt like more than that too. I was just too delirious with need to define it. He dropped his head back. "Oh, God, that's it, baby, more, please," he grunted.

I slid down lower until he was buried in me to the hilt. *Oh.* For a few seconds I simply breathed, getting my bearings, experiencing something completely new.

"Are you okay?" he asked. He sounded pained, but I had no doubt that if I said I wanted to stop, we would.

But I didn't want to stop. "Yes," I said. "Better than okay."

His breath released. He held on to my hips as I moved slowly up and down on him, experimenting, feeling every inch of him. "Your face, Grace. I love your face right now. You're so beautiful."

And when I met his eyes, I saw the sincerity of what he'd just said. He was looking at me like I was a goddess. I smiled and leaned forward, kissing him for a minute before pulling back and experimenting with the movement of my hips again, bouncing and rotating. I gasped as he adjusted his hips and hit that internal spot again. "Oh Godddd," I moaned. "Right there, please don't move." And then I began riding him in earnest, as he leaned back slightly and watched me with heavy-lidded eyes, his lips parted, and his cheekbones stained with color. So beautiful. He was beautiful too. And then I closed my eyes so I could focus on the feel of him. Of this.

When my internal muscles began clenching and that tingly heat started spreading downward, I opened my eyes and looked right at Carson. "I'm gonna come!" His eyes darkened and his hips bucked upward as I threw my head back and screamed his name—again and again. *Carson, Carson, Carson.* It rang in my head long after the pleasure began to fade.

Carson

As Grace repeated my name, my own climax surged and I jerked my hips as I spilled into her, the pleasure pulsing through my cock in blissful spasms. I watched her ride out her orgasm, grinding down on me to milk out every last drop of pleasure, unknowingly doing the same for me. *Fucking beautiful.*

I recalled the look on her face as she'd begun lowering herself onto me. Curiosity. Amazement. *Pure delight.* I'd never in my life seen that mix of emotions on anyone's face, especially when it came to me. It'd fucking *moved* me.

I couldn't remember being moved during sex before. Ever. Wasn't that the weirdest thing? I mean, sex was... *sex*. It was supposed to cause the earth to shift. And of all the sex I'd had, I'd never experienced that.

As she raised her head, a small, satisfied smile on her face, she leaned forward and kissed me sweetly and then touched her forehead to mine. For a moment, we simply breathed together, staring into each other's eyes. "What if this backfires and you just end up ruining me for anyone else?" she asked with a teasing quirk of her lip, sitting back and pushing the hair that had fallen low on my forehead out of my face.

What if.

"What happens if you end up ruining *me* for anyone else?" I told myself I was teasing too.

She laughed, lying down on my chest. I was still semi-hard inside of her, just enjoying the feel of her skin on mine, running my hands up and down the silk of her back. I liked the feel of her in my arms. Too much.

What I needed to do was lighten up, put this solidly back in the category of *"fun weekend."* "I feel so damn sorry for that first guy," I said. "Never getting to hear you scream his name. Missed out. Sorry fucker."

Her body shook on top of mine in gentle laughter. "Who knew I was a screamer anyway? Think the manager will be by to kick us out soon?" She grinned against my chest and nipped at my skin with her teeth.

"Probably. We should stay in your room tonight—give the people on this floor a little rest." I grinned into her hair and she laughed again. *There we go. Back on track.*

After a few minutes I gave her a gentle nudge. "Okay, up. I'm not going to keep you locked in this room all day.

Although it's tempting. We're gonna walk around and you're going to experience Vegas."

"Okay." She yawned. "Nap later?"

"It's a plan, buttercup."

She shot me a wink. "Okay, good, come rinse off with me."

That sounded dangerous, but I was nothing if not a risk-taker.

An hour, a bottle of bodywash, and another orgasm later, we were dressed and ready to go.

I didn't have a specific destination in mind—we just walked down the Strip, people watching and stopping in a casino here and there. She loved the casino at the Paris which didn't surprise me. I teased her that she was like an old lady with the slot machines. She took out a couple of dollars and sat feeding them into the machine, sucking in a breath when she won twenty-seven back. We brought her ticket up to the redemption kiosk, and I couldn't keep the grin off my face just watching her excitement. It was like this girl had lived under a rock all her life and someone had finally lifted it to show her the sky. I realized that I hadn't had just plain *fun* with a girl maybe ever. And who would have guessed that the girl I first thought was an uptight little princess would be the one to give that to me? I had said it to Grace and it was fucking true; *life is wild*.

I told her that while she was in Vegas, she needed to experience a buffet and so we walked to the Bacchanal Buffet at Caesars Palace. She got a plate and a half of food and then sat back with a look on her face like she had gorged herself. "I guess I didn't really get your money's worth, did I?"

I laughed. "Well, considering that your first plate was all dessert, I'm not surprised."

"I just didn't want to get full and then miss out on all those cakes." She grinned but it slipped into thoughtfulness. "I can't even remember the last time I ate cake, much less… eight!"

"Then it was worth every penny."

She waved her hand toward my lunch, the plate piled high with ten different items from four different food stations. "You must work out to keep that physique of yours. Because you sure don't diet."

I laughed around a mouthful. "I don't work out at the gym, but I surf and snowboard anytime I'm not traveling for work—any extreme sport and I'm there."

"Snowboarding? In California?" She wrinkled her brow.

"Yeah! Mammoth Mountain is less than five hours from LA and Tahoe is about seven. The snowboarding is great. I go with my buddies all the time."

"Really? Hmm. Sounds fun."

"Where are you from originally, Grace?"

"Ohio," she answered.

"I'm gonna assume you've never surfed. Have you ever snowboarded?"

She shook her head. "No, I've never done either. After my parents divorced, money was kinda tight. We never traveled."

"When did your parents divorce?"

"A couple years after my brother, Andrew, died. My mom just never really pulled herself out of the depression she sunk into," she said quietly. "My dad tried everything to help her move forward, but nothing worked. Eventually, she asked my dad for a divorce. I think just being around him, watching us all try to get back to life, it was too hard for her. She resented us and thought we were the reason she couldn't ever feel okay." She shrugged, but I saw the grief flash in her eyes. It still hurt her to think about what had happened to her family.

"So your dad raised you. Where did your mom go?"

"She moved across town. We went to her house on the weekends for a while, but eventually those visits stopped. It was miserable for us to be there. And confusing. She would just start crying in the middle of dinner, and if any of us ever raised our voice for any reason, she couldn't handle it. She checked into a hospital to try to have her depression treated when I was fourteen and she seemed to get a little better. But she's never completely come back. My sisters and I see her once a year or so, usually around the holidays. She's living with a boyfriend now who's pretty nice. She seems to be doing okay. Better anyway." She fiddled with her napkin.

Jesus, no wonder she was such a control freak. Her whole fucking world had fallen apart when she was just a kid.

"Hey," I said, reaching for her hand across the table. "Thanks for sharing that with me."

She gave me a smile, but it still held the sadness of what she'd just told me. "I didn't even make you sink a basket for that one."

I smiled back. "We're too good at that game anyway—let's just skip the formalities from now on and move straight to the secret." I held up a finger. "But fair is fair. I owe you one."

She grinned and tapped her chin. "Hmmm. Okay, tell me about why you traveled around Europe—and where you went." Her eyes shined. It must sound cool to someone who had never been out of Ohio her whole life.

"Well, like I said, when my granny died, I got a little bit of money. I had lived in Massachusetts with her briefly, but other than that, I hadn't ever lived outside of California, and so I decided to bum around Europe for a little while, just go wherever I wanted, see where the wind took me."

Her eyes widened. "That sounds terrifying."

I laughed. "No, it was awesome. I loved traveling. Just me and my backpack—no itinerary, no specific destination. I went to Rome, Barcelona, Florence, Venice, Paris... the most incredible places in the world. Then I ran out of money and came home."

She considered me for a few beats. "You're a really brave person, Carson."

A felt a warm flush inside and looked away. "Nah, not brave, just open-minded."

"Don't sell yourself short," she said softly.

I looked back at her and for a few seconds our eyes held before I smiled and dug back into my food.

When we got back to the hotel, it was about three o'clock and so we decided to enjoy the pool for a little bit. We parted ways at her floor and planned to meet in the lobby in twenty minutes.

I let myself into my room and noticed right away that it had been cleaned. Fresh sheets for me and Grace to dirty up again tonight. I whistled as I grabbed my swim trunks and began to change.

Before I could go to meet Grace, though, I needed to call my agent, Tim. Shit, this was not going to be pleasant. I had been scheduled for three fan signings today—all of which I had blown off. And Tim had flown in this morning to help manage them. I didn't regret my choice, spending time with Grace made me happy as hell and signings did not. But I needed to do some damage control.

I sat on the end of the bed as his phone rang.

"You had better be dead and calling me from the afterlife right now."

"Would that get me off the hook?"

"No, but you'd be safe from me. Otherwise, I'm going to kick your ass all over Vegas. Where the fuck are you, Carson?"

"Uh, I'm still in Vegas. I just came down with a nasty, nasty virus." I forced a cough. "Seriously, I couldn't even get out of bed."

"Really? Because Chastity Aurora said she saw you gorging yourself on cake at Caesars Palace today with some little blond."

Oh. I grimaced. *Fucking Chastity Aurora. Little tattletale.*

I sighed. "Listen, Tim, I'm gonna be up front with you. Those signings? I hate that shit, you know that. It was unprofessional of me, but I blew them off. I'm sorry I put you in a bad spot, but I can't do those anymore. If you set me up with more of them, I'm gonna have to find a new agent."

"Carson, this isn't exactly the time to threaten to fire me. I should be firing you *after* I kick your ass." He paused. "Listen, I already put out a press release apologizing to your fans on your behalf. I said that a family emergency came up, so roll with that if you're asked. You don't have to give details. And then don't *ever* make me look bad again in public, you got it?"

"Yeah, I got it." He was right. I should have at least given him a head's up.

"All right, go back to your *virus*. You don't have any other scheduled events this weekend. Your room's paid for and you have to give twenty-four-hour notice for cancelations or I'd send you back to LA tonight. But, Carson, I'll see you at your shoot on Monday. Ten a.m. Be there."

"I'll be there, Tim. Thanks. And... sorry."

I threw the phone on the bed and sat with my head in my hands for several minutes, trying to get back in a better headspace. The only reason Tim had even been as lenient with me as he'd been was because I'd already made him a good amount of money with a couple films. And my potential to make him more was off the charts. I knew that. And so did he.

Grace. I just wanted to see Grace. I didn't want to think about any of this shit. I didn't want to think about what I had to return to on Monday.

CHAPTER 8
Grace

I took a few minutes to freshen up before pulling on my suit and cover-up. When I checked my phone, I saw there was a message from my sister, Julia, just calling to chat. I texted her quickly telling her I was in Vegas for my law conference and that I'd call her when I got back Monday. She texted back right away.

Totally forgot that was this weekend! Enjoy? Haha. Talk Mon. xxoo

Oh, I was enjoying. She had no idea. My little sister was more of a free spirit than me and she liked to tease me about my drive, telling me constantly that I needed to loosen up. Would she be happy or horrified by what I was up to this weekend? Probably both. Of course, I wouldn't tell her—she was my nineteen-year-old baby sister and I wanted to be a good example to her. I didn't think what I was doing this weekend exactly fit the bill.

There was also a call from Abby asking me to give her the go-ahead to paint the kitchen "Green Apple."

I sat on the edge of the bed and dialed her number. "Hey, babe, do I have the green light on the Green Apple?" she asked in greeting.

"Aren't you supposed to be lying around *not* scratching yourself?"

"Ugh. I need a distraction. Scratching myself is better than sex right now. If I don't do something, I'm going to start master-scratching. Scratchy-bating? What's the proper term for self-pleasuring through vigorous, non-recommended scratch-athons?"

I laughed. "You have the green light on the Green Apple. *Please* go distract yourself. Paint my room while you're at it."

"Okay. I just might. How's the ultra-stimulating law conference?"

I paused. "Um, ultra-stimulating just about says it, Abs. You have no idea." I let out a nervous laugh.

Abby was quiet for a beat. "Spill, Grace. What in the world is going on?"

"You might be worried about me, Abby. I'm kinda worried about myself."

"Well, now I *am* worried. *What*, Grace?"

I speed-talked. "Remember how you told me to take the hot porn star I mentioned up to my room and let him teach me a few tricks? Well, I did. Only we went to his room. And he did. Teach me some stuff. Some really great, amazing, stuff I nev—"

"WHAT?" Abby screamed so loudly that I had to hold the phone away from my ear.

"Who *are* you and what have you done with Grace?"

"Abby! I know, I know, okay, quiet. Listen, it's kind of a long story. After I talked to you, we got trapped in an elevator and he...well, he grew on me, I guess? It's hard to

99

explain. He has this really soft side, and yes, I *know* what he does. But God, he's really sexy, like in a way that I had no idea even *existed*. And I just thought, what does a weekend hurt, you know?"

"Uh…um, huh. I'm just stunned. My little type-A Gracie Hamilton, the girl with a plan? Are you sure this is a good decision? I mean, are you using condoms? Geez, I can't believe we're even having this conversation."

"I'm having fun, Abby. And I haven't had fun, really, well, *ever*. Don't judge me."

"Oh, honey, I'm not judging you. Listen, I trust you, okay? And if this guy got you to bend your own rules and put that excitement in your voice, then there must be something special about him. Just…please remember what he does and keep reminding yourself that it's just a weekend, okay? And then when you get back, you're spreading the porn-star sex-trick wealth."

I laughed. "Deal. I love you, Abby."

"I love you, Gracie. Oh! What's his name, in case you go missing?"

"Abby! I'm not going to go missing! His name is Carson Stinger. He's from LA."

"Okay, stay safe. Call me tomorrow morning. Seriously."

"Okay, I will. Bye, Abs."

"Bye, Pod Person."

I hung up the phone smiling and then headed down to the lobby.

When I stepped off the elevator, Carson was standing with one hip propped against the wall at the corner of the bank of elevators, doing something on his phone again. He pressed a button and stuck it in his pocket, and then looked up and saw me coming toward him. God, that little dimple below his mouth practically put me over the edge each time he smiled. I was a slave to that tiny dimple. I smiled back at it, at him, shaking my head slightly. "What?" he asked as I met him and we started walking toward the pool.

"Nothing, I was just thinking that right where you were standing, that's where we ran into each other. Who would have ever guessed after *that* encounter that less than six hours later, I'd be moving in to your hotel room?"

"Not surprised at all. I predicted that one. It just took you a little while to catch up." He put his arm around me.

I elbowed him in the side. "You probably did, you egomaniac."

He laughed, but then his face went serious as he steered me out another exit from the one we were headed toward. "Sorry, I just saw some people who might recognize me and I didn't want to deal with them."

I frowned. People from his business, here for the expo, I was assuming. My chest felt tight and I pushed the feeling away—nothing good could come from thinking too much about his "coworkers." Did he see a woman he had made a film with? I couldn't bring myself to ask.

Carson looked down at me with regret on his face. "Sorry, Grace, do you mind if we go to one of the pools farther away from the entrance?"

I shook my head. "That's probably a better idea for me too," I said quietly. There were people here from my school. It probably wasn't a great idea for it to get back to the faculty that I was skipping presentations to cavort with men in general, and porn stars in particular.

We walked through the pool area to a less-crowded section, closer to the back, and put our towels and my bag down on two loungers with a little bit of shade.

"Need me to put some sunblock on for you?" he asked.

I nodded. "If you could get my back…" I said, taking off my cover-up.

He took the bottle I handed him and started lathering up my back. Then he kissed the side of my neck and handed the sunblock back to me. "Thanks." I smiled, applying sunblock to the rest of my body. I felt more relaxed here, away from the entrances, away from our real lives, away from the reminder that we weren't really free to be spending a weekend together, even though we were.

I sat down on my lounger, but he turned and walked over to a family sitting a few loungers down and asked them a question. They nodded and pointed to an orange raft lying to the side of them. Carson picked it up and started walking back toward me calling behind him, "Thanks! I'll return it."

Then he took my hand and pulled me up. "Wait! I thought we were going to lay in the sun for a little while before going in the water."

"Who said that? There wasn't a plan. We do what we do when we wanna do it, remember? And right now, I wanna swim with you."

"Okaaay. Well, what if I don't want to swim right now?"

"Then I do this." And then he dropped the raft and picked me up and tossed me right in the water.

I came up sputtering, madder than a hatter. The water was only about as high as my shoulders where he had tossed me and so I stood up, glaring at him as he grinned at me from the side of the pool. "I cannot believe you just tossed me in the pool!"

"Well, believe it. I did," he said, not remorseful in the least. He threw the raft in the water and then walked his perfect body to the deeper end and executed the most perfect dive I'd ever seen, slicing straight through the water. *Oh. Well that was hot. Why is he good at everything?*

Before I could barely blink, he had swum underwater to me and was pulling me down by my legs. I opened my eyes under the water, making my most angry face at him as he met my eyes and grinned. God damn him, he was even beautiful underwater, with air bubbles coming out of his nose.

He let go of me and I surfaced, smoothing my hair back. He surfaced a second later laughing and pushing his wet hair back out of his face. "Don't be mad, buttercup. I just couldn't wait to get slippery again with you."

I glared at him for another second, but I couldn't maintain my anger at him, as he gave me that innocent expression, water droplets sticking to his impossibly long eyelashes.

I shook my head, my lips tipping in a smile. "You really are an asshole. I can't believe you threw me in the pool. No one has ever thrown me in a pool."

He pulled my body to his and swirled us around in the water. "That's a shame. You're so pretty soaking wet." He leaned in and kissed me lightly on my lips, and then kissed each of my eyes and then my nose. Okay, he was forgiven.

"You're a really good swimmer," I noted.

"When you grow up in hotels and cheap apartments, all with pools, you tend to spend a lot of time perfecting your swim strokes." He paused. "I didn't have much else to do. Some kids play basketball. I swam."

I studied him from this close vantage point. When he wasn't smiling, there wasn't even the barest sign of that dimple. It was like a little secret. Happiness just under his skin. "I guess I was under the impression that because your mom was…famous…that you had money."

"It's hard to keep much when you spend almost

everything you have on *nonprescribed* prescription drugs. And I know I used the word 'famous' before, but I would probably say 'well-known' is a better term. But in the business, that doesn't always translate into 'well paid.' It just means she was willing to do things others weren't."

I stared at him, a pinching sensation in my chest. What must it have been like for a little boy to know what his mom was doing every time she went off to a job like that? My own mom had been emotionally unavailable for most of my life, and that had hurt. Sometimes it still did. But I forgave her because her pain stemmed from a terrible tragedy that she hadn't been responsible for. I wondered what complex emotions Carson felt about his own mother's choices. *Stop, Grace. You're only going to know him for another day or so.* And the more I wondered, the more attached I'd get.

I changed the subject. "Why'd you borrow that raft?" I asked, nodding my head toward where it was floating nearby.

"Because I want to prove a point," he said, letting me go before swimming to it and pulling it back to me.

"Oh God, is this part of your *Titanic* therapy?" I asked. "Listen, I'm not a professional. And I really think this requires someone board certified."

He winked. "Never let go, baby. Come on, work this through with me. I need you, Grace."

I laughed. And then we spent the next half an hour trying to get us both up on that narrow raft without tipping over. Every time he rolled off, he would sink under, holding one hand up in his imitation of a human popsicle. I was laughing so hard my face hurt.

Finally he was able to hold himself steady enough that he could drag me on top of him and we both lay there, eyes wide, moving as little as possible. A slow grin spread across his face and he whispered to me, "I knew it."

"Never let go, baby," I whispered back.

He laughed and that was all it took for us to capsize.

Carson

We got out of the water and dried off and collapsed on the lounge chairs. I kept one eye on Grace's bikini-clad body as she closed her eyes and dozed off for a little while.

I walked over to the bar and ordered us a couple beers, and when she stretched and opened her eyes fifteen minutes later, I handed her, her drink. "Thanks. Sorry, was I out for long?"

"I'm glad you were. I need you well rested for tonight."

She smiled teasingly at me. "Why? Are we going to work through more emotional cinematic issues?"

"Same one. Only we're gonna use the bed as the flotation device."

"You really do need extensive help, don't you? I might have to start charging."

I took the beer out of her hand and pulled her over on top of me. "Name your price. I'll pay it," I said, squeezing her ass and tickling her ribs.

"Ahhh! Carson, you're gonna make me pee on you," she squealed.

"Kinky. But not at the pool, baby. Not everyone's into that kinda smut. You're gonna shock some—"

"Grace? Is that you?" a male voice asked.

My head came up and Grace's whipped around. She

105

sat up and was over on her own lounger so fast, my hands were still positioned where her ass had been milliseconds before.

There was a tall, brown-haired guy in swim trunks standing at the end of our lounge chairs looking at Grace with a worried expression on his face.

"Parker! Hi. Oh my goodness. I didn't even know you'd be here this weekend! Hi!"

"Hi," he said, looking over at me, clearly waiting for an introduction.

Grace ignored it.

"So, how are you enjoying the conference so far?" she asked, tilting her head and smiling at him. I saw his eyes dart down to her practically naked body before he answered, and I felt my hands curling into fists.

"Uh, it's good. I really liked Professor Fulton's talk this afternoon. What did you think? I didn't see you there."

"Oh, um, I've been sitting in the back mostly. Yeah, the talk was good. Very informative." She nodded her head vigorously. I wondered if this geeky bozo could see how full of shit she was. If he couldn't, he didn't know her very well. My muscles relaxed.

Finally, he just stuck his hand out to me and said, "Parker Gray, I'm in school with Grace."

I shook and opened my mouth to speak when Grace cut in: "This is Rick...Ryder. He's in law school at, uh, Stanford."

What the fuck? Was she kidding around? I glanced over at her. By the distressed look on her face, I could see she wasn't. Something heavy formed in my stomach.

Parker looked dubious. "Stanford, huh? Great school. How do you two know each other?"

"Oh, Rick's parents are friends of the family. You know. We go way back. Right, Rick?"

"Sure, Grace. Way back."

"Oh, well, it's cool that you two got to see each other here then. What's your law focus, Rick?" Parker asked.

I gave Parker a thin smile and glanced at Grace. She still looked panicked. My eyes traveled down to her cleavage.

"Well, Parker, I would say my focus is... parts inspection."

Parker looked confused. "Oh, you mean like the law surrounding industrial labor laws?"

"Sure, Parker."

Grace laughed nervously. "Well, it was great to see you, Parker. We'll have to do coffee when we get back."

Parker turned his confused face from me and grinned at Grace, his eyes sweeping her body again. "Sounds good. I'll call you."

"Okay." She gave him a little wave, tilting her head. Why did it feel like I'd shrunk several inches since Parker had shown up?

I watched him turn his scrawny body and walk away. I was legions above him in the looks department, so why did I fucking hate Parker Gray?

I turned to Grace. "Rick Ryder?" I asked. "Nice save if you didn't want him to know what I do."

"He's too straitlaced to get it. Hell, yesterday, *I* wouldn't have gotten it." She fell back in her lounger, exhaling.

My chest felt tight and I wanted to punch something. "Ready?" I said, gathering our things.

"Oh, okay...if you are." She looked at me nervously. "Carson, I'm sorry, it just wouldn't look good for my career if it got out that I was canoodling with a porn star."

"Canoodling, Grace? Jesus, I don't even know what the fuck that is."

"You're mad," she said, biting her lip.

"No, I'm not mad. I'm just ready to leave."

She nodded and started grabbing her stuff too, putting it into her bag. It was then that I spotted Tawny Anderson, a girl who worked for the same company I did. She was a beautiful redhead with a killer body. I hadn't ever made a film with her, but she had propositioned me for some extracurricular time on many occasions. I had never taken her up on it.

She was standing at the bar a couple feet away with a girl I didn't recognize. "Hey, Tawny," I called, and she turned around, her eyes lighting up.

She walked over to me and met me right in front of Grace's chair. "Carson!" she squealed, kissing my cheek and pressing her large breasts into my chest.

I smiled suggestively at her. "Hey, baby, how are you?" I asked, pulling her into me and gripping her ass.

"I'm great, gorgeous. I heard you had a family emergency. Anything I can help with?" She ran one finger down my chest.

"Maybe. What did you have in mind?"

"I'm sure I could think of something." She giggled. "But I thought you didn't mix business with pleasure."

"I might be able to make an exception for you," I said, raising my eyebrows and squeezing her ass tighter.

That's when Grace cleared her throat, and me and Tawny both turned our heads to see her standing there with her shoes and cover-up on and her bag on her shoulder, looking for us to move so she could get by us.

"Who's she, Carson?" Tawny demanded.

"She's no one, babe," I said, and the look that came over Grace's face nearly brought me to my knees. She looked like I had just slapped her in the face and kicked her while she was down. I felt that look like a punch in the gut. *Shit.*

Grace didn't wait for us to move but instead pushed past us, knocking Tawny off balance. "Watch it, girlie!" Tawny said angrily.

Grace didn't even look back. *Shit, shit, shit.*

"Anyway," Tawny said, turning back to me and taking my hand and replacing it on her ass, "where were we?"

I was such a stupid fuckup. Holy Christ. What had I done? I was so fucking hurt when she made me feel like an embarrassment, like a *nothing* in front of her friend. I had automatically reacted, trying to make her feel the same way too. And I'd succeeded. And I felt like shit. "Sorry, Tawny, I gotta go," I said, taking her by the shoulders and physically moving her out of my way.

"Wait, what? I thought we were gonna hang out!"

"You were right," I said over my shoulder. "I don't mix business with pleasure. I almost forgot for a minute there."

I jogged in the direction Grace had gone, looking around and finally spotting her going through the door to the hotel. I raced after her.

When I got inside, I ran to the elevators, hoping to find her waiting for one. I had fucked up. Jesus, I had fucked up. My heart pounded and I broke out in sweat even though I'd run into the air conditioned building. I flashed my room card to the guard and pressed the up button furiously, swearing under my breath. When the elevator finally came, I jumped on and when a few people tried to follow me in, I held my hand up and said, "Sorry! Emergency! No one else is gonna ride this elevator!" They stepped back, confused, as I pushed

Grace's room floor. No one else was gonna slow me down in getting to her. Panic coursed through me. *Shit, I did this. I fucking did this.*

When the elevator doors opened, I leaped from the car and raced down the hallways and as I turned the corner, I saw Grace almost at her door, just removing her key card. When she heard me behind her, she turned, her mouth opening slightly, eyes widening. The hurt was still clear in her large, blue eyes.

She turned back around to her door.

"I'm sorry, Grace," I said desperately.

She halted, her back still to me. "There's nothing to be sorry for. You obviously have a life. I got in the way of it for a minute there. Please, don't let me interrupt the plans you have with *Tawny*."

"I don't have any plans with Tawny. I did that because I didn't like what happened with Parker. It made me feel like nothing and I wanted to do the same to you. I wanted to make you feel like nothing too. It wasn't fair and I fucked up, and I'm sorry."

She studied me for a minute. "I understand. I'm sorry too. But this"—she gestured between me and her—"isn't going to work. Not even for a weekend. I've had a nice time. But we both need to get back to our real lives. We don't make any kind of sense and this is just a recipe for disaster."

She slid her key in the slot at her door, and when I heard the click indicating that it was open and she was about to go inside, my heart leaped with panic and I took a step forward. "No one else has ever made me feel the way you do," I blurted. She paused and then turned toward me slowly, her hand dropping from the door. "Not even close," I went on.

"Shit, I don't even know what to call it because it's totally unfamiliar. And down by the pool, it scared me, Grace, and I reacted. But it's because you are far from nothing to me." I took another step forward. "You are far from nothing to me," I repeated.

She stared at me for another couple beats, expressionless, and my heart dropped. She looked down at the floor for a few moments and then slowly raised her gaze to mine. I was caught there, at her mercy. *Please forgive me.* "Do you wanna come inside, Rick?" she asked.

I breathed out a laugh. "Yes, buttercup, I do."

She nodded and held her door open to let me in.

CHAPTER 9
Grace

I held the door open as Carson walked in behind me. The lump that had been in my throat during the entire walk from the pool up to my room was starting to recede, but I still felt the lingering hurt over watching Carson with Tawny and what he had said to her about me. I had asked myself all the way up to my room why that stung so damn much that I wanted to roll into a ball and cry. But I had hurt him too. I just hadn't realized it at the time. I thought he would understand why I couldn't flaunt the fact that I was spending time with an adult film star in front of my classmates. That was the kind of thing that could come out later and ruin my career as a lawyer—especially in DC, where politics always came into play. I had thought he would roll with it and laugh it off after Parker walked away. It's why I had come up with that dumb name on the spot—trying to put a private joke out there for Carson. To unite us in that awkward moment. I hadn't meant to make him feel like he was nothing, that's not how I felt.

But our lives didn't mix. Those encounters at the pool made that blatantly obvious. This was supposed to be a weekend of fun, of letting go temporarily, and then returning to exactly what I had been doing before I arrived in Vegas. Was this *thing* with Carson morphing into something dangerous for both of us?

I don't know what to call it because it's totally unfamiliar.

Yes, I could relate. And if feelings got involved, even on a basic level, where did that leave us when all was said and done?

I didn't know what to do. The logical part of me was telling me to end this and walk away, despite the fact that I liked him and we had this electric chemistry. The emotional part of me was holding on, but to what, I didn't know and it didn't make sense.

He was an enigma to me, stinging me one minute and then soothing me the next—with his words, his touch, his smile.

God. This *had* become complicated and I'd only spent a day and a half with him.

I dropped down on the bed and looked at Carson, now standing with his hip against the corner of the wall, arms crossed, studying me somewhat warily. Why did he have to be so gorgeous? It was his poison and he'd injected me with it—I was infected. I laughed humorlessly, ending on a sigh.

"What?" he asked, cocking his head to the side.

"Us." I raised both arms and dropped them. "What are we doing, Carson?"

He looked down, sliding his teeth up his bottom lip and worrying his brow. "What do you want to be doing, Grace?"

I sighed. I wanted to be spending time with him. But I wanted it to make sense. I was pretty sure the whole "Guy

Number Two" cover was blown, for me anyway. I had done a good job of convincing myself that that was the reason I agreed to spend the weekend with him, but had it ever actually been the case? Maybe not. Something about him drew me in and made me want to stay, break all my rules, throw all my well-made plans out the door, experience things I'd never allowed myself to experience, want things I'd never allowed myself to want.

The truth though? Carson wasn't part of my plan as I'd convinced myself—he was the *antithesis* of my plan. And I wasn't sure anymore if that was bad or good. But did it even matter? We couldn't be any more than a weekend; it wasn't possible. For too many reasons to count. And I was pretty sure that it was going to be hard to walk away Monday morning, knowing that that was it. *Definitively*. Was it worth it to make it that much harder by spending another day with him?

Carson pushed off the wall and walked to the bed and then squatted before me, resting his arms on my knees and looking up into my eyes. "Listen, Grace, clearly this weekend arrangement has changed into something that we didn't necessarily expect it to. We're friends." He smiled but it appeared a bit wobbly. "Who would have guessed? And I for one, want to spend the rest of the weekend with my friend. Do you want that too?"

I gazed into his eyes. Is that what we were? Friends? Friends who had sex for the weekend? I guess maybe that was better than strangers who had sex for the weekend. And really, how much harder was it going to be to walk away in thirty-six hours rather than right now? I couldn't see things changing much by Monday morning. I would survive. It would suck because I liked him, but I would do it and it would be okay. By the time I'd touched down in DC, reality would be back in focus and I'd resume my life.

"Yes, I want that too."

That heart-melting smile bloomed across his face, the dimple emerging. "Good," he said, standing. "I'm going to go up to my room and get dressed for dinner, and then I'm taking you somewhere nice. Can you be ready in half an hour, buttercup?"

I cocked my head to the side. "Why do you call me buttercup?"

His smile gentled. "Maybe because you're so small."

"I'm not *that* small."

"I forget. Come here."

I breathed out a laugh, standing and walking into his open arms where he held me for a few moments and then kissed my forehead. *Somewhere nice.* He'd said it in reference to dinner, but this was somewhere nice. In his arms. *Damn.*

When I stepped back, I said, "Remember, I have that gift certificate."

"Yeah, but I want to take you out so I'm not using your gift certificate."

"Why? We both earned it for getting stuck in that elevator."

"Because it's important to me to treat you, that's all. End of story."

"Okay." I paused, looking off to the side for a moment. I needed to say one final thing about what happened at the pool before I could put it to rest. "I hated seeing you touch her, Carson, and that scared me too," I said quietly.

He closed his eyes for a beat, dropping his head. When he looked back up into my eyes, his own were filled with regret. "I used her to get back at you. It was wrong on so many levels." He shook his head slightly. "I didn't know what to do with it. I've never been...jealous before. It was unchartered waters."

"You were jealous?" I asked. "Of Parker?"

"Yeah. I wanted to drown him in the pool."

I laughed but quickly covered my mouth and shook my head. "That's not nice."

He smiled. "No, it's not. It's also illegal. So I held myself back and chose to be an asshole instead." His expression turned serious. "I really am sorry."

I smiled and said softly, "Me too." I pulled in a breath. "Half an hour?"

"Yeah. Half an hour." He brushed his lips across mine. "See you soon."

When the door had clicked shut behind him, I fell back on the bed. "Life is wild," I reminded myself quietly.

After a few minutes, I got up and hopped in the shower. When I got out, I felt better, more optimistic that things would be just fine. I spritzed on some perfume, just a little, and then blew my hair dry and used a curling iron until it fell down my back in soft curls. I applied a little more makeup than I usually did, including two coats of mascara to darken my light brown lashes. They wouldn't be anywhere near as lush as Carson's, but nature was cruel that way, giving long, dark lashes to boys who didn't appreciate them. I kept my mind on mundane things while I got ready, turning on the radio and singing along to a few songs as I got dressed.

Not knowing if I'd go out to a nice dinner or not while I was here at the conference, I had only brought one cocktail dress, a little black number that I had borrowed from Abby that was hanging in the closet. It was short and strapless with an eyelet lace embellished waist and skirt that flared out. It was sexy yet demure. I loved it and I hoped Carson would too. His knock at my door sounded just as I was slipping on my black heels.

When I flung the door open, Carson was standing there in a pair of black dress slacks and a light, sage-green shirt that did all kinds of crazy things to the color of his hazel eyes. He had obviously done a little something with his hair, slicked it back slightly. He shook his head, giving me a pained expression as he looked me up and down. "Not nice, buttercup."

I laughed. "What do you mean?"

"How am I supposed to sit through an entire meal when all I'm going to be thinking about is getting you back up to my room and fucking you senseless? That dress does crazy things to me."

Sex. Yes. Let's keep the focus on sex. I laughed and shook my head as I grabbed the small clutch and he took my arm and led me out the door.

"Where are we going?" I asked as we stepped on to the elevator.

"I made a reservation at Olives. Is that okay?"

"Yes. I mean, I haven't been to any of the restaurants here."

He pulled me to him as the elevator made its descent, enveloping me in that singular scent that made my hormones flash fire through my body. I couldn't help leaning into him and sticking my nose in his neck, inhaling deeply.

He chuckled. "You like the way I smell, buttercup?"

"Mmmm," I breathed, not coming up for air.

"I like the way you smell too," he whispered. "It makes me hard." And I could feel that indeed it did.

I leaned back and looked up at him, that spark flaring between us.

"Do you have running shoes?" he asked.

I raised a brow, confused at the unexpected change of subject. "Planning on ditching the bill?"

He laughed. "No, I was thinking we could go hiking tomorrow morning if you're up for it. Red Rock Canyon has some beautiful trails. We'd have to go early though. In the summer, it gets pretty hot by the afternoon."

"I'd like that," I said as we stepped off the elevator. "I did bring running shoes. Remember though, I have to be back for the one conference presentation at two. I'm trying to get into a law class in the fall and the professor who teaches it is presenting tomorrow."

"We'll be back in plenty of time for that." He looked at me. "What time does your flight leave on Monday?"

"Six a.m." I said quietly. "Yours?"

"Seven. We could ride to the airport together."

I nodded but decided I didn't want to think about that. We were here now and I was going to enjoy the last of our time together.

We arrived at Olives and I looked around. It was beautiful, with the same Mediterranean style as the rest of the Bellagio. I waited back a bit as Carson leaned in and spoke to the hostess. She giggled and nodded her head and he smiled back at me, offering me his arm as we followed the hostess to our table. We walked out onto the balcony, overlooking the man-made lake in front of the Bellagio, where we had watched the fountain show, and I gasped. "It's so beautiful."

Carson just smiled and pulled out my chair. "It's not hot dogs on the strip, but I figured, we gotta eat, even if we have to downgrade the venue this time."

The waiter approached our table and we each ordered a glass of wine. I sat back, looking around in wonder.

Everything surrounding me was filled with light. The glow from the strip shined in the distance, the water sparkled, and the twinkle lights adorning the balcony danced. It felt magical, like another world. I met Carson's eyes and saw that he'd been watching me. "I like that look on your face," he said quietly.

He'd said that to me in bed too. I brought my hands to my cheeks as I thought back to that moment, realizing he was saying he liked to watch me enjoy new things. My heart gave a little squeeze.

"What are you thinking?" he asked taking my hand across the table.

I smiled, deciding that just for tonight, I was going to experience everything I could and enjoy every minute of it. *Life is wild*—Carson was right. Or it could be, if you let it. I was going to let it. I was going to clear my mind and soak in the beauty of everything around me—the location, the food, the man sitting across from me. I was going to live for all the years I had rejected relationships that might have come naturally if I hadn't been overly focused on other things, and for all the years I had made choices that I thought would make other people happy, never considering what would make *me* happy. I'd worked so tirelessly to make sure I was steady and dependable for my dad and my sisters who'd already lost so much, never taking into consideration that I'd lost too. Never admitting that I'd sacrificed parts of myself that Carson was just bringing to life.

Carson had infected me, it was true, but his looks weren't the only part of his poison. It was his spirit too. His bravery. And maybe when it came to Carson, just like a vaccine, a little poison was also the cure.

There would be consequences to this weekend, I knew

that now and I wasn't lying to myself anymore. But maybe they wouldn't all be negative. Maybe I would walk away a better person because of my encounter with this man.

"What I was thinking, Carson, is that I feel lucky to be here with you tonight."

His eyes warmed and a smile tipped his full lips.

The waiter set down our wine and when he'd left, I raised my glass. "To life being wild."

He raised his glass to mine. "To well-made plans," he said with a smile.

Carson

Grace's eyes shined as she looked around at all the sights. I loved it. I wanted to show her more. I wanted to give her all the experiences I could. I wanted to watch her big, blue eyes widen with awe, not just at the things I could do to her body, but with all the experiences she had deprived herself of for so long. I wanted to show her things she'd never seen before. I wanted to take her snowboarding on a mountain at twilight, I wanted to worship her body in the bright sunshine on a beach somewhere exotic. For the first time in my life, I felt like I had something to offer other than just the physical. But the wanting felt like a double-edged sword—it made me feel alive in a way I'd never felt alive before, but it filled me with regret to know that I could never have any of it with this girl.

But maybe the wanting of it in and of itself was a good thing. Maybe Grace had opened my eyes to the possibility that I could be more, that life could be more. Something about that filled me with a feeling I couldn't identify in that moment—something I'd think about later.

We ordered dinner and Grace smiled across the table at me. "So, Carson," she said, "should I trust you to take me hiking out in the desert *all alone*? I'm not going to mysteriously disappear tomorrow morning, am I?"

I chuckled. "Not because I'm planning on burying you in a shallow grave, but there is a real risk of me pouncing on you like a desert hyena because you're irresistible."

She laughed. "I guess the authorities could trace me by following the trail of torn and discarded clothes?"

I took a sip of wine. I never drank wine. But tonight seemed to call for it. "And the scream of my name echoing through the canyons," I said. God I loved to hear Grace scream my name. There was nothing like it.

She cleared her throat. "Speaking of which, should we stay in my room tonight? It hasn't even been used."

"No, I decided I like having you in my room."

"Why?"

"I don't know. Something about having you in my lair."

She rolled her eyes. "More like your sex den, desert hyena."

I laughed. "I like that even better."

Our food came—I had ordered the ribeye and Grace had ordered the salmon. We ate quietly for a few minutes. "Mmmm, this is fantastic," Grace moaned.

"Do you go out to eat a lot?" I asked.

"No, rarely. I have a scholarship that pays my expenses too, but there's not a lot left over at the end of the month." She shrugged. "I don't have a lot of time to do anything except study anyway. It'll pay off." She took a drink of her wine, looking over the rim at me.

"I'm sure it will," I said. "What's your law focus

anyway?" I cut a piece of meat and speared it and stuck it in my mouth.

"Corporate law."

"God, that sounds about as exciting as the patented burp of the Tupperware container."

She laughed. "What?"

"My granny used to say that. I suddenly understood what she meant."

She brought her hand to her mouth as she swallowed the sip of water she'd just taken. "Corporate law is actually very interesting."

"Oh yeah? What's interesting about it?"

She looked up, thinking for a minute. She opened her mouth, and then shut it, finally letting out a small laugh. "Nothing. There's nothing interesting about it at all."

"Then why did you choose it?"

She sighed. "My dad works in the criminal justice system. He sees all the stuff that goes down every day with prosecutors and defense attorneys...all the BS they have to deal with, all the awful stories they hear. I asked for his advice and he thought corporate law would be a good, safe, solid career choice." She played with the food on her plate for a moment.

"So... your dad chose it, huh?"

"Carson," she said, laying her fork down. "This isn't all about me pleasing my dad. It was also about asking someone who has a lot of experience in the field to guide and direct me, that's all."

"Hmmm...okay, so if you hadn't had your dad to *guide and direct you*, what would you have chosen?"

She looked at some distant point beyond my shoulder, a small frown tilting her lips. "I'd really like to be a prosecutor," she said quietly, lowering her gaze, her cheeks turning pink and shame filling her expression, like she had just admitted that she wanted to eat my liver with a fine Chianti.

I nodded, but she remained quiet. I didn't want to make her uncomfortable with this line of questioning, and so I changed the subject. "So Las Vegas is known for its night-clubs. Do you wanna go to one after dinner?"

She took a sip of her wine and looked up at me with warmth in her eyes. "Actually, Carson, if it's okay with you, I'd rather go back up to your hotel room."

"Check please," I said, pretending to look around for our waiter.

She laughed, and the moment turned light again. We chatted through the rest of dinner, and then the waiter cleared our dishes and I paid the bill. I took Grace's hand in mine and we headed back upstairs. My body was humming with anticipation, but more than that, something had deepened between Grace and me today. I couldn't experience *all* the things I wanted to with her, but we still had time left together—and I wasn't going to waste a second of it.

CHAPTER 10
Grace

We hopped on the elevator with several other people and began our ascent to Carson's room. A couple got off at the next floor and we rode in silence with the remaining people, until they too exited on their floors.

As soon as the doors shut, I found myself pressed to the elevator wall by six feet of hard, *really amazing-smelling* man. His mouth came down on mine. I expected the kiss to be wild, filled with passion, but he took his time as he pressed against me, his hands moving down the sides of my body, our tongues tangling slowly. The leisurely kiss didn't seem to match the location—on an elevator where anyone could potentially catch us—and for some reason, this fact sent excitement zinging over my nerves. Carson had kissed me in lots of different ways in the last day and a half. But this kiss was my favorite. This kiss felt like it was personalized—I couldn't pinpoint exactly why, but something about this kiss was different than any before it. He fit his body to mine, our tongues moved together like a slow tango. We had clearly begun learning each other. I reached up and linked my arms around his neck pulling myself as close as I possibly could.

The doors opened and Carson leaned away from me slowly, leaving me blinking and breathless, apparently unconcerned about anyone seeing us kissing in the elevator. I walked on legs that felt like Jell-O down the corridors to his room.

Once the hotel room door had shut behind us, he was on me again, pushing me up against the door, kissing me hard and deep. When he broke away, he gazed down at me, rubbing his thumb over my bottom lip. "I can't get enough of you," he whispered, his eyes stormy, his expression tense and maybe even a little troubled. But then his mouth was on mine again, my tongue meeting his, my hands in the silk of his hair, and my thoughts melted in the flames of my desire.

Carson suddenly scooped me up and carried me to the bed, setting me down right next to it. He took my shoulders and turned me around slowly, unzipping my dress. I felt his warm mouth kiss down my back as the zipper sliding down revealed more and more skin. I shivered, my nipples puckering at the erotic sensation of his mouth touching me somewhere unexpected.

My dress dropped to the floor and I stepped out of it and moved it aside with my foot. I turned slowly, standing before him, naked except for my small, black thong. His expression was intense and hungry, his eyes moving down my body and back to my face. "You're stunning," he said. I *felt* stunning under his perusal. Stunning and completely unembarrassed. Compliments usually made me uncomfortable, but not now. His gaze met mine and there was something so serious in his expression. For a moment I faltered before I stepped toward him. I almost had this strange notion that he needed *me* to take the lead. I reached up, putting a palm on his cheek. He leaned into it, closing his eyes and letting out a sigh.

"Grace," he said softly, my hand dropping from his cheek as he turned me toward the bed. He'd taken charge after all. Maybe I'd read him wrong. Maybe he didn't know any other way.

His warm body moved up against mine. He brought his hands around me to palm my breasts, his fingers drawing lazy circles around my nipples. I laid my head back on his shoulder, sighing with the pleasure his touch brought. "Carson," I breathed as he continued to rub my nipples gently, causing butterflies to take flight in my rib cage and sparks to shoot between my legs. In minutes, I was wet and ready for him, just like always.

I rocked my hips gently against his hardness and he sucked in a breath. "The things you do to me, buttercup," he murmured. "I didn't know…" But he trailed off there, not finishing the thought. I wondered what he had been about to say, but my need was so all-encompassing that when his hand wandered down between my breasts and dipped lower, all questions vanished, and I held my breath with the sweet anticipation of his touch right where I so desperately needed it.

Just as his hand reached my belly button, he stepped away from me and I made a whimpering sound of loss. "Shh, buttercup," he said, "I just want to be able to feel you skin on skin."

I didn't look around as I heard him taking off his clothes. Then he was back against me, and I moaned at the sensation of his warm muscles against my body, his erection hot and hard, poking into my lower back. He was so supremely masculine, I felt feminine in a way I never had before. I relished it, discovering this side of myself for the very first time. I didn't have to be in control here, nor did I want to. I trusted him. I loved the way he talked, the things he said when we were intimate, the way he took control and told me what to do. It made me feel safe, taken care of, and hotter than I'd ever in my life felt before.

But I was also beginning to realize that Carson had needs too, maybe even ones he didn't admit to. Maybe even ones he didn't recognize. And I would respond to those if I could. Sex had to be give and take, didn't it?

My dreamy half-thoughts were interrupted when he flicked my nipples, causing a lightning bolt to shoot between my legs. I moaned as he kissed and licked down my neck and then he said, "Bend over the bed, Grace." His voice sounded strained. He was losing some control.

Heat rolled through my belly at his words and I started to take my thong off, but his hand stopped me. "Leave it on."

"But—" I started to say, looking back around at him.

"Leave it on," he repeated.

Okay, then.

"Spread your legs," he said gently.

I did as he said and then bent forward over the bed. For several seconds, there was no movement behind me again. "So perfect," he whispered, right before I heard the condom wrapper being ripped open. Not knowing exactly what was happening behind me and when it would happen added an edge to the excitement. I wanted to cry with the desperation that was clawing through my body now, the deep ache pulsating in my core.

Carson moved my thong aside, his finger grazing my tender skin and then he paused, waiting, driving me just a little bit crazy. When he finally moved, I expected to feel the blunt tip of him push inside me, instead what speared inside my opening was his warm, wet tongue. I jerked and cried out with the unexpected sensation, made up of equal parts physical pleasure and the mental shock of the picture of him behind me, lapping at me from that angle. *Holy God.*

He reached underneath me, using his middle finger to draw lazy circles on my clit as he continued to plunge his tongue slowly in and out of me. I couldn't help it, I writhed down on his face, gasping, feeling an orgasm just within reach. "Faster, *please*, Carson," I panted. How was it exactly that he always managed to make me beg? I wanted, *needed*, to come so badly, and his movements, although delicious, were just too slow to tip me over the edge.

He ignored me though, instead licking backward, over my, oh my God! Was he really licking me *there*? I tensed up slightly, but he kept moving upward, licking up the seam of my ass until he hit my lower back and then kissed my skin lightly. His movement stopped again and I almost screamed out in frustration. If he wasn't inside me in the next three seconds, I was going to take matters into my own hands. I was so worked up, I thought I was going to combust.

But he pushed my thong aside again and then *finally* the blunt tip of his cock at my entrance. I leaned back into it, moaning. He pulled it back though and I made an angry sound of frustration in my throat. "Stay still, please," he said. Despite the *please*, it sounded like an order, not a request. ·

I nodded, too desperate to form words. I briefly considered turning around and jumping on top of him, and forcing him to take me, right before I felt him at my entrance again. I was trembling with the effort to stay still, but when he saw that I was going to, he pushed in a little bit. We both moaned in unison. "You're even tighter from this angle, Grace. Jesus."

I dropped my head and he pushed in all the way, filling me completely. *Oh God, that's amazing.*

He started moving slowly, his hands holding my hips steady. I tilted my backside up toward him, wanting him as deep as possible. "Grace," he moaned as his thrusts picked up in speed.

"I wish you could see this, baby. I wish you could see me pumping inside of you. It's so beautiful. You're so beautiful." His voice pattern staggered with his movements, sounding thick and disjointed.

I closed my eyes and pictured what it must look like and moaned at the image my mind created. He reached around and put his hand under my thong and started massaging my clit again to the rhythm of his thrusts, one hand still on my hip. He had never made any sounds during any of the other times we had had sex, but this time he let out little grunts with each thrust. Something about those little sounds and the idea that it was another sign that he'd lost a bit of control, sent me over the edge and I screamed his name as I came, hard and fast, intense ecstasy tightening my body.

"Oh fuck," Carson grunted behind me slamming into me one final time and then groaning in release.

My whole body was vibrating with the receding waves of pleasure, my legs shaking from the effort to support the rest of my body.

Carson pulled out of me and I turned around and fell onto the bed. I looked up at him and his expression made my breath halt. He looked awestruck... I blinked, right before he came over top of me and took my mouth, kissing me slowly and deeply, then leaning up and looking into my eyes. "Damn," he murmured.

I smiled lazily. "Yeah," I said, smiling bigger. "Damn."

He disposed of the condom and then we climbed into bed together, me snuggling into his warm, hard chest.

Carson

I held Grace, stroking lazily up her arm for a few minutes, reflecting on what we had just shared. It was a base position to have sex in, and despite that, I had felt more connected to Grace than I ever had to anyone I had been with. *Emotionally connected*. I had been about to tell her that I didn't know it could be this way, but as the words came to my lips, I thought better of it. That felt dangerous. This was about *one* weekend, nothing more. I was confused, and I didn't ever remember being confused. It was a new feeling for me. Confusion indicated possibilities, *choice*, but what were my choices in this situation? There were none.

I was floundering.

I looked down at her and she smiled before she closed her eyes. I kissed both lids and she opened them again to look at me. She leaned up and put her hands flat against my chest, one on top of the other and then rested her chin on them.

"Hi," she said casually. "How are you?"

I laughed. "My granny used to say 'fine as frog hair!' when anyone asked her that. I never knew what the fuck it meant. That just popped into my mind." I loved that my granny's phrases were coming back to me. Just mentioning her a few times to Grace had brought her back to life in some sense.

Grace moved her hand slightly and kissed my chest. "Tell me about your granny."

"She was a sweet lady. I went to stay with her most summers and then, like I said, when my mom went to rehab. She taught me things." I was silent for a minute, picturing her, hearing her voice in my head.

"What kinds of things?" Grace asked gently.

"How to mow the lawn, how to sneak up on a grass-hopper, how to choose a cantaloupe at the store." I grinned down at her. "Completely worthless things to a kid from LA. It wasn't what she taught me so much as that she cared to do it."

She nodded up at me like she totally understood what I meant. I thought she probably did. "How *do* you choose a cantaloupe at the store?" she asked.

"You smell it, right at the top. If it smells cantaloupe-y, it's ripe."

"Cantaloupe-y." She repeated with a smile. "Is that true?"

"Probably. Granny was right about almost everything." I paused. "She had a sadness about her too though, because of how my mom turned out." I pictured the way she'd turn her head when she talked about my mom, like she couldn't bear to look in my eyes. "She never talked much about my mom, but I could tell there was lots of regret there."

"Where does your mom live now?" she asked.

I paused. I didn't usually talk much about my mom, even to my closest buddy and roommate, Dylan, but I had already shared things with Grace that I hadn't shared with anyone else. Any question she asked felt comfortable now, normal. I trusted her.

"My mom still lives in LA," I answered. "Not too far from me."

"Do you have a relationship with her?"

"Yes and no. I talk to her every once in a while, but

we're not close. She's gotten her life together more than she had when I was a kid, but there's just too much water under the bridge now. We don't really know each other. Being around her is just awkward."

She looked sad, her eyes moving away from mine for a couple seconds. "She doesn't…"

"Make films anymore?" I finished for her. "No. She lives with some guy. He's a jackass. We got into it one time about eight months ago when I went to see her and I haven't been back. But she's off the prescription meds now—or at least as far as I know." I actually didn't even know if she'd heard that I had made a handful of films. I had no real idea what she'd think about that. Being in the business obviously hadn't given her much satisfaction if any at all, but she knew better than to try and tell me what to do at this point.

"I'm sorry," she whispered. "I know what it's like not to have a mom—or at least, not one you can count on. But at least I had mine for the first eleven years of my life."

I thought about that. "Maybe that makes it harder, not easier, buttercup."

"What do you mean?"

"I just mean that maybe having something good and then having to let it go is more painful than never knowing what you're missing."

"Yeah, maybe," she murmured.

We were both quiet for a few minutes. I looked down at her and put a piece of hair behind her ear. "So pretty," I murmured.

She made a small sound in the back of her throat. "Do compliments make you uncomfortable?" I asked. She always looked just a little uncertain when I gave her one, or brushed it off in some small way. Surely she had to know how beautiful she was.

"They usually do, but I love hearing them from you," she said quietly. "I grew up with a dad who's a guy's guy, the strong, silent type. He was a great dad, but he didn't ever tell us girls we were pretty. He wasn't the type to dish out compliments on any subject really." She paused. "If he was happy with you, you knew it by the silent, prideful look in his eyes and maybe a chin lift in your direction. I learned to get that look and that chin lift with my accomplishments, never my looks." She gave a small shrug.

I nodded, thinking that, in that regard, we were probably polar opposites. I got by on my looks alone, rarely with the things I did, or didn't do. "Well, just for the record, you're beautiful. A beautiful little buttercup."

"And you're a beautiful desert hyena," she said.

I laughed. "I've been given a lot of compliments in my time, but I think that may have been the best one."

We were both quiet for a few minutes. "Tell me about your first time." She said after a few minutes.

I put both hands up behind my head and gazed at the ceiling, faking dreamy recollection.

"Sandra Daniels. We were fifteen. I liked her *a lot*. We spent one beautiful afternoon together at my apartment. The next day at school, as I was walking up to her locker with her favorite breakfast bagel in hand, I heard her telling her friend that now that she had gotten rid of her virginity, she could move on to someone serious who was more suited to a relationship, not just sex. I was crushed."

I grinned down at Grace, but Grace was the one who looked crushed. "Carson—"

"Oh, no, no, don't get that look on your face. I was

133

fifteen, buttercup. I'm over it. Scout's honor." I held up two fingers in the Boy Scout salute.

She didn't smile and instead blinked and then looked down. When she finally met my gaze, her eyes were filled with regret. "It's exactly like my stupid plan, isn't it?" she said. "It's awful. *I'm awful.*"

"Whoa. Wait. I didn't tell you that story to try to compare you to her. I swear. You asked and that's how it happened. Like I said, we were fifteen. It's different."

She was still and quiet for several long moments, a small frown on her face. "Carson, I want you to know something," she finally said. "I know that our little 'arrangement' this weekend started out like that, but well, I don't consider you 'Guy Number Two' anymore, and I never will. You're more than that to me. To me you're Carson, my special desert hyena." She attempted a smile, but it pretty much failed. She was being way too hard on herself—we had arranged this together. She didn't have anything to feel badly for, at least not in my book.

I kissed her forehead. "Well, I'll tell you what," I said. "I'm just glad this bed is so nice and big, because if you fall out in the middle of the night, I'm not going to have any problem dragging you back up. Never let go, baby."

She let out a small laugh, and I saw her relax. She brought one hand down to tickle my side.

I laughed, turning to tickle her back. She squealed and we play-wrestled for a few minutes until I looked into her eyes and saw that she was turned on again. So was I. Fuck, my buttercup was really going to be the end of me.

I leaned in and slanted my mouth over hers, kissing her until we were both panting and lust was shooting through my veins again, stiffening my cock.

I pushed the hair back out of her face and looked into those clear, blue eyes before I ran my nose down hers and then brushed my lips over her mouth.

I reached my hand down between her legs to make sure she was ready to take me, and when I felt the slippery wetness there, I moaned.

I lowered my head to lick her nipples, sucking one into my mouth and taking long pulls at it until she was grinding against me and pulling at my hair. I knew what I was doing in the bedroom, but Christ, how was it that this girl hadn't had *one* orgasm from the first doofus she was with? She was so damn responsive, *perfect*. He must have been the most unskilled loser on the planet. I put him out of my mind as quickly as he had entered it. No one else was gonna be in this bed right now, just me and her.

I dragged my lips along her ribs and she let out a sound that was half laugh and half sigh, a shiver moving through her. That shiver inspired one in me and caused my breath to hitch. Her body was a playground and I wanted more time to explore every inch of her. I wanted to discover secret, sensual spots that no one else knew about, maybe even her.

I moved those thoughts away, the ideas twisting through my mind and making me feel raw and shaky.

I reached over to the nightstand and grabbed a condom and slid it on as she watched, her eyes widening slightly when she took in my straining erection. Our eyes met and something passed between us, intense but tender. It made the world tilt slightly so that the whole room suddenly seemed off balance. Grace's eyes widened, and she reached up, wrapping her arms around me and pulling me back to her mouth as though she'd known I needed an anchor.

We kissed and touched until I couldn't take it any longer.

I took my cock in my hand and guided it to her opening and pushed inside her tight, silken warmth, never taking my eyes from hers. "Grace," I breathed out as I started to move inside her. Her eyes closed on a moan and she wrapped her legs around me. Another anchor. Her. All around me.

I kissed her deeply, possessing her with my tongue and my cock, feeling something powerful surge up in my chest. I brought my mouth to her neck and licked and kissed the satiny, soft skin there as she made gentle sighing sounds. "Mmmm...feels so good, Carson," she said.

I loved that I was making her feel good, loved hearing her say my name, loved the tender look in her eyes as she watched me above her.

I moved in and out of her slowly and deeply, not speeding up the tempo, wanting it to last. "Carson, I want..." she moaned.

"What, Grace? What do you want?"

"Everything. I want everything," she panted. "Everything you have to give."

My head came up from her neck, and when her eyes met mine, they widened. Those beautiful eyes. She was my anchor and yet I was drowning in her.

Heat pooled in my balls and pleasure circled through my abdomen as I sped up my rhythm. I reached down between us and circled my finger on her pleasure spot, eliciting a long moan from her. That moan shot through my body, ending at the base of my spine, the first tingles of an orgasm taking hold. She was going to be my undoing, in ways I didn't want to consider.

As I felt her internal muscles begin to contract around me, I let go and my own climax exploded, hot and intense, blissful. I brought my mouth back down to hers and kissed her deeply as she spasmed and pulsed around me.

I lay with my head buried in her neck for a few minutes until our breathing evened out and I registered that she was running her fingernails up and down my arms. I sighed in happiness. Then I leaned up and kissed her on the mouth and smiled as I pulled out of her.

As I was flushing the condom, it registered that that hadn't been fucking. That hadn't even been just sex. I had just made love to Grace. It also occurred to me that I knew how to fuck but knew very little about sensuality, and that maybe she had far more to teach me than the other way around. I grabbed the sink, letting it be my anchor for the next few minutes until I felt my heart rate return to normal.

CHAPTER 11
Grace

Someone evil and cruel, a demon from the depths of Hades, shook my shoulder in the early morning darkness. I smelled Carson's scent close to me and inhaled deeply on a smile and tried to nestle back into the blankets. I loved that smell. It was just a dream, a dream I thought was bad at first, but was turning good—very good. "Wake up, sleeping buttercup," I heard whispered into my ear on a minty breath.

I forced one eye open. "What did I ever do to you?" I croaked out.

He chuckled. "If you want to go hiking this morning, we need to get going. Up!"

I groaned. What had I ever seen in him? He was a sadist. I heard him walk into the bathroom, and I drug myself out of our warm, happy nest. I loved that nest. I wanted to return to it and stay there indefinitely. It was warm and it smelled good—it smelled like him.

I walked into the bathroom and Carson was standing at the sink running his hands through his wet hair. He looked at me in the mirror and chuckled. "Hey, Fraggle Rock." He grinned. "Not really a morning person are you?"

I grunted. But when I looked at myself in the mirror, my eyes widened. I *did* look like a fraggle. Good call with the nickname. My hair was sticking out in every direction and I had deep pillow creases on one cheek. *That's what you get when you wake me up at the butt crack of dawn,* Carson. I frowned and picked up my toothbrush and started brushing my teeth.

Carson came around behind me and put his arms around my waist and whispered into my ear, "Did I ever tell you I have a thing for crazy-looking Muppets with wild hair?"

I snorted, spewing a little toothpaste out. "I knew your weird fetishes would come out eventually," I said around a mouthful of foam. "Did anyone ever tell you you should go into the military where enjoying getting up at the crack of dawn is an asset?"

He laughed softly, patting me on my ass. "Hurry up. We need to get going if we're going to beat the heat."

I hurried through a shower and blew my hair dry and pulled it back into a ponytail. I felt a little more alive when I walked out into the hotel room. Carson was sitting on the bed pulling on his sneakers.

I dressed in the workout outfit I had brought—intending on using it at the hotel gym. Lucky for me, I'd been getting much better workouts in than a run on a treadmill. No workout clothes required. I pulled on my sneakers and a ratty, gray, zip-up sweatshirt.

I glanced at the clock and my eyes bugged out. "Five fifteen?" I yelled. "You have me up at five fifteen?"

"Shh," he said. "People are sleeping."

"Right. Exactly!"

"Come on. It takes at least twenty minutes to drive there. If we want to really get a good hike in, we need to get going."

"You're crazy."

"So I've been told."

We made our way down to the parking garage and he guided me over to a red Chevy Trailblazer. I frowned. "I thought you flew in."

"I did. Rental car. I like to have the option of going somewhere farther than the strip if I want to."

I climbed into the passenger seat and we drove out of the garage. A few minutes later and Carson pulled into a McDonald's drive through. "Coffee?" he asked.

"God yes."

He shot me a grin. "Don't you get up early for classes?"

"I never schedule classes before nine a.m. Eight o'clock is about the earliest my brain is functioning."

"Ah. Well then, this is good for you. Watching the sun come up in the desert is something everyone should experience at least once."

He ordered and then drove forward, paid, and took our coffees from the teenager at the window. I took a grateful drink from the paper cup.

"And how exactly are you so chipper at this time of the morning?" I asked after I'd dosed myself with several sips of caffeine.

"Well, for one, I had an amazing night"—he winked at me—"and for two, I'm used to getting up this early to go snowboarding. We usually leave at four or five in the morning."

We drove in silence for a little while, both sipping our coffees. He turned up the radio a little bit and I leaned my head back, sighing in contentment. I was still sleepy, but riding in the car with Carson, sipping coffee, was nice—peaceful. Just as I was finishing my coffee, we pulled into the Red Rock Hotel and Casino.

"What are we doing here?" I asked.

"Quick stop," he said. "This is the perfect place to watch the sun rise. There's a great view to the east from the top parking deck."

It was still dark out as we got out of the car, me stretching. Carson came around to my side and put his arms around me from behind, pulling me close to his body. "Look, Grace," he whispered.

I followed his gaze in the dim light and my breath hitched as I saw the glowing red sun rising in the sky, casting golden rays of light out to every side. "Oh, wow," I breathed. "I literally don't think I've ever watched the sun rise, Carson."

"Never?"

"Not that I can remember."

"Then maybe… maybe from here on out, they'll make you think of me," he said softly.

My breath caught at his words. What he meant was, when we parted, perhaps the sunset would always be a reminder of this weekend. Of him. Sadness welled inside me, but I didn't want to lose this moment. This beautiful *now* that would soon become a memory. I managed a smile over my shoulder, nuzzling in to him.

He pulled me back harder to his chest and kissed my temple. We stood watching the miraculous display of nature's wake-up call to the world for a good twenty minutes, the sun dancing over the mountains as it creeped higher in the sky, the vivid reds and whites of the canyon on full display. It was breathtaking. When the whole sun was showing over the horizon and the landscape was bathed in light, Carson pulled my hand and we got back in the car.

Ten minutes later, after paying at the pay booth, we pulled into the parking lot at the Red Rock Canyon Visitor Center. Carson went to the trunk and grabbed a backpack that I hadn't even noticed him putting in as we got into the car in the Bellagio parking garage.

"No rope and shovel in there, I hope," I said, looking at his backpack with mock suspicion.

He laughed. "No, buttercup. Just some bottled water."

"Whew."

He took my hand and we began walking toward one of the trailheads.

The landscape was mountainous and rocky, the colors bursting all around me as the day grew lighter and lighter.

The rock formations in the distance were rusty red, the cacti bright green, and various colors of desert wildflowers were sprinkled beside the trail. The orangy-red, glowing sun in the distance was a backdrop for the beauty all around us. I was struck by how *vivid* everything was. Las Vegas had manufactured glitz—in spades—but this was a kind of radiance too and I marveled at it.

We walked along in silence for a little while. I was fully awake now, watching the amazing view of Carson's muscular backside in a pair of khaki shorts moving up the trail in front of me. It was as awe-inspiring as the natural wonder around me and I smiled to myself, drawing in a big breath of dry desert air.

After a little bit, we started chatting. I told him about my sisters, Julia and Audrey, both younger than me. I talked about my dad, how he was still a cop but was planning on retiring in the next couple of years. I described what it had been like to grow up in the Midwest, in the same house all my life, and what it was like to leave Ohio for the first time at eighteen years old.

I told him about my best friend Abby and her boyfriend Brian and how Brian went to Georgetown with me. I described the night I had introduced them at a school function I had dragged Abby to.

He talked about what it had been like to grow up in Los Angeles, staying in the same city but moving around constantly. He told me about his best friend and roommate, Dylan, who was his snowboarding partner-in-crime and was finishing up his final semester at a computer-programming technical school. Carson said that Dylan was such a computer genius that he could have taught the classes himself, but in order to get a decent-paying job, he needed the degree.

We talked about everything and nothing, filling each other in on our lives. There was something about talking as we walked, looking ahead at the trail and not at each other, that made it feel like we could say anything. The boundaries naturally in place when looking someone in the eye were gone, and it seemed even easier to open up. To me, it felt like our own private place away from the world—there, it was just me and him, our own stories, what we liked, what we felt, and absolutely nothing else.

I was shocked at how quickly time was going by as we walked and chatted. I glanced at my cell phone ,in the pocket of my sweatshirt, now tied around my waist, and it was already seven thirty. We stopped and he took a couple bottles of water out of the backpack, and we took long drinks from them.

When he offered me a granola bar, I asked, "Where'd you get these?"

"Vending machine when I woke up this morning," he said. "Always prepared, buttercup."

"Lucky for me," I said, eyeing him. "Why do you call me buttercup?"

"Maybe because your skin is satiny like a flower petal." And he trailed his fingers up my arm, tickling me lightly. I laughed and shook my head.

We ate and drank and then got back on the trail. We stopped again in another hour, and after we drank more water, he leaned against a rock and pulled me against him, kissing the side of my neck. "Mmmm...I love the way you smell even more when you sweat. It's irresistible."

I laughed at the tickly feeling of his lips trailing lightly down my neck. "Is this where you turn into a desert hyena?"

"Probably. I feel him coming out. He's strong, baby. He's hard to contain. Ah!" He contorted his head in at an awkward angle and brought one arm out stiffly. "Run, Grace! Run!"

I laughed as he grabbed me around the waist and brought me against him hard, growling into my face. "Too late, baby. You had your chance."

He nipped at my neck and ground up against me while I laughed and writhed in his arms.

After a few minutes, he turned serious, his gaze meeting mine as he leaned closer. He kissed me slowly and deeply, our tongues tangling, our breath mingling. I gasped, my eyes opening , when he took my bottom lip into his mouth and sucked on it gently. His eyes were open too and our gazes locked. A coil of heat unwound in my belly.

Finally, he broke away, tucking a strand of hair behind my ear that had come loose from my ponytail. "It feels good to be up here with you. I didn't know if I'd like company while hiking. Who knew it could be even better with the right person?" He smiled at me gently.

I smiled back and then cocked my head to the side. "Do you go hiking alone a lot?"

"Any chance I get, yeah. I love being outdoors."

"I can tell. Hiking, snowboarding, surfing. What don't you do?"

"There's nothing I won't do, buttercup. But you already know that." He gave me an exaggerated wink.

I rolled my eyes. "Seriously, though, what do you love so much about it all?"

"Adventure sports?"

"Yeah."

He looked over my shoulder and was quiet for a minute. "I love the physical challenge. I love the fact that if you do something enough, you can become great at it. With enough practice, you can master things that, at first, seem impossible. It has nothing to do with who you are, how you look, nothing superficial. It's just about not quitting. And then, you get to take credit for it, because it's something you accomplished." He was quiet for another minute, his brow furrowed. I could practically see the wheels turning in his head. "Huh. I never actually thought about it until I just put it into words for you." His smile was startling in its intensity, that dimple doing its worst.

Hi, dimple. I grinned right back.

He pulled me closer. "Know what else I really like?"

"What?"

"You."

"Yeah? And what exactly do you like about me?"

He gave me a considering look. "I like, no I *love*, the

145

look on your face when you're seeing or doing something new—almost like it's a religious experience."

I'd realized that over dinner the night before and I loved hearing him say it.

"And I like how you let me see beneath that perfect exterior because it turns out that what you were hiding is even more stunning, Fraggle Rock hair and all."

I laughed. He grinned back and kept looking into my eyes. My heart constricted.

"And I really, really like how you make me feel—like if you looked at me every day the way you're looking at me right now, I could do anything, be anything, *be more*." He ended on a whisper, the laughter leaving his expression.

I reached up and touched his cheek. No one had ever complimented me quite like that. I wasn't sure how to respond except by saying, "I like you too, Carson."

"Yeah? What do you like about me?" he asked. He gave me a boyish smile. I saw the vulnerability in it. My answer meant something to him.

"I like how you make me want to be brave like you, to listen to my own desires and make my own happiness." I kissed his nose. "I like how you let me see beneath your sex-on-a-stick exterior because as unbelievably amazing as you are in that respect, as it turns out, that's the least of what you have to offer."

Our eyes held for several moments and I wasn't sure what I saw on his face. That same vulnerability, yes, but also a hint of disbelief. I'd meant what I said, though. And I wondered... I wondered if he'd think about... choosing another life path.

That's dangerous thinking, Grace, and not part of the arrangement. No, it wasn't. And so I pushed it aside as he pulled me in to an embrace, kissing the top of my head.

"And," I went on, leaning my head back, and attempting to reclaim the lightness we'd been enjoying, "I like how you make me feel, how you make me laugh and have fun and feel more alive than I've ever felt before."

He stared at me for several heavy beats. "I think you should know something, Grace," he said after a moment.

"What?" I asked suspiciously.

"In the tradition of the Native American people who lived in this desert ten thousand years ago, we just got married, baby."

I burst out laughing. "Vows at the top of the mountain?"

"Exactly," he said, laughing too.

After a minute or two, we joined hands and moved on.

At a little before ten a.m., we returned to the car, sinking into our seats and turning up the air conditioner to high.

"Wanna go see the visitor center before we get back on the road?" Carson asked.

"Okay," I said, glancing over at the outdoor, shaded center.

We spent a half an hour looking at the four themed areas; earth, air, fire, and water. Carson stood next to me and put his arm around my shoulder as I read about agave roasting pits and I nuzzled into him and kissed the side of his neck. Things felt so natural between us now. Too natural. Painfully natural. I was aware of the hurt—the goodbye—in the very near distance, waiting for me, but I'd vowed to enjoy the last of our time together, and though it might take some effort, I was committed. *Light. Fun. You can do it.*

We drove back to town and stopped at a small burrito bar and sat on the outdoor picnic benches as we ate. Carson pulled me onto his lap halfway through, and it felt completely comfortable to continue eating sprawled across him as we reminisced about the things we had seen on our hike.

"Thank you for showing me my first sunrise," I said. "Thank you for the whole morning. It was one of the coolest things I've ever done."

He nodded, his mouth full of burrito. After a minute, he said, "My pleasure, buttercup. And by the way, a sunrise will always remind me of you too."

I leaned in, kissing him softly and smiling against his salty, burrito-flavored lips.

We drove back to the hotel, and I reminded him that I was going to the seminar presentation and wanted to get there a little early. We stopped by my room so I could grab some clothes and then went up to his room to each take a quick shower.

When I emerged in my bra and underwear, Carson was drawing the curtains so the room was dark and cool. "Nap?"

"God, that sounds so good," I sighed.

He set the alarm and we snuggled together under the blankets, skin to skin. It felt warm and cozy and his smell was intoxicating me again. But my body must have needed sleep more because before I knew it, the alarm was going off. Carson untangled himself from me and rolled over to shut it off. We snuggled for a few more minutes, waking slowly. *Delicious.* I wished I could stop time for a few hours and live under those covers with him.

"Meet me back in my room at four o'clock?" he asked. "It's our last night. I want to do something special."

I nodded, a lump forming in my throat. I swallowed it down with effort. "Four o'clock," I repeated. Wish as I might, time would not be stopped, or slowed.

I dressed in a conservative outfit of black slacks and a black-and-white polka-dotted blouse. In some odd way, I felt like I was slipping on an old version of myself. But that wasn't accurate. This buttoned-up version still existed. It was just that I'd become *more*. My stomach knotted at that line of thinking and I wasn't sure exactly why. That was a good thing, wasn't it? It was the positive I was going to walk away from this weekend with. I slipped on my shoes and leaned over Carson, still lying in bed. "Four o'clock," I said again.

His expression was so serious as though those words made a lump form in his throat too. "Okay," he said. "See you then. Oh, take the extra key card on the desk so you can let yourself in."

"Okay," I said. Then I kissed him softly, grabbed the key card, and left the room.

As I walked down the hall, another burst of melancholy swept through me, and it occurred to me that this was the first time Carson and I would be apart for longer than fifteen minutes since we had first stepped onto that elevator.

Carson

I lazed around for a little while, flipping on the television and watching *Die Hard* for half an hour or so when I found it on a movie channel. Finally, I shut it off and pulled on some clothes. I was still feeling the depression that had overcome me when Grace closed the door behind her. I was going to see her in a couple hours and yet I was already missing her. This wasn't good. I suspected that I was somewhat fucked when it came to Grace, but I didn't want to think about it. It was going to suck to watch her walk away tomorrow morning. I stood at the bathroom sink, looking at myself in the mirror. "You are such a dumb motherfucker," I said to my reflection. I turned, leaning against the counter and crossing my arms. Maybe we could keep in touch. Maybe I could fly her out to LA. We needed to talk—I couldn't let her go permanently. I suddenly realized that it was an impossibility for me. I had no idea what we'd do, but we had to do something. I tried to work through it in my mind for a few minutes but couldn't come up with a solution. "Fuck!" I yelled to no one.

I was antsy as hell and needed to get out of my hotel room while she was gone. I'd come back up and meet her at four and we'd talk, figure something out, but to sit and drive myself crazy for the next hour sounded less than appealing. And so I headed to the lobby and decided to stop by the end of the expo, probably just finishing up about now. I'd make an appearance, chat with a few people, pass the time.

When I entered the conference room, it was still crowded with fans, lines formed at tables where the most popular performers sat signing anything from photos to body parts. This was good. A crowd was good. *Distraction*. Speaking of which… I shook my head on a smile when I saw one woman bent over, as a male performer I didn't know signed her bare ass.

"Carson Stinger!" I heard shouted and looked over to see Bobby Prince, another male performer who worked for Courtney at ArtLove.com.

"Hey, man." I said as I walked toward him. Bobby was just packing his stuff up and so we stood and shot the shit for a little while before his girlfriend, who was in the business too, came over and put her hand around his waist asking, "Ready, baby?" We shook hands and he took off. I looked around and saw a grandma who must have been ninety years old having her saggy cleavage signed by a woman I didn't know in a short, red leather dress with a zipper up the front. The old woman sort of reminded me of my granny. She probably knew how to pick out a cantaloupe too. *Okay, that's enough.* I turned away. This was not my scene and exactly why I had told Tim that I wasn't doing this type of stuff anymore. Why I thought it'd be a good idea even to walk through, I didn't know.

Suddenly, everyone I looked at had a *story.* I wanted to know why they were here, doing what they were doing. I let out a harsh breath. *Christ.* No, I didn't. Did I? I really had no fucking idea. It was just because I'd spent the weekend hearing Grace's story, a woman who I'd judged to be completely different than she actually was. A woman who had a family, and a past, and hurts and fears. A woman who made decisions based on things I'd have never known about if I hadn't fucking asked.

Oh, Jesus. I was reeling.

I headed for the exit doors and just as I was almost there, I heard my name shrieked. I pivoted with a jolt to see a twenty-something blond jumping up and down and pulling her friend's arm. "Oh my God!" she yelled. "Carson Stinger, I LOVE you!" Then she ran over to me and pulled her shirt all the way up, exposing her tits. "Sign me!" she demanded, sticking a Sharpie pen in my face.

I managed a smile and scrawled my name across her breasts. "Thanks for the support." I smiled, handed her back the pen, and started to walk off.

"Wait!" she yelled. "Will you take a picture with me?"

I sighed. *No.* "Sure." I returned to where she stood and put my arm around her shoulders. She pulled her shirt back up to expose my signature, as her friend snapped a picture.

I said another goodbye and as I turned, I heard one of

the girl's whisper to the other, "Grab his dick so you can say you felt up Carson Stinger."

I heard them rushing at my back and turned toward them saying, "Whoa, ladies, I appreciate your fan support, but no one's grabbing my junk." I tried to laugh it off, giving them my most charming smile, the one that always got me off the hook with women, the one that suddenly felt very hard to bring forth.

They obviously didn't hear me though, or didn't care what I said or didn't say, because their eyes remained directly focused on my crotch, and their hands continued to reach forward.

"Back off!" I yelled deeply, shielding myself with my hands and causing them to startle and halt. I saw several people in my peripheral vision stop and turn toward me.

I started walking for the exit again as the blond yelled after me, "What the hell? You fuck for a living and your dick's suddenly off-limits? Whatever, asshole!"

Anger spiraled in my gut. I was not public property. I clenched my jaw but kept walking. They didn't deserve a response. When I got out into the hall, I kicked a plant over, dirt spraying over the carpet.

I returned to my hotel room and slammed the door behind me, and then kicked it for good measure. I sat down on the corner of the bed, staring blankly at the wall. I was pissed, and I couldn't seem to shake it off the way I usually did when fans got overly "friendly". Those girls were bitches, but who fucking cared? Who cared what they thought? Who cared what anyone thought?

A minute later, I heard a click and the room door opened. Grace came in with a smile, her blue eyes softening when she saw me. "Hi, handsome," she said. "Miss me?"

I opened my mouth to say something full of sexual innuendo about exactly what I missed about her, but I snapped my mouth closed. She'd been right about that being a reflex when I felt a lack of control. And now, she'd see right through it. I loved that. I hated that. She'd stripped me of my defenses and now it was just *me,* standing here bare in a way I'd never been bare before.

Her face morphed into concern. "Carson? What's wrong?" She came over to me and tilted my chin up with her finger and looked into my face, her eyes searching mine. I didn't answer but wrapped my arms around her and lay my head on her belly, taking in long inhales of her soothing scent. She stilled as though she sensed my turmoil. She probably did.

After a couple seconds, she started running her hands through my hair gently, soothing me further. "Talk to me. What happened?" she asked quietly.

I took in a deep breath and pulled back. "Nothing, Grace. I just ran into some bitchy fans from the expo. Just a hazard of the job."

When her eyes skittered away from mine, I knew that she didn't know what to say—my job was probably something she really didn't want to think about. Frankly, it was something I really didn't want to think about either. She appreciated some of my personal attributes. But she didn't appreciate my career.

This is Rick…Ryder. He's in law school at, uh, Stanford.

She'd lie about it if we were in public, like she'd done with Parker. I got it. She had an image to uphold. And I was bad for that image. That depression again, cramping my stomach.

I stood. "I'm gonna take a quick shower, okay? Then we can get ready for dinner?"

She smiled a small confused smile but nodded. "Okay." She took her hand and brushed a piece of hair off my forehead and then brushed her knuckle over my cheek. I leaned toward it and closed my eyes. I didn't really need a shower, but it would give me the time to get into a better headspace and allow my emotions to settle.

It was my last night with Grace. I didn't want anything to ruin it. But, we needed to talk. We needed to figure something out.

I wasn't worthy, but I couldn't let her go.

CHAPTER 12
Grace

I heard the shower turn on and sat down in the chair at the desk to check my phone and shoot Abby another quick text. I had been sending them intermittently since I'd told her about staying with Carson. She wanted to know that I was okay. If the positions had been reversed and she was spending the weekend with a stranger, I'd want her to check in frequently too.

Carson hadn't described to me exactly what happened with his *fans*, but he looked disturbed. Upset. And truthfully, just hearing about that aspect of his life upset me too. I needed to shake it off because that wasn't fair to him and I wanted to enjoy our last night together. I sat still, picking at a hangnail on my thumb. There was so much push and pull inside me, so many things I was trying to embrace, and several I was actively attempting to set aside. When I was with him, it was easier to quiet my mind, but once I was left to my own thoughts, they continually wandered to Carson and my feuding emotions. I'd only halfway focused on the presentation I'd attended, mostly distracted by the fact that we were going to be saying goodbye in the morning. My stomach twisted at the very thought.

Maybe we could keep in touch somehow? Was that completely stupid and unrealistic? We needed to discuss this. I was pretty sure he'd be open to the topic, but what if he wasn't? What if he was still planning on the quick, permanent break we had arranged? He had called us friends. Did he want to remain friends? Maybe at some future time, when circumstances had changed, we could—

A knock sounded at the door and snapped me from my chaotic thoughts. The shower was still running so I walked to the door and pulled it open. A middle-aged, short, balding man in khakis and a sport coat was standing on the other side. He looked surprised to see me. "Carson here?" he asked.

"Oh, he is but he's in the shower. Do you, uh, want to wait for him, or..."

He tapped on the doorframe, looking annoyed. "I'm his agent, Tim." His gaze ran over me, his eyes filling with something that made me squirm. "Well, I can see why he shut off his phone and blew everything else off this weekend," he finally said. "You're quite the hot piece of ass, aren't you?"

Excuse me? My eyes widened in shock. Who the hell talked that way to a stranger? "I—"

"Listen, just tell him I stopped by, since he's not taking any calls, and I apparently missed him downstairs earlier at the naked boob signing." He snickered. "Let him know his shoot tomorrow morning has been moved back to eleven. And, girlie, do everyone involved a favor and go easy on his cock tonight. The whole shoot depends on him being able to get it up. If you've worn him out, no one is gonna be happy—especially Bambi, his costar. Capeesh?"

There was a lot there that made my heart drop into my feet, and I felt bile rising up my throat, but I wasn't going to let this greasy sleazeball see that. This was a member of Carson's team? *God.* I stood taller and formed my face into what I hoped was a bored expression. "I'll tell him, Tim," I said, my voice cracking slightly, but my eyes remaining steady.

"Good," he said, starting to turn away. Then he turned back and his beady, little rat eyes assessed me again. "You know," he said, running one finger down my cheek to which I flinched away, "you've got a really good look—sexy yet innocent. You'd look great on film. When you're done with Carson tonight, why don't you come down to my room and we can do some role-playing, see what your acting skills are like…among other things." He adjusted himself in his pants as his eyes moved down to my breasts and lingered there.

I pushed the door closed in his face. I felt like I was going to throw up. I had no words. If this weekend had taught me anything, it was that I was a lot more frazzle-able than I thought.

I leaned unsteadily against the wall, trying to get hold of myself. Carson had a shoot tomorrow morning. With a girl named *Bambi*. His costar. Which meant… I clenched my eyes shut for a minute as a small sob clogged my throat and made it hard to breathe. *Stop it, Grace.* I was not going to cry about this. It was what he did. I *knew* this.

Yes, I knew it, but it was the one thing I hadn't allowed myself to truly dwell on during our time together. I hadn't let my mind stray to the mechanics of Carson's job… or the fact that another real-life person was involved. In this case, a person named *Bambi*. I'd kept the specifics of his job in the back of my mind, not denying them exactly, just refusing to fully consider the reality. We were going to spend the night together; he was going to be inside me tonight and then inside Bambi in the morning? My heart clenched painfully. I hated the thought of that. I hated it.

Carson suddenly emerged from the bathroom, a towel wrapped around his waist. He smiled, but it quickly disappeared as he took me in. "Buttercup?" he asked worriedly.

"Your agent Tim came by," I said, my voice shaky. "He wanted to let you know that your shoot with Bambi in the morning has been moved to eleven."

He froze and his eyes closed for a couple beats. Then he opened them and said simply, "I'm sorry, buttercup." And that's when I felt my heart truly crack.

Carson

My guts churned as I took her in from across the room. *Shit, shit, shit! Fucking Tim!* I hadn't wanted Grace to know about my shoot. I had avoided thinking about it myself. But it was reality, and I knew I'd have to face it eventually. I was just sorry as hell that Grace had to face it too. And that Tim—the sleazebag—had delivered the news.

"Grace," I started, walking toward her. She crossed her arms and the movement made me want to slam my fist into the wall. She was drawing away from me, not purposely maybe, but her body language spoke for her. "I'm sorry you had to find out about the shoot like that." I hesitated. I didn't really know what to say. I felt ashamed, confused, still unsteady. "You knew what I did…" I started, the words fading because they weren't right. Maybe those didn't exist.

"I know," she whispered. "I guess I just didn't think you'd

be going so directly from me to someone else. I guess... I guess I didn't think about it."

I understood that, I did. But I also wanted her to understand that what I'd be doing tomorrow was professional, nothing more. "It's not like that, Grace. It's work," I said quietly.

"I know." She nodded, a jerky movement that wasn't quite convincing. "What I wonder is, how do you separate the two? I never asked you anything about what you do because I didn't want to think about it—not truly. But now I want to know. How do you separate real life from 'work'?"

I watched her for a minute, taking in the way she held herself. She was ashamed of what I did, which made me fell low, but I thought, mostly... she was hurt. Because it was personal to her now. I couldn't blame her for the way she felt. We'd started this weekend with a different set of rules: no strings, a smooth parting of ways. And somehow, everything had been flipped on its head. "I've only made four films, Grace. Like I told you in the elevator, I don't exactly enjoy it, but it was always easy enough for me. Before."

"Before what?" she asked, her gaze rising to meet mine, searching.

"Before you. You've changed things for me." And as the words tumbled from my mouth, I realized how true it was. I had no idea of what that meant exactly, but I couldn't deny it.

"So what are you going to do then?" she asked quietly.

I scrubbed a hand down my face. "What can I do?" I asked, raising my voice, feeling the anger and frustration of the situation. "I have a two-year contract, and I'm only six months into it. I'll get sued if I break it. And what the fuck else am I going to do, anyway, Grace? Work at a gas station? I don't have a college degree. I don't have any other prospects. The truth is, I don't have anything to offer you." The statement caused misery to fall over me like a net. Trapped. I was trapped. I'd never felt more worthless.

Her eyes filled with tears. After a moment she sighed and walked toward me. "I'm sorry. This isn't fair. I knew what you did and now it must feel like I'm holding it against you. It's just…it didn't hurt two days ago. It hurts now."

"I know. I know, Grace." My shoulders slumped. This was a no-win situation. I had thought we'd figure out a way to make *something* work, but how? What? It was true—I had nothing to offer her. She couldn't deal with what I did and still be a part of my life, and I got that. How would I feel if Grace was going off to make a film with some other guy tomorrow morning? I wouldn't care that it was "work"; it would freak me the fuck out. I'd be sick and jealous at the thought of anyone touching her the way I had.

I had told her that we were friends, and we were, but we were more too—what exactly, I wasn't sure and there was no way for us to explore any of it. The fact that we lived in two different cities was the very least of our challenges.

And as far as my job, I had few to no good options aside from what I was doing right in the moment. I had spent a lot of money in Vegas, not that I'd tell her that, and I needed the contract installment that tomorrow's shoot would bring to replenish my bank account.

"Isn't there anything else you've thought of doing?" she asked warily. "I mean, surely you couldn't have planned to do this forever."

"I don't have a plan, Grace! You're the one with the plan!" I yelled, hating myself, so filled with regret and frustration that I lashed out at her.

Her lip trembled. She was obviously holding back tears. I wanted to make it better for her, but I couldn't. I was worthless and powerless and the girl I cared about was standing in front of me trying not to cry, and there wasn't a damn thing I could do about it.

I took a deep breath and closed my eyes very briefly. "I don't want to lose you, buttercup, but I don't have a plan," I said miserably. "I'm so sorry, so sorry." I raked both hands through my hair, grimacing and turning away from her.

"Come to DC, Carson. Stay with me. We can figure something out." I turned to face her. "Maybe you could enroll in college there...or..." She trailed off, her eyes losing the look of hope that had been in them a moment before. Now she was frowning and looking sad and uncertain.

I studied her. My sweet buttercup. "I can't stay on your couch mooching off of you, Grace. If this"—I waved my arm around the room indicating where we had started—"was an unlikely way for anything real to begin, that situation would be the worst idea in the history of bad relationship ideas. What would your dad think? Your sisters? I wouldn't do that to you—to us." Plus, whether I liked it or not, I was still tied to that damn contract. I had a job to do in the morning, and then as many as they booked me for in the next year and a half.

Her eyes met mine and we looked at each other for long moments. The air was heavy. My heart was heavy. I could see that she was out of ideas too. She was slipping away from me and I was desperate to hold on, but it felt impossible.

She let out a breath, looking away. "This is going to hurt more if I stay with you until tomorrow morning," she said quietly. "I can't stand it hurting any more than it does now, Carson. I can't..."

"I know," I said, something inside pulling tight and snapping.

She nodded and stood up and started gathering her

things. I felt both numb and hot, my skin prickly. I sat silently, staring ahead, hating life, hating myself and my stupid choices, and most of all hating the fact that we could never explore what had just started blossoming between us.

When she was done, she knelt down in front of me just as I had done to her yesterday. Tears shimmered in her eyes and my heart beat so slowly I thought it might stop. "I'll always think of you when I get on an elevator or see a sunrise," she said quietly, her voice breaking on the last word.

I managed a small smile, my heart giving a hollow thud. Maybe it'd cease beating, right here in this hotel room. I was so fucking sad. I would never know what we could have been together, and it felt so damn unfair. My gaze moved over the lines of her face, the shape of her lips. I tried to memorize the shade of her eyes, the exact way her hair fell around her shoulders, so I could keep the image of her in my mind's eye forever. I thought of all the things that would make me think of her—too many to mention them all. "I'll always think of you when I watch *Titanic*...or see a buttercup," I said. I hated this. It was exactly how it was supposed to end, or at least what we'd planned, and yet it was all wrong.

Stay. Don't go.

She smiled sadly, standing slowly and then leaning in to kiss me, her lips lingering on mine. Then she turned away too quickly for me to see her face and she opened the door and closed it quietly behind her.

Thud, thud...thud.

Fuck!

I stood and grabbed the vase of flowers off the desk and hurled it at the wall. Glass shattered and water and flowers rained down as I sat back down on the bed heavily and put my head in my hands.

CHAPTER 13
Grace

The tears started to fall before I was halfway down the hall. I knew this was the right thing to do—I couldn't stay a minute longer knowing where he was headed in the morning and admitting to myself that my heart was involved. But it didn't change the fact that I was forcing myself to leave. It didn't change the fact that it *hurt* to leave. It didn't shut out the memory of the stark misery that had washed over his face when he realized I was leaving. As I stepped on the empty elevator and the doors closed behind me, I swiped at my cheeks and leaned back against the wall.

This is where it had started. On an elevator. And now here I was on an elevator again—only this time it was ending. *And I don't want it to.* I wanted to go back in time and do it all over again, even knowing what I now knew, just to spend a couple more days with him.

When I made it back to my room, I dropped my things on the floor, and sank down on the bed. I curled into a ball, allowing myself to release the sobs that I'd barely been holding back as we'd said goodbye. I missed him. I already missed him, and we'd only been apart for fifteen minutes.

I couldn't stay here. Once I'd managed to gather myself, I stumbled to the bathroom and washed my face. Then I threw on a pair of jeans and a T-shirt and started packing. There was no way I could remain in this hotel with Carson a couple floors above me. There were several reasons for this, mainly that I simply didn't trust myself not to run back to his room and fling myself at him. But to what end?

Grace, Grace, Grace. What did you do? Yes, I had gotten myself into this situation. But how would I have known that I would develop feelings for Carson Stinger, Straight Male Performer? If someone had told me two days ago that that would be my reality, I would laugh and say such an idea was ludicrous. Now? Now it wasn't ludicrous at all. Because what I hadn't known, was that he had an impossibly sweet side and that he was exciting and brave and generous in every way possible. Would I rather not know? Would I rather go back to the time when it was easy to walk away from him if I had to agree that I would never experience the beauty of our weekend? I was too hurt and confused to answer those questions right now.

I hefted my large purse over my shoulder and pulled the handle up on my suitcase and rolled it out the door.

Thankfully the checkout process was quick and in mere minutes I was outside stepping onto a shuttle that would take me to the airport. I prayed that there was a flight I could get on tonight, but if not, I'd sleep in the terminal. It wasn't much of a plan. I almost laughed but caught myself. Then I almost sobbed and caught myself again. All my well-laid plans had gone out the window.

As the shuttle pulled away, I looked back over my

shoulder at the Bellagio. I'd become a different person this weekend. Carson had changed me in ways that I suspected were going to make me look at all my decisions differently, make me reevaluate all my future *plans*.

Deep breath. I turned forward, watching the road ahead. The best I could do was take the lessons from this weekend with me and think of them—*of him*—as a gift, even if now, my heart was breaking with loss. My hands gripped the strap of my purse as I forced myself not to demand the shuttle driver stop and let me out so that I could go running back to Carson. Instead, I leaned my head back on the seat and let myself feel the mixture of heartbreak and hope mingle inside, bathing my heart in both darkness and in light.

———

The wheels of my suitcase bumped over the threshold of my apartment the next morning at seven thirty and for a minute I stood looking around, feeling like a different person than the girl who had walked purposefully through this very door, spine straight, future set, all plans firmly in place. I closed the door behind me, stifling a yawn. I was completely exhausted in every way possible. I had been able to change my flight to a red-eye and had sat around the airport for several hours waiting until boarding started. Once on the plane, I'd tried to sleep, but my mind wouldn't let me, too active to shut down and allow me some rest.

I went over every minute of my weekend with Carson, trying to pinpoint the exact moment when I handed him a piece of my heart. Had it been over hot dogs that first night? After the amazing sex? Laughing in the pool? When he told me he was jealous of Parker, revealing that he had feelings for me too? Or had it been sooner than that? Maybe in the elevator when he sang to me to keep me from panicking? When I discovered why he put on that false front? Was it possible to connect to another person that quickly? I wanted to scream! *Shut down, brain!* Did it really even matter? It was like I was trying to investigate the scene of a crime, attempting to find the smoking gun that had resulted in the mangling of my life as I'd known it.

I sighed, my shoulders slumping as my purse slid down my arm, and I let go of my suitcase.

"Hey, pod person!" I heard called from the kitchen.

"Hi, Abs," I said, meeting her in the doorway. She gave me a quick hug and then sat back down at our small kitchen table, reaching for the mug of coffee sitting next to some papers and a pen in front of her.

When I remained standing, she looked up at me over the rim of her cup, her eyes widening as she set the coffee back down. "What'd he do to you?" she demanded, standing up again and walking to where I stood.

I shook my head as my face crumbled and my raw emotions welled up in the midst of the safety and comfort of my best friend. "He didn't do anything to me, Abby. I did it to myself. I—" I choked and the tears started flowing.

Abby pulled me to her, stroking my back and hugging me silently for several minutes as I got ahold of myself. When my tears had subsided, she pulled away and looked into my face, her expression stern. "I can't believe you did this to us, Grace."

I laughed a soggy laugh. "To us? How do you figure I did anything to *us*?"

She pushed a piece of hair behind my ear. "Because, Gracie, I love you, and so we're going to deal with the aftermath of this weekend together. I'm busy. And still itchy. I hardly have time for this." She let out an exaggerated sigh, a corner of her lip quirking up. She was trying to make me smile.

It worked. I loved her.

"Sit," she said. "I'll get you a cup of coffee and you tell me all the details. I don't have to be at class until eleven." Abby was in school at one of the best culinary institutes in the DC area. Her cooking was to die for. If I ever indulged, it was to try out one of her recipes and I was never disappointed.

She poured me a cup of coffee and added cream and sugar to it just the way I liked, and set it in front of me. I wrapped my hands around the warm mug and brought it to my mouth, taking a small sip of the hot liquid.

"At least tell me you didn't fall in love with him, honey," Abby said.

I released a breath. "It was a weekend, Abby," I said back, my gaze shifting away.

When I looked back at her, her mouth was agape. "Oh shit. *You idiot.* You totally did! You fell in love with the porn star!" She groaned, leaning back and sliding down in her chair, flailing for a second and slapping a palm on her forehead. "Oh God," she practically yelled. "This is much worse than I thought. No wonder you never let loose! When you do, you really go all out, don't you, girlfriend?"

"Abby, stop the hysterics. I didn't fall in love in two days." *Did I?* I felt momentarily confused. No, of course not. That wasn't possible. "I just… I care about him. I didn't want to say goodbye." *I miss him already. So much.*

Abby sighed, pulling herself up. "Start at the beginning, Gracie. I want a play-by-play, and I know you're sad, but don't gloss over sexy times." She pulled a piece of paper and her pen forward as though she was going to take notes.

I laughed and then sniffled. "You're really a perv, you know that?"

"Uh-huh. I make no apologies. Now start talking."

We talked until she had to shower and leave for class. I cried a little more, but it felt good to get it out. Another emotional release that I'd needed—the sharing of the experience with my best friend. Then I went into my room, did a face-plant on my bed, and didn't wake up until Abby was walking back in the door at six that night.

Carson

I traveled straight from the airport to the hotel where my shoot was being held, knowing that I could shower there. They'd need to prep me for the cameras anyway. I was used to the drill.

I had barely slept for two hours the night before, listening to every sound in the hallway, hoping against hope that Grace would decide to come back. There was no way I could go to her after the way we'd parted... We had said our goodbyes. I couldn't make it any harder on her. But I thought maybe she'd change her mind and decide to stay just one more night with me. And so instead of going to the airport like I'd thought about, I stayed in the room where she'd know I'd be. But she hadn't come back. I understood. I wasn't surprised. It still fucking sucked. And the worst part of it all was that I missed her in a way I'd never missed anyone else before. Every instinct in me told me to charge after her, claim her as mine. But that caveman shit I'd joked about that first night wasn't going to cut it. We had gone over the reality of our situation… of *us*. Our lives didn't mesh, and there was nothing we could do right now to make that happen.

What was it about her that had gotten under my skin so deeply and so quickly? Maybe I was trying to figure it out so I could talk myself out of the feeling of loss that I couldn't shake. In the end, I decided that. But maybe there simply wasn't a clear-cut answer. It was just because she was *her*, and it was really just as simple as that. *Her*, who'd charmed and mesmerized me. *Her*, who'd made me question things I hadn't questioned before. *Her*, who'd made me see myself in a different light— one that cast shadows, but also, one that offered a perspective I hadn't noticed before, one I hadn't even fully investigated yet because I was still half-dazed from the experience.

I knocked on the door of the suite number Courtney had texted me that morning and was let in by a cameraman I'd worked with before. "Hey, Joe," I greeted him.

"Hey, Carson, how's it going?"

"Great. Is makeup set up in there?" I asked, indicating a closed door leading to what I assumed was the bedroom and bathroom.

"Yeah. They're waiting for you."

"Okay." When I opened the door, I was greeted by Courtney who mouthed *hi*, a cell phone held to her ear as she moved away.

"Hi, Carson," I heard a high-pitched voice say. "I'm Bambi." A naked blond with large, obviously fake breasts said from a makeup chair over by the window. A woman with a small makeup brush was applying something to Bambi's nipples.

I smiled tightly. I was so not into this. *Just get through it and get paid*, I reminded myself. "Hey, Bambi, nice to meet you," I said, walking over and shaking her hand.

"We may as well start getting acquainted." She smiled, standing and swatting the makeup person aside as she leaned in to kiss me softly, running her tongue over my bottom lip before leaning back on a look clearly meant to be seductive. Why she was bothering, I wasn't sure. I thought it was pretty obvious that I was a sure thing here, whether I wanted to be or not. *Fuck.* Why was I suddenly feeling ill? Bambi was beautiful. And she had a killer body.

"Is this your first shoot?" I asked.

She bobbed her head. And her breasts. The makeup person stepped forward, bent, and began applying something sparkly to her stomach. "Yes," Bambi said, "and I specifically asked for you for my first time." She looked briefly shy which was a strange contradiction to her nudity in the midst of a crowded room as she ignored a woman now rubbing the sparkly stuff down her thighs. It struck me that this whole scene was just... odd. "I've had a crush on you since I saw your picture on Courtney's website," she said with a small giggle.

Interesting. The thing I focused on though, was that she'd never done this before. The least I could do was make it as comfortable as possible for the both of us. Maybe she was putting on a front. Maybe it would help if I made it clear she didn't have to. "What's your real name, Bambi?"

Her expression went blank. "Huh?"

"I'm assuming Bambi is a stage name?"

Her eyes darted around. She swallowed. "Rose," she finally said. "My real name is Rose."

Rose. It made me think of the *Titanic.* It made me think of Grace. *Ouch.* I grimaced, shifting that thought aside. *Rose.* Think of Rose, the woman in front of you right now. Someone had once named her Rose. Did they know she'd tossed it aside and now called herself Bambi? *Oh God.* My head pounded. I backed away. "Pretty name," I managed. "Well, I gotta shower, but I'll be out in a few," I said, practically running away from her.

"I'll be ready," she called after me. I heard the confusion in her voice.

Get it together, Stinger. I took a quick shower, relaxing for a minute under the warm spray, and then asked the makeup people if they could pull the chair into the bathroom. I wasn't in the mood to chat with anyone. I needed some time to get my head in the game here, so to speak. Or at the very least, my body.

Unlike the longer-length films I had done, this was just a one-day shoot, so at least it'd be over after today.

Thankfully makeup wasn't a big production on a shoot like this one, especially for me. Anything applied would just rub off so not much was used. Courtney came in and kissed my cheek. "Hey, handsome," she said. "You look tired." She looked at the girl touching me up. "Put some concealer under his eyes, Marcia."

"I'm fine, Courtney. Dim the lights," I muttered.

"Even dim lights won't hide those bags, love. What'd you do? Stay up all night partying?"

I snorted. "I wish." No, I'd stayed up all night pining after a girl.

Marcia rubbed something under my eyes and powdered it and then signaled that she was done.

Courtney looked pointedly down at my boxers. "Need some time alone, hon?"

"Yeah," I answered, already wondering if I'd be able to get it up at all.

"Okay, the shoot calls for Bambi to touch herself for a

171

few minutes on the bed and then you come join her, ready to start the party, got it? You'll move out onto the balcony after a few minutes and continue there."

"Yeah. Okay."

"Good." She looked at me for a couple beats, but then cleared out and closed the door behind her.

I stood, waiting a couple minutes until I heard the music start in the bedroom beyond. I dropped my boxers and leaned back on the sink and tried to get in the mood. Not a twinge.

I envisioned all the sex I'd had this weekend with Grace. Maybe I had overdone it. *Grace.* There it was, that twinge, as I pictured her bent over the bed in heels and a thong, begging for me to take her, I hardened. *There we go. Okay.* I pictured all of the ways I had taken her over the weekend and after a couple minutes, I was painfully hard.

There was a soft knock on the door indicating they were ready for me. I walked out, naked, my erection jutting in front of me, and watched for a minute as Bambi writhed on the bed, moaning in an over-the-top way, her hand between her legs. *Rose. Her name is Rose.* I almost lost my erection, but clenched my eyes closed and pictured Grace again. *All right. Back in business.* I moved toward the bed to join Bambi and as I sat down beside her, she sat up slightly and started kissing me, thrusting her tongue in my mouth and moaning loudly. I almost grimaced. Her breath was fine, but she didn't taste like sunshine and sweetness. I cracked my eyes and looked down her body. Her skin was rouged and glittery. It'd look great on camera. But I couldn't help picturing the way Grace's smooth skin had flushed naturally with color when I made her cum.

Don't think. Just stop thinking. My heart was beating too quickly now, but not with arousal. With panic. This wasn't working for me.

It has to work for you. You have a job to do.

I didn't want to think of Grace, but thoughts of her were the only thing keeping me hard. I shut my eyes quickly and tried to bring her to mind. I reached up to touch her hair and it wasn't heavy silk in my hand—it was crispy with hairspray. We continued kissing and Rose brought her hand up to my cheek, the one that she had used to touch herself. I smelled her essence on her hand and that was it. I broke away from her and stood up. "Sorry," I muttered. "Not your fault but this isn't working for me."

"Cut!" I heard yelled.

I walked into the bathroom, retrieved my clothes and started pulling them on as Courtney's voice sounded at the door. "Carson, babe, if you need a little more time or maybe a blue pill, I've got you covered."

I opened the door, pulling on my shoes. I pushed past Courtney. "Sorry, Courtney, I really am. But I can't do this anymore." I looked around the room in general, catching sight of a stricken-looking Rose pulling on a robe in the corner. "Rose," I called. She looked up, blinking at me. "This has nothing to do with you. I promise. Maybe… just think about if this is what you really want, okay? There are… repercussions. There just are. And… Rose is a great name." I looked around at the crew staring at me with looks ranging from confusion to flat-out annoyance. "I'm sorry for wasting all of your time. I don't know what to say. I'm just…sorry." Then I walked to the door of the suite, opened it, and closed it behind me quietly.

I returned to the elevators and pushed the down button. My head was spinning. *Oh, shit.* What the fuck had I just done?

I was gonna get sued and I'd never make a film again after that meltdown.

I stood there, staring at the closed elevator door. I was screwed. I took a deep breath, pulling it through my body. So...why didn't I give even a small rat's ass right now? I let out a small, humorless laugh. I was basically penniless and jobless, and I felt...fine. Lighter.

What exactly are you going to do now, fuckwit? What about a fucking plan before you do some shit like that? I laughed again, only this one was real. A plan. I reached both hands up and laced my fingers together, putting them on my forehead and letting my head fall back. I stood like that for a minute until I heard the elevator ding and the doors start to open. I dropped my hands and started stepping toward it when I saw who was getting off. Tim. Fucking, Tim.

He looked surprised as he stepped from the car. "Carson," he said, "you can't be done already." He looked down at his watch. The elevator doors closed behind him and he took a step closer to me.

"The shoot *is* over, Tim. But only because I walked out."

His brows snapped down. "You walked out? What the hell is going on?"

"Listen, Tim, I would have called you later to let you know. But I'm done. I'm not gonna be making films anymore."

His eyes narrowed slowly. Then he let out a sharp laugh. "Well, goddamn. She must have been one hell of a fuck for you to throw your whole career away. Now I *really* wish that little blonde had taken me up on my offer to join me in my hotel room."

I jolted. "Your *offer?*" I asked, the air around us taking on a red tinge. "Your fucking *offer?*" I repeated, the realization that Tim had propositioned Grace when he came to my hotel room the day before making my blood boil. *Disgusting pig.*

I moved on him before he even knew what was coming, grabbing his dress shirt and walking him backward until I slammed him against the wall. Rage was pumping through my blood as I got right up in his face. "You sick, depraved motherfucker. How dare you speak to her like that? How dare you even fucking look at her? I should beat the living shit out of you."

"What the fuck are you doing?" he yelled. "Over a piece of ass, Carson? Over a fucking piece of ass?"

My limbs turned to ice as I balled my fist, and smashed it into his face. Blood spurted from his nose and I let go of him, letting him sink to the floor. He looked up at me dazedly.

I stepped over him, entering the elevator car. That coldness was seeping all through my body, making me feel disconnected, like I was watching the scene from some perch high above. I had a moment of vertigo—almost a soaring feeling—and then I gave a slight jolt, suddenly grounded again. The world around me came into focus, everything appearing sharp and clear. I pulled myself straight. "I'll no longer require your representation, Tim," I said without emotion. He let out a groan, pulling himself forward and beginning to sit up. I felt nothing for the sleazy asshole bleeding in front of me, nothing but hollow contempt. I pressed the lobby button, my eyes never leaving him as the doors between us closed.

———

I hopped in my car, a black Nissan Pathfinder that I had bought six months before, after signing with Courtney, and sat there for a couple minutes, staring unseeing out my window. I leaned forward and rested my head on the steering

175

wheel as I cleared my head. When I finally sat up and started my car, I drove like a homing pigeon to the entrance of the freeway. I had no real destination in mind. Maybe I'd just drive for a while and attempt to gather some more clarity about where to go from here, literally and figuratively.

Traffic slowed, coming to virtual halt. Fucking LA traffic. Truthfully, I didn't really care. It wasn't like I had to be anywhere. I let out a small laugh, attempting to run a hand through my hairsprayed hair. Oh Christ. I was still wearing fucking makeup. I let out a sigh, sitting back, my gaze holding on a billboard I'd seen a thousand times before driving through this part of the city. Huh. I tilted my head, my eyes moving over the photograph of men in uniform, guns drawn, running through mud.

Did anyone ever tell you you should go into the military where enjoying getting up at the crack of dawn is an asset?

Grace's words wound through my head, bringing with them a strange energy that suddenly pulsed through my veins. She'd been joking. But…an asset? Maybe I did have a few of those. I was adventurous. I was strong. I enjoyed getting up at the crack of dawn.

She'd told me I was brave.

The traffic started moving and I pulled past the billboard, still traveling slowly enough to grab my phone and look up an address on the internet. Then I turned on my GPS and exited at the next off ramp, following the prompts until I arrived at my destination thirty minutes later. The sign on the building in front of me read: *Navy Recruiting*. I took a quick moment to thoroughly wipe the makeup off under my eyes, and then got out of my car.

My heart was beating swiftly, but I was also filled with this sense of surety, of *purpose,* when I had just been feeling lost and without direction. I pulled the door open. *One chance to change your mind, Carson.* I paused for a second but then stepped inside.

"Can I help you?" a man wearing a khaki uniform, with a name tag and a few ribbons on his shirt asked as he stepped forward.

Was I really going to do this? Grace's face swam in my mind, the way she'd smiled at me, the way she'd looked proud when I told her why I loved challenging myself with physical sports. "I'm here to enlist," I said.

The man smiled. "Well, okay then, I'm your guy. Come on over with me. I'm Petty Officer First Class Duane Mitchell," he said, shaking my hand quickly and then gesturing for me to follow him to his desk. He sat behind it and indicated a chair on the other side.

"What's your name?" he asked as I took a seat.

"Carson Stinger."

"Okay, Carson, well, before we get started with anything, let's chat for a minute. What's brought you to this decision?" He leaned back in his chair, studying me.

I cleared my throat. "Well, to be honest, I don't really have any options that look a whole lot better. I'm not the college type. I already know that. I want to do something worthwhile with my life."

He nodded. "Well, that's as good a reason as any. Now let me ask you this: Have you thought about what job you'd like to do?"

"Uh, not really. I kind of just decided I was gonna do this about half an hour ago."

He laughed. "Right. Well, what are you good at?"

"I'm a great swimmer and I'm good at extreme sports."

Petty Officer Mitchell studied me again for a couple

seconds. He tilted his head toward a poster of a group of men in dive gear, machine guns in hand emerging from the water. "Ever heard of a Navy SEAL?"

"A SEAL? Yeah, of course. I'd be suited to be a SEAL?" Those were...well, those were badasses.

"Well, I don't know. You'd need to score really high on a test called the ASVAB and then pass a physical test during basic training that will ensure you a spot in BUD/S, which stands for Basic Underwater Demolition SEAL Training." He paused, eyeing me, but I remained silent. He went on. "Then you have to make it *through* basic training and A school. Even if you make it through all those steps and end up in BUD/S, only about twenty percent of men actually make it through, which means eighty percent fail. So, are you suited to be a SEAL? Not many men are. But if you're a good swimmer and you like sports that are dangerous and take a high level of skill, it's a decent start. I'll be honest with you, though, BUD/S is the most rigorous military training on the face of the planet earth. Think on it carefully."

I nodded. I'd already done as much thinking on the way here as I needed to. Add to that the fact that I didn't have any other options, *and* that this whole sudden idea had excitement buzzing beneath my skin, and I knew my answer. "Let's get started," I said.

CHAPTER 14
Grace

I sat on my bed half-heartedly studying. My heart was heavy and I felt a longing inside that I couldn't quench. I missed him, plain and simple. When was this feeling going to let up? It had been a few days since I'd gotten home from Vegas and it felt like my emotions were intensifying instead of weakening. I had only known him for two and a half days. Didn't it make sense that I could forget him in that amount of time too?

I sighed and lay back on my pillow, staring at the ceiling. What was he doing right now? Was he on set? I cringed at the though. Then again, he'd told me he had only done four films in six months and he'd just shot one a couple days before. A fierce surge of jealousy rose up in me when I pictured him with someone else, even someone he'd never see again. I wanted to scream at the very thought. And then I wanted to throw myself on the floor and cry until I was exhausted and numb. *That's what you get when you develop feelings for a porn star, Grace.* I *was* an idiot, just like Abby had jokingly called me.

But how had *he* handled it? Had it been hard for him too, like he'd told me it would be? He'd said I'd changed things for him. And realistically, what that might mean was that my short-term legacy would be that I made his life more difficult. I had a hard time hoping for that. And yet, he could do so much *more*. I couldn't be the one to dictate that for him though. He'd have to decide that himself. It's why I had walked away. It's why I had had *no choice* but to walk away. God, he probably wished he'd never met me.

I didn't feel that way about him though, as much as I hurt. I knew what he did, but he was more to me than that. If he weren't, it would have been easy to walk away. I might have even run. And therein lay the problem. An impossible problem.

I lay there for a little while longer, lost in my thoughts, when I got a very, very bad idea. I wrestled with it for a few minutes before I stood up and grabbed my laptop off my desk. I powered it up and sat cross-legged on my bed, my hands shaking as I typed his name into Google search. The first site on the list was a website called ArtLove.com and against my better judgment, heart racing, I clicked on it. I knew this was a bad idea and yet it was like I was possessed. I was powerless to stop myself.

"Grace?" Abby called as I heard the front door shut.

"In here," I called back, reducing the screen before it had fully loaded.

I heard her footsteps and looked up from the computer when she appeared in my doorway in her school uniform, black pants and a white chef's coat.

"What are you doing?" she asked suspiciously, taking her hair out of the ponytail it was in and massaging her scalp. "Your cheeks are bright red."

180

"Um, looking up porn," I said, half-grimacing, half-smiling.

Abby's hand froze in her hair. "Uh, okay. You do have a lock on your door, you know?"

I rolled my eyes. "I'm looking up Carson, Abby."

She stared at me for a minute. "Is that such a good idea?"

"Probably not, but it's like I have to see it. I have to know the reality of it. I have to move on." Would this help? I didn't know, but it seemed like it might.

She hesitated but then came and sat down on the bed next to me. "All right then, doll, I'm gonna hold your hand."

"Thanks, Abs," I said as I clicked on the reduced screen to bring it up.

I had never looked at porn before and so I had no idea what to expect. My eyes grew large as I saw naked people engaged in all manner of sex acts. "Oh my God," I breathed.

I looked over at Abby and her head was tilted and a small smile was on her face. "This is the site he works for?"

I nodded. "He said he has a two-year contract. It must be with this site. Why?"

She looked at me. "Have you ever seen porn, Gracie?"

"I mean, I've seen images here and there, pop up ads... whatever," I said. I felt defensive like I sounded totally uptight. Porn had just never really... called to me. Romance books were more my jam. When I had the time to read for pleasure. Which... wasn't often.

"Well, compared to what's out there," Abby said, "this is actually very...artistic."

I turned my gaze back to the screen. I could see what she meant. Most of the scenes were on beautiful beaches or in opulent-looking homes or patios. The people were all good-looking. I scrolled down, looking more closely. Seriously, the women looked like they could be supermodels. Why did they do this? The same reason Carson did, I guess. Didn't it cause real relationship problems for them too? Both now *and* later? I shook my head, attempting to clear it. I had a hard time making sense of why people chose this profession. I'd thought the majority didn't *have* much of a choice, but looking at this site made me realize I was probably wrong.

When I tried to click on one of the videos, a pop-up box appeared saying that if I wanted to watch the full video, I would need to become a member and spelling out the different membership options.

I glanced at Abby, my heart still beating rapidly, and then typed Carson's name into the site search bar. Immediately, a page loaded and I let out a tiny gasp. There were stills of Carson *actively* having sex with different women in multiple screen shots. My brain couldn't keep up with my eyes as I let out a small, choked noise of distress and Abby squeezed my hand, saying "Let's turn this off…"

"No, not yet," I said, my voice sounding very far away to my own ears. I needed to see this. I needed to see the truth of what he did. What he'd done the day after we'd said goodbye.

"Gracie, these are things he did before he even met you," she said quietly.

"*These* ones are, Abby, but if I come back here and look next month, there will be a new one, maybe two," I said miserably.

Abby squeezed my hand. "You won't do that though right?"

I shook my head. "No, just this once. I just need to remind myself why I can't contact him. Why I *have* to let him go."

She shook her head sadly and we both looked at the photos in silence for a minute.

"Holy hell, sweetie, you were right—he's *hot*."

I looked at her, my lips thinning.

"Sorry, not helpful," she muttered, looking back at the screen.

As I too forced myself to look back at the images, feeling simultaneously empty and sickened, it registered that the expression on his face was...*wrong*. It was...it was the same look I had seen on his face in the lobby of the Bellagio when we first met and then again at the bar.

What position *did we make our two kids in? Doggy-style? Reverse cowgirl? The Garfield?*

I couldn't even remember the rest of the positions he'd described to shock me that day. What I did remember was the expression on his face when he was with me in bed. And this wasn't it. *He has his mask on in these pictures.* But it was little comfort. I felt the vomit rise up my throat, and I slammed my laptop shut, refusing to look at Carson being intimate with other women for one more second.

Carson

Shit, this is gonna suck. I took a deep breath and pulled the door open. Irene, Courtney's elderly receptionist looked up from her computer screen. "Hey, Carson." I gave her a wary smile and she smiled back. Well, at least her reaction to me wasn't calling security like I thought it might be.

"Hey, Irene. Is Courtney in?" I leaned on her desk and

she batted her lashes up at me. I usually flirted with her when I came in. I just didn't have it in me this time.

Irene's brow furrowed. "She is, hon. Do you have an appointment with her?" She started flipping through her book. "I don't see—"

"No, Irene, I don't. I'm actually—"

"Carson."

I looked up and Courtney was standing in the doorway of her office, in a gray skirt and a light pink blouse, her black hair hanging straight and long down her back, her face expressionless. *Shit.*

"Courtney, hi." I walked toward her. "I'm sorry I haven't called you and I didn't make an appointment. I just—"

"Carson, come on into my office."

I followed along behind her, like a kid who had been called to the principal's office, a kid who knew he was guilty and deserved exactly what he was about to get. After the way things had gone with Tim, I was not hopeful that this meeting would go well. Again, this was gonna suck.

Courtney sat down behind her desk and I took the chair in front of it. Courtney leaned back in her chair, steepling her fingers and studying me quietly. "What happened, Carson?"

I lay my hands on my thighs. "I'm done, Courtney. I'm sorry. I know it wasn't the professional way to do it. You've been good to me and I really do hate that I'm ending things this way between us."

She was silent for a minute. "You cost me a lot of money that day."

I took a deep breath. "Yeah, I know. That's part of the reason why I'm here." I reached into my pocket and removed my wallet and took the check out of the billfold. "I sold my car. I had them make out a cashier's check and I signed it

184

over to you. I don't know if it's enough to cover all the expenses of the shoot, and I know it's not enough to cover what you would have made off of the video itself, but I hope it's a start, and I can make payments for the—"

"First, tell me what happened to spur you running out of that suite half-dressed and looking like you were about to lose your lunch."

I looked down at the check in my hands and set it on the edge of her desk. The sound that emerged from my throat was pained, but it ended on a sigh. I liked Courtney. She'd always been good to me, always been someone I felt like I could trust in a business full of untrustworthy people. "I met someone, Court," I said softly.

She studied me, her expression softening. "Ah, I see. You fell in love. Now I get it."

"No, not exactly. I only spent a weekend with her, but—"

"Carson, you fell in love. I see it in your eyes."

I shook my head, frowning. "No, really, two and a half days, Courtney. That's it. Not weeks, days. I've just never felt that way about anyone. We... she... it's just—"

"Carson." She let out a soft laugh, but it wasn't unkind. "Love doesn't always make sense. And that's the great beauty of it, the great mystery—the thing cynics who scoff at so-called 'insta-love' would bottle if they could. But you can't manufacture mystery, honey. Believe me, I know."

I stared at Courtney, taking in her words, letting them swirl around in my head. I hadn't expected this reaction at all. "I don't have anything to offer her," I told her.

"So change that."

I nodded, looking down at my hands. I was going to try to become something more, someone better. But I wasn't going to fool myself into thinking that by the time I achieved that, Grace would be waiting around. She'd inspired me, changed me, but I had to do this for me.

"I think we might have a few things in common," Courtney said. "Can I tell you a little about my background?"

"Yeah. Of course."

"My mom was in the business too. I never said anything about it to you because I know I never liked people bringing it up to me when I wasn't prepared to talk about it. I only know your history because I make it my business to know about the people working for me. Also, my mom's story ended a little differently than yours did. My mom overdosed on heroine when I was fifteen. She was a runaway who got into the business when she was sixteen. She lied about her age and started making films. I can't say that I watched her decline because I never really knew her when she was anything other than the shell of a person. She could be fun and even vivacious when she wanted to be, but those times became few and far between as I grew into a teenager. Thankfully, my dad was a decent guy who stepped into my life fully when she died. They had had a three-month affair, and although he could have tried to deny me based on what my mom did for a living, when she told him she was pregnant with me, he never tried to play that card. I think he had truly and honestly wanted to take care of her, but she just wasn't in a place to let him do that. So after she died, he took me in and he gave me the stability I had never had. He was a good man...He passed away two years ago from lung cancer."

I couldn't even utter a word. I was so shocked by Courtney opening up to me like this.

"Anyway," she went on, "you can probably put two and two together about why I started this website. A lot of undignified, soul-stealing stuff goes on in this business. And this is a business that attracts people who are the least likely to be able to deal with that kind of thing to begin with." She studied me for a minute. "I started my site because I wanted to inject some heart into a business that's sorely lacking in that. True, the people in my videos are virtual strangers. But I think that portraying sex as a natural expression of our physical selves, while also showing that it doesn't have to be degrading to either party, is the best I can hope to accomplish here. If porn is always going to exist, and I believe it will, then I want to be responsible for doing it in a way that respects the fact that none of us is only our body—all of us have a heart and a soul, and they can't be separated."

I stared, processing her words. I'd said yes to working for Courtney's company after viewing her site and the work her team did. It'd looked... classy to me, I guess, after the raunchier nature of the studios my mom had worked for. But I'd never really thought about the overall message she'd been trying to convey. I felt a small sense of relief at the realization of exactly how much integrity she had, and that her company was the only one I'd ever worked for. But that didn't change that I was no longer interested in doing the job.

She was watching me, a small smile on her face. "What I'm trying to say," she finally said on a laugh, "is that I'm a fan of love." She rifled through some papers on her desk, choosing one from the pile. "Now, Carson, from what I recall, we made a change to your contract that amended it to be six months instead of two years. You remember initialing that change, right?" She looked pointedly at me.

"Uh, yeah, I do?"

Courtney lowered her chin and looked up at me through her dark lashes.

"Yeah, I do," I said more confidently.

"Good. Then according to my calendar"—she flipped her desktop calendar back a couple pages—"your contract ran out last week. Good luck in your next endeavor, Carson Stinger. It's been real."

I stood up and rubbed my palms on my jean-clad thighs. This was not how I'd expected this meeting to go and I was so damn relieved and grateful. "Courtney, I don't know how to—"

"Take care of yourself, Carson," she said, not rising from her seat. "And take your cashier's check. If you don't, I'll tear it up."

Right. I picked up the check and stuck it in my pocket. "Courtney. Thank you. You take care of yourself too."

"Oh, I intend to." She smiled.

I nodded and moved slowly to her door. I looked back once as I put my hand on the doorknob but she'd already picked up her phone to make a call.

PART 2

CHAPTER 15
Grace

Two months later, August

I pulled up in front of my childhood home and smiled as I stared out at it. I was tired from having made the eight-hour drive from DC to Ohio, but seeing the house gave me a burst of energy. *Home.* I already knew exactly where my dad was sitting inside that brick Cape Cod—in front of the TV in his slipcovered ratty, brown recliner, the one he would never give up no matter how much my sisters and I begged him to upgrade. One year, when my sister Audrey was eleven and taking sewing classes, she sewed a slipcover for it with little yellow daisies all over it. My dad looked like he was going to blow a gasket when he saw it, but then he glanced at my sister who was clearly about ready to burst with pride over the perfect fit she had accomplished, and he sat down in it and said, "Well, Audrey Bug, I didn't know anything could make this chair more comfortable, but I think you've done it." Then he made a big show of adjusting himself just right and laying his head back with a satisfied smile. Yeah, my dad was a good guy.

"Dad?" I yelled, unlocking the door and walking inside.

"Is that my Gracie?" He called, right before he came out of the living room with a smile. He kissed me on the cheek. "Law school must be agreeing with you. You look great."

"Thanks, Dad. It is," I said with a smile.

"How was the drive?"

"Not bad. I listened to an audiobook so it went by quickly."

"Audiobooks, GPS…" He scoffed. "Pretty soon people will have no reason to learn to read a book *or* a map. I'm telling you."

I rolled my eyes. "You should try it, old timer. You might change your mind."

He laughed and took my small suitcase and brought it into the living room, where we sat down. Fall classes started in a week, and I had driven home to visit my dad and sisters between summer classes ending and the new semester beginning. I only had a couple days, but I missed them. I missed home.

"Jules and Audrey aren't here?" I asked.

"No, they'll be home soon. They both get out of class at five."

I nodded. My sisters were both in college at Wright State where Audrey was studying to be a teacher, and Julia, a nurse. I was proud of both of them. They did well in school and worked during the summer to help with their tuition.

I stood. "I'm gonna get some iced tea. Can I get you something?"

"Yeah, grab me a beer. Thanks."

I went in the small kitchen and grabbed a can of

Budweiser out of the refrigerator, the same beer my dad had been drinking for as long as I could remember. I poured myself a glass of iced tea and returned to the living room, handing my dad his can.

He popped it open, took a drink, and said, "So tell me about your classes."

I took a long drink of my tea. "Actually, Dad, I have something to talk to you about," I said nervously.

"Oh yeah?" he asked, eyeing me.

"Yes." I took a deep breath. "The thing is, I changed my law focus." I took another gulp of tea.

When I lowered my glass, my dad was staring at me seriously. "Okay. What'd you change it to?"

"Well, I know how you feel about the criminal court system. I know you have a lot of experience—"

"Gracie, spit it out."

"I decided that I want to work in the prosecutor's office." I set my glass on the side table and played with the hem of my sweater. Silence. After a couple seconds, I raised my lashes and looked at my dad. He had a small frown on his face and his lips were pursed. My heart sunk. I had worked my whole life to avoid that look, *my whole life*. I almost took it back, right then and there. I almost spit out *just kidding!* But then for some reason, Carson's face appeared in my head, smiling, encouraging me with that *look* I'd memorized. I knew it was my own mind conjuring his image, but it comforted me anyway, spurred me on. *Be brave, Grace.*

"Gracie, you have no idea the things I've seen, the side of humanity *you'll* see if you get into criminal law. I know our family has had our share of heartbreak, Grace. But I want to protect you from more of that. Corporate law—"

"You can't protect me from heartbreak, Dad," I said

softly. And maybe we'd all tried too hard to do just that. There were consequences to exposing yourself to potential pain. But there were also consequences to ignoring your own wishes toward that effort. I'd recently learned that very lesson.

My dad tapped the bottom of his beer can on the armrest. "You don't make any money working in the DA's office," he tried. "Corporate law is a good, safe field of law, you'll make a great salary, and you won't take your work home with you every day of your life. You won't see all those victims faces when you lay your head down at night."

I looked down, frowned, took a deep breath, and met my dad's eyes again. "The thing is, I'm tired of being safe all the time," I said. "I'm tired of doing things because they make sense for everyone else except me." My voice hitched on the last word and my eyes swam. I looked down, unable to keep eye contact.

My dad sighed and then was silent for long minutes. Finally he said, "I only ever wanted my girls to be happy. You think this is going to make you happy, then that's all I need. I just never wanted you to be jaded and bitter, like your old man."

I let out a short laugh and then sniffled, my tears mixing with my laughter. "You're not jaded and bitter."

He sighed. "In some ways, yeah I am. I accept that. And, Gracie, I'm sorry I never made it clear to you that your happiness is important to me. You stepped right in and started taking care of this family when your mom left. I saw it and I let you do it, and that probably wasn't fair to you."

"No, Dad," I said quickly, shaking my head, "I wanted to do that. It made me feel like I was helping to make things better for everyone. Better for you."

"You were, darlin', but I should have made that more my job than yours. It was too much pressure for a kid. And you always put enough pressure on yourself as it was. Go make yourself happy, Gracie. Live your dream. Take care of others like you've always taken care of us. You're damn good at it."

I let out another little sob and launched myself at him, almost tipping that damn flower-covered recliner right over. My dad wasn't big on physical affection, but I just couldn't contain myself in that moment. I loved my dad so much. It was like a ten-ton weight had been lifted off my chest. And as it turned out, *I* had been the one who had let it sit there all that time. I hugged him tightly, and after a minute, he wrapped his arms around me too, and we sat like that for a while, me whispering, "Thank you, Dad," in his ear.

"What the HELL are you doing to my dad?" I heard screeched from the living room doorway. I sat up and laughed.

"I'm hugging him, you nutjob," I said to my sister Julia, smiling and getting up.

She was grinning too. "Hi, big sis," she said, hugging me to her and squeezing me tight. What my dad lacked in shows of physical affection, us girls made up for, at least with each other. We were each other's anchors, each other's comfort.

"God, you make me feel short," I said, looking up at her beautiful face. Julia was blond like me, but she had gotten our dad's height and towered over me at 5'9". I was insanely jealous of her long legs and supermodel figure. She could and did eat anything she wanted.

"Audrey should be right behind—" Julia started to say, just as I heard the door slam and Audrey's voice call out, "Hellooooo!" A brunette head peeked around the doorway and Audrey's pretty grin lit up her face. Audrey had gotten my mom's side of the family's height like me but had brown hair like my dad. She was adorable in every way—I had practically raised her when Andrew died and my mom had checked out. I considered myself almost more of an aunt to her than a sister.

She ran in the room and launched herself at me, practically toppling me over as we both laughed and jumped up and down.

My dad cleared his throat.

All three of our heads turned toward him.

"Do you girls mind? *Jeopardy!* comes on in five minutes and I can't hear it over all the clucking."

I started moving first. "Of course! Here, you sit down." I pushed him into his daisy-covered recliner and handed him the beer that he had set down on the table next to him before I had launched myself into his lap, and I turned the TV on the right channel.

Julia and Audrey were both rolling their eyes at me as I went about making our dad as comfortable as possible. Well, whatever, some habits were hard to break. He was my dad. I took care of him. That's what I did. And I was going to follow my dream! With my dad's blessing. I threw an afghan over his legs and grabbed my small suitcase and all of us girls ran up the stairs, pushing and giggling like kids.

We went into my old bedroom and Audrey and Julia flopped down on my bed as I opened my suitcase and started putting clothes into the dresser drawers.

"So what's new, chickadees?" I asked.

Silence. I looked over at them and they were shooting looks back and forth. I put my hands on my hips. "What?" I asked, narrowing my eyes.

"Julia has something to tell you," Audrey offered, grinning broadly.

My eyes swung to Julia, who was looking at me nervously. "Yeah?" I let the word drag out, raising my eyebrows.

She started playing with a string on her ripped jeans. "Well, the thing is, I kinda met someone."

I raised one eyebrow. "As in a boy?"

"Yes, a boy—"

"Well, that's not all. Tell her the big news," Audrey said, and Julia shot her a warning look.

I sat down on the bed with them. "Julia, just spit it out," I said.

"I'm not a virgin anymore," she blurted out. "I'm de-virginized. I'm a woman!" she finished, giving me a small, nervous laugh.

"The cherry is popped," Audrey offered reverently.

I looked back and forth between them. "You were nervous to tell me, Jules?" I asked on a small frown.

"Well, no, I mean, a little, it's just..." She took a deep breath. "Yes, I was nervous to tell you." She took my hand. "You've just always been kinda like a mom to us, and face it, you're kinda straitlaced, Gracie. I mean, are *you* a virgin? We talk about everything, but you've never talked about sex with us. At least not on a personal level. You've just always been so driven, so focused on other things..."

I stared at her, thinking. We joked about sex. We made references to sexiness and hot guys, stuff like that, but I guess she was right. I had never talked about sex on a personal level. I had never really gone to parties or dated boys much in high school and so there really wasn't anything to talk about there. I had never told anyone, except Carson, about my guy plan. That stupid plan that didn't even exist anymore.

I took a deep breath. "I'm sorry, girls. You're right. I haven't been a good older sister in that category. I should have been more open with you. I just…I had all these dumb ideas that, up until a couple months ago, I didn't even know were dumb ideas. I probably needed the talk more than either of you. It's just, without Mom here…I never… I've treated you both like babies. I'm sorry."

"No, Grace, we're not trying to make you feel bad. You've always taken care of us. We love you for that. We just didn't know how you'd react to this kind of specific information." Audrey gestured her head toward Julia.

I grabbed Audrey's hand and squeezed it, and then looked at Julia. "Who is he?"

She grinned, her eyes sparkling. "His name is Evan and he works as part of the hospital administration where my class has been doing some training. He's twenty-two. We've been dating for three months and I'm in love, Grace. Truly in love. He treats me like a princess, like I'm the most precious thing on the planet," she finished dreamily, flopping back on the bed.

Audrey rolled her eyes. "You're really not sorry you missed all the gushing over the last few months, Grace. It's been truly vomitous."

I laughed. "So, did you…enjoy it?" I asked.

Julia propped herself up on her elbows. "The sex?" She bit her lip. "Well, we've only done it a couple times so far, and…well, no, not really. I mean, I'm sure that's kinda normal…" She frowned, looking over at Audrey.

Audrey raised her hands. "Don't look at me. I'm untouched. Pure. I don't know what to tell you other than you could be broken in some way."

I laughed, but Julia narrowed her eyes at Audrey.

"You're not broken, Jules. The first couple times usually aren't that good. It gets better, I promise. And if you're with the right person, which hopefully you are, it can be incredible. Beyond incredible."

I looked over at them and they were both staring at me. I laughed again. "Okay, girls, we need to talk, and I think I have something to tell you that will make up for the years and years of sex-talk repression in this house. Settle in and buckle up," I said seriously, biting my lip with nervousness. I laid down on my side and propped my head up on my hand and started talking, wondering if I'd get through the story this time without crying because I still missed him so damn much that, even two months later, I got emotional saying his name. "So you know that conference I went to a couple months ago..."

Carson

"I still can't believe you enlisted in the NAVY, you crazy motherfucker!" Dylan yelled from the kitchen as he grabbed us both a beer.

I chuckled. "You and me both, bro."

Dylan came back in the room and handed me my beer. He took a seat on the other couch, studying me over his bottle as he took a long sip and propped his feet up on the coffee table. "You gonna tell your mom you're taking off?"

"Nah, you know what happened the last time I was over there. I'll send her a postcard *if* I make it to SEAL training in Coronado."

He nodded. He had seen me, or rather my busted lip, after I had gone to see her the last time and gotten into it with her current boyfriend who sucker punched me like the bitch he was.

"So," he said, taking another pull on his beer, "you ever gonna tell me about this girl you spent a weekend with and changed your whole life for?"

I laughed. "I didn't change my whole life for her, dude."

"Uh, yeah, you kinda did, man. What kind of pussy voodoo did she cast on you?"

"Funny. No, I meant, I'm not making all these changes because of Grace. I'll most likely never even see her again." I paused as the pain in that statement hit me yet again. I had thought about contacting her and letting her know my plans. But what if I failed? No. I needed to actually accomplish something before I let Grace know. If I decided that made sense. "I just realized it's time, that's all. I can't do porn forever, man. It was time for me to come up with some kind of life plan, some direction at least."

"I can't disagree. I mean, as badass as it was to have women porn stars showing up at our house parties." He grinned. "Not that there's been any partying going on here lately, you monk."

I chuckled, but then I grew serious, putting my hands behind my head and leaning back on the couch. "Man, I might be right back here next year. Do you know what a long shot this is going to be?"

Dylan shook his head. "Nah, you won't be."

"No, seriously, the odds are not in my favor when it comes to becoming a SEAL."

"How do you figure?" Dylan asked, adjusting his feet on the table.

"Dude, I explained the whole twenty-percent thing, I explained about all the insanely talented athletes that try out every year and don't make it—"

"Yeah, you did, but here's how *I* see it. It doesn't all

come down to how great of an athlete you are, or how fast you can swim however many yards in the ocean while on the verge of hypothermia." He set his beer down, took his feet off the coffee table, and sat forward on the couch. "What it comes down to is how much heart you have and how you will give this your all, not because anyone will toss you accolades, but on the contrary, because no one *ever* has, and you don't depend on that for your success. Those guys out there who have been coddled constantly and cheered for their whole lives, they'll be the first ones to quit when they don't have anyone to depend on but themselves. But not you—because you've never known any different. And that sucks. But in this case, it's your strength. It's your ace in the hole. I'd bet on you, Carson Stinger."

He picked up his beer, sat back, and kicked his feet up on the coffee table again as I stared at him, not knowing what to say. *Well, damn.* "Thanks, Dylan," was what I finally came up with.

"Did I tell you *I* was making a career change too? Motivational speaking. Don't all line up at once, people."

I laughed. "You should. That was inspirational. I mean it."

Dylan grinned but then went serious as he raised his beer to me. "I meant every word of it, bro."

"I know you did, man, I know." I held up my bottle in cheers to him. In cheers to good friends who have your back.

CHAPTER 16
Grace

Eight months later, April

I sat in the semidarkness, staring at the horizon, hearing the bird conversations begin all around me. Moments later, I watched in awe as the first slip of yellow glow rose in the distance. It was like those birds sensed the glory of the sunrise even before it appeared and were singing its welcoming praises. I sat there until the full, round sun had fully emerged from beyond the horizon. I thought of Carson, as I always did when I watched the sun rise. *As I'd promised I would.* I wondered where he was and if he was happy. But I didn't let myself wonder any more than that, still *couldn't* let myself wonder any more than that.

I continued on my run along the C&O Canal with the other early-morning joggers, and when I was done, I drove home and took a quick shower. I was desperate for coffee. I guess I'd never really be a morning person. But I made it a priority to set my alarm to run outdoors rather than on the treadmill, so that I could watch the sun rise as often as I could. I'd missed too many of them already.

I'd be graduating law school at the beginning of the summer and the next two months were going to be jam-packed with studying and test taking. Plus, I'd been applying for jobs in DC, hoping to get a position in the prosecutor's office. I was filled with excitement to see where life would take me now that I was headed in a direction I had chosen for no other purpose than I wanted it and it felt *right*. And that felt like a pretty good plan.

Carson

"Get your dicks out of the dirt, shitbags!" Instructor Wegman yelled. Holy mother of Christ, every muscle in my body was screaming out in pain. We had been at this for almost five hours straight now, our punishment for failing a knife inspection during our first week of SEAL Training. We had been about to do an ocean swim, and the instructors came around to inspect our gear, an inflatable vest, CO_2 cartridge and KA-BAR knife. When Instructor Flynn had rubbed my knife on his arm hair, he had looked up at me and yelled, "FAIL!" *Fuck me.* By the end of inspection, seven other men and I were told to join the instructors at the Grinder—our workout area—at ten p.m.

I was already worn completely out from a day of brutal workouts that started at five a.m. We had begun with a Grinder PT, a four-mile timed run in our boots and pants, in the soft sand, which we were expected to do in thirty-two minutes or less, we ran sand dunes, and then we did a two-thousand-meter swim, and that was only *before* lunch.

But there wasn't a choice. All eight of us had lined up shoulder to shoulder as the instructors stood before us, looking at us disgustedly. "If you can't even be trusted to take care of a piece of equipment, how the fuck are we supposed to trust you with our lives in the field, shitbags?" We stood silently as the instructors berated us, telling us what fuckups we were. That was okay. Because it meant at least a small break.

But then the beating had started. They had told us to run to the surf, get wet, and run back in two minutes. When we got back, Instructor Wegman had looked at his timer and shook his head. "Two minutes, ten seconds, shitbags. For every second you're late past two minutes, you do that number of eight-count body-builders." And so we had done our ten body-builders and then ran back to the surf again to try to do it in less than two minutes. The second time, it had been two minutes and twelve seconds. So we did twelve eight-count body-builders. Each time, we took longer and longer, our bodies physically unable to pick up speed in our exhaustion. This had been going on for five hours. We were now doing sixty eight-count body builders, barely able to move, limping back from the water each time, wanting to crawl.

As my legs buckled beneath me on the way to the water, a guy next to me grabbed onto my waist and pulled me up. "Whoa, steady. I got ya. Take it slow and give it a minute to recoup in the water. There's no way we'll make it back in under two anyway. Let's just try to make it back."

I gave my legs a minute to stop shaking and continued on with him toward the surf. "Thanks, man." I groaned, grimacing as bolts of pain shot up both legs.

"My first name's Noah."

I nodded. I only knew him by his last name, Dean. "Carson."

Noah muttered, "Fucking hell," as he dunked himself in the cold, nighttime ocean water and then stood up and closed his eyes for a minute, unmoving, letting his body rest. I followed suit and after a few seconds, we turned and started moving toward the shore again, this time our teeth chattering, shivering with cold. It was fucking miserable.

"I can't do this anymore," I ground out, my jaw unwilling to move it was shaking so hard.

"I bet you said that three hours ago too," Noah ground out. "I know I did. And yet, turned out we were wrong because here we are, still doing it."

My face twisted into something maybe resembling a smile as we limped up the shore back toward the Grinder for another set of body-builders. Maybe a hundred this time.

I stumbled away slightly as a classmate next to me vomited onto the beach.

"Shitbags, don't fail knife inspection again," Instructor Flynn said, getting up from the platform the instructors had been sitting on watching us all night. We were dismissed.

As we started limping away, Instructor Flynn said, "Hold up. Before you go in, clean up all this sand you got all over the PT area."

An hour later, we limped inside to sleep for an hour before morning PT would start. As Noah turned to go toward his room, I said, "Hey, thanks again." I'd been seriously on the verge of quitting. I'd always been good at physical challenges, but this was beyond anything I'd imagined.

Noah just nodded, giving me his own version of something resembling a smile.

When I pulled myself out of bed an hour later feeling

like I had fallen off a cliff and hit every jagged rock on the way down, I thought to myself, *There is no fucking way I can do this for another day. How the hell am I going to make it through Hell Week when I can't even make it through one brutal punishment for one night?* Hell Week was going to be *five* days and nights like the one I'd just endured, probably much, much worse, *on zero sleep*. I was losing it from only having an hour of rest. How would I make it a full week with no sleep and being tortured constantly? From what I heard, by Friday, most men were delirious and swollen so badly, they were asked not to go out in public. I simply wasn't cut out for this. It was a wrap.

I limped outside intending to ring the bell. In that moment, nothing seemed more important than getting back in bed and trying not to move. I felt half-crazed with pain and exhaustion.

As I stepped outside, the sun was just breaking over the horizon. I turned toward it and stood still, my eyes trained on that small sliver of brilliant orange. My breath released. I closed my eyes and pictured Grace standing in front of me, my arms around her as we had gazed out at the same picture. *Grace.*

You're a really brave person, Carson.

I'd taken another step forward but now I hesitated again. The thing was, getting through this wasn't going to take mere physical strength. Honestly, I'd run out of that, which was why I was standing here intending on ending this torture. But… God, Dylan had been right when he'd said this was going to come down to how much heart I had. I stood a little taller. He believed in me, and Grace had looked at me sincerely and told me I was brave.

Now it was up to me. I'd taken what I'd thought was the

easier route once before, following in my mom's footsteps and doing something that was never very personally appealing. And it had only brought unhappiness and dissatisfaction.

Either I was going to quit right now, or I was going to take Dylan and Grace's words in and bet on myself. I was going to find out exactly how much heart I really had. Their words could only go so far.

A small slip of sand stood between me and failure.

I glanced out to that vibrant sunset again, beautiful and unceasing. And then I turned back around and limped inside, away from the bell and toward the showers.

CHAPTER 17
Grace

Fourteen Months Later, June

I picked up the glass of ice water and held it up. "To Brian passing the bar exam!" I said to Abby who was sitting next to me at our kitchen counter. "And the fact that he'll now be able to support you in a style to which you'd like to become accustomed."

Abby grinned and held up her own water, clinking mine softly. "To Brian. Thank *God* all that studying is over and I get my fiancé back. I mean, unless *your* work hours are any indication, and then, never mind. Nothing will change."

I laughed, shaking my head. "I'm not that bad."

"Yeah you are," she said, disagreeing. "But luckily I don't have to live with you for very much longer."

"Ha-ha. You're gonna miss me," I said, taking a bite of the takeout salad I'd picked up. "But you chose a good one, you know that, right?" I said, nodding my head toward her solitaire engagement ring.

She sighed and smiled. "I know. He's a keeper. I mean as long as he doesn't piss me off in some toothpaste-cap kind of way, this should work out."

I laughed.

Abby and Brian had gotten engaged at Christmastime and were getting married in September. Next week was the big move-out weekend for all of us. I had found a great apartment in the U Street Corridor area and although I was a little nervous to be living by myself for the first time in my life, I was excited too.

The last piece to fall into place was Brian finding out the day before that he had passed the bar exam. We were all going out later to a celebratory dinner.

"Now," Abby went on, "all we need to do is find *you* a great guy."

"Oh no. Uh-uh. I'm too busy to date. Don't even think about some weird setup. My job barely leaves me enough time to go to the grocery store on a regular basis. I hardly have time for a guy." I speared a cherry tomato and brought it to my mouth.

I had gotten my first job in the DC prosecutor's office and was working in juvenile court. It wasn't necessarily exactly what I wanted to be doing, and I was looking to work my way up. But as of now, there were no other positions and very low turnover in the other courts. I knew I was lucky to be in the office I had strived to be in, and so I worked hard to make a good name for myself.

I looked over at Abby to find her studying me. "You still think of him?"

"Who?" I asked, knowing exactly whom she was referring to.

Abby snorted. "You know who. Don't try to give me that."

I put my fork down and turned to her. We hadn't talked

about Carson in a while, but I couldn't lie to Abby about this. She knew me too well. "Yeah. But it's not a bad thing, Abs. It doesn't hurt anymore." *As much.* "I just…wonder how he is sometimes. I wonder what he's doing. I wonder if he ever thinks of me."

Abby nodded. "As long as he's not the real reason you've apparently sworn off all men since you returned from Vegas two years ago."

I let out a brittle sounding laugh. "I haven't sworn off all men. I went out on that date with the guy from my law class that I ran into last year."

Abby raised an eyebrow. "Grace, you grabbed coffee with him when you saw him on the street and you wouldn't even let him pay for yours."

"I forgot to tell you we had sex in the bathroom."

Abby almost choked on the sip of water she'd just taken. "I wish!" She laughed, knowing I was lying.

I laughed too. "For real though, Abby. We flirted! It was date-ish."

"Grace, he told you, you looked nice and you said he looked well too. That is not flirting. I had that same conversation with my grandpa when I saw him last month."

I gave her a face. "*Anyway*, it's not about swearing off men. You know I didn't date much even before I met…before I went to Vegas. I'm just busy. Really, Abby, that's the only reason. I'm not closed off. If I meet someone who appeals to me, I'll make an exception, okay? I promise. Don't worry about me."

"So the super hunk who lives downstairs doesn't appeal to you? Because you certainly appeal to him."

I shook my head. "No, he's too…super hunky. All those muscles are intimidating. Like he could crack me like a walnut."

"You need to be cracked like a walnut." She moved her brows up and down and I rolled my eyes in response. "What about the really cute guy who asked you out at happy hour at Marvin last month? He wasn't your type either?"

"Him? He kept pulling on his ear. I didn't know what it meant. It seemed like a secret signal I wasn't interpreting."

"Oh geez," she moaned.

"Abby! Seriously. Really. Not closed off. The right guy will come along. I'm just waiting for that...certain something. I'll know it when I find it. When I find *him*."

Abby looked at me with narrowed eyes for a second but then took a deep breath and said, "Okay. If you say so." She threw her napkin and plastic fork inside the Styrofoam container and stood up, carrying it to the trash. "All right, I'm off. See you tonight. I'll be home about seven. Reservations are at eight." She grabbed her purse and coat and headed for the door.

"Bye, Abs!" I called. I continued eating my lunch, placing my fork down and pushing it aside after a couple minutes. I took a deep breath, putting my elbows on the counter and resting my face in my hands. A shiver moved over my skin and I raised my head in confusion, the particles in the air almost seeming to change direction, as though something nearby had disrupted them. I closed my eyes and allowed myself to picture Carson's face. I didn't let myself linger on the thought of him often, or picture him in my mind's eye. But for some reason, in that moment, I indulged myself because I felt him so strongly, almost as if he were in the room with me.

After a few minutes, I forced myself to stand up and clean up my lunch, and then I went about my Saturday.

Carson

As I stared out the cab window, watching DC stream by, I rubbed my hand over my short, military-style haircut and I thought of everything I'd been through in the past year and a half. I thought of Hell Week, how I had somehow, impossibly, survived that miserable five days, consisting of the most hellish simulated conditions that would assure the navy that they were sending men into the field that would never quit, no matter how much misery and pain was thrown at them, no matter how delirious they were from lack of sleep. *I was one of those men.* I was still trying to wrap my own head around that.

Noah Dean and I had helped each other through that week. I didn't know if I could have done it without his encouragement. Noah told me afterwards that he had gone meal to meal—knowing if he could just survive long enough to make it to the next meal, he'd have that time where he sat in a warm cafeteria with food in front of him before he faced the torturous conditions again. I understood that. But I hadn't gone meal to meal. I had gone sunrise to sunrise, that bright light breaking over the horizon, the motivation that kept me from giving up. The thought of Grace in my arms spurring me on, even in the midst of the worst physical trial I had ever endured.

Dylan was the first person I had called that Friday afternoon when we were secured and received the brown shirts that meant we had made it through Hell Week. "Not surprised, buddy," he had said, and I could hear the emotion in his voice. "Not surprised at all."

I had finished BUD/S twenty-four weeks later, was

assigned to SEAL Team Two, went to SEAL Tactical Training, and finally, finally, earned my Trident. *I had done it.*

And now I was about to deploy overseas on my first assignment. Anything could happen. But first, I was in DC to attend an award ceremony for a former instructor who I respected highly. Me and a few other guys who'd trained under him had flown out to be there for a quick two-day trip, and then I was going to meet back up with my platoon before we all flew out together in about a week.

There was a buzz of anticipation under my skin. Grace was still in DC. When I'd booked the trip, I hadn't been able to resist looking her up on whitepages.com. I'd found her address but hadn't been able to find her on social media. I'd wanted to message her and let her know I'd be in town, and more than that, I wanted to tell her that she had inspired me to become a SEAL, that I had accomplished something I was proud of. I didn't know what her life looked like now, but I wanted to tell her that I still missed her, even after all this time.

Just showing up at her apartment seemed intrusive. What if she lived with a man? What if she just wasn't interested in seeing me? Still I was here…in the town where she lived. It was like I could practically feel her presence, feel *her*, somewhere very close by.

It's just because your mind is stuck on her, Stinger.

I opened my phone again, looking at the address I'd typed into my notes app. I pulled in a big breath, steeling my nerves, and then opened my mouth to ask the cab driver to take me there instead of back to my hotel. But before I could, my phone rang. *Noah.*

"Hey, man," I said.

"Hey, Carson. Did you get the call yet?"

I was suddenly on alert. "What call?"

"Word just came down. Our flight's been moved up. I guess there's a situation that they need us to move on."

My heart jumped. *A situation.* We'd been doing intensive specialized training for *situations* for the last eighteen months. Was I ready? I guess I was about to find out. "How soon do I need to be there?"

"As soon as possible. We leave tomorrow morning."

Shit. I'd need to pack my stuff and head to the airport now in order to be back in time to leave in the morning. "I'll call you when I land," I told Noah.

"Talk to you then."

We hung up and I opened my phone again, looking down at that address, yearning like I hadn't felt in a long time welling up inside me, tightening my ribs. *Buttercup.* I stared at it another few moments before closing my phone. Fate had intervened, making the decision for me. I wasn't going to Grace's apartment. I was heading to Afghanistan.

CHAPTER 18
Grace

Six Months Later, December

The branches of the tree tickled my nose and I giggled as I scooted a little to the left to be closer to Julia. It was midnight, now officially Christmas, and my sisters and I were lying under the Christmas tree, staring up through the branches at the white twinkle lights—our tradition. We would sneak down after Dad had put our presents out and we would put our gifts to him under the tree, and then lie beneath it, talking until we were so sleepy that we couldn't keep our eyes open.

"I think Evan's going to propose today," Julia whispered.

"What?" I whispered back. "Jules, oh my God! Are you sure?" I whispered back a little louder than her.

"Pretty sure." I could hear the smile in her voice. "He confirmed the time he was going to get here this morning about fifteen times, and I saw the name of a jewelry store on a receipt in his car a couple days ago, right before he snatched it up and stuck it in his pocket."

"He could have just gotten you a necklace or something for Christmas," Audrey offered.

"Maybe, but I just have a gut feeling," Julia said.

"Me too actually," Audrey said. "That boy is crazy about you. I'm surprised it took him this long."

I found Julia's hand next to me and squeezed it. "I'm so happy for you, Jules. He's a really great guy."

"Yeah." She sighed happily. "He really is."

After a minute of silence, I said, "God, I'm really going to be an old maid now."

Audrey giggled. "At twenty-five? I think you might have a few good years left in ya, Sis, not to worry."

I shook my head, the branches tickling my nose again with my movement. "My eggs are drying up as we speak."

"Oh, stop," Julia said. "Anyway, if you want to meet someone, you have to actually leave your apartment for more than work. From what you've told us, that's the only place you go."

I sighed. "Yeah, yeah. I know. I get enough of that from Abby. I'm just too tired by the end of the day to want to do anything except collapse on my couch."

After another minute of silence, Audrey asked, "Any more wild porn star weekends you haven't told us about? Not that I could take it if there were—you really turned my world upside down with that story."

"Ha-ha. You and me both. No. That was a one-time thing. Promise." I bit my bottom lip, wondering where Carson was celebrating Christmas. I changed the subject. "Andrew would be twenty-four this year," I said quietly.

"Yeah," both girls said at once and we were all quiet for another minute and I knew that like me, they were thinking of our brother and who he might have been. And though

215

time didn't heal all wounds, it certainly made the pain more bearable, especially if you had others to help carry it.

Carson

It was Christmas day, the shortest day of the year in Afghanistan, pitch-black outside though it was only six o'clock in the evening. The sounds of the desert winter night picked up all around us as me and four other SEALs sat on the dirt floor of an abandoned cave in the mountains outside Kabul.

Noah, my buddy since SEAL training, and now a member of my platoon, was the quietest of us all. When Noah spoke up, we all listened, knowing that if he took the time to say something, it was gonna be important. And there was Josh Garner from Dallas, a cocky shit-talker on the outside but a man you could trust with your life if it became necessary. I knew that because, on several occasions, it *had* become necessary. Also, Leland McManus, our lieutenant, the son of a casino tycoon from Las Vegas, and Eli Williams who we nicknamed "Preacher" because he was always saying some profound shit, even though he liked to talk smack as much as the rest of us.

We had just opened our MREs and were "enjoying" what was a disappointing take on a Christmas feast. Josh held up a spoonful of what looked like beef stew. "Cheers, assholes, Merry fucking Christmas," he said through a mouthful.

We all snickered and then raised our instant coffee up to each other. "Merry Christmas," was mumbled all around.

"God!" Eli moaned, leaning his head back. "This is better than my mama's turkey and gravy!"

"Your mama must cook like shit then," Leland offered up.

Eli nodded over at him. "Yeah, I gave that one to ya, didn't I, asswipe? Merry Christmas. Consider that your gift."

Noah and I both shook our heads, me chuckling softly and Noah smiling. We all ate in relative silence for a minute and I glanced out into the night. Never in a million years did I imagine myself spending Christmas in a cave in the desert in a far-off land. I felt like I was living an alternate life... one almost completely disconnected from my first twenty-three years. It was a good thing because I loved my job, I respected the hell out of the guys I worked with, and I felt a sense of purpose that I never had before. But sometimes, when I had a quiet moment to sit and think about it, it threw me for a small loop.

And it always made me think of Grace.

If you could see me now, what would you think?

I took a bite of fruit, deciding maybe it wasn't fruit after all. "The first thing I'm gonna do when I get back to the US of A is get myself the biggest, juiciest cheeseburger—maybe two," I said, setting my fork down.

"First thing I'm gonna do is get myself the biggest, juiciest pussy—maybe two," Josh said, spooning some rice into his mouth.

Eli made a disgusted sound.

Josh looked over at him. "What? Don't tell me that just because you're married, you're looking forward to getting home to your wife so you can engage her in a good game of checkers?"

Eli chuckled. "No, but I don't talk about making love to my wife in vulgar terms. You'll see, intimacy with a woman you're in love with is the ultimate experience. You have no idea, you sorry fucker."

Josh was silent for a beat, a horrified expression on his

face. "Man. That's...that's beautiful. You know, when we get back home, you should think about putting out a book of poetry."

We all laughed, even Eli, but he finished it with a "fuck you, bro."

"I just might...pretty mouth on you, all that 'making love' talk. We could put on some slow jams, talk about our feelings—"

BOOM! We all startled and went silent, looking around at each other and starting to gesture with our hands and eyes about what moves to make.

Gunfire erupted not too far away and we all dropped our meals and went for our weapons. It was on.

CHAPTER 19
Grace

One year, seven months later, July

"Crap!" I swore, as the bottom dropped out of the box of books I was carrying down the hallway to my new office, the books landing on the carpeted floor with a loud thud.

I put the now-empty cardboard down on the floor, squatted, and started piling the books up so that I could carry them to my desk.

My desk. In my new office. In Las Vegas, Nevada. I still couldn't believe I was here—in Vegas, again, only this time, not for a law conference, this time starting my new job.

When it had become clear that moving out of the juvenile court in DC was going to be a long time coming, I had started half-heartedly applying to jobs in other cities. I didn't necessarily expect anything to come of it, but I had been surprised when I had heard back from the DA in Clark County almost immediately. After a lengthy interview process, I was offered the job of a prosecutor in the Clark

County Criminal Division, serving Las Vegas. *My dream job.* Taking a job in Vegas felt…strange. I wasn't sure how being back in the city where I had spent a life-changing weekend was going to affect me. But I reminded myself that it wasn't like Carson lived here—he lived in Los Angeles; at least as far as I knew, he still did. But just driving past the Bellagio when I had flown in for my in-person interview caused a swarm of butterflies to take up flight in my stomach. I had to believe that that reaction would fade over time, as, after all, it had been almost five years since that weekend. It was just because it was the first time I had been back and it dredged up the distant memory. That was all. Pretty soon, seeing it enough, it would just be another hotel on the strip.

"Can I help?" a male voice asked and I looked up into a smiling pair of the bluest eyes I'd ever seen.

I picked up one of the two piles of books I had already made and stood. "Thanks, that would be great," I said, returning his smile.

He bent down and picked up the other pile and followed me to my office, less than fifty feet down the hall. I set the books I was carrying on my cluttered desk and he did the same with the ones in his arms.

I turned to him and rubbed my hands on my jean-clad thighs and held one out. "Grace Hamilton," I said.

"Ah. I've heard great things about you, Grace. Welcome aboard," he said, his handsome face breaking into a warm smile and his hand reaching out to shake mine. "I'm Alex Klein. I'm a prosecutor here too."

"Nice to meet you, Alex. I'm happy to be here." I smiled again. There was a lot of smiling going on between Alex and me.

"Well, Grace, I'll leave you to the unpacking. I'm

working late and was going to order a pizza in a little bit if you have time to join me for a slice or two?" He gestured down the hall to where I assumed his office was.

I watched him as he backed out my door. "Oh, um—"

"I could brief you on who you'll be working with around here... who to get in good with and all that." His lips tilted, and he raised a brow.

"Well how can I resist that offer? Sure, Alex. Thank you."

"Okay, great, I'll come get you when the pizza's here." And with that, he turned around and walked back to his office. I watched him walk away and when he got halfway down the hall, he looked back and smiled. I laughed and turned around, grinning now as I started unpacking.

Carson

We closed in, Leland putting a finger over his lips and cocking his head to the left to indicate our target was in the next room. We all nodded and moved in, none of us making a sound. Josh counted on his fingers as we stood to each side of the door, turning as he kicked it in on three. The door flew inward and we moved in as one unit, surprising four men holding weapons but sitting on chairs, their feet propped up, clearly not expecting trouble.

We fired on them before they could even raise their guns, killing them instantly.

There was another small door beyond that room, and when Josh kicked that one open, we moved in and immediately took in a man cowering on the floor in the corner. "Mehran Makar?" Eli demanded.

The man narrowed his eyes, cursing, calling us dirty pigs, and Eli fired, killing him. A breath gusted from my mouth, my heart rate slowing. He'd victimized innocent people. The world was better off without him. And as for us? Our mission was complete.

We cleared the rest of the room, letting down our guard only slightly until we were confident that no one was hiding. We had been given intel that there were only four guards, but we couldn't rely on that one hundred percent until we had checked it out ourselves.

"Clear?" Noah asked, coming back in the room.

"Yeah," I said. "All clear out front?"

"Yeah. Let's check out back." There was a small building behind the larger warehouse that Leland was now covering. There was only one door and no windows, so no way for anyone to escape. But we needed to go in carefully, in case someone was waiting inside.

Ten minutes later, we had the door open and had moved inside the small structure. It looked to be deserted.

Josh flicked a light switch on the wall, and Leland and I sucked in a breath. Noah swore, "Holy shit," and Eli muttered, "Motherfucker."

At the back of the room was the biggest stash of weapons I had come upon, Russian-made surface-to-air missiles and rocket-propelled grenades. It was a fucking stockpile.

"Jesus, that fucker had some serious plans," Josh said.

We all stilled as we heard a quiet scraping sound in the back. When I examined the back wall, I noticed a small door next to the shelves of weaponry. It almost blended into the wall.

I nodded to the other men, making sure they saw it too, and we moved in.

Noah kicked the door in this time and as Josh shined his flashlight into the pitch-black space. We all recoiled at the smell. "God damn." Josh coughed.

My gaze flew around. *Oh, God.* We'd walked into hell. The sight that met our eyes was straight out of a horror movie. My brain struggled to make sense of it, thoughts careening, attempting to organize what we were standing in witness to. A pair of dark eyes met mine and I took a step forward, inexplicably pulled as a hand reached from the dark.

"You okay, man?" Noah asked quietly. I brought my head up from out of my arms, resting on my knees and looked up at him. I felt numb, heavy. "I will be. You?"

His chin went up in a jerky nod. "Same."

I nodded back, watching the other four men walk up the rocky slope toward us. "The other team will be here in about an hour," Eli said.

When we had called in the night before, we had been ordered to stay with the weaponry until another team could get there to inventory it. The sun was already high in the sky.

Noah and I nodded, Noah speaking quietly, holding up his radio. "We're supposed to be at our rendezvous point in six hours."

"We'll be ready to leave as soon as the other team gets here, then," Leland said, emotionless, a faraway look in his eyes that I didn't like. Even Josh was somber, patting Leland on his back as he walked by him.

Half an hour later, we had briefed the second team and were ready to leave. I stood up, hefting up my gear and securing it to my back as the other men did the same. We started walking. I only looked back once.

It had taken us longer than we'd thought it would to jog the distance to our rendezvous point, and we were still about an hour away when the sun started to set in the desert sky. It was the end of October, when night temperatures dropped rapidly in Afghanistan. Our breath came out in short, white bursts as we hiked quietly, all of us aware of our surroundings, as we were trained to be, but quiet in our own thoughts.

I tried to keep my thoughts at bay. It wouldn't serve me to go over what we'd experienced now. I felt the emotions of the night before hovering just in the distance, but instead of allowing them to creep closer, I focused my mind on the sunset we'd watched that morning, and my thoughts of Grace. I thought of her a lot now because we were always up with the sun. And though it may or may not be a good idea to dwell on a woman I hadn't seen in so long, thoughts of her soothed me and so in a time of little comfort, I took them for the gift they were.

Suddenly, Josh, who was walking in the lead, stopped and held up his hand to indicate we stop as well. We all came to a halt, listening. When none of us heard anything, we moved forward again. A few hundred feet later, Josh halted again and we all followed suit, readying our weapons. We were trained well enough to know that one hunch based on the snapping of a stick in the desert might be dismissed but *two* most definitely shouldn't be. We moved so our backs were to each other and circled slowly, squinting our eyes to see as far as possible in the darkening distance.

"Shit!" Leland grunted as one shot rang out and his leg buckled and he went down next to me.

The rest was a blur of gunfire, blood, explosions, and pain. So much fucking pain.

I heard someone moaning from faraway, and for just a second, I was lucid, the noise exploding back into my brain as I came to and lifted my head from the ground, where somehow I had ended up.

Leland was next to me and I could see that his leg was in bad shape, part of the bone broken and protruding almost straight out of the skin. He was moaning and trying to drag himself toward me.

I went to push myself off the ground and bit my lip to stop myself from screaming out in agony, my hands were covered in blood and blisters, the skin hanging loose in several areas. A surge of adrenaline pulsed through me, and I sprung to my feet and hefted Leland under his arms, bearing his weight on my forearms as I dragged him away from the gunfire that was still hitting rocks to the left of us, where I could also hear Eli, Josh, and Noah yelling and returning fire. There was too much smoke for me to see what was going on. My job now was to get Leland out of the line of fire. As I moved away, I tripped on something, my body jerking strangely. I struggled to stay upright with Leland's weight in my arms and, after a second, kept moving.

Leland grunted in pain as I dragged him with me, my own grunts of exertion mingling with his. I looked behind me and saw a rock big enough that I thought we could both fit behind it and picked up my pace. I rounded the rock a couple seconds later and lay Leland down and collapsed to the right of him, just as a spray of bullets took out a piece of the top of the rock, small pebbles raining down on us as we covered our heads.

Leland looked at me, pale and expressionless and passed out again. I saw more blood coming through his jacket and moved it open with my forearms. Thank God it was

225

unzipped. "Fuck! Fuck! Fuck!" I grunted out. He had been shot in the chest too, and the blood was slowly spreading, soaking his shirt underneath. I glanced back down to my mangled hands, so swollen now, they were entirely useless. I leaned over him, putting pressure on the bullet wound with my arms, closing my eyes and again, picturing the only thing that brought me true calm—the sunrise. I envisioned it coming up slowly over the horizon, bathing the world around it in yellowy light, in hope.

The world swam around me. I heard the sound of a helicopter propeller and more shots rang out, followed by more yelling and another explosion, and then finally, quiet. I looked down. My arms were now entirely drenched in Leland's blood. Distantly, I registered that if he lost much more, he wouldn't survive.

The helicopter landed and I heard footsteps running toward us. "Here," I called out. "He needs a medic." Why did I feel so damn cold and tired? Why did the SEAL kneeling down in front of me look like he was moving farther and farther back, through a long tunnel? I blinked slowly, my head feeling heavy on my shoulders. The last thing I heard was, "He's shot too—he's going down." Who? Who was going down? The world went dark.

PART 3

CHAPTER 20
Grace

Present day

I walked into my boss's office and greeted him as I took a seat in the chair sitting on the other side of his desk.

"Grace," he said, with a smile.

Lawrence Stewart was the DA in Clark County, a robust man with kind eyes and an easy smile. He was fair and generally easy to work for, although he could be a little set in his ways. I hadn't found any reason to go up against him yet, but I knew from observation that I should pick my battles wisely.

"How are you, Larry?" I asked. It's what he had asked me to call him the first day we spoke, during my phone interview.

"Good, good. And you? How's wedding planning?"

"We haven't even set a date yet. You know, we work for a slave driver."

He laughed, lacing his hands over his stomach. "I could probably spare you both a weekend."

I grinned. "A whole weekend? Okay, then, we'll get on it."

I had initially been nervous to let people at the office know Alex and I were dating, especially since I was new. But at a company gathering, two months after I started, Larry had come up to me and smiled warmly as he said, "Alex is a good kid. I'm glad you've found a friend in him."

After that, we still didn't make a show of the fact that we were dating, but I knew it wouldn't be frowned upon. The whole office had been happy for us when we'd announced our engagement.

It was easy to work with Alex, even though we were engaged too. We didn't live together yet and so that probably helped, but I thought it would be fine when we saw each other both at the office and at home. Alex was easygoing and calm, very go-with-the-flow. In the courtroom, he came across as the trusted boy next door, and his win record reflected that.

Even though I'd basically scrapped my grand plan as far as it pertained to getting married, and let life play out as it may in the romance department, things had ended up working out in pretty much the exact way I'd laid out for Carson in that elevator so long ago. Carson... what would he think if he knew? Would he think he was Schmuck Number Two after all? God, I hadn't thought about that conversation in a long time...

I snapped back to the moment as Larry sat back in his chair. "There was a murder two nights ago, Grace. The police found a young girl shot in the head, left on the side of the road near Red Rock Canyon."

I blanched. I could picture the area. I had been there once upon a time... Speaking of Carson...

"Was there any evidence found at the scene?" I asked.

"Plenty. The police got a print off a bracelet the victim was wearing. And she was holding a rock with blood on it. They ran the print and it came back to"—he picked up a piece of paper off his desk and read the name—"Joshua Garner, twenty-eight. He was recently honorably discharged from the navy—served as a SEAL for almost ten years and had just started life as a civilian again. He moved here a couple months ago. No family in the area. When the police went to his address to arrest him, they found that he had a head wound that matched the rock the victim was holding. When they tested it, blood on the rock was a match to Mr. Garner. Not to mention, the bullet in the girl came from his gun. They arrested him yesterday for murder."

I furrowed my brow as I tapped the pen I was using to write down the case information on the legal pad on my lap. This case sounded about as foolproof as you could hope to get as a prosecutor. "Is he talking?"

"No. He lawyered up right away."

So I won't be able to talk to him. "Place of employment?"

He glanced down at the paper in front of him again. "He works security at the new hotel on the strip, Trilogy."

I knew of it—it was a luxury hotel with three towers. I'd heard it was incredibly lavish. I wrote the name down and then looked back up at my boss. "Do we know who the girl is?"

He shook his head. "She wasn't carrying any identification and she hasn't shown up in any missing person reports yet. She looks Hispanic, late teens to early twenties. All the crime scene photos are in here," he said, tapping the case jacket in front of him.

"Is there any evidence of sexual molestation?" I asked.

"We don't have any autopsy information yet. What I've

told you is about all we know. Now that you're closing up the Montega case, I want you to work this one. Your first homicide—I know you're up for the job. Grand jury is on Friday."

His phone rang and he glanced at the screen. "I've gotta take this." He slid the case jacket across the desk and I picked it up and stood.

"Thank you, Larry. I won't let you down." I turned to leave his office.

"I know you won't."

I walked back to my office and sat down at my computer. My first homicide. It didn't seem right to be overly happy about it; after all, a young woman had died. But I was excited that Larry thought I was competent enough to handle it. I had held my own with many felony cases so far, but this was the first one that involved a murder.

I called down to homicide and asked for the lead detective on the case, Detective Powers. She had time to meet with me in a half hour and so I told her I'd be there.

I started turning off my computer and gathering my papers as Alex walked in the door. "How's my beautiful girl? Can I take you to lunch?" he asked, leaning on my desk.

"I wish. I thought I had an easy wrap-up day. But I just got a new case and I've gotta get moving on it. Larry gave me my first homicide."

Alex raised his eyebrows. "I'm not surprised. You're an amazing lawyer. I'm gonna be wrapped up with clients tonight, but dinner tomorrow night and you can catch me up?"

I stood, putting my arms around his neck and looking up into his kind eyes. "Sounds great," I said.

He kissed me quickly on my forehead and let me go,

whistling a catcall as he walked behind me toward my door. I laughed and grabbed my purse and coat from the coat rack and blew a kiss over my shoulder as I headed to the stairs.

I got in my car and made my way to police headquarters, where I sat down with Detective Powers and went over the details of the case to make sure our testimonies were ready for grand jury. I grimaced as I looked at the pictures of the dead girl again, a bullet hole straight through her forehead. I had seen violent crime scene photos before, but this time, I felt a fierce responsibility come over me. It was *my* job to get justice for this girl. A lump formed in my throat as I took in the horrific details. No one's life should ever end that way.

"If you ever get used to seeing that kind of thing, it's time to retire," Detective Powers said with a bit of humor in her voice. But her eyes said she was completely serious. I liked her. She was about forty, pretty, with short, blond hair. She was direct but kind.

"I agree. It makes it that much worse that she's so young," I said quietly, closing the file and pushing it away from me.

"Detective, do—"

"Please, call me Kate," she said, smiling warmly.

"Okay, Kate." I smiled. "Do you have any ideas about a motive here?"

"Not yet. But I do have a couple people to follow up with that have proven hard to pin down so far. They may be helpful in shedding light on Mr. Garner's state of mind, among other things."

I nodded. "Well, it looks like we have plenty to present to grand jury on Friday. I don't see any problem getting an indictment."

"No, there won't be a problem. If you have any questions,

give me a call, but otherwise, I think we're in sync. I'll see you at the courthouse?"

"Yes, sounds good. Thanks for meeting with me today. I know you have a busy schedule."

"Not a problem."

We both stood and shook hands, and she walked me to the door. I thanked her again and headed back to my office. I had two days to prepare for grand jury.

Carson

I walked into Leland's office and closed the door quietly behind me. He was on the phone, but when he saw me, he told whomever he was talking to that he needed to go.

I sat down in the chair across from him and leaned my elbows on my knees, running my hand over my hair, which I had kept short even after leaving the navy.

"Anything?" Leland asked, looking at me warily.

I shook my head, my jaw tensing. "No. Not a damn thing."

Leland paused. "Okay. But you're in agreement that we can't visit him. It's too risky. And even if we sent someone else in there, everything's recorded. Josh couldn't talk anyway."

I let out a frustrated sigh. "I know. We'll just have to wait until bail is set. *Fuck!* We've always been like a well-oiled machine. How did this happen?"

Leland frowned, drumming his pen on his desk. I knew that if anything happened to Josh—hell, any of us—Leland was going to take it the hardest. He had presented this operation to us in the first place after he and I had been medically discharged from the navy.

"Fuck is right," he mumbled, looking out the window at the midday Vegas strip. I looked out the window too, breathing out some of the frustration. It wasn't going to help anyone—especially Josh—if I totally lost my cool. I could see a small slip of the Bellagio and I had the sudden flash of who I'd been the weekend my life had changed. The weekend I'd met Grace. I'd been so disconnected. Directionless. She'd made me see that and because of it, I was sitting here, burning with purpose. I sat up a bit straighter. So yeah, this specific situation sucked. But when I thought about other turns my life might have taken, other places I might be, I was fucking grateful to be where I was. Now? Now we needed to get Josh back with us too. Any other option was unacceptable.

I made a point of relaxing my muscles. "Leland, this is a bad situation, about as bad as it fucking gets, but we knew the risk going in, and so did Josh." *And we still deemed it worthwhile.*

He took a deep breath, moving his eyes back to me. "Yeah." After a minute he continued. "Josh has gotta know we went back in for him, right?"

"Fuck yeah. He knows the motto. Hell, we've proven it enough times over the years." I paused. "Yeah, he knows."

Leland pursed his lips, still drumming his pen. "Okay, what's next?"

"Well, the operation halts, obviously. We keep a low profile. We can't be seen together. We keep trying to pinpoint Bakos's location because there's no one else who could be responsible. And we do it before he starts putting the pieces together and we all have targets on our backs." *Bakos. The fucker who was behind this. The only one who could be.*

"Well, why didn't you say it was a fucking cakewalk? Shit, is that all?" He laughed a humorless laugh.

I chuckled and it sounded just as hollow. "Yeah, it's in the bag."

We were both quiet for a minute. "Any idea why he'd set Josh up like that rather than just shooting him in the head?"

"I figure he has him shot in the head, he'd never know who he was. We don't carry ID. Frame him, get him arrested, it not only goes down harder, but it's an easy way to get him identified. I mean, I've gotta give him credit."

Leland huffed. "Damn. We underestimated him."

I shook my head. "No. We got caught."

"Well, yeah, that didn't help either. So now it's just a waiting game."

"Yeah, now it's just a waiting game. We're doing everything we can."

"Have you talked to the detective yet?"

"I put her off, but I have an appointment with her Friday. I couldn't hedge any more than that. I'd appreciate it if you could call my office phone, so I can cut the meeting short though. If she wants to meet with me beyond that, she'll have to bring me to the station." I wasn't going to make it easy, and for good reason. I was involved too.

Leland nodded. "Yeah, no problem. Does the detective know you were in the navy with Josh?"

"Yeah, I didn't really have any choice but to tell her. I figured it'd look suspicious if I didn't offer that up and it came out later."

Leland frowned. "Probably true." He paused, obviously thinking. "Is there any way us serving with Josh could get back to Bakos?"

"I don't see how at this point, but again, we need to find him before he has time to gather information we don't want him to have. He'll be keeping an eye on the investigation. It's just normal police protocol to question an accused's boss at his place of employment. Hopefully Bakos takes it at face value and doesn't look any closer."

"Yeah, let's hope."

"I've tightened security throughout the hotel. No one is gonna get in here to ask questions without us knowing about it."

Leland was quiet for a minute and then nodded. "Thanks, man."

I nodded back, standing up to leave. "How's forty-five?"

"No problems. Dylan's still working on flights and paperwork. He said he'd have it all scheduled by tomorrow. The priority is Bakos though and so that's what he's focusing on."

"Okay, good," I said. "Keep me updated."

"I will. Thanks, Carson."

I started walking toward the door when Dylan walked in. "Hey, speak of the computer genius. Tell me you have something," I said.

Dylan had moved to Vegas a month earlier, when we realized we needed someone to help with the computer side of our operation—someone we could trust implicitly right off the bat.

"Not yet. That motherfucker moves around so damn much." He frowned. "I have some ideas though. They'll just take time."

I nodded. "Yup, a waiting game," I said to both Dylan and Leland. "A fucking waiting game."

Dylan clapped me on the back. "I have some programs running, so I'm scheduling flights right now. I ran into a couple problems with paperwork though. That's why I'm here," he said, addressing Leland.

"I'll let you figure it out," I told him, starting to leave again.

"Okay, see ya," Dylan said.

I nodded at Leland again and walked out the door, headed back to my office.

CHAPTER 21
Grace

I walked out of grand jury feeling accomplished. It had gone perfectly and we had gotten the indictment. No surprise, but it still felt good to be done with that part of the process. Now I could really get to work preparing my case.

Kate Powers was standing in the hall when I walked out. "Hey, Grace, great job in there."

"Thanks, Kate, you too."

We started walking toward the front of the courthouse. "Hey," Kate said, "I'm actually heading to Trilogy where Josh Garner works. I finally pinned down his boss, the head of security there. I met with him briefly the other day but he got called out on an emergency and so I rescheduled with him for today. Wanna come along?"

I thought about that. "Sure," I said. "It'd be helpful to hear Josh Garner's boss's read on him."

"Well, he's not just his boss. They were actually SEALs together before coming to Vegas. Another guy they served with owns Trilogy and offered them a job. Hopefully one or both of them have some information on Josh Garner that might help at least establish his character."

"Oh, even better. They know him well. I'm in."

She opened the front door and held it for me before walking through. "Um, hmm. And wait until you get a load of this guy. I roll my eyes when my teenage daughters use the word *hot* to describe every good-looking male they see, but oh, honey, this guy is H-O-T. Not to mention, he won a silver star for valor, which makes him even hotter."

I laughed. "Should I clear my schedule for the rest of the day so I can recover after getting an eyeful of this brave and perfect specimen of man?"

"Not a bad idea, I'm telling you," she said, laughing.

We parted ways agreeing to meet in the lobby at Trilogy and I got in my car and started driving toward the strip.

As I passed the Bellagio, I smiled to myself. When I first moved here, I had wondered if it would be hard for me to pass that hotel all the time. In the beginning, it had been. That old familiar longing would set in, and I would want to know how he was so badly, it felt crushing. But as time went on, I came to see that hotel as a symbol of all my life had become. I had made the choice to follow my own dreams because of my weekend there. I was doing what I loved. And in very large part, I had Carson to thank for that. Before him, I had always felt like if I lost control in one area, I would lose control in all areas. He had shown me that that didn't have to be the case—that I could trust myself, and it was okay to let go a little bit and experience life. And so that's how I had gone forward. And I was happier for it.

Life is wild, he'd said. Fate could be wild. Putting you just where you should be at just the right time. And perhaps intervening in ways you never even realized until you could see the big picture later.

I parked in the Trilogy garage and rode the elevator up to the lobby. I had never been here before and I was taken aback by how stunning it was. Trilogy didn't have a theme per se, like many of the other luxury hotel/casinos in Vegas, unless luxury was considered a theme. There were huge, dramatic chandeliers hanging everywhere, plush seating in deep jewel colors, and gleaming gold walls and ceilings.

I spotted Kate talking on her cell phone on a deep blue chaise lounge and walked toward her. She smiled and hung up her phone. "Ever been here?" she asked.

"No, it's stunning."

"Yeah, it really is. Each tower is slightly different but equally luxe. The water features outside are the most incredible I've ever seen. You should walk around for a few minutes after we finish this meeting."

"I might," I said, still looking, distracted by the opulence.

We walked up to the beautiful gold-adorned front desk, and I stood back as Kate talked to the desk clerk before returning to where I stood. "We can go on back. He has an office to the right of the casino. I was back there the last time I was here."

I looked around as we walked through the casino. I had been to plenty of them since I had moved to Vegas, but they still managed to make my eyes go wide with all the sights and sounds. The people-watching was my favorite, some animated, some sitting stoically as they fed dollar bills into a machine.

We stepped out of the casino and Kate rounded a corner into a hallway. We took several turns and ended up in a hall that dead-ended, and Kate knocked on the first door to the right. I stood waiting with her for a couple seconds before the door opened and I looked up into the face of the very fine specimen of man that Kate had referred to. My heart gave a sudden slam and then began beating furiously as my bones turned to liquid. *Oh. Oh, oh, oh.* I almost sagged against the doorframe. I felt dizzy and yet adrenaline spiked through my veins, the only thing holding me up.

"Carson," I breathed.

Carson

I heard my name released as a whisper and when my eyes moved over to the little blond standing next to the detective in front of me, my muscles froze, shock pulsing through my body, time seeming to halt entirely as my eyes met with hers.

"Grace?" I said on a harsh exhale.

We all stood there, silent, me and Grace staring at each other with mouths hung open. I tried to gain my equilibrium as she blinked rapidly at me. I had been in a lot of unexpected situations through the years, and I had always managed to gather my shit quickly. As I stood staring at Grace, I did not gather my shit quickly.

Holy hell.

Grace.

In my office.

Is she real? My eyes did a quick survey of her from head to heels. Her blond hair was pulled up in a twist just like the first time we'd met and she was wearing a navy-blue skirt that showed off her slim figure and a pale gray blouse. She was beautiful. Beautiful and professional.

Grace.

"So, you two know each other?" the detective asked.

It broke the spell. I glanced at the detective to see she was looking back and forth between us, a small, curious smile on her face. I moved into my office, making room for them both to enter. I kept looking back at Grace though as though she might disappear into the ether at any moment. "Yes, I know Grace" is all I managed in answer to the detective's question.

Grace remained silent, appearing shell-shocked as she followed us into the room. *Okay, deep breath.* This wasn't the time to deal with the emotions currently assaulting my system at this unexpected turn of events. *Grace.* I needed to get the detective out of my office and get Grace alone. Questions were exploding through my brain that had nothing to do with why they were here.

I took a seat behind my desk as the detective and Grace took the two seats on the other side. "Thank you for meeting with me again, Mr. Stinger," the detective said.

"Call me Carson, Detective." I'd told her that the first time we'd met, but either she'd forgotten or preferred the formality. What was her name again? Kate? God, I couldn't fucking think straight. And I needed to think straight.

I glanced over at Grace, who was still staring at me with the same bewildered expression. God, she was even more beautiful than I remembered her, and I had done a lot of remembering when it came to Grace Hamilton.

"Yes, right, Carson." The detective laughed. "We established that, didn't we? And again, call me Kate," she said. "We won't take much of your time. We just have some questions about Mr. Garner."

"We?" I asked, glancing at Grace again.

"Yes, we. Ms. Hamilton is the prosecutor working on this case. I'm sorry, I thought you said you knew each other?"

I froze for a second, my eyes flying back to Grace and my stomach tightening. *Prosecutor?* Oh fuck. *Oh no.* This wasn't good. Or was it? Could this be… a good thing for Josh? My brain was going a million miles a minute. "It's been a while," I said, my eyes remaining on Grace as my brain cartwheeled.

Kate was glancing back and forth between the two of us again. "Okay, well, I'll make this quick and you two can catch up."

Neither Grace nor I said anything, but Grace crossed her legs, seeming like she was relaxing a little bit. Kate cleared her throat. "Okay, Carson, I understand you were in the navy with Mr. Garner and that you both moved here recently to work at Trilogy. Has he ever exhibited any behavior that seemed unusual to you, especially in more recent months?"

I focused my gaze on Kate. "No."

"Care to elaborate?"

I leaned back in my chair. "Josh Garner has always acted sound of mind and body. He's an extremely stable man. I never observed any unusual behavior."

Kate nodded and jotted something on a small pad she had placed on her crossed knee.

"What kind of soldier was he?"

"He was a trustworthy teammate who did his job well."

She nodded. "I'm assuming you were in situations where violence was necessary. How did he react to those situations?"

I glanced at Grace, who was reaching into her bag for a pad and a pen too. As she took the pen in her hand, I noticed the slight tremor. I also noticed the ring on her finger. My heart dropped. *It's been almost five years. What did you expect?* I locked my feelings down and looked back at Kate, trying to recall her question. *Violence. How did he react. Right.*

"In a professional manner," I answered. "He did what he had to do to complete the missions we were on. If you're asking if he seemed to like the violent aspect of his job, the answer is no. He did what was required and no more or less than that."

"Any idea why he left the navy?"

"He had served as a SEAL for ten years. He was ready to get back to civilian life, and his job here was a good offer. He didn't elaborate any more than that to me."

"Okay. Did you see him Sunday during the day or Sunday night?"

"He worked Sunday, but we didn't have very much interaction. I was mostly in the security rooms downstairs and he worked the casino floor."

Kate nodded again. "Good employee?"

"Very good employee."

"Did you socialize personally?"

"Not much since we've been in Vegas. We've both been busy."

Kate tapped her pen on her paper. "Okay, I think that's all I have for now." She put her pad and pen in her bag. "If I have any more questions, I'll be in touch." She smiled and stood.

Grace started standing too, but Kate put a hand on her arm. "Grace, I'll be in touch. Have a good rest of the day." She nodded to me and turned and walked to the door, exiting quietly.

Grace stood up quickly and so did I. "Carson, what—"

"Grace, how—"

We both laughed a little uncomfortably and then both went silent, just looking at each other.

"Hi, Grace." I smiled. I wondered if I looked as thrown as I felt.

She let out a breath and smiled back. "Hi, Carson."

I came around my desk and sat down in the chair Kate had been previously occupying and Grace sat back down. I wanted to reach for her hands, but I didn't. I could still hardly believe she was real—sitting right here in front of me.

"You went into the navy?" she asked, eyes wide.

I nodded. "Yeah. Right after we left Vegas."

"Right after..." Her brow furrowed and she gave her head a small shake. "Why didn't you tell me?" she asked. I thought it was hurt in her tone, but I wasn't sure.

"At first, I didn't know if I would even succeed," I told her. "I was spinning after that weekend, Grace." I let out a breath. "And then right after I became a SEAL, I tried to look you up on social media but I couldn't find you." I ran my hand over my short hair. I didn't mention the two days I'd been in DC, or that I'd almost gone to visit her. I hadn't had the chance, so what did it matter? "Anyway, I shipped out after that." *And then the years and the timing.*

And the mission.

She sighed and gave a small shrug. "Oh. Well, no, I'm not much for social media. I have a few accounts but they're under iterations of my name..." Her voice faded away and for a moment she appeared confused as though she'd forgotten what she was talking about.

I didn't respond right away, didn't save her. I felt lost too. And truthfully, I wanted to quietly stare at her forever. But she fidgeted slightly under my gaze, bringing me back to the present and causing something to occur to me suddenly. "You didn't go into corporate law," I said. "You became a prosecutor."

She let out a breath on a smile. "Yes."

Her dream. It'd been her dream, the one she'd barely been able to admit to. I wanted to know everything—when had she made the decision? Did our conversation play any part in it? Had it been hard? And how was she *here?* "How did you end up in Ve—" I started to ask but was interrupted by the ringing of the phone. "Damn. Hold on."

I leaned across the desk and picked up the receiver. "Leland, it's taken care of."

"Uh, okay, man. The detective already left?"

"Yeah. Nothing much to update. We'll talk later."

"Oka—"

I hung up, relaxing back in the seat. I was restraining myself from scooping her up and hugging her. I knew there were things I should be addressing here—first and foremost the fact that she was the prosecutor on my friend's case, a case that had more to do with me than she could know. We needed to discuss that. Or maybe we *shouldn't* discuss that. *Shit.*

Her hands moved in her lap and that ring caught my eye again. "You're engaged," I said. My voice sounded kind of flat, even to my own ears. It didn't surprise me, but I could admit—to myself at least—that I didn't like it. I hadn't seen her in so many years and yet that ring on her finger made my guts churn.

She looked down at her hand, a confused expression on her face, almost as if she didn't know what I was talking about for a second. "Oh. Yes."

"When's the wedding?"

"The wedding?"

I tilted my head. "I assume an engagement means there'll be a wedding at some point?"

"Oh, um, well, we haven't set a date yet." She fiddled with her ring for a second before clasping her hands together and clearing her throat. Then her gaze shot quickly to my hand as if it had suddenly occurred to her I might be wearing one too. Her gaze was lowered. I couldn't see her eyes in order to discern her reaction to my bare finger. But her gaze lingered there and after a moment she asked, "And what about you Carson? Anyone special in your life?" She seemed to go even more still than she already was—or maybe even brace—as though my answer was going to cause her an emotional response and she wasn't sure what it would be. I dragged the moment out, watching her, noting her body language. Finally, I shook my head. "No. No one special."

We stared at each other for a few beats before she broke eye contact and started to stand. "I should go," she said suddenly, her words tumbling over each other, the notepad on her lap falling to the floor. I stood as she did and then bent to scoop up the paper. When I straightened, I was closer to her, and we stood staring at each other again for several seconds. A feeling of déjà vu hit me and it took me momentarily off balance. "Grace—" I started.

"I have to go," she said before she pivoted and began walking to the door.

Stay. Don't go.

"Grace, wait, have dinner with me," I blurted.

She halted in her tracks.

"Just to catch up," I said.

She turned slowly to face me. "Catch up?" she asked. God, her expression almost looked… fearful.

"Yeah. Just catch up. A lot has happened for both of us. I'd love to hear a little more about your life."

247

She stared at me and I could see the internal battle she was waging. "Just dinner," I said.

After a moment, she bobbed her head. "Dinner. Okay. Yes. Dinner would be fine."

Fine. "Great. I can pick you up. If you'll write down your address. I mean, do you live with your fiancé?" I asked. Goddamn, I was feeling so many emotions at once, I felt all tangled and out of whack.

"No, I live alone."

That knot untangled just enough that I could pull in a full breath. I reached behind me to grab a pad and a pen off my desk. As she started to write, her hand paused as though she was having second thoughts. But then her hand began moving again and finally she handed the pad and pen back to me. I had this insane urge to run over to the safe in the closet and put her address in there in case she tried to take it back. *Dial it down, Stinger.*

"Carson, I—"

"Seven o'clock?"

She hesitated but then nodded. "Okay, seven."

"Okay."

We stood there awkwardly for a second before she turned and opened the door, glancing at me one more time before walking out. *Holy shit.* I sagged down against my desk.

Grace. Prosecutor Grace. Engaged Grace. *Grace.*

I didn't know whether to laugh or throw something. I did neither. After a few minutes, I opened my office door and got back to work, because despite the jittery state of my emotions, people were depending on me.

CHAPTER 22
Grace

Somehow, on shaky, unstable legs, I made it back to my car in the garage. Emotions were dipping and soaring strangely. My body felt like I had just drunk seven pots of coffee in a row and then gotten slapped across the face repeatedly. I sank down in my seat, closed the door, and let out a long, trembling breath. *Carson Stinger.* Holy hell! I felt like a bomb had just gone off in front of me and I should check myself for shrapnel.

I had the vague impression that it was my life that had just exploded, but I didn't know exactly how or why.

God, when I first saw him, I had thought I would pass out. I hoped that Detective Powers hadn't been able to see how much that encounter affected me. How embarrassing.

I attempted to gather myself and clear my head. *Get it together, Grace. You're acting like an emotional wreck. And over what?* Okay, so I had just unexpectedly run into a man that I had spent a weekend with almost five years ago. He had helped me to discover some important things about myself and what I wanted that had had a positive influence on my life. Great. Good. We had both moved forward with our lives. I was engaged now to a man who was good for me, a man who loved me. Carson had obviously done pretty great for himself too. He had gone into the navy, become a SEAL. *Holy crap!* A strong surge of something I could only call pride rose up in my chest. I pictured him standing in his office, so professional, so poised, so different than the young man I remembered.

When he'd told me he had tried to look me up, a feeling of deep disappointment had formed a ball in my throat. Immediately, I hadn't been able to help wondering how that might have changed things. Would we have reunited—even if only by phone, or by mail? I chewed at my lip, finally deciding there was no point in attempting to answer that question. We *hadn't* reunited. And that was reality. If we had, in some shape or form, I may not have the life I had now. I may not be with Alex…

I leaned up and looked at myself in the car mirror and frowned. I looked shell-shocked. "Shake it off," I whispered to my own reflection.

I exited the garage and turned back onto the Strip, blasting my AC. As I traveled to my office—and despite my best efforts—my mind continued to stray to Carson.

I had made dinner plans with him. I groaned out loud, hitting my hands lightly on the steering wheel. What was I going to tell Alex? I had tried to rush out of there—so overwhelmed with the emotions pummeling me, I could hardly think straight. But he had stopped me and I was weak. God, after all this time, I was still affected by him. But holy shit, what woman wouldn't be affected by him? I had thought he was hot five years ago. Now he was a blazing inferno. That boyishness that had charmed me so completely back then was still there but roughened up a bit—not gone but chipped away, giving him an edge that he didn't have before. And that damn dimple still worked its magic, entrancing me every time he flashed a smile and it made an appearance.

His hair was shorter, and although he was still lean, I could tell that his muscles were more chiseled, even hidden under the suit he was wearing. And there was something behind his eyes that hadn't been there before—maybe a worldliness? I wanted to know more. God help me, I did. I stopped at a red light and brought my palm up to my forehead. I shouldn't be thinking about him like this. It was highly inappropriate.

Not to mention the fact that he was well acquainted with the man I was prosecuting. Was there a conflict of interest there, even having dinner? No, I didn't think so. It's not like he was involved in the case. He was just the man's employer. But still, I wasn't going to lie to myself and say that it was just two old friends grabbing a bite to eat. We were two people who had spent a weekend having sex...lots of sex...lots of *great* sex.

My mind started to wander to places it shouldn't wander and I pulled up short. *God, stop, Grace! What is wrong with you?*

So... yes, having dinner with him felt more complicated than just catching up with an old friend. But I longed to know how his life had come to the place where it was now. I longed to know how he was doing. I had thought about him so often over the years. So I'd satisfy my curiosity, and then we'd go our separate ways. He lived in the same city I lived in. Okay. That was fine. I would make sure—

A car horn blared behind me and I jolted out of my thoughts, moving forward through the light. I forced myself not to think about Carson the rest of the way back to my office. I had the second half of the workday to get through and I needed to focus.

Alex was out of the office for the rest of the day, tied up in court, and I was thankful. I couldn't help feeling guilty about making dinner plans with Carson.

I closed the door behind me when I got back to my office and sat down at my desk, resting my head in my hands and sitting quietly for a few minutes, trying to get back to a place of calm. I massaged my temples. Geez, what were the freaking *odds* that I'd run into Carson, and right here at home? What were the chances that almost five years later, completely unexpectedly, I would walk into Carson Stinger's office in a city neither one of us had lived in when we parted? I sat up, letting out a short, incredulous laugh. *Life is wild, indeed.*

Carson

After Grace left, I went up to see Leland to update him about the detective's questioning. I didn't mention Grace.

Dylan was working on hacking into some databases that may or may not pan out in helping Josh's case. He was also still trying to get a lead on Bakos that would give us enough time to move in on him. Josh would enter his plea in a day or two and then we could figure out bail. It was just a waiting game at this point.

I sat downstairs in the security room, watching the tables for a while, and then I texted Leland and told him that I was leaving a little early with a headache. It wasn't a lie. I had been sitting down there thinking of Grace the whole damn time. My head was splitting.

Still, I made time to go upstairs to the forty-fifth floor to check on the girls. This was something Grace couldn't know about. I was looking forward to catching up and telling her where my life had gone, but I knew I couldn't be completely honest with her. Especially not about the girls. That was something she wouldn't like and something she might be required to report.

A half an hour later, I drove my truck home and as soon as I slammed the door behind me, I went to the kitchen and took a couple Advil, followed by a long, hot shower. When I got out, I felt a lot better.

I pulled on jeans and a long-sleeved, black shirt and grabbed my phone. I had forgotten to check in with Dylan before I left.

He answered on the second ring. "Hey, man."

"Hey, Dylan, I left a little early. Did you get all the paper-work squared away?"

"Mostly. I'm hoping it will be by tonight. I'm just waiting on a few things."

"Okay, cool. I just wanted to check in."

"Okay, you all right?"

"Yeah." I hesitated and Dylan remained quiet. "Hey, Dylan, you remember that girl I met in Vegas five years ago or so? The one—"

"Yeah. Pussy voodoo?"

I chuckled. "Yeah." Only, I wished that was all it was. Then I might not be spinning like a top.

"What about her?"

"She walked into my office today. She's the prosecutor on Josh's case."

"You're shittin' me."

"No. I'm not. What are the odds, right?"

He paused for a minute. "Geez, man. That's either really bad luck or really good luck. I don't know. Shit's pretty complicated right now. Are you still interested in her?"

I sighed. "Interested? It doesn't matter anyway. She's engaged."

"Engaged, huh? Well, engaged ain't married."

I made a small agreeable sound in the back of my throat. "I'm taking her to dinner tonight. Just to catch up."

"That sounds interested, Carson. Be careful."

"I will. I will. Thanks, Dylan."

"All right. I'll see you in the morning."

"Okay, I'll be in early. I'm meeting the dignitaries from Saudi Arabia." It was part of my job as head of security to secure high-priced items that Trilogy guests brought with them.

"Oh, right, okay. I'll see you then."

We hung up and I glanced at the clock. It was ten to seven. I grabbed my jacket and my keys and headed for the door.

CHAPTER 23
Grace

I was just finishing blow-drying my hair when my cell rang.
It was Abby.

"You're going to die when I tell you who I'm going to
dinner with, Abby," I whispered into the phone.

"Are you answering your phone from an under-
ground bunker?"

"What? No."

"Then why are you whispering like that?"

I whispered into the phone again, "I don't know. Maybe
a hear-no-evil thing?"

"Oh God. The last time you sounded like this, you were
spending a weekend in Vegas with a porn star."

I laughed nervously. "Well, funny you should mention
that actually."

I heard a shriek come from the other end of the line and
held the phone away from my ear, grimacing.

"Jesus, Abby," I said, raising my voice to regular volume.
"Are you trying to bust my eardrum?"

"Tell me you are not going to spend the weekend with another porn star, Grace. I let it go once, but twice is just too outrageous. Plus, you know, Alex and all…"

I laughed. It felt good. I needed the relaxation a little laughter brought. I had taken a long, hot bath when I got home, but I was still strung up as tight as a bow over the thought of going to dinner with Carson. Not to mention the fact that I hadn't yet told Alex about my evening plans. He was still with some clients and I'd only heard from him via text.

"Yeah, no." I cleared my throat. "I am, however, going to dinner with *the* porn star." I was whispering again.

"Say what?" Abby practically yelled.

"Abby, stop it. You're going to scare the baby." Abby was eight months pregnant.

"The baby's fine. It's you I'm worried about. What is *up*?"

I sighed. "I went along for an interview with a detective today for a case I'm working on and walked into Carson Stinger's office. No joke. I thought I was gonna faint, Abby."

"Carson Stinger's *office*?" she asked, sounding completely confused. "What office? Where?"

"He's head of security at a new hotel on the Strip. Apparently he went into the military after we parted ways and he's been overseas most of this time. I don't even know all the details. He asked me to dinner to 'catch up' and I said yes."

Abby was quiet for several seconds. "He joined the military… Wow. *That* is a story I have to hear. You better call me the minute you get back. What does Alex think about your dinner plans?"

I paused. "I haven't actually told him yet. But you know Alex, he's easygoing. I think he'll be fine with it."

256

She huffed out a breath. "That's what I'm worried about."

"What does that mean exactly?" I asked, frowning as I put Abby on speaker and took my robe off so that I could pull on my underwear and bra.

There was another short silence before Abby spoke. "I just... Remember how that guy hit on you when we were out at Thanksgiving?" Abby and Brian had come to Vegas a couple weeks before to spend Thanksgiving with me and Alex because I was wrapping up a big case and hadn't been able to get home to see my dad and sisters. We had gone out for Thanksgiving dinner, deciding to make a big night out of it, and when I had left the table to use the restroom, a guy stopped me and made a pretty big show of hitting on me.

"Yeah? And?" I asked.

"Alex didn't even bat an *easygoing* eyelash. He really couldn't have cared less."

"That's not true! He just trusts me."

Abby huffed out a breath. "I can't hold it in any longer, Grace." And I swore I heard Brian's voice in the background saying her name quietly in a warning manner. "Shh!" I heard her say back.

"Abby, what can't you hold in any longer?"

"He's boring! Alex is boring!"

I sucked in a breath. "No he's not! He's...he's kind and sweet and..."

"Safe?" she asked.

"Yes! Safe. So what? What's wrong with that? He loves me. He's good to me."

Abby sighed dramatically into the phone. "Grace, I can see that he is. He's a nice guy. It's just, you two act like brother and sister. It's almost creepy."

I laughed. I couldn't help it. "We're creepy? That's just...*mean*!"

"I don't mean that you're creepy. What I mean is... how's the sex?"

"Abby, stop. I'm not talking about this anymore. Alex loves me. I'm marrying him. That's it."

"Please don't be mad at me. I just couldn't not say anything to you. And since we're talking about Vegas five years ago, I've gotta say it—after you came home, I saw you change in so many good ways. It was like you blossomed after that. In all areas except one. Where men were and are concerned, it's like you went *backward*. What's up with that? What's up with the whole 'safe' fiancé? What's going on there? Is that what you were really waiting all that time for? *Safe?* I love you. I'm only saying this because I love you. I don't want you to end up regretting marrying him."

I sighed. "Abby. I know you're looking out for me. But when it comes to Alex, I know what's good for me, okay? I really do. I won't regret marrying him. I won't. Thank you for sharing your concerns. Now, speaking of bad decisions, I gotta go get ready for dinner."

"Okay," she said, sounding uncertain. "Just one more thing and I won't bring it up again—you keep saying that he loves *you*. You don't have to answer me now, but do you love *him*? That's it. I've said my piece. Please know this is coming from a good place, okay?"

"I'm not mad. I love you. I'll call you tomorrow, okay?"

"You better. I love you too."

"I will. Bye, Abs."

"Bye, Grace."

I hung up and sat on my bed in my underwear, chewing on my thumbnail. *Brother and sister?* Is that really what Alex and I acted like together? No. He loved me. I mean, I loved him? No, I loved him. Of course I loved him. I was attracted to him. He was handsome and sweet and good. I was lucky to have him. He *did* make me feel safe. So what? Was that a *bad* quality? I loved Abby, but she wasn't the one who had to live my life. I needed to get this straight in my head before I went out to dinner with walking sex on a stick.

How's the sex?

Before my mind could follow that line of thought, my phone rang again. Alex. Perfect timing.

"Hi," I answered quickly.

"Hi yourself. What are you up to?"

"Actually, I'm getting ready. I ran into an old friend today and I'm going to dinner with…him."

"Him?"

I nodded and then realized he couldn't see me. "Um, yeah. I ran into him at Trilogy today when I was there with Kate Powers on a case. I met him at a law conference I went to years ago and he asked me if I wanted to grab a bite with him tonight. Of course, he knows I'm engaged. Do you mind?"

"No. That's fine. I'm going to turn in early anyway. I have to be back in court early again tomorrow." He yawned. "Have a good time, okay?"

"Oh, okay. Love you."

"Love you. I'll see you in the office tomorrow afternoon."

"Bye, Alex."

I hung up and sat chewing my thumbnail for a few minutes longer. Then I got up and did my makeup. I wasn't sure what to wear since I didn't know where Carson was taking me, so I pulled on a pair of dark jeans, heeled boots, and a dressy top. It'd work pretty much anywhere.

The doorbell rang and I ran a brush through my hair quickly, took a deep breath, and went to answer it. When I pulled it open, Carson Stinger was filling my doorway, six feet of male, every inch of him beautiful. I knew. I remembered every inch of him. I almost shivered but forced myself still. This was already off to a very bad start.

"Hi," I said, opening the door so he could come inside. I backed up and hitched my thumb over my shoulder. "I'll just grab my coat."

He didn't say anything, just gave me a smile that was decidedly tight. Tense. *Is there a problem?*

Coat and purse in hand, I rejoined Carson, who remained standing in my doorway, glancing around as though casing the joint. He still hadn't said a word to me.

He waited as I locked up and then we walked in silence down my front path to a black truck. He held the door open for me as I climbed inside. As his truck roared to life, and he pulled away from the curb, I glanced at him again, wondering at his stoic demeanor, and feeling like I was going to dinner with a total stranger.

Carson

I glanced over at Grace sitting in the cab of my truck. She looked beautiful, and my blood was humming with her proximity alone. But as much as I wanted to enjoy dinner with her, I had worked myself into a shitty mood over the fact that there were roadblocks between us again that were going to make it very challenging for this to go anywhere.

Engaged ain't married.

Dylan's words had rung in my head as I'd driven to Grace's address, and though at first they'd lit a fire of hope, the more I thought about the reality, the grumpier I'd gotten. What the fuck was I doing? It had been hard enough to get over her the first time. And now I was willingly putting myself back in the same situation? Where I pined for her and she was unavailable? The reasons were different now, but the results would be the same. I was some kind of masochist when it came to this girl. The first time, I hadn't known how she would end up affecting me. This time I did, and I was back for more. It had really become obvious to me when she opened the door, her cheeks all flushed and her hair flowing over her shoulders, and everything in my body yearned to rip her clothes off and take her up against her wall. I needed to get a handle on that. She was engaged. Shit. And I was unavailable for a relationship anyway, for all intents and purposes. So why did I have this suspicion that when it came down to it, I was going to act like a fucking idiot and push all those very good reasons aside? I didn't trust myself with Grace Hamilton, plain and simple. So much had changed in my life, but evidently that remained the same.

Grace looked uncertain, her hands fidgeting while she chewed at her lip. I let out a slow breath. God, I hadn't even greeted her properly. I forced myself to relax. "Sorry for the mood," I told her. "It's been a challenging day."

"That's okay," she said. "I have those too."

"Let's start again. Hi, Grace."

"Hi, Carson."

"Guess what," I said.

"What?" she asked, tilting her head.

"I live about five minutes from you, in this same neighborhood." When I had gotten into my truck and put Grace's address into my GPS, I had almost laughed out loud. She hadn't written her zip code down, so I didn't realize until that moment that she too lived in Summerlin, a neighborhood northwest of Vegas. Something about it struck me as funny. Apparently, her pull even spoke to me in some psychic manner. I was fucked. Either that or fate was just messing with me. *Again.*

"Really?" she asked on a smile. Then she frowned as if she'd realized it was not a positive. I'd wondered the same thing honestly.

I got on the highway and I drove toward the Strip, both of us silent for the first few minutes as I continued to relax in her presence. *You smell the same,* I wanted to say. Some mix of vanilla and flowers that brought to mind tangled sheets, and gasps of pleasure. And yearning. Lots of that.

"So this is really weird, isn't it?" she finally asked, breaking me from the memories that made me feel simultaneously turned on and sorta sad.

"Us being together?" I asked.

"Yeah. Running into each other after all this time. It's just…almost…unbelievable."

I nodded but paused. "Yes and no."

"How so?"

"It's hard to explain. I was shocked but almost not surprised at all. Maybe I always expected to see you again." I hadn't even really thought about that, but as the words left my lips, I realized how true they were. Maybe I'd kept it there, in the very back of my mind…the knowledge that Grace Hamilton was not a one-time experience. What that meant exactly, I had no clue.

She raised an eyebrow. "This is some kind of weird stalking thing, isn't it? You spent years planning this."

"I was wondering the same thing about you." I gave her a mock suspicious look.

She laughed. "Okay, you got me. It's been quite the operation...tracking you all over the world." She turned her body so she was facing me in the cab of the truck. "Speaking of which, Kate said you just moved here a couple months ago. Where were you deployed?"

"I served in the Middle East."

She gave her head a small shake. "Wow. I mean, wow, a SEAL, Carson. I'm so impressed. What made you decide to go into the navy?"

I paused for a minute, wondering if complete honesty was a good idea or a bad idea. Finally, I answered, "You."

Her eyes widened. "Me?"

I nodded. "After that weekend, Grace, I wanted to be more. I wanted to have something to offer someone like you."

She was staring at me, her lips slightly parted as if she had been about to say something but decided not to.

"Anyway," I said, rescuing her, "the navy idea kind of came to me in a blinding flash of light and I just did it before I really had time to think about it."

She let out a breath. "I don't know what to say. I, well, I'm...honored that you consider me the catalyst for changing your life in such a positive way." She paused. "I'm just... Thank you for telling me that."

I grinned over at her. "Don't take too much credit. I did all the hard work."

She laughed. "Yes, you certainly did."

We smiled at each other in the dim cab, something flickering and jumping between us.

"So," she said, looking away, "how did you end up in security in Vegas?"

"Me and my buddy Leland got injured in the same ambush. His family owns Trilogy. He and I got medically discharged and he asked me if I'd like to come to Vegas with him and take the head of security job. It sounded like a good opportunity." I shrugged. There was so much more to it than that, but I couldn't tell her about that part, not now.

"Where did you get injured? What happened?" she asked quietly.

"I was shot in the back," I said. "Luckily the bullet went straight in and out, causing minimal internal damage. And my hands were burned." I held one up but in the dim light of the car, even I could barely see the scarring on the palm side of my fingers.

Grace sucked in a breath. "My God..."

"Wait," I said, changing the subject, "you just got my whole story out of me in the car ride to dinner. What are we gonna talk about now?"

She laughed. "We'll probably figure something out."

"We always did," I said on a smile. I pulled into a parking garage and drove up a couple levels before finding a spot. In just a few minutes, things were easy and comfortable with Grace again.

"Where are we going?" she asked as we headed toward the garage elevator.

"Well, I didn't exactly make reservations. But I have three or four ideas for you to choose from that shouldn't need one."

"Can we do hot dogs?" she asked in an excited rush of words.

I laughed and looked over at her. She was grinning. "Seriously?" I asked, raising a brow.

"What? You don't like hot dogs anymore?" she asked as we came to a stop in front of the elevator.

"I love hot dogs. I just don't think I've had a hot dog since…well, since I had a hot dog with you."

"Me neither! Let's do it."

I let my eyes linger on her. God, she was so pretty. My hands were itching to touch her. I fisted them at my sides.

A couple seconds later, the elevator doors opened and we stepped in. As it jolted, starting its descent, my eyes met Grace's and we both laughed, knowing exactly what the other was thinking. Here I was riding an elevator with Grace Hamilton again. *Life is fucking wild.*

We walked to the entrance to the strip. It was December and the air was cool, but not cold, perfect walking weather.

"Do you come to the Strip a lot?" I asked as we headed toward the restaurant.

"Rarely. My best friend, Abby, and her husband came in for Thanksgiving and I took them here to see the sights, but Abby's pregnant so it was the tame Vegas tour."

"The roommate you lived with when I first met you, right?"

She glanced over at me, looking slightly surprised, and nodded.

"Your fiancé doesn't ever take you to get a hot dog?" I had to bring him up. I had to know what her relationship with him was like. The word itself, *fiancé*, told a story. But it didn't necessarily tell the whole story.

She was quiet for a beat, then two. "Alex is more of a homebody, I guess you'd say," is all she said, but I thought a look of disappointment swept over her features. *Interesting.* That hope again. *Engaged ain't married.*

We got to the restaurant and Grace grinned as she walked

through the door I held open. The hostess led us to a table, and I pulled Grace's chair out for her. "Milady," I said with a slight bow.

She laughed as I scooted her close to the table and took my own seat. When the waiter came over, we both ordered a beer.

"So tell me more about why you decided to become a prosecutor," I said.

She looked down and played with her napkin for a minute before responding, "Actually, Carson, I have you to thank for that. After we talked about it here"—she waved her arm toward the window, indicating Vegas—"I realized that it was what I really wanted. And I made it happen. So...thank you."

I leaned back in my chair and smiled. "Really?" I'd recalled our conversation about her secret career aspirations and briefly wondered if I'd influenced her decision at all, but I hadn't realized what happiness it would bring me to hear her confirm it.

"Yeah, really." She smiled. "Anyway, I took my first job in DC but there just weren't any openings in the court I wanted to be in, and so I started applying to different cities and ended up here. And I love it. I really, really love it."

"That's great, Grace."

She continued to fiddle with her napkin, a worried look coming over her face. "Speaking of my job... Your friend—"

I tensed. "We can talk about that another time, okay? It's a weird situation, but...let's just catch up tonight." I'd been going over the situation with Josh all day, every day. I needed a mental break. And I wanted the opportunity to get reacquainted with Grace without all that hanging over us. That probably wouldn't be possible for much longer, and so I was going to actively keep it at bay tonight.

She nodded slowly, pressing her lips together. The waiter delivered our beers and took our orders, saving us from any more awkwardness.

When the waiter walked away, Grace said, "That's what you ordered the last time."

"I know. You ordered the same thing too."

She nodded and laughed.

I held my beer up. "To fate," I said. "She's a tricky bitch." I meant that in more ways than I could explain. Even to myself.

She huffed out a breath and raised her eyebrows. "That's for dang sure," she said and clinked my bottle.

Our food came a few minutes later and Grace dove right in. "See," she said around a mouthful of chili cheese dog, "I learned from last time."

I laughed at her and dove into mine too. I could feel cheese sticking to my chin and something gloppy on the side of my mouth.

Grace shook her head at me, her eyes dancing. "How in the world are you not taken yet, Carson Stinger?" she asked on a laugh. I grinned and used my finger to bring the cheese to my mouth, and then watched as the smile faded from her face and she just kept looking at me, blinking as I wiped my chin with my napkin. Her eyes took on a sort-of faraway look as she licked her bottom lip. At that small gesture, I felt my cock jump in my pants. *Fuck*.

"Grace—" I started.

"So!" she said brightly, crossing her legs under the table. "This was a really good idea. I need to eat more hot dogs." She stopped and furrowed her brow. "I mean, you know, you can never eat too many hot dogs." Her frown deepened. "I mean, you probably can. There *is* probably a recommended hot dog limit." She waved her hand around. "Phosphates and all that, but what I mean is I fall too far beneath—"

"I'm gonna save you from yourself here, buttercup." I laughed. "You can stop now."

Her eyes flew to mine and her cheeks flushed. We stared at each other in silence for several beats before she finally whispered, "I missed that. That nickname."

"Yeah," I breathed. "Me too."

Her eyes softened. "Why do you call me buttercup, Carson?" she asked quietly.

I breathed out a smile. "Where'd I leave off?" I asked.

Her lips parted slightly, and she shifted her eyes to the side, away from me. Her fingers fluttered in the air momentarily as though she was looking for something to do with her hand. "Something about satiny skin from what I remember." She reached for her beer, taking a quick sip.

What else do you remember, Grace? Do you re-live it in your head like I do? "Ah," I said. "Right. Hmm." I gave her a small smile. "Well, maybe it's because you're as pretty as a flower."

She stared at me for a couple beats, opened her mouth as if to say something and then closed it again, grimacing slightly. "I'm sorry. I shouldn't be doing this…flirting this way. Carson, I'm engaged."

I took a sip of my beer. "Yeah, Grace, I know that," I said as I set it down.

She searched my face and then shook her head and looked down again. "I'm sorry, that sounded…bitchy or something. I didn't mean to imply that you—"

"Grace," I interrupted, "it's okay. Really. I got you, all right? Let's talk about something else. I'm having a good time with you."

She nodded, but still looked troubled. "Okay, thank you."

I took another big, sloppy bite of my hot dog, keeping eye contact as I did it. I was rewarded with a laugh before she too took a messy bite.

We finished our food and the waiter cleared the table. We chatted about living in Vegas for a few minutes as we each finished our beers. When the waiter delivered our bill, I paid and we started to put on our coats.

"This was fun," Grace said.

"Yeah, it was. I've wondered for a lot of years how you were doing and it's great to see you so happy."

"I am," she said. "And same here. It's great to see you doing so well, looking so...well."

Our gazes lingered on each other, but then she moved, breaking the spell.

"Do you want to walk past the Bellagio fountain?" I asked her as we exited the restaurant. "For old time's sake?"

She gave a soft laugh. "Why not? I haven't been there since...well, you know, since *you.*" She glanced up at me, her smile fading. We walked in silence for a few minutes before she said, "So, Carson, can I ask you something?"

"Of course," I said, as we started across the street.

"It's sort of personal."

We were sort of personal...once. "Go for it," I said.

"Did you do that film that you were scheduled to do the morning after you left Vegas?" she asked quietly.

That film. The one with Bambi/Rose. The one I'd bolted from. I glanced at her, and she lowered her eyes but kept looking straight ahead. I hesitated in answering as we made it past a small group of people, and then I took her hand and pulled her to an empty spot at the edge of the stone railing looking out to the lake at the Bellagio.

When we stopped, she pulled her hand back and waited for me to answer. "I showed up," I said.

Her eyes darted away from mine but when I continued with, "But I didn't follow through with the shoot. I left and I didn't go back," her eyes returned to my face and I thought I saw her shoulders relax.

"Oh," she said. She let out a little huff of breath. "Is it wrong that that makes me glad?"

"For me or for you?"

"Both," she said without hesitating.

I regarded her for a moment. "Did the thought of it cast a shadow over our weekend?" I asked.

She looked away, appearing to really consider that. "I hated the idea of you with someone else so soon after you'd been with me. But... did it cast a shadow over the weekend?" She shook her head. "No. No, I didn't let it do that. That weekend was so special to me. I wouldn't let anything cast a shadow over it."

My heart gave a hard thump. "Thank you for that honesty. That weekend was so special to me too." We didn't break eye contact. God, I wanted to kiss her so badly.

She switched from one foot to the other, looking down and then peeking up at me. "I looked up your films," she admitted after a moment.

I froze. What. The. Fuck?

She brought her hands up to her cheeks. "I'm sorry. That was highly inappropriate to say... I—"

"Why did you look up my films, Grace?" I *hated* knowing that she had seen those. I hated thinking of her sitting at her computer watching me fuck other women. It made me sick. I looked away, out to the water. "Goddamn, Grace, why'd you do that?" I muttered.

A feeling that I hadn't felt in a really damn long time slithered its way through my guts—*shame*. Yes, shame that I'd participated in the sex trade—that was still there. But mostly, shame that she'd watched me doing it. Watched me perform an act publicly that we'd experienced personally. Had she wondered if what we'd done contained some elements of acting too? Or had she realized that the intimacy we shared was something completely different? Sometimes I didn't even like to think about how I'd approached having sex on camera for money. That person felt so far away… And I hated that I was confronting him now in front of Grace who I wanted to see me as the man I currently was, not the one she'd walked away from.

I rubbed my jaw. Yes, that life felt so far away, so distant from who I was now. But Grace didn't necessarily see it that way.

"Hey," she said, leaning her head to the side to get my attention. I turned back toward her. "I'm sorry. I shouldn't have told you that. It was so long ago, and—"

"Why did you do it?" I asked, needing to know.

She paused. "At the time, I guess I just needed a reminder about why I shouldn't contact you," she said. "And then when I… when I saw it… I realized that what we'd done… what that weekend was about, was different. You were real with me. It made me miss you more," she said.

I let out a harsh exhale of relief. She'd known. And I hated that she'd seen me with anyone else, but… she'd known.

"I missed you too, Grace," I said. It felt like there was so much more to say, but we were skating a thin line here, and I had to be mindful of that too.

She smiled sadly and opened her mouth to say something when a collective "oooh" sounded from the group around us and the water show started.

We stood watching it for several minutes and then I moved closer to Grace, our sides barely touching, but the heat of her felt like it was scorching me, moving through me, taking over. I was itching to move behind her and hold her in my arms like I had the last time we were here. And then I wanted to take her back to my house and—I slammed the brakes on that line of thought. It was only going to lead to pain on several different levels, most notably at the moment, a serious case of blue balls.

She looked up at me and our eyes met, that same old electricity passing between us. She swallowed. "We should go," she said.

"It's not over," I said back quietly.

Our gazes locked and her lips parted slightly. "Huh?" she asked.

I gestured my head toward the water. "The show," I said quietly.

She blinked as if coming out of a trance. "Oh. Well I...I work early. I should...get home..."

I cleared my throat. "Okay," I said, turning and leading her through the light crowd of people still watching the water.

We walked back to my truck, and I held the door open for her and took her hand to help her climb inside. Another rush of warmth passed through our hands and she glanced down at me quickly before pulling her hand away.

I exited the garage and started driving back toward Summerlin. We were both quiet, thinking our own thoughts. The lines of Grace's body looked tense in my peripheral vision. It was clear that we still had the same chemistry we'd had the last time we were together. I wanted to see her again. But how was that supposed to happen exactly? I hadn't asked a lot about her fiancé, but I figured although he might accept one dinner out with an "old friend," he'd probably question two. He'd also probably frown upon me kissing his fiancé up against the door of her house when I dropped her off. But I had gotten a few signals that, fiancé or not, Grace might not be completely opposed to that—at least not physically. I was remembering how she felt, how she tasted. Need was pumping through my blood and I couldn't do a damn thing about it.

As I pulled in to Summerlin, I glanced at Grace and she was chewing on her lip again. "What are you thinking?" I asked. As our time together was coming to a close, the mood between us had shifted.

"It's probably better if we don't see each other again," she said, twisting her ring.

"Better for whom?" I asked, a mixture of anger and fear filling my chest.

Her head snapped up. I could just make out her tense facial expression in the dark cab. I pulled up in front of her house and kept the engine idling.

"Better for me," she said. "Spending time with you tonight, it's brought up..." She trailed off.

"Brought up what, Grace?" I asked quietly, moving closer to her, her words making the anxiety in my chest fade slightly, hope taking over. This was my chance. I might not get another. "Feelings? Feelings that never faded?"

She closed her eyes for a couple beats. "Don't."

I stopped. "Don't what?"

She gave her head a shake. "Just don't," she whispered, her hand gripping the door handle as though she was going to flee.

Stay. Don't go.

"Call it off, Grace," I ground out, suddenly filled with

intense possessiveness and purpose. Fuck skating thin lines. I'd just trampled right over one. But… fuck… why would fate bring us back together only to have us part a second time? I didn't want to say goodbye to her again. There were reasons I should, I knew that. But all the reasons other than her damn fiancé seemed far away and unimportant.

Give her a reason to stay. Ask her not to go. You have something to offer her now, where you didn't before.

She choked out a bitter sounding laugh. "Call it off?"

"Yes, your engagement. Call it off," I said, moving in closer and putting my hand on the back of her neck and gently pulling her toward me.

Her eyes moved down to my lips and she didn't pull away. "Stop," she whispered, sounding desperate, her voice cracking.

I stilled, hissing out a breath, and then moved back, letting go of her. A small sound came from her throat right before she thrust her face into mine, taking her own hand and wrapping it around the back of my neck to pull me in closer. Our lips connected and a shuddery sigh passed between us. I had no idea who it originated from. All I knew was that the mixture of lust and relief that flooded my body at the feel of her mouth on mine was so intense that I vibrated with it.

She slipped her tongue into my mouth first as she scooted closer so that our chests were pressed together too. I swallowed the sexy sounds she made as our tongues met and tangled, tasting each other, stroking and caressing. I refamiliarized myself with the taste of her, the feel of her mouth moving on mine, the tiny sounds she made. God, I had missed this, everything about her, everything—

She pulled back on a small sob. "This isn't right. I knew you were going to do this to me," she said, her voice breaking.

I was silent for a second, gathering myself. A zing of hurt stabbed at my insides. "Do this to you?" I asked. "Buttercup, I think *you* were the one who jumped *me*."

Her eyes narrowed. "I…you! I…" She made a frustrated sound of anger in her throat and started reaching for the door of the cab.

I reached out and grabbed her hand. "Call it off," I repeated again, only this time I said it quietly, as gently as possible. This was all wrong. I wanted to pull her back into my arms and make my case. *Give me time. Call it off. Give me time.*

She stared at me for a couple beats, threw the door open, and fled inside her house. I watched her door close behind her.

I started up my truck and roared off. "Fuck!" I yelled. That had not gone well.

CHAPTER 24
Grace

I slammed my front door behind me and took a deep, shuddery breath. That had not gone well. The worst part was that it *had* gone well for a while there. Very well. I had had fun with him. I had laughed more than I had in a long time. But then that damn sexual tension slipped in and ruined everything. How had I even doubted that it would? This was Carson Fucking Stinger I was talking about here. I had duped myself again because I *wanted* to go out to dinner with him. I was such an idiot. And I had kissed him. *Oh my God*. That was cheating. I had cheated on Alex. And Carson was right—it had been *me* who jumped on him. I had told him to stop and he had, and then the stark disappointment that had rushed through me was so intense that I practically attacked him—as if I were suffocating and his mouth contained lifesaving air.

I had come to such a good place where Carson was concerned. We had parted the first time knowing we couldn't be a part of each other's lives, but under the circumstances, we had said goodbye on the best possible terms. And I had been thankful for the role he played in my life. When he came to mind, I thought of him with…fondness, I guess, and yes, perhaps some lingering sadness too. But now? Our most recent parting had not been on good terms. And just like that, my peace was totally disrupted.

I made my way over to my couch on legs that felt like rubber and sunk down onto it, not even bothering to take my jacket off.

I let out a short growl that faded away into a groan. Why did I have to run into him again? Why did he have to live in Vegas? And just around the corner for Pete's sake! I had been going along happy…*fine!* And suddenly he was back, shaking my life up, making me question things again, just like he had the first time. *Damn him!* I grabbed my phone out of my purse. I was going to call him and give him a piece of my mind. Who did he think he was exactly anyway? How arrogant could one person be? Asking me to call off my engagement five minutes after he walked back into my life? Seriously? The nerve! I stared at my phone and then threw it down on the couch when I realized I didn't even have his number anyway. I slumped back. That was probably for the best. Angry calling could be as bad as drunk texting. Bad idea all around. I went to my room and got ready for bed. This day needed to end.

My alarm went off at five a.m. and I dragged myself out of bed. I had not slept well. I was cranky and still deeply perturbed. I couldn't identify exactly what I was so restless about other than the fact that Carson had managed to tilt my world on its axis—*again*. I should have bolted out of that hotel like a bat out of hell the second I laid eyes on him, standing there in all his muscled, male beauty, flashing that damn dimple for good measure.

"Stupid dimple," I muttered through a mouth of foamy toothpaste.

I took a shower and wrapped a towel around my hair and my body, and then plunked myself down on my bed. *You're being overly dramatic, Grace.* Okay, so he had taken me off balance. But so what? All I had to do was make it clear to him that I was happy with my life. I was *not* going to call off my engagement for him, a man whom I had spent *one* weekend with once upon a time—a man I really didn't know when you got right down to it. Or did I? Well, anyway, that didn't matter.

I paused, confusion swooping in again as I considered what I knew about Alex, the man I was planning on spending my life with. I knew his family. They lived in San Francisco and I had met them several times when they visited Alex in Vegas. Lovely people. Upstanding. I knew that Alex had wanted to be a lawyer since he was a kid. He was kind, gave to charities, and loved to read cozy mysteries. He was a brilliant attorney. We never fought and he was always considerate. Was he boring like Abby had said? Okay, maybe a little, if I was totally honest. But so what? He was also stable and solid, and he didn't have my emotions in a constant free fall like *some* people did. I wouldn't hurt Alex—I couldn't.

How's the sex?

I shot up off the bed and dressed in my dark gray suit, and then did my makeup and hair, deciding to leave it down. Then I pulled my jacket on, grabbed a bagel, slid my heels on by the door, and locked up behind me. On the way to work, I pulled through a Starbucks drive-through and ordered a grande latte.

By the time I had drunk half my coffee, I felt better, calmer. I just needed to remember a few important facts. Carson had fulfilled his role in my life all those years ago. He'd been a positive influence. But he was my past. Alex was my future. Alex also wasn't a prior porn star like Carson, who probably had a different woman in his bed every night of the week. A horn blared, and I realized I'd started drifting into another lane and made a quick correction, my car whipping back the other way as the remainder of my coffee tipped onto the passenger seat. "Great!" I yelled. I gripped the steering wheel, feeling another surge of anger. I wanted to scream at him. Look what he was doing to me! I didn't even recognize this version of myself.

I made a spur-of-the-moment decision.

After a series of turns, I pulled into the garage at Trilogy. I needed to get this over with right now. He needed to know exactly how I felt about him. I would be kind but firm and reiterate to him the fact that I was *one hundred* percent certain about marrying Alex. I couldn't live, couldn't focus, if this wasn't put to rest. I just wanted my life to go back to the way it had been two days ago. *Easy. Calm. Predictable.*

I parked my car and made my way upstairs, weaving through the lobby and the casino until I was in the hallway where his office was located. The door was closed. Maybe he didn't even get in this early. I paused but took a deep breath and knocked twice on the door. I heard voices and some scuffling. A few seconds later, the door was pulled open and Carson was standing there in suit pants and a crisp, white shirt, a girl in a small, gold cocktail uniform appearing behind him, straightening her outfit. His eyes filled with surprise when he saw me.

"Thanks, boss," the girl said, stopping to wipe some

imaginary lint off Carson's shirt and then winking at him and stepping around us.

Carson nodded at her and turned back to me. "Grace. Hi." He smiled, leading me into his office and closing the door behind us.

"Were you…*in here*…with that girl?" I demanded.

Carson parked himself on the edge of his desk and crossed his arms, his biceps pulling the white cotton of his shirt tight.

Amusement, and something that looked like satisfaction, lit his eyes and he chuckled.

"What's funny?" I asked.

"You. You're jealous."

"Jealous?" I sputtered. "I'm not jealous. Why would I be? That's ridiculous. I just don't see how you could ask me to call off my engagement last night and then be in here with another girl this morning."

"Did you call off your engagement?" he asked quietly.

"What? No! No," I said, shaking my head. "Of course not."

"No?"

"No."

We stared at each other for a few beats, my pulse kicking up another notch and a tick starting in his jaw.

I stood taller, pulling forth my resolve and setting my hands on my hips. "I just came here to tell you we couldn't see each other again."

"You already told me that last night."

"Oh. Yes, well, I did, but I'm telling you again. To make sure you heard me."

"That's why you came here? To make sure I heard you?" he asked.

I nodded. "Mm-hmm. To make sure you heard me," I repeated, my words faltering slightly. *What are you doing, Grace?* I suddenly began doubting myself. *Why are you really here?*

"Yes, I heard you," he said. "I was two feet away from you when you said it, Grace."

I huffed out a breath. "Well, I know you heard me. But I want to make sure, you know, you *heard* me."

Carson's eyes narrowed, his chest rising and falling steadily. I could practically see the wheels turning in that head of his.

Suddenly, he stood up from the edge of his desk and stalked toward me. I backed up, but he kept coming until my back hit the wall. My pulse skyrocketed and I sucked in air. The delicious smell of him—clean soap and Carson Stinger—was suddenly all around me, intoxicating.

"Yes, I heard you, buttercup. Did you hear me when I told you I didn't agree?"

He leaned in toward me, taking one finger to lift my chin so that we were staring at each other eye to eye. He studied me for a few seconds. "Look at you, buttercup. You're all worked up—that brain of yours going a million miles a minute, isn't it? You've been trying to solve this *problem* since you jumped out of my truck last night, haven't you? Maybe since you walked out of this hotel yesterday afternoon. It's got you all twisted up, turned inside out. How'd you sleep last night, Grace? Did you want to shut that brain of yours off? Give the control over to me? Let me take charge until you were mindless, the only thing coursing through your system pure pleasure? Wouldn't that have been sweet relief, buttercup?" His voice was like silk, flowing over me, making me shiver with want. *This is why you're here, Grace. You know it is. He read you exactly right.*

I stared up at him as his eyes glittered down at me. Yes, I wanted that. God, I wanted that so badly I ached. I wanted him, needed him. The memory of what he could do for me was so vivid in my mind, I wanted to scream with frustration.

Carson moved closer, putting his hands on the wall to either side of my head and bringing his thigh up so that my core was resting on it. He reached a hand down and lifted my skirt so that I was pressed firmly against him. *Oh, God, oh, God.* My thoughts scattered and I moaned with the pleasure, pressing down harder, my eyelids fluttering closed. I couldn't *think* and it was blessed relief.

"Does he do this for you, Grace?" He leaned forward and whispered in my ear, "Do you scream out his name when you come?" My eyes felt heavy and I was vaguely aware that I was moving on his leg, bolts of pure arousal pulsating through me. God, it had been so long.

"Answer me, buttercup, does he do this for you?" Carson ground out, sounding angry now.

My eyes focused on him but skittered away at his question. He stilled and I cried out in frustration.

He brought his right hand down and nudged my chin again, turning my face until I was forced to look into his eyes. He studied me for a couple beats. "You haven't slept with him," he said finally, almost expressionless.

My eyes tried to look somewhere else, but the rest of his fingers came up to grip my chin, not allowing me to look away. "Why, Grace?" he breathed, his eyes so intense I felt like they would scald me.

I tried to shake my head. "I…I just…" I whispered.

He studied my face again for several seconds and he grunted, as if he was satisfied with something that he saw. And then his thigh started moving against my core again and I moaned. I was lost, the sweet relief of the mindlessness he was bringing me more addicting than any drug I could imagine.

"Do you want me to stop?" he asked. "If you do, just say the word, and I'll stop."

I shook my head from side to side. "No, don't stop. Don't stop," I breathed out, sweet, heady pleasure coursing through my veins.

As he moved, he started talking. "I'm not going to play games with you, Grace," he said, his voice smooth and low. "I got a whole lotta shit that I'm pushing aside, against my better judgment, to give things a shot between us."

His hands came down from the wall and moved up my rib cage, opening my jacket. "Why?" I breathed.

"Because apparently when it comes to you, I'm a damn fool," he said, but there was something close to tenderness in his voice even though my eyes had fluttered closed again.

His hands came up to my breasts and his thumbs rubbed my nipples through my thin blouse. I gasped, a surge of heat blossoming between my thighs. Something was... I should stop this. A shot between us? What? I... that... I just...I couldn't think. And I didn't want to.

"I never could purge you from my blood, buttercup," he whispered. I moaned. I could feel an orgasm just beyond my reach and I wanted it. I wanted it so badly, I was desperate. "I don't think I ever wanted to," he said, moving closer to my ear. "I want you to give us a chance too," he said.

He leaned in and started kissing up my neck, his lips as soft as butterflies against my skin, his thigh circling faster against my core, his thumbs moving over my nipples until I became aware of my own panting.

"Has anyone else fucked you as good as me, Grace?" he asked. I almost laughed. The nerve! But then he sped up his movements and all thoughts fled. Nothing mattered except the intense pleasure just beyond my grasp. "Answer me."

"No! No!" I admitted. "Ahhh. Oh God, Carson. There hasn't been anyone since you," I breathed out.

I felt his body give a small jolt, but then his movements resumed. "God, I like that," he growled into my ear and then kissed up my neck, licking and sucking the skin gently. The combined sensations of his thigh, his mouth and his hands tipped me over the edge, intense waves of pleasure making my muscles clench deliciously. I shuddered and just as I was about to scream, he plastered his mouth on top of mine, drinking in my moan and adding one of his.

The kiss slowed, and then he lifted his lips from mine. As I came down, my foggy brain clearing and reality rushing back in, I looked up dazedly into his eyes. Carson was gazing at me intensely, his eyes dark with hunger but with something tender too. I was mesmerized.

He opened his mouth to speak when there was a loud knock on the door. It jolted me fully back to reality. I gasped and started moving to the side, away from him, shimmying my skirt down over my hips as he lowered his leg and took a step back.

"Stay there," he said quietly. "Who is it?" he called.

"It's me, man," I heard from the other side of the door.

Carson swore under his breath and glanced over at me, his eyes running down my body as if checking me over for signs of what we'd just done. Then he walked to the door and pulled it open. "Hey, Leland. What's up?"

"They're almost here," I heard Leland say in response.

Carson paused and huffed out a breath. "Okay, I'll be right there."

I heard Leland let out a small laugh. "You got a woman in there or what?"

The reality of what had just happened become blindingly clear. *Oh my God.* I needed to leave. Immediately. I smoothed my skirt down and walked around Carson. "Um, if I have any more questions, I'll call you," I said, stepping around a large man about our age with dark, almost-black hair, wearing a navy blue suit. I caught the surprised expression on his face just as I turned and started walking quickly back up the hallway, toward the casino.

"Grace," Carson called, but I ignored him and sped up, my legs weak as I practically ran to my car.

As I pulled out of the garage and waited to turn onto the street, an entourage of black limousines and SUVs with international flags made their way across the intersection and pulled to a stop in front of Trilogy. I craned my neck to watch as Carson walked out the front doors of the hotel and shook hands with a man stepping from the first limousine. I supposed foreign dignitaries stayed in Vegas all the time. I looked away and turned in the other direction, driving away as quickly as possible. Surprisingly, my hands were steady on the wheel.

Carson

I was alone in the small room. I walked to the corner and stood the tiny Dixie cup upright. It had fallen over with my last throw. I moved back to my chair and sat down and aimed again.

"He shoots! He scores!" I said quietly as my dime plunked straight into the small cup.

I retrieved the dime and shot a couple more times, making each shot easily. I was bored. I stood looking at the closed door for a few seconds and finally walked over to it and turned the doorknob.

Someone was usually in here with me, but today there wasn't anyone. They hadn't had anyone extra to "babysit" me. I rolled my eyes. I was hardly a baby. I was eight years old. The man of the house.

I knew what my mom was doing and I didn't like it. It made my stomach hurt to know that she was under the covers with some man, naked, while they made a movie. She called herself an actress, but I had heard other people, people who whispered behind my back, call her a whore. I knew what a whore was. I knew it meant that she screwed people for money. But the worse part was, I knew it was true, so I couldn't defend her. I couldn't call them liars. Every time I asked her to stop doing the job she was doing, she would yell at me and ask me how else I expected to eat.

I knew it would also mean that she had to stop taking the pills and sleeping for most of the day.

I snuck around the corner and heard the music coming from the front room. I also heard grunts and other strange noises. I knew they were sex sounds and that I should go back to the room they had told me to stay in. But for some reason, my legs kept moving forward.

I peeked my head around the corner and my eyes grew big, and I put my hand over my mouth to keep myself from yelling. My mom was in the center of a bed and there were three men around her, all naked—

I turned away, and I choked out a small sound, tears springing to my eyes.

But I wanted to save her! I had to. Those men shouldn't be doing that to her. She was my mom. I turned and ran toward her and suddenly, those men were gone, and she was on the bed on her back and I was over her sobbing, "Mom! Mom!" She was beaten and half-dead, blood caked on her face. She looked up at me through cracked, swollen lids and...smiled. The sweetest smile I had ever seen. As she smiled, her face transformed, her features growing younger, becoming someone else. I could see that she was pretty, even despite the blood and the swelling. "Ara," I breathed out. It was Ara. I had another chance to save her. This time I would.

I shot up in bed, panting. My phone was ringing.

"Hello," I said, my voice both groggy and slightly panicked.

"Hey, Carson," Leland said. "Josh's bail was just set. Two million."

I closed my eyes for a beat. *Shit.* "Can we cover it?"

"We? No. Trilogy? Yes. I'm on my way to the bank now. I just wanted to let you know."

"Okay, keep me posted."

"Will do."

I hung up and collapsed back on my pillow, glancing at the clock quickly. I had slept in after working late the night before and then tossing and turning most of the night once I finally fell into bed. I stared up at the ceiling. *That fucking dream.* I'd had it before but not for a couple months now. I wondered if it was because Grace was back in my life—*sort of.*

Grace.

Josh was being taken care of, and so I took a minute to think about Grace as my heartrate returned to normal.

Had I messed up with her? Maybe. But I was having a hard time feeling too sorry about it because seeing her come again was fucking fantastic, even if it might have also worked to scare her off.

Kissing her in my truck the night before had just gotten me all crazy possessive—and fucking horny. Let's call a spade a spade. And so when she had burst into my office, talking about *him* again, I had taken charge in a way that I knew she'd probably respond to—and she had. And she'd asked me not to stop. But the fuck of it was, she probably regretted it. And that made me feel like shit.

What didn't make me feel like shit? The fact that not only hadn't she slept with her fiancé, she hadn't slept with anyone since me. But why? That was the question. There had to be something there. Something we needed to talk about. And the sooner, the better.

Grace lived in her head *a lot*, and she was hard on herself. I had known that about her an hour after meeting her four and a half years before.

I put my hands behind my head, picturing Grace. Now she was almost certainly walking around convincing herself that she was a bad person who had done something immoral to her fiancé, which wasn't entirely untrue. And that wasn't going to help my case. She was going to feel guilty now, and guilt didn't bode well for her telling him to take a hike like I had asked her to.

I swung my legs out of bed and headed toward the shower. I had to fix things. I wanted her. Plain and simple. I had told her that I was pushing a lot of shit aside to give the two of us a shot. That was true, but it wasn't... I *couldn't* push a lot of the shit I had going on aside, and some of it, I'd be asking *her* to push aside, or at least accept. The situation was complicated. But I knew how to multi-task if something was important to me.

If Grace would just tell me she wanted what I wanted, we could try to work through the complications together. But before that, I couldn't risk confiding in her. There was too much at stake. Yeah, we needed to talk.

CHAPTER 25
Grace

I brought my legs up under me and wrapped the blanket around my shoulders, leaning back on my couch. I had just gotten home from the office, after a twelve-hour day, pulled on my pj's, turned on the TV, and settled myself under a blanket. It was eight o'clock and I hadn't eaten dinner yet, and I was starving. But a few minutes of couch time felt like the priority. I felt… guilty and vulnerable.

God, I had told Carson I couldn't see him again and then humped his leg like some horny, little lap dog. Mixed message much? It was beyond humiliating. And wrong. I was a terrible person.

I was *supposed* to be a professional. I'd convinced myself I was. I showed up at work every day in conservative suits and sensible shoes. In court, I was efficient and confident. In my personal life, I paid my bills on time, called my dad at least once a week, was a good friend, a loyal girlfriend, and an all-around honest person. But enter Carson Stinger, and suddenly I was a crazed basket case. A nutjob. A lying, deceiving nutjob who let him manhandle me against his office wall. And he hadn't even had to work very hard to get me there. I had practically begged him. I didn't necessarily need a plan for every aspect of my life anymore, but I did like things well-ordered. And Carson's presence didn't even allow me to maintain that. I put a hand over my forehead and squeezed my eyes shut.

Beyond the embarrassment though, was sadness and shame. I had betrayed Alex. And worse, I had told Carson that I hadn't slept with Alex or anyone which wasn't only none of his business, but was going to give him the wrong idea.

How's the sex?

Nonexistent, actually. It wasn't that I wasn't attracted to Alex—it was just that everything had gone so fast for us. We had started dating practically the day I moved to Vegas, gotten engaged quickly, and were talking about getting married as soon as this spring. We had been intimate in other ways, of course. I just wanted to wait until we were married to have sex. I hadn't even told Abby we were waiting because I knew she'd give me flack. And okay, maybe it was a little old-fashioned, but why not? I thought it was romantic. And Alex, being the gentleman that he was, was okay with that. I thought the anticipation added some spice. I thought—

I was startled out of my thoughts by a loud, pounding knock on my door. Who the heck knocked like that?

I shrugged off the blanket and tiptoed to the door, standing to the side of it as I called, "Who is it?"

"It's me, Grace," I heard a deep voice say. *Crap!* Carson.

I stood there, biting my thumbnail for a minute, thinking about what I should do.

"Grace, please open the door," he finally said from the other side. "Please," he added again after a couple seconds.

I sighed and pulled the door open, the cool December night air chilling me as I stood there in my cotton shorts and tank top.

My gaze ran over Carson. He was wearing a pair of dark jeans and a leather jacket and he was so damn good-looking, I hated it. I really did. It made me bitter and also turned on. "What do you want, Carson?" I asked, folding my arms over my chest.

"Can I come in? I just want to talk for a minute and then I'll leave."

I paused but stepped back, allowing him entrance. I supposed we did need to put this to rest, since I hadn't exactly been very convincing the day before.

He walked past me and then stood waiting as I closed the door. I didn't lock it though. He'd be leaving soon.

I moved past him and parked myself back on the couch, bringing the blanket around me again. He took a seat on the opposite side of the couch, leaning forward, his forearms resting on his thighs as he studied me.

"Josh Garner made bail this morning," he said. "I guess you know that."

"Yes," I said back. "A bail bondsman posted it. It was pretty high. I wonder how he got it."

He gave a small shrug, but then remained quiet. It appeared he was struggling with whether to say something. Finally, he gave his head a shake and looked away. When he looked back, he said, "We should talk about yesterday morning. I owe you an apology."

I let out a breath. "Carson…" I leaned back, bringing my hands up over my face. I ran them back through my hair and met his eyes again before letting out a soft, humorless laugh.

"What?" he asked.

"You don't owe me an apology. I let you do what you…

did. I *wanted* what you did." I looked away as I felt my cheeks heat. "That was probably obvious. But it wasn't right. On *my* part. Not on yours. You're not the one who made promises to someone and broke them." Again, terrible person.

He was silent for a second, his forehead creased. "What I was trying to say with my apology," he said softly, "is that I'm sorry for coming on so strong." He paused, squinting very slightly as if he wasn't exactly sure if he really was sorry for that. "But I meant every word I said. Every word. No games on my part. I'd like to give us a chance."

I shook my head slowly. "Carson, you had just been messing around with a cocktail waitress in your office before I walked in."

He drew his head back and then burst out laughing. "I wasn't doing anything with Lara. She flirts relentlessly, but I've never touched her." He squinted. "You didn't come to that conclusion after what happened with us?"

Oh. And dammit. I hated that happiness uncoiled in my belly to hear that he hadn't been with *Lara* right before I'd walked in his door. Truth be told, I'd sort of been carrying the vision of the satisfied-looking cocktail waitress like a small shield. What we'd done had meant little. He gave women orgasms in his office all the time. I was just one of many in a long line-up. "How would I know that?" I asked sullenly. " It's been a long time, Carson."

"Whether you realize it or not, you know me better than just about anyone, buttercup." He paused. "And I think I know you better than anyone too. Even after all this time."

My mouth fell open. "Well, that's presumptuous. I think my fiancé knows me better than anyone."

As he stared at me, I saw a small tick in his jaw. "Are you sure about that?"

I narrowed my eyes. Again with the nerve. I knew exactly what he was referring to—the fact that Alex and I had a sexless relationship. Temporarily, of course. But now Carson was going to use it against me. Hostility felt good. Another shield to carry since I'd lost one in *Lara*. "I should have never told you that. It's none of your business and I refuse to speak about it with you again. God, look at us. We can't even spend three minutes together without fighting or kissing."

He laughed. "Is that such a bad thing?"

"Yes! Yes, it is. I need to focus… I need to…stop cheating on my fiancé!"

Carson's face went completely serious. "You're not in love with him, Grace. I don't want you to cheat on your fiancé either. Call it off." He looked into my eyes. "Let's figure out what's still between us. Is it really fair to the guy that you marry him when you still have feelings for me?"

My mouth fell open again. Carson had obviously changed in many ways, but that cocky self-assuredness was still there. Only, I had this inkling that where once it'd been at least somewhat contrived, now it was authentic. He'd come by it honestly through grit and—

A light knock sounded and I jumped while Carson's eyes flew to the door. "Expecting someone?" he asked.

"Oh my God, Alex said he might come by with dinner. I thought it had gotten too late. That's probably him," I hissed.

Carson stood, and I leaped up next to him. "Break it off with him, Grace," he said, taking a few steps toward the door. "For him. For you. For me."

"For the future of mankind?" I asked sarcastically.

A slow grin lit his face, and that dimple popped out. "Absolutely," he said. "The world needs us, Grace."

Ugh. He was so sexy. "Wait!" I whispered. "You can't open that door!"

He turned and made it back to where I stood in just a couple steps, taking my face in his hands. "I need to tell you one more thing before I go." His eyes searched mine as another soft knock sounded that we both ignored. "I haven't been with anyone else either. Not since you."

Huh? "What?" Was he joking? I was caught off guard, shocked. How could that possibly be true? In almost five years, Carson Stinger, sex-on-a-stick, hadn't been with anyone else? "Why?" He'd asked me the same question and I hadn't answered it, but it appeared that he would as he opened his mouth to speak. But just then, a second knock sounded, this time louder.

Alex. I came back to my senses. "This won't look good. Please, you need to go out the back door, Carson," I whispered. "Can you do it quietly?"

His lip quirked. "I might have some expertise in stealthy getaways, buttercup," he said, letting go of my face and walking backward away from me. "But next time, I'd like to leave through your front door." *Next time.* He opened the sliding glass door that led to the small patio at the back of my house and stepped outside.

I blinked and he was gone.

Carson

As I slunk around the side of Grace's house, I heard her front door open and a male voice say, "Dinner delivery! What took you so long to answer?"

He sounded like a fucking loser. Nah, that wasn't really fair. If Grace liked him, he was probably a decent guy. And that was the part that fucked with me even more. I really wanted to hate him, but why should I? He hadn't done anything wrong except not know how to sexually satisfy his woman. Which actually made me like the hell out of him. In this case.

"Oh, I was getting out of the shower!" I heard Grace lie. She was kind of bad at it, but apparently, the fiancé didn't pick up on that.

I walked to my truck, parked in front of her neighbor's house. I hated sneaking out like I was some kind of thief. But I had made it clear what I wanted. Now I just had to hope she figured out that she wanted the same thing.

I sat in my truck, watching their shadows move beyond the blinds. Maybe Grace and *Alex* weren't fucking, but I still bet he was in there holding her and kissing her. So yeah, maybe I could hate him.

I'd surprised myself by telling her about not being with anyone else since her either. I didn't even know if she'd believed me. I wanted to explain why. I wanted to tell her what I'd gone through. I longed to open up to Grace. I hadn't opened up to anyone since her—not in any true sense. The truth was, I just wanted her in every way possible, despite…everything.

Circumstance had been our downfall once. And fate had stepped in the second time I almost contacted Grace. But I would be damned if I wasn't going to take advantage of this opportunity now. I had a whole lot going on and so did she, and maybe in the end, we'd been put back in each other's lives for a different purpose and eventually we'd go our separate ways. But everything inside me fought against that idea. I knew what I wanted, and I was at least going to put up a fight. Now I just had to hope Grace came to the same conclusion.

I fired up my truck and turned onto the road that led to my house. All these years, I had thought of Grace and not known where she was, what was going on in her life. Now I knew she was five minutes from me. And in some ways, it hurt worse than knowing she was a continent away.

CHAPTER 26
Grace

Christmas was a week away. I immersed myself in last-minute shopping and work, including the Garner case. The trial was set for the end of January and so I had time to prepare, not that there was very much new evidence. The autopsy on the victim had come back and other than the obvious cause of death, a gunshot wound to her head, there was no physical trauma, no drugs in her system, and from what the ME could tell, she was a virgin. She hadn't been sexually molested so that ruled out that possible motive. But even without a motive, the DNA evidence was irrefutable. The accused's blood was at the scene on the rock, and the victim's blood was found on clothing at his apartment. Not to mention that the bullet removed from the victim was from Josh Garner's registered firearm. I didn't think we'd need to provide a motive with evidence like that.

There were no witnesses to prepare other than the ME and a DNA expert, so I felt like I was on top of the case. Which was good because I had taken a week of vacation time to go home for Christmas. Alex was coming with me and I couldn't wait to spend family time basking in the comfort of home and tradition. I needed it for the mental health care it would bring. I was in dire need of mental health.

I hadn't talked to Carson since he had left my house via the back sliding glass door a couple of days before. I needed space. Everything with him had come on so fast, so unexpectedly. *Just like the first time.* I guess that was just us. Not that there *was* an us. But still. I was emotionally discombobulated. And I was still feeling guilty and brittle over what I'd done to Alex, something I didn't have any intention of telling him about. We weren't married yet. Yes, technically, I knew I had cheated on him. But would it really hurt him if he never knew that once his fiancé had kissed another man? Oh okay, *and* had an intense orgasm on another man's muscular thigh as he held her up against his office wall? I groaned out loud in shame as I sat at my office desk. God, I hated myself.

Apparently, Carson was respecting the fact that I needed space from him because he hadn't contacted me. That was good. Although I was intensely curious about why he hadn't been with anyone else since me in almost five years. I wanted to ask him. And I had to admit to myself that a thrill raced up my spine whenever I thought about that. I was the last woman Carson had ever touched.

Was it simply because he had been overseas most of that time? That had to be it. Still, weren't there willing women in ports all over the world? And why hadn't he taken *Lara* up on her advances? What were his reasons? I shouldn't care so much about knowing. After all, I had my own life now—and my own man to think about. I shouldn't be thinking so much about Carson. But I simply couldn't help it.

I had also been wondering more and more if Carson had anything to do with the case against Josh Garner. They were friends who had a military history and had both moved to Vegas at the same time for essentially the same reason. That didn't mean Carson knew more than he had told Detective Powers when she interviewed him. But I got this strange feeling that he did. Add to that the fact that another teammate owned the hotel they both worked for and the large bail that had been posted, and questions kept rolling through my mind. Something nagged at my brain. There was a connection; I just couldn't fathom what it could be.

I sighed loudly and sat back in my chair. Getting away for a week would be good. I'd talk to my sisters—get a better perspective on this whole confusing, mind-boggling, distressing…

Unsettling…

Annoying…

Disruptive—I'd bust out the entire thesaurus as I explained the—*situation* to my sisters. It was just what I needed.

I worked until nine o'clock that night. Alex had started his vacation a day early as he'd put all his Christmas shopping off until the last minute and needed the day to hit the mall. How typically male. I wondered where Carson was spending Christmas. I knew about his mom, and if their relationship was still the same as it'd been when I first met him, then surely he wouldn't be going back to LA. I sighed, trying to clear the constant thoughts of Carson away. Whatever he was doing for Christmas was not my business.

When I got home that night, I immersed myself in laundry and packing and by the time I was done with that, I was exhausted. Alex would be picking me up at five the next morning in order to catch our flight. I was so tired and yet I lay in bed for hours, unable to sleep, watching the reflection of my neighbor's Christmas lights twinkle beyond my curtain.

Carson

I sat across from Josh as he leaned back on the couch in the condo I had delivered him to secretly. No one had followed us here, I was sure of that. Leland had just called to make sure we had arrived safely and I'd assured him we had.

"How are you doing?" I asked Josh.

He sighed. "Great, Carson. The last couple weeks have been like a dream come true."

I frowned, not in the mood to banter with him. "What happened, Josh? We weren't supposed to split up. Number-one rule."

"Yeah, no shit. I fucking made up that rule," he said bitterly.

I studied him. The guy was on trial for first-degree murder. I was gonna give him a break. "What happened?" I repeated.

He sighed, scrubbing his hands down his face. "You guys were on your way out with the merchandise. I was clearing the last room of the warehouse when I heard a girl crying. I thought we had missed one. I turned back and went to investigate, and lights out, man. The next thing I knew, I was waking up in some abandoned house with a lump on my head the size of a beach ball. I made it home and the police were knocking at the door an hour later. That's all I know."

I took a deep breath. "Just like we thought. An ambush.

Fuck. You know we went back in for you, right? We realized you were gone and went back in for you. You had disappeared like a ghost."

"I know you'd never leave a man behind. I didn't question that for a second."

I gave a quick nod. "He knew we were coming."

"Yeah. And he fucking shot a girl in the head, Carson."

"He's a sick fuck. We already knew that."

He frowned and then laced his fingers together behind his head and leaned back. "Yeah. No surprise."

I studied him for a second. "All right. I gotta get out of here. We *are* going to get through this. Dylan is working on it; we're all trying to figure this out. We're gonna get a break, okay? We've got your back."

Josh closed his eyes for beat. "Never doubted it for a second." He looked up at me. "Thanks, Carson."

I nodded and stood up. "Stay put. Anything you need will be delivered. The police know where you are, but no one else does and you cannot come near Trilogy. No going out to pick up some woman. No going next door to meet your pretty neighbor. Stay put."

"Sounds like fun," he said. "Merry fucking Christmas." But when I frowned at him, he said, "Yeah, yeah, stay put. I got it."

"Hey, beats MREs in a cave, right?"

He chuckled softly. "Barely. But yeah."

I said goodbye and left the condo. Twenty minutes later, I was pulling into the garage at Trilogy.

I walked into Leland's office later that night. "Are you taking off?" he asked.

I sat down in the chair across from him. "I don't know if I should. If there's anything—"

"There's not. If you stay here over the holiday, you'll just end up pacing in your office. It's better if we don't show our faces very much. Dylan is staying here to work on the digital side of things, but there's nothing any of us can do to help him with that. Plus, if anything comes up, you're only six hours away. It's probably best that you get out of town."

"All right. Are the girls all taken care of?"

"Yeah. I wish we had gotten them all out before the holiday. I don't like to have to keep the guards posted over Christmas. But that's the way it goes. We just didn't get the paperwork in time. Dylan did everything he could."

"I know. Sucks, but another week and it'll all be worked out."

"Right. Have a Merry Christmas, man." He stood up and walked around his desk to shake my hand and clap me on the back.

"You too, Leland."

"I will. Drive safely."

Back in my office, I grabbed my duffel bag and then made my way to my truck. Fifteen minutes later, I was driving out of town.

I wondered where Grace was spending Christmas. She hadn't contacted me since the night I left her house. I wasn't going to harass her. She knew what I wanted. The ball was in her court. Still, it left a knot in my gut. I had a shitload of stuff going on and I still couldn't stop thinking about her. Getting out of town was going to help—or so I hoped.

I pressed down harder on the accelerator, putting Vegas behind me as quickly as I could.

CHAPTER 27
Grace

"I swear I forgot something," I said to Alex for the fifth time.

"Sweetie, you've gone through the list. You didn't forget anything. And if you did, you can replace it when we get there. Relax." He patted my knee.

"You're probably right," I murmured as the plane doors opened and the line of people started to move forward. "Yeah…" I trailed off as we both stood up.

Alex grabbed our small suitcases from the overhead bin, and I moved out in front of him, taking the handle of mine and pulling it up so that I could wheel it behind me.

I had woken up feeling distracted and just *off*. Maybe I was coming down with a bug. I was going home for the first time in a while and I should be feeling relaxed and excited. Instead, I couldn't shake a nagging feeling that I had left something behind, something necessary. Something vital.

What's so vital that you can't borrow it from Audrey or Julia, or pick it up at the mall?

It didn't help that I had tossed and turned all night, sleep evasive, those glittering lights lulling me into mindlessness, but not enough to drift off. I was overtired, that had to be it.

Plus, I *was* just a little nervous about this trip. Alex had only met my family once, when they came to Vegas after I'd first moved there. We had just started dating at that point and we all went out to dinner. So this was a chance for Alex to really get to know them better. Which was *good*…right?

We had an hour layover before our next flight to Dayton, and so we decided to get a bite to eat at one of the restaurants near our boarding gate.

We stepped onto an escalator and started descending and I glanced over at the people traveling upward, an old woman catching my eye. *I've seen you before.* She smiled at me and winked. I blinked, something so familiar about her… I craned my neck as she moved upward and away from me, but she didn't look back.

As we traveled through the airport, we passed a little girl sketching in a notebook. Just as we walked by her, she smiled and held it up to her mother who was standing in front of her. I turned my head to see what it was and time slowed, my heart constricting as I saw the delicate, little, yellow flower she had drawn. It looked like a… I snapped my head forward, time resuming as I kept moving.

When we got to the terminal where our gate would be boarding, we sat down at a table in a food court, and Alex went to place an order at an eatery that served soup and sandwiches.

As I sat there waiting for him, I looked around. A man sitting at a table near the entrance, with his back to me, caught my eye. Short, dark-blond hair and broad, muscular shoulders. My heart rate picked up and I sucked in a breath. *Carson?* It couldn't be. How? I started to stand, just as he did too, and air lodged in my chest. As he turned toward me, deep disappointment hit me and I sank down in my chair, deflating. It wasn't him.

You know what you left behind, don't you, Grace?

You know what's missing... what's been missing all these years.

My hand gripped the table edge. I stared straight ahead for several minutes, the truth of what I was feeling washing over me. *Oh God...* It hit me, sitting right in the middle of a food court in the Atlanta airport. It was Carson I was missing. It was Carson I was *wanting.* Carson. The one who made me feel out of control in so many ways—the one who was anything but *safe.*

Realization dawned like the first light of sunrise bursting over the horizon. It hadn't been our time so many years ago in Vegas. We'd still had things to accomplish, growing to do. But... we'd been given a second chance. *Now.*

Take it. Hold on tight. Don't let him go this time.

My eyes moved to Alex standing at the counter waiting for our order. Alex. *Oh, Alex.* I had chosen him because he was almost the exact opposite of Carson. And I had been afraid that if I didn't choose someone who was blatantly different in every way, that I would always compare the man I ended up with to the man I really wanted. I released a breath of regret. I'd made a mistake. A big one. Not one that was only going to hurt me, but one that was going to hurt Alex too. But I owed it to him... I owed it to him to tell him the truth before he wasted one more second with a woman who didn't love him enough. I hadn't done it with realization or malice, but the truth was, I'd treated him like a consolation prize. Alex and I should have just been friends all along.

Call it off.

Alex turned and headed my way, a tray of food and two water bottles in his hands.

He sat down and started doling out the order.

"Alex," I said, reaching across the table and taking his hand. He stopped moving, looking down at it in surprise.

"What's wrong?" he asked, obviously having heard the seriousness in my tone.

"Do you love me, Alex?"

He gave me a small, confused smile. "Of course I do. You know that."

I closed my eyes momentarily, giving my head a shake. "No, I mean, do you feel passionate about me?"

He let out a short laugh, pulled his hand away and uncapped his water bottle. "I'm not the most passionate person, Grace. You know that."

Right. He was far too rational for passion. Only..."I don't think that's true," I said.

He took a drink of water and then set the bottle on the table. "Huh?"

I grabbed both his hands this time, nearly knocking the bottle off the table. "I think there's passion in you, Alex. If you meet the right woman, the one who knows how to bring that out, the one who sets fire to your soul, the one who knows how to save you from yourself. Oh, Alex, you deserve that, and I believe she's out there."

He brought his head back, looking at me like I was crazy. "She? What are you saying, Grace?"

"I can't marry you, Alex," I whispered.

"You can't...what? What's going on here?"

I closed my eyes for a couple beats. "I'm so sorry. I wish I had realized this sooner."

He took a deep breath and then resumed splitting the

food between us. "Grace, you're nervous about having me spend quality time with your family. It's normal. It's a big step. Almost as big as getting engaged."

I shook my head. "No, please. Listen to me."

He stilled, looking up into my eyes, obviously seeing that this wasn't some cold feet situation that he should simply wait to pass. "Okay, I'm listening," he said quietly.

I licked my lips, my heart beating loudly in my ears. "I'm so sorry. I love you too... I really do. But not enough." *Like a friend. Or... a brother. Oh, God, Abby was right.*

His eyes moved over my face. "You're not *in* love with me? Is that what you're saying?"

My shoulders crumpled. "No, I'm not." I looked into his eyes. "And I think, Alex, if you really search your heart, you'll realize that we were never right for each other as more than friends."

He tilted his head, but didn't reply. I could see he was taking stock of this, evaluating the facts as he knew them, sifting quickly through the evidence he might have overlooked, coming up with an argument, or perhaps determining if there was an argument to be made.

"I never ever wanted to hurt you," I whispered. "If I had figured this out before now, I wouldn't have done it in the middle of an airport right before Christmas. Because I know this is shitty, Alex. But now that I've admitted the truth to myself, I can't possibly keep it from you. You deserve to know."

He let out a long, slow exhale. Sadness filled his expression. Hurt. He looked away and then tapped the pads of his fingers on the edge of the table for a moment. I sat still, waiting for him to digest what I was telling him, to make his argument if that's what he'd decided to do. After a minute, he met my gaze again. "Maybe I'm not completely surprised by this," he said.

"You're not?"

He shook his head. "No. You've been distant lately, distracted. I noticed it, Grace, and it made me wonder why it didn't bother me more. I'd decided to think about that after the holidays, when I had more free time."

Rational Alex. It almost made me smile. Even if he was slightly passionless—at least for me—he really was a good person and I really did care about him.

"And maybe you're right," he went on. "I don't know. The timing has kind of taken me by surprise here." He paused, studying me again. "Is there someone else?"

I closed my eyes for a couple beats. "Yes. But he isn't the reason why we shouldn't get married." *It's just that he challenges me... He excites me... He saves me from myself in ways big and small.* It was becoming clearer and clearer by the moment. I hated hurting Alex, but this was *right*. I knew it was.

"Who is he?" Alex asked.

"Someone from my past... It doesn't matter. He's not the reason we're not right together. He just helped me to see what I already knew deep inside."

"Would you be breaking up with me if he didn't exist?"

"I think so, yes. Maybe not today, but yes. I'm so sorry," I repeated.

He paused, staring off behind me. After a minute, he said, "Maybe this is right, for both of us. It still doesn't make it easy. Especially in the middle of an airport."

"I know... I just, I couldn't pretend everything was fine this week..." I said, a lump forming in my throat, my words dying.

We stared at each other across the table, and though

there was pain in his expression, there was also understanding, and I thought… a glimmer of… relief. Maybe he didn't even realize that that emotion was skating at the edge of whatever else he was feeling, but I was pretty sure that in a short amount of time, he would. I blew out a breath. After a minute, he said, "Work…"

"I'll find a new job if you want me to. I'd never make this worse for you. I—"

"Of course I don't want you to quit your job. I actually… well, I was going to talk to you about this when we got back from Ohio, but I was offered an assistant DA position in San Francisco, near my family. I didn't know how you'd feel about possibly moving…"

"You mean, you're considering taking it?" I asked softly.

"Well, like I said, I was going to talk to you, but…yeah, I was hoping you'd agree to move."

"Oh."

He cleared his throat. "Anyway, it might be right for both of us…"

"Alex, really, if you want to stay in Vegas and you think it would be awkward to work with me—"

"No, I think we're mature enough to work together. That's not it. I just…well, I have a lot to think about."

I nodded. "Okay, but if you change your mind about me leaving the office, will you tell me? I care so much about you."

"I know you do," he said sadly. He looked down for a second. "I'm going to get a flight to San Francisco from here and join my family. Will you be okay flying by yourself the rest of the way to Dayton?"

"Yes. Of course." I slid the ring off my finger and held it out to him.

He took it from me, staring at it for a moment before putting it in his pocket. Then he stood, grabbed his still-wrapped sandwich, pulled the handle up on his suitcase, and walked around the table. He kissed me softly on the top of my head and said, "Be happy, Grace."

I watched him walk off and wiped away a tear. As sad as I felt, I knew what I'd done was right. I had fooled myself into thinking it was a good choice to marry someone I had lukewarm feelings for. And that had been deeply unfair to Alex too. He was a good man. He deserved to find a woman who brought out the best in him—and especially that passionate side he swore he didn't have. You be happy too, Alex.

I sat for a few minutes longer, coming to terms with what had just happened, when suddenly it registered what song was playing over the airport sound system. Celine Dion's "My Heart Will Go On" played softly beneath the clanking of trays and the sound of chairs scooting across the tile floor. I laughed a soft laugh. As the song continued to play, my nerve endings began vibrating with purpose.

I knew what I was going to do. I wasn't going to go to Dayton. I had a flight to change.

I had to pay a hefty fee, but I was able to book a flight back to Vegas that left a couple hours later. My body was humming with anxiety, but I also felt filled with gleeful anticipation, the knowledge that this choice was right singing in my blood. I was going to Carson.

Call it off. Give us a chance.

I wondered if I should call Trilogy and get ahold of him before I just showed up there. But I somehow knew it would be better to go to him in person, to explain my feelings while standing right in front of him. He had been brave, as usual, and put it right out there that he wanted us to try again, to try for real this time. And I had pushed him away not once, not twice, but all three times he made his feelings known to me. I'd had a good reason—another person's feelings to consider. But still, it had to have been hard for him to lay his pride on the line and to be rejected. I wanted to look in his eyes when I told him that I wanted him too. *I have always wanted him.* If I had been honest with myself, I would have known as soon as I looked in his eyes again that I had never stopped.

As I waited for my flight to board, I took my phone out of my purse and dialed Julia's number.

"Hey, Sis," she answered. "I thought you'd still be flying right now."

I cleared my throat. "I'm actually about to board my flight, Jules," I said, "um, back to Vegas."

There was a slight pause. "Why? Is everything okay?" she asked worriedly.

"Well, yes and no. I broke up with Alex."

"Oh, Gracie, I'm so… I mean, are you okay?"

"Yes, I'm good, Julia. We…weren't right together. It took me a little while to figure it out, and I'm sad about that but relieved too." I took a deep breath. "Anyway, I'm headed home, and, Julia, I'm nervous to tell you this, but I'm heading home because Carson Stinger is back in my life—you know, the man I spent a weekend with almost five years ago. And he's not a porn star anymore. He's a SEAL, or rather, a former SEAL who now works in security, and I, well, he wants me, I mean, I hope he still wants me." I paused. "My behavior toward him, well, it wasn't awesome. I've been all over the map because I was confused and… anyway, I want him too and I'm going home to tell him that.

And I hope you all will forgive me for ruining Christmas, but I have to do this because he taught me to follow my heart. And I am, and he's my heart." I started crying at this point, but I couldn't stop talking. "He's had my heart all this time, Jules, and I carried that and deep inside it scared me so badly because I didn't think I could ever have him again. But—"

"Grace!" Julia came over the phone and I heard the laughter in her voice, but then I heard a little sob in the background.

"Am I on speaker?" I whispered.

Julia and Audrey started laughing and crying and talking over each other.

"People! I can't even hear what you're saying. Audrey, I didn't even know you were there." I shot a look over my shoulder. Thankfully, no one was close enough to hear my teary rambling.

Audrey's voice came over the line. "Go get him, Gracie!" she laughed. "Alex wasn't for you. We knew that when we met him in Vegas."

"Why didn't you say anything?" I cried.

"Because we didn't know you'd get engaged to him! And then we felt bad. We were going to try to bring it up this week. But it would have been hard because he would have been here.... We, oh, it all worked out! Go get your guy, Grace. We'll talk Dad down from the ledge."

I laughed but then groaned. "Oh God, Dad. Will you tell him how sorry I am and that I'll explain? Tell him I'll call him as soon as I can, okay?"

"Don't call him too soon. We got this. Give him some time. It'll be fine. But you know Dad. He blows up first and asks questions later."

"Yeah, I know. Thank you so much. I love you both so much."

"We love you too," they said together.

I hung up and went to the restroom to clean myself up. An hour later, I was boarding my flight back to Las Vegas. *Back to Carson.*

I touched down in Vegas at seven o'clock that evening. I had been traveling all day and I was right back where I had started, and yet the course of my life had just changed dramatically. Alex had driven us to the airport, and so I took a cab back to my house to get my own car.

I wished I knew exactly where Carson lived. I would go there first to see if he was home. But if he wasn't at Trilogy today, hopefully they would call his home number for me and I could get in touch with him that way.

As I drove out of my neighborhood and toward Trilogy, a case of nerves attacked me. What if he had changed his mind and decided that he didn't want me anymore? No, that couldn't be the case, could it? Surely that wouldn't have changed in less than a week?

He hadn't been with anyone else in all this time. A lump formed in my throat and I didn't know whether to laugh or cry when I considered the fact that neither one of us had had sex with anyone else since each other. I had half a mind—and plenty of hormones—to make that the first priority, right after I told him I wanted him.

But my head was clear and the confusion and guilt that had been clouding things ever since I laid eyes on him again vanished. He was mine. And I wanted to be his. That was all I needed to focus on right now.

The only challenge left between us—I hoped—was what was going on with him and this case I was working. I couldn't figure it out, and I knew that if things were going to go anywhere with us, we'd need to talk. Somehow though, that didn't feel like the immediate priority. Suddenly, I knew with every fiber of my being that whatever he'd have to tell me, wasn't anything that was going to make me run. I trusted him. I trusted the man that he was. Despite the time and the distance, I knew he was good and decent. I *knew* it.

I pulled into the garage at Trilogy and rode the elevator up to the lobby and then made my way through the casino to Carson's office. With each step, my heart rate quickened and my excitement grew.

His office hallway was deserted and his door was closed. I stopped in front of it, and pulled in a deep breath before I knocked lightly and waited. No answer. I knocked one more time, but when it became clear that he wasn't in, I turned around haltingly, feeling disappointed. I guess I could go to the front desk and find out if he was in at all—maybe somewhere else in the hotel or casino.

As I started walking away from Carson's office door, a tall, young, blond man wearing glasses turned the corner toward me. His eyes traveled over me and he smiled a warm smile. I smiled back and when I noticed that he was going toward Carson's door, I said, "Oh, do you work with Carson?"

He stopped. "Yeah, can I help you?" he asked.

"Um, well, I don't know. I'm looking for Carson, but he's not in his office—"

"No, he's gone for a couple days. He'll be back next week. Do you want me to leave a message on his desk? I was just going to leave some other paperwork in there for him."

Back next week? My heart dropped and my shoulders sagged. "Oh," I said.

The man was looking at me closely. "Wait, are you Grace?"

"Yes. How did you—"

"I'm Dylan," he said. "I work with Carson now, but I also lived with him in LA, before he went into the navy."

"Oh!" I said, surprised and still not fully understanding how he knew my name but finding it interesting that another friend of Carson's worked at Trilogy.

"Well, it's nice to meet you, Dylan. Do you know where Carson went or how I can call him? I just wanted to...tell him something kind of important."

He paused. "I do know where he went, but you won't be able to reach him by cell. I've tried a few times today and evidently he isn't getting reception."

"Oh," I said again, tilting my chin down and frowning. "Okay, well, can I leave you my phone number so you can give it to Carson if you get ahold of him?"

He paused, looking like he was considering something. Finally he said, "This *something* that you have to tell him, will he be happy to hear it?"

I gave a small laugh, holding back the tears that threatened. "I think so," I whispered. "I hope so."

He studied me again for a few seconds before saying, "Well, Grace, if you're up for a six-hour drive, I can tell you where he is. If I know Carson, and I do, I'm pretty damn positive he wouldn't mind that."

I straightened. "Really?" I asked, my heart lurching. He had the address where Carson was!

He chuckled. "Yeah. What kind of car do you have?"

"Um, a Honda Accord."

He shook his head. "That won't work. Switch with me. I have four-wheel drive. Just take care of her."

He turned back in the direction of the casino and gestured for me to follow him.

I ran to catch up, asking, "Where is he exactly, Dylan?"

He glanced at me as we walked toward the elevators to the garage. "He rented a cabin in Snowbird, Utah. Wait until you see that boy snowboard." He grinned and held the garage door open for me.

"He rented a cabin to go snowboarding by himself?"

He nodded. "That's Carson for you. He hasn't been in the snow since he was discharged. He was itching for it. We're all working, so none of us could go with him."

"We?" I asked.

He nodded as he stopped next to a large black SUV. But he ignored my question and instead handed me his keys. I took them, hesitating only briefly before digging around in my purse for my own. I was giving my car to Carson's friend—a stranger. I held back the smile that threatened at the knowledge that once again, I was tossing all plans and reason for Carson.

I pointed up the row of cars and hit my electronic door lock, making my car lights flash. Dylan looked at me and nodded, taking my keys.

"Hand me your phone," he said. I did, and then he took a few minutes and programmed something in, looking between his own phone and mine.

"I put the address of the cabin he's staying in into your GPS. I put my phone number in there too, just in case you need to reach me."

I blinked as I took my phone back. I was beyond grateful for his help and his kindness, but I was confused. This was the first time I'd ever met this man. And if he knew my name, surely he knew that I was the prosecutor on Carson's—and possibly his friend's—case. "Why are you doing this, Dylan?"

He returned his phone to his pocket "I'm not sure, Grace. But it feels right." With that, he smiled and walked off, calling behind him, "Drive safely."

Carson

I threw another log on the fire, watching as it jumped and sparked, forming shadows on the walls. I sat back down on the leather couch, lacing my fingers behind my head and leaning back. It was early morning, still dark out, and the temperature was near freezing.

I had always been an early riser, but after being in the military, it was a habit that was even more ingrained.

I had been snowboarding all day yesterday and my muscles were still a little sore. But God, I had missed it. And apparently it was just like riding a bike because after an hour or two, I felt all my skills return.

I felt a little bit guilty about enjoying something so much with everything Josh was going through, but Leland was right—there was nothing we could do right now except pace the floor. At least Josh was free of the cage they'd put him in and we knew for now, he was safe. This was a stress outlet for me and in the end, it would help Josh if we all were on our best mental game.

Out the window, the first light of day was casting the woods in a silvery glow. I watched it for a few minutes as the snow sparkled and the trees took shape.

My mind returned to Grace for the tenth time since I had gotten out of bed. I knew the ball was in her court, but it didn't stop me from thinking about her all the damn time. I didn't know what I'd do if she didn't contact me when I got back, but my choices were limited. For now, I had to trust. It was all I had.

My head rose when I heard a light scraping sound coming from the front door, my muscles immediately primed. I stood quickly and grabbed my gun from the drawer of a side table. I didn't expect trouble, but it was always good to be prepared, especially with everything going on in Vegas.

I started walking quietly toward the front door when a knock came and a female voice called out weakly, "Carson?"

I froze. Was that…*Grace? What? How?* There was no way. I had just been thinking about her—my mind must have conjured her up somehow. Even so, wild hope made me feel momentarily woozy. I stuck the gun in the waistband of my jeans and headed to the door.

"Carson?" I heard called again, louder this time. *Holy shit. It is. Grace.*

I flung the door open, the sunrise blaring in at me, almost blinding. And there she was, standing in front of me, cheeks flushed bright red, her long, blond hair wet and covered by snow, shivering violently, with one boot on.

What the…? I grabbed her in my arms, pulling her inside. "Grace, what…? How?" I didn't even know what to ask first. My mind was going in ten directions.

She grabbed my face in her freezing cold hands, her eyes moving over my features. "I never let go, Carson."

"What, Grace?" I asked, confused and filled with worry. She had hypothermia. She was delirious. And how was she *here?*

She shook her head, trying again, "Never let go, baby," she said. "I never did. I never let go. Of that weekend. Of you." Tears made her eyes sparkle and she made a strange sound that was a sort of laugh, but mostly a sob. Then she tried to smile but her teeth were chattering so violently that it looked like a terrifying grimace. "You… save me from… myself. You… thrill me and you… scare me, but in a good way that makes me… throw all caution—"

"Grace," I breathed, pulling her into my arms as the understanding of why she was here lit my heart and caused a lump to fill my throat.

"I never let go," she repeated at my ear. "I never let go."

I scooped her up in my arms and carried her inside, kicking the door shut behind us.

CHAPTER 28
Grace

Carson sat me down in front of the fire and took my drenched jacket off. He grabbed a blanket from the couch and wrapped it around my shoulders. My teeth were chattering so loudly, I could barely hear my own thoughts.

"Grace, baby," he said softly, "what happened? How are you here?"

"I called it off," I said.

His eyes moved to mine as he peeled off my wet socks. They were filled with surprise. With joy. With hope.

"I was flying home for Christmas when I realized," I chattered out. "I knew it all along, but…I just…I realized in the middle of the airport and I told Alex. We weren't right together, Carson. We never were. I think he knows that too. So I broke up with him and I flew home, and I went to Trilogy to find you, to tell you." I was crying again. "To tell you that all these years… all this time, I never really let go. I never did."

He was rubbing my freezing feet between his hands now

as he gazed at me, watching me as I talked, that same gentle expression on his face.

"Your friend Dylan told me where you were and he gave me his car."

"Really?" He grinned and shook his head slightly. "Damn I love that guy. Stay put." He stood up and walked out of the room, and when he returned a minute later, he had a towel in his hand and he began tenderly drying my hair.

"Keep going," he said gently. "Get to the part where you lost your boot."

My shivering had mostly stopped now and warmth was flowing to my extremities, the heat from the fire seeping into my cold flesh. I sighed and wrapped the blanket around me more tightly.

"Well, as I started getting closer to you, I got distracted, and…I ran out of gas. I was just down the hill from here though. I was able to pull Dylan's SUV to the side of the road and I walked the rest of the way."

Carson frowned at me. "You could have been hurt," he said.

I reached up and put my hand on his cheek, the slight stubble there rough against my skin. He closed his eyes for a couple beats, leaning in to it. "I didn't get hurt. Just cold. And I lost my boot a couple hundred feet from your door, and I didn't care. I just kept going because the sun was coming up and"—I let out a small sob moving my face closer to his—"I told you the sunrise would always remind me of you, and it has, all this time, all these years."

"Did you wake up to see a few?" he asked teasingly.

I laughed softly. "Yeah. More than a few. Because I felt you with me each time I saw one."

He closed his eyes again for a second and kissed my

lips gently and then kissed each one of my eyelids and my nose. "Me too. You've come to me with the sunrise all these years too."

I sniffled as I found his full lips and rubbed mine over his softly, not tasting, just feeling, soaking in his warmth, his presence.

"I never let go, but I still turned into a human popsicle," I said softly.

Carson laughed, his eyes twinkling. "On the positive side, I think I'm cured. No more cinematic therapy needed," he said.

We both smiled into each other's eyes, warmth shining from his. He smoothed my hair back. "We have so much to catch up on," he said quietly.

I nodded. We had time.

"But first, I'm taking you to the hot tub, and then to my bed," he said.

"Yes," I whispered, desire coursing through my suddenly very-warm veins. "Yes."

He pulled me up from the couch and I took his hand as he led me to a door at the back of the cabin. Then he grabbed a couple large towels on a shelf behind him. "Take off your clothes and wrap this around you. It'll be cold for a couple seconds but it'll be worth it, I promise."

He started removing his clothes and when he pulled his long-sleeved T-shirt over his head, I gulped down a lump that got stuck in my throat. He had been beautiful before, but now...I didn't even know real-life men looked that way. He was all sleek, hard muscle, not an ounce of fat on him, covered in smooth, golden skin. He looked so *large*, standing before me, like some kind of god. "Carson, you're...so..." I said, staring unabashedly at his naked chest and then moving

322

my eyes down to his tented boxers. "We can skip the hot tub," I suggested.

Carson chuckled. "No, you need it—not just for the warmth but for the relaxation. At least for a few minutes. You've been driving all night," he said gently.

I noticed the small scar to the left of his heart, near his shoulder. It must be where the bullet exited from his body. I closed my eyes briefly as it hit me all at once that if things had been just a little different, I might not be here with him at all. I leaned in and kissed the scar and when I straightened, Carson's eyes were warm and tender, but he didn't say a word.

He reached for the hem of my sweater and started lifting it. I closed my eyes as it came over my head and then reached down and unbuttoned my jeans. My eyes tangled with Carson's and heat flared in his, making the hazel color deeper.

My jeans were damp, so it took a minute to get them down far enough that I could step out of them. Then I stood back up as his gaze roamed my body, covered only in a black bra and underwear. "So damn beautiful," he murmured.

He'd always made me feel beautiful, and so desired. Time had done nothing to change that.

I reached in front of my breasts and unhooked my bra. It fell open and Carson's eyes drank me in as a small groan came up his throat.

He reached out and pulled the straps down my shoulders and let my bra fall to the ground. My nipples pebbled under his hot stare.

As his eyes traveled over me, he whispered, "You take my breath away."

God, I was already turned on by a simple striptease. A less than elegant one considering the dampness of my clothing. And apparently, having very recently been a human popsicle did nothing to cool my blood. At least not under Carson's slow perusal and the way he sucked at his bottom lip as his gaze roamed my body. Maybe it was also that it had been so long. And that this time, he was mine. We hadn't discussed it specifically, but I knew it was true. He was mine and I was his. That knowledge alone was a heady aphrodisiac.

We both reached down simultaneously and removed our bottoms, each watching the other. His cock sprang free and unconsciously, I clenched my thighs together and shivered, not with cold but with arousal. Carson quickly secured a towel around his hips and then wrapped another around me before he picked me up in his arms. I laughed and he smiled. "I don't want your feet to get cold again," he said, and then he used one hand to unlock and open the back door.

The blast of cold, snowy air hit us and I wrapped my arms around him, putting my face in the crook of his neck, breathing him in and humming contentedly at the scent of his skin right against my nose, that individual smell that I would recognize until the day I died.

I couldn't help darting my tongue out to taste him there. He tasted slightly salty and I relished it on my tongue. I wanted to taste him everywhere.

A small growl came from his throat and a slight tremor moved through his body as he walked to the hot tub a few feet away.

As I climbed in the hot, steamy water, he placed our towels underneath a bench behind him and pressed a button to turn on the jets.

Oh, God, heaven. As I sunk down into the water with a sigh, Carson climbed in and moved right next to me.

My eyes fell closed and I moaned at the delicious feel of the hot water swirling around me. I let every muscle in my body relax, letting the stress and emotional buildup release from my tense body. After a few minutes, I grew so hot that I felt perspiration break out on my forehead. The desire that had been pulsing through my body a few minutes ago was still there, but it had taken a back seat momentarily.

I looked at Carson to see him smiling at me. "I missed that," he said.

"What?" I murmured.

"The look of pleasure on your face."

My lips tipped, and I took a moment to really study his face for the first time since he had come back into my life. Those deep hazel eyes with the long, dark lashes, always watching, observing, taking in everything around him, the beautiful lines of his face, and those full lips that I constantly wanted somewhere on my body. "I missed *you*," I said. "Everything about you." I reached out my finger and traced his strong jaw, a day or two worth of scruff making it rough beneath my touch, and then used my thumb to trace his lips, right before I leaned over and kissed him gently. He wrapped a hand around the back of my neck and pulled me closer to him, slanting his lips over mine.

Snow was falling gently around us, the sun now almost entirely up in the sky, casting a warm glow over the quiet morning. The trees around us shivered and so did I. With happiness. With pleasure. With deep gratitude for this moment that seemed both destined and dream-like.

We kissed slowly for a few minutes, our tongues meeting and dueling gently, but then he moaned deeply into my mouth and thrust his tongue deeper, and that shivering went everywhere. Down my limbs. Into each cell. Oh God, the taste of him. How had I lived without it all these years?

I pressed my breasts against his chest and rolled around

on top of him so that I was straddling him, his erection pressing into my stomach. I slid my wet body against his, glorying in the glide of our slick skin.

Our kisses went deep and wild until we were both panting into each other's mouths. My body was relaxed yet filled with electricity, making me needy and desperate again.

Carson suddenly pulled away, breathing hard and looking so strained he almost seemed to be in pain. "Grace, baby, we need to slow this down. It's not gonna take much to—"

"Let's go inside," I whispered against his mouth, moving off of him.

He stood quickly, grabbing the towels from under the bench and handing me one as I pulled myself from the water. He reached to the side of the hot tub and switched off the jets. I couldn't look away from his body as he performed each small task, his muscles flexing under his skin as he moved. God, he was exquisite.

When we got inside, he locked the back door behind us and led me down the hall to a small bedroom.

I glanced around at the cozy room, filled with distressed, black furniture. The bed was a large, four-poster with white, down-filled bedding. It was unmade, as if Carson had gotten out of it not too long ago.

I turned back toward Carson and he moved closer to me. I studied his face as he took the towel from around my body and rubbed it gently through my hair again, our gazes clashing. I loved the look on his face, intensity hardening his features and yet his eyes filled with tenderness. I saw his desire, and I saw his heart. Both were mine.

"Never let go, baby," I repeated from earlier.

He smiled, the dimple appearing, and suddenly I was

being walked backward until I hit the bed and he was over me. "Never," he said and then his mouth came down on mine.

———————

Carson

I pulled the comforter all the way over us and then pressed into her softness as we kissed deeply for long minutes, reveling in the feel of each other. I was lost in her, lost in the sounds she was making as I kissed her and ran my hands over her skin. My Grace was naked, beneath me. It was as if I had never woken up this morning but was still in a dream. Only I knew it wasn't, and the joy that was pulsing through me, along with the arousal, was unlike anything I'd ever experienced.

I broke from her lips and gazed down at her, running a thumb over her cheek. She was here. She'd come to me, over the miles and through a snowstorm. And I knew now that, like me, a part of her had never left. My heart squeezed tightly. She was mine. *Finally.* A fierce protectiveness filled my chest and I both reveled in the feel of it and accepted the emotional vulnerability that came with it. This was the way it should be—always. I leaned back in and kissed down her neck as she arched her head back into the pillow and sighed out my name.

Her fingers danced over my thigh, causing goosebumps to break out on my skin. I was as hard as granite, my cock throbbing and my hips rising on instinct. I wanted to thrust and take. It'd been a fucking long time and I likely wasn't going to last more than a few minutes, if that, once I got inside of her. I hoped she would understand—I'd make it up to her the second time…and the third…and the fourth.

"What's funny?" she whispered and I realized I'd been smiling against her skin.

"Nothing's funny," I said. "I'm just happy. And I want you."

"You have me," she said.

I took one of her nipples into my mouth, licking and sucking it until she was rolling her hips against me and reaching her hand down between us, trying to put me inside of her on her own.

"Hold up, Grace," I whispered. "I want that too, but—"

She shook her head from side to side. "Please, I don't care. I just want you inside of me. I need that. Please."

I wasn't capable of arguing. My hand shook as I lined the head of my cock up at her entrance. She put one leg around my back and I surged inside of her tight, wet heat.

"Oh, God bless America," I groaned at the exquisite feel of her all around me, gripping me tightly from inside. "You feel...oh God..." I felt like I might start talking in tongues. The pleasure had stolen my capacity for language.

She let out a small laugh, her internal muscles gripping me more tightly with her movement and I resumed kissing her, nipping at her lips, wanting to be attached in any and every way possible, all at once. I started moving, my body demanding to take over, movements jerky as I attempted to go slow.

As though she understood my struggle, she raised her hips slightly and said into my ear, "I don't want slow."

Oh, thank God. With her words, I started moving, relishing the feel of not only the physical pleasure but the reality of being connected to Grace in the most intimate way possible.

I moved in and out of her as she wrapped both legs around my back and tilted her pelvis up so that I could go deeper. My body was moving of its own accord, pounding, pushing, and taking the pleasure it had been denied for so long. "Grace," I panted. I felt drugged yet hyperalive, each nerve ending singing with pleasure.

"Carson, Carson," she breathed, sending me spiraling higher.

I felt the tingling begin at the base of my spine, an orgasm swirling through my abdomen, and I moved even faster to claim it, wanting it, needing it.

Just as my climax hit me and I began to jerk inside Grace, she screamed out and I felt her pulsing around me as I came, spilling inside her as I thrust forward. I buried my face in her neck, moaning at the same time I breathed her in.

I lay still for several seconds, feeling our mutual pulsating recede and finally fade slowly away.

I pretended to let out a snore against her neck and she laughed, and my cock, still halfway hard, slipped out of her a little bit with the movement.

I brought my head up and looked into her eyes, dancing with laughter. I grinned into her beautiful face and leaned forward and kissed her. As my lips met hers, something occurred to me. I closed my eyes for a beat before grimacing. "I didn't use a condom. I'm so sorry. I don't even have one here anyway, but fuck, I didn't even—"

"It's okay. The timing's off anyway. I just ended my period a couple days ago. I think we're good."

"Okay," I said, rolling off and pulling her against me. I was quiet for a minute. In all the years that I had had sex, except on film, I had always used a condom. As I considered it now, I couldn't bring myself to care that we hadn't used one this time. I knew I probably should, but I just didn't.

After a couple minutes, I felt her breathing slow. I pulled

the comforter all the way up to our necks and grinned up at the ceiling. She was asleep. I wasn't surprised considering she'd been up all night.

I could hardly believe that Grace was in my arms. Gratitude and a deep peace fell over me, bringing calm and relaxation. I gave in to it, drifting into a restful sleep, warm and cozy inside, while outside it continued to snow.

CHAPTER 29
Grace

I woke up slowly and snuggled into the warmth surrounding me. Memory filtered in and I sighed in happiness and contentment. *Carson*. I didn't know how long I'd been sleeping since the shades were closed and the room was dark. But Carson wasn't here. I remembered waking briefly to hear him talking in his sleep. What had he said... Ara? Was it a name? I had a moment of insecurity... but no. No. We were beyond that.

I lay there for a minute, thinking about how natural it'd felt to be with him again, and how I couldn't wait to spend more time with him, here in this dreamy cabin that felt like a refuge from the world.

I sat up and saw his duffel bag sitting near the closet and so I got out of bed and went over to it, peeking inside. The cabin was chilly but not freezing, and I smelled the very faint smell of a wood fire burning.

There was a thermal, long-sleeve shirt right at the top of Carson's bag and so I pulled that over my head. I dug through his clothes a little bit more and found a pair of boxers, pulling them on and folding the waistband down so that they would stay up on me.

After using the bathroom right across the hall and brushing my teeth, I headed toward the front of the house. *Where is he?*

A blazing fire was burning in the stone fireplace, and now that I wasn't frozen and overwhelmed, I took a moment to really look around the cozy cabin. The kitchen was right behind the living room—an open floor plan, although because of a bar with upper cabinets separating the two, I couldn't see it in its entirety. The furniture was comfortable and rustic, plenty of throw blankets draped on the arms of the couch and side chairs. It was a room that made you want to snuggle up and stay awhile.

There were large windows on every wall with a view of the snow-covered pine trees surrounding the cabin. Snow was still falling gently outside.

"Sleep okay, buttercup?" I heard as Carson's arms came around me from behind. He kissed the side of my neck and I tilted my head to give him better access.

"Hmmm," I sighed. "There you are. Why do you call me buttercup?" I tilted my head a little more, relishing the feel of his lips on my skin.

There was a slight pause behind me as his body stilled against mine and I turned to face him. "When I was a boy," he said, his eyes filled with warmth, "I used to pick butter-cups in my granny's yard. She would hold one underneath my chin and I would hold one under hers. She said that if it reflected yellow, it meant we liked butter."

I smiled, tilting my head, charmed by the picture of him as a little boy, holding a flower beneath his grandmother's chin as she played a silly little game that made him feel special.

"When I asked her how the buttercup made a glow," he went on, "she told me that when something brought you happiness, its glow became a part of you and made you glow too. The very first time I saw you Grace, to me, you glowed. I thought I disliked you"—he laughed softly, his expression tender—"but I couldn't deny that you glowed. You made me so happy, Grace, in a way that I never even knew was possible. And that weekend, even when you left, I kept your glow with me and I've never let it go."

"Oh, Carson," I breathed. I pulled him to me and kissed his lips. We stood there for long minutes, cuddling and hugging each other close. "Thank you," I said softly. What he had given me hadn't come in bright, shiny paper, hadn't been tied up with a bow. But it was a gift nonetheless—he had given me the gift of his heart. And finally an answer to the age-old buttercup question that was better than I could have expected. The sun slanted in the window, falling over us and I asked, "What time is it anyway?"

"It's only noon. You slept five hours or so."

I turned back around in his arms, looking out the large windows again. "It's so beautiful here," I said.

"I know. I love it. Someday I'd like to buy a place here." He brought his chin down to my shoulder. "Are you gonna let me take you snowboarding? Maybe tomorrow?" He nuzzled his nose along my neck.

I laughed softly and moved away from him, sitting down on the leather sofa and pulling a throw over my bare legs. "Sure. I just hope I don't show you up. I hear you're decent but…"

He laughed. "Well, now I'm nervous. Maybe I'll just save my pride and keep you in bed for the next couple days."

He sat next to me and pulled me into his arms so that my head was resting on his chest. I laughed. "Hmmm...you are good at that. It's not a bad idea actually."

He chuckled and we were quiet for a minute as he played with my hair gently and I watched the snow fall.

"Are you hungry? I have coffee made."

"Coffee sounds great. And I'm starving." I couldn't even remember the last time I'd eaten.

"Okay. Oh, I went and got Dylan's SUV while you were sleeping. There was a can of gasoline in the garage. I brought your suitcase in." He indicated with his head toward my suitcase sitting by the door, the one I'd packed for Dayton what seemed like a hundred years ago.

"Thanks. That was pretty dumb of me to run out of gas. I'm usually slightly more competent than that."

"Nah, your mind was just preoccupied with other things," he said. "Like my hands and my mouth and my... indoor plumbing."

I laughed. "Is that a euphemism?"

"Not one that sounds very sexy."

I made a face and he pretended to bite me to which I laughed.

Carson got up and went to the kitchen and I watched the fire contentedly and listened to him preparing the food behind me for ten minutes before he came back into the room with a cup of coffee and a plate of scrambled eggs and toast.

"I remembered how you like your coffee," he said, "but I don't know how you like your eggs. I hope that's okay."

"This is how I like my eggs," I said with a smile. "Thank you."

I dug into the food and Carson took a seat on the couch. When I looked up, he was sipping his cup of coffee and watching me with a small smile.

I finished eating and set the plate on the coffee table. Carson scooted down slightly and I sighed, leaning my head on his shoulder as I sipped at my coffee.

"What are you thinking about?" he asked.

"Umm, you, me, us."

"I like that topic," he said. "What about us?"

"I was just thinking how right this feels. I was thinking how sorry I am that it took me so long to realize it."

Carson chuckled. "It took you a week, Grace."

I smiled, turning my head and kissing the crook of his neck. "Too long."

"You had a few things going on. It was normal that you got spooked by me. I came on sort of strong."

"I like when you come on strong."

"I know you do, buttercup," he said with a smile.

I lifted my head and looked up at him, warmth filling me now that I knew the meaning of my nickname. "Just don't get carried away," I warned.

He laughed. "Please. You're the real boss here. You think I don't know that?" He looked down at me tenderly. "I'd do anything for you, Grace. I'd slay a dragon for you."

I kissed him softly and then we cuddled for a few minutes before I remembered being pulled from sleep by his dream. I leaned back so I could look at him. "You said a name in your sleep this morning," I told him.

He seemed to still. "I did?"

"Yes." I paused. "Carson, who is Ara?"

335

Carson

My heart gave a strong knock. Who is Ara? I leaned back and ran my hand over my short hair.

Grace studied me, obviously seeing the heaviness in my expression as she frowned and then sat up to look more directly at me.

I was silent for a minute, getting my thoughts straight as she waited me out. I was ready to tell her about this. If we were together now, then she needed to know. This was part of my life.

"Ara was a fourteen-year-old girl who was raped and beaten by a high-value target we had been sent in to kill in Afghanistan. We found her, half-dead from her injuries, and we stayed with her as she died."

Grace brought her hand up to her mouth for a second. "Oh, Carson. I'm so sorry." She paused. "When you say we, you mean your unit?"

"Yeah. We had gone in on the mission and we were successful pretty immediately. But when we went into the warehouse the target had been hiding in, we found some things we weren't expecting, including a whole room of women and girls in the most deplorable conditions you could imagine." I was silent for another minute, picturing opening that door, the smell hitting us immediately as we all recoiled and then shined our flashlights in to see terrified eyes staring back at us. They hadn't given them access to toilets or water. They were being held like cattle, worse than cattle.

"They were being trafficked?" she asked warily.

I nodded. "Yeah. Girls as young as six were in that room, fated to become some sick fuck's sexual plaything."

She stared at me silently, eyes wide with shock and sadness.

"One of the girls, Ara, had seen a chance for escape when they threw some dinner in for them. The guards caught her and they raped her—raped her in any and every manner they could. They hurt and degraded her in ways I still don't want to think about." My voice faded at the end as I swallowed down the lump that always formed when I thought of Ara, of what she'd endured in punishment for her attempt at freedom. "They all took turns with her and then they beat her so severely that she was barely conscious. We learned the details later, when our translator talked to some of the other women being held."

Tears had gathered in Grace's eyes, and she grabbed my hand and held it to her heart as I continued to talk.

"After we killed the traffickers and found Ara, we carried her outside and we cleaned her wounds as best as we could with what we had. But the internal damage was too much. She needed a hospital and we had no way to get her to one. We gave her morphine and we stayed with her through the night, taking turns holding her hand and telling her stories—any story we could think of. As the sun started to rise, it was my turn to hold her hand and I told her about you, how I thought of you every morning when the sun came up in the sky. And I swear, she smiled at me, Grace. She looked right in my eyes, and she smiled. And then, then she was gone."

"Oh God," Grace said on a pained whisper.

I stared out the window, a stark desert appearing before me as I recalled that morning. I remembered the way the light had reflected back at me in Ara's eyes, a young girl from a distant land, who'd slipped from this world, her hand gripping mine, as orange streaks blazed across the sky.

"How do you handle that memory, Carson? How do you get over that?" Grace finally asked.

I thought about her question. I thought about how you ship off to fight for your country, and no one ever tells you that the inhumanity you might witness will seep into your very soul and irrevocably change who you are. They never tell you that a thousand miles and many years away, a singular moment will suddenly come back to you—where you were, what you felt, what you saw, that one frame on repeat, over and over and over. They never tell you that it will be so strong that you'll want to fall to your knees and grip your head and reject living in a world where horrors like that one occur, and the sun keeps rising and setting over and over day after day.

"I'll never get it out of my head. I'll never get over it," I said. "But I'm okay with that. I prefer it to forgetting. Ara lived it. She held on until that first ray of light shattered the darkness around her. I like to think, to her, it was a small piece of freedom, that light. Or maybe I just hope so. But the very least I can do is remember."

Grace released a staggered breath. She picked up my hand and held it to her heart and then brought her lips to my scarred palm, kissing it softly.

I watched her, pain etched into her expression. The clear heartbreak she felt for a young girl she was only hearing a story about moved me and brought me peace. When she leaned back, she asked, "What happened to the other victims?"

"They were all from small, poor villages in the surrounding areas. The townspeople helped locate their families and get them back where they belonged. They had mostly been told that there was a housekeeping job or something like that in a nearby town or city. That's the usual MO when it comes to trafficking. In some cases, families even sell their daughters into what they believe will be a better situation than they can provide."

"And Ara's family?" she asked quietly.

"We had to leave before Ara's family was located, but the townspeople thought they knew where they were and promised to take her body to them."

Grace put her head on my chest and her arms around my waist and squeezed me gently. God, it felt good to talk about this with her and let her comfort seep into my heart. The guys and I had talked about it afterward, but it wasn't the same. It wasn't the same as being wrapped in Grace's arms as she took part of my pain and made it her own. I didn't want her to hurt, but to share my scars with another human was a relief that I not only wanted, but had needed so much..

We were quiet for a few minutes, just holding each other. Finally, I said quietly, "Grace, there's more, and this part concerns you."

She brought her head up and frowned. "Okay," she said, worry lacing her voice.

I paused. "Listen, when I tell you what I'm about to tell you, I understand if you need to take some time to think about it. I pray to God that you don't get back in Dylan's SUV and drive back to Vegas, but if you want to do that, I'll understand."

"Carson, you're scaring me."

I took a deep breath. "That day in Afghanistan, the initial plan was to kill the target and get in and out of there, but because of the unexpected situation we found, we were later making our way to the rendezvous point. It gave men who worked for the high-value target time to ambush us. You already knew I was injured along with Leland, but not the circumstances."

She nodded, expression wary. I grabbed her hand and squeezed it. "Anyway, after that, we were shipped back while we healed. Leland got medically discharged and I was given a choice to stay or go. When Leland offered me a job, I decided to take the discharge too."

"Yes, you told me all this."

"I know. But I didn't tell you what my real job is."

Her brows lowered. "You're not the head of security at Trilogy?"

"Well, yes and no. That's my full-time job. The rest of the time, I plan and execute operations with my friends to rescue women being sexually trafficked. We use the forty-fifth floor of Trilogy to house them while we locate their families and obtain the necessary paperwork to fly them home."

"What?" she breathed, her face losing color.

I turned more fully toward her. "After what happened with Ara, with what we saw in that warehouse, we were all pretty messed up over it. We talked about it and decided we needed to do something that mattered, something that made a difference, using the skills we had, not in foreign countries, but right here in the US. Leland had the means and the location to offer us all jobs as cover for the operation we'd agreed to put into effect. As SEALs we're able to gather intel and break into locations where victims are being held. In Vegas, most of the women come from Latin American countries. So far, we've located and rescued six groups of women since we've been in Vegas. The last rescue was the night before Josh got arrested."

"Oh my God, I don't even... I don't even know what to say. Wait, what does this have to do with Josh's arrest?"

"Josh was framed, Grace. There's a man in Vegas who makes it his business to sell people. The women we rescued were his merchandise. What happened to Josh was his way of letting us know he didn't appreciate what we had taken from him."

CHAPTER 30
Grace

I believed him without a doubt. I trusted him implicitly. The story about Ara broke my heart and my mind was reeling with everything he'd told me about the undercover operations. *My God*. How had my whole world turned upside down, yet again, in the space of half an hour? Carson seemed to have a special knack for throwing me for a loop rather quickly. I sat on the couch with my hand on my forehead, trying to collect myself enough to ask more necessary questions. But only one came to mind. "How should we handle this?" I asked.

I looked at Carson and he paused for a couple beats before he smiled. I stared, then frowned. "Why are you smiling?" This didn't seem like the time to smile.

"You said, 'we,'" he said, still smiling.

"Yeah," I confirmed, "I said we."

"Just like that?" he asked, his smile fading, but hope remaining in his eyes.

I pursed my lips, studying him for a minute. "I understand why you wouldn't tell me this before now...before I

told you I wanted to be with you. Before there was an…
us. But did you think I wouldn't believe you when you
did tell me?"

He scratched his chin. "No, I guess I didn't think you'd
doubt my story. I just wondered if you'd want to have any
part of it."

I breathed out a humorless laugh. "I don't know if I
do, exactly." I paused, thinking about this tangled web. "But
here's the thing: it comes with you. It's what you do. And,
Carson, I don't know if anyone's told you this lately, but
you're a hero."

"Oh, no, buttercup. I'm no hero."

"Yes, Carson, you *are*. I've worked cases that involve
women who've been sexually victimized in some form or
another. I've been witness to the haunted look in their eyes.
I've seen the devastation. Yes, you're a hero. So again, how
should we handle this?"

His eyes softened. "Dylan's working on it. He's trying
to pinpoint a location for the guy we're tracking, the one
we're all but positive is responsible for the setup. His name
is Gabriel Bakos. The problem is, he moves around so damn
much, it's hard to track him. If we can just pin him down,
we can go in and we can *make* him talk."

"That sounds dangerous."

"It's a man's life we're talking about. My friend's life—a
man who not only didn't kill a woman but who has saved
hundreds. And who, if set free, will save hundreds—perhaps
thousands—more."

I sighed, closing my eyes briefly. I could only imagine what
Josh Garner was going through. God, his case looked like such
a slam dunk. And he had been framed by someone so evil that
he not only sold human beings but also didn't blink an eye

at murdering an innocent young woman and then ruining a man's life. I felt scared and sickened at the mere thought of his "business." "I know. Okay, what else? Tell me everything."

"It's just a waiting game right now. A fucking frustrating as hell waiting game."

I chewed at my lip for a minute, my mind sifting through possibilities. "I can get a continuance to give you more time," I offered.

His brows rose. "That'd help. I'd never ask you if I didn't know for a fact—"

"I know. It wouldn't be questioned. DAs ask for continuances on cases all the time."

"It wouldn't affect your career? Your reputation?"

I shook my head. "No. Not if I asked for it within reason." He nodded.

I breathed deeply and sat back again, trying to solve this puzzle in my head, using all the evidence that I knew I had against *an innocent man*. *Shit! Shit! Shit!* "Can't you go to the police regarding this Bakos person?" I asked. "I mean, surely they'd be able to collect some evidence…somewhere or question him, or *something*."

"No. First of all, if we went to the police with our story and told them what we'd been doing, all of us could face arrest and then Josh would really be fucked. Also, police are restricted by search warrants and other red tape. We have all the expensive technology the police *don't* have, and we're still having a hard time tracking him. Even if we got his location and gave it to the police, by the time they got in there, Bakos would be cleared out and so would all the evidence. We need to get to him first. We can't work under the restraints of law enforcement if we want to be successful."

I gave a nod, going over what he'd said. I knew how the

legal system worked, better than most people, and unfortunately, he was right. Vigilante groups, even ones doing good work, couldn't be encouraged by the police.

"I've gone over it a thousand times," Carson said. "There's no solution yet."

I sighed. "How do we simply…wait, though? How are you not pacing the floor right now?"

"Because if I do that, I'll go crazy. I have to have faith that with all of us working together, we'll figure this out. I can't consider the alternative. Until there's a reason not to be optimistic, optimism is what I'm choosing."

I huffed out a breath, my shoulders sagging, still doubtful about whether I could follow his lead or not in that regard. I was a worrier. When my brain got hold of a problem, it liked to work it to death. Sometimes that was helpful. And sometimes it drove me crazy.

"Go take a shower, buttercup, and then we're going to run to the grocery store. I only bought some necessities yesterday."

I sighed but stood up, intending on doing as he said. When I was halfway out of the room, I turned around and walked back to Carson. I sat down next to him again and when he turned his face to mine, I whispered, "All those years ago, I knew, *I knew* who you were. I felt it, your goodness, *here*," I tapped my heart. "Thank you for proving me right."

Carson

I sat on the couch and listened to the shower come on. I couldn't help the smile that tipped my lips and the happiness that emanated from within. My buttercup was fucking amazing. Had I really ever doubted that? No. That was the reason I wanted her back so fiercely it had been like an ache in my bones. But I hadn't known just how strong she was.

Grace had seemed shocked by my story, but she had been on board before I even finished telling it. And she was proud of me. I saw that pride shining in her eyes and it fucking undid me. I had changed my life for *me*, but she had been the catalyst, and I would never deny that. And so the fact that she was proud of me, well, that meant everything.

I brought the dishes into the kitchen, put them in the dishwasher, then stoked the fire a little bit and sat back down on the couch. By the time Grace came out of the bathroom fully dressed, her hair falling loose, I was feeling relaxed and so damn happy. There were no secrets between us now. We were a team, she was with me, and despite the current predicament, I felt a deep serenity settle inside.

She walked over to me, straddled me, wrapped her arms around my chest, and just held me to her for several minutes as I breathed in her shower-fresh scent.

But when I tipped my head back, I saw that her eyes were distant and she had a slight frown on her face. "Grace, you need to try to shut off your brain for a couple days while we're here. I know I just dropped a whole shitload of information on you. But trust me, you will just give yourself a migraine if you keep working the information around in your mind while there's nothing we can really do. The guys and I have gone over every angle, and we have more information than you do right now about the players involved."

She sighed as she met my gaze. "I'll try."

"Good. Oh, I almost forgot, I went out earlier while you were sleeping and got you something."

"What?" she asked, moving off me.

I got up and grabbed a bag by the door. "I looked for your missing boot this morning, but it was nowhere to be found. It's snowed so much, the path from where Dylan's SUV was to the cabin is completely covered over. So I bought you some new boots and a waterproof coat, some gloves, and a hat. They're from the local supercenter so choices were limited, and I'm also sure my fashion sense is lacking, but they'll do the job." I handed the bag to her.

She took it and dug around inside for a minute, checking everything out as I put on my gear. "Not bad actually, on the fashion front. Thank you."

"You're welcome. Put them on and we'll get going. I looked at your one boot to get your shoe size so hopefully those fit."

She pulled on the black snow boots with some kind of fake fur showing at the top and the gray-and-black jacket and smiled. "Perfect," she said.

"Try on the gloves and hat too. I want to see the complete snow-bunny look."

She raised one eyebrow but pulled the gloves on and then put the hat on too. Goddamn, she was cute. I couldn't help grinning as my eyes wandered over her.

She laughed, then took my hand and we walked outside. Before I had even locked up the cabin, the worried expression was back on her face and a small crease had formed between her brows. As she started walking in front of me to my truck, I bent and scooped up some snow and started forming a snowball. "Carson, what about the rock the girl was—"

I nailed her right in the back of the head. She stopped dead in her tracks, interrupted midsentence, and turned

346

toward me, her expression incredulous. "Did you just throw a snowball at my *head*?"

"Yeah, I did. Bullseye."

"I see," she said, bending down and gathering up some snow and then beginning to make a snowball.

I laughed. "Oh, buttercup, you have another think coming if you—" And with that, she nailed me right in the face and then laughed out loud, doubling over.

I closed my eyes and wiped the snow from my face, blinking wetness out of my lashes.

"That's it. It's on," I said, scooping up some snow and starting toward her.

She shrieked and ran as fast as her big, clumpy snow boots could carry her, which was to say, exceedingly slow. I laughed and watched her, giving her a head start. It was the least I could do.

She ducked behind some trees, and I went wide around the grove and came in behind her several minutes later. I surveilled her for a couple minutes as she peeked out in front of her and then went back to work on her stockpile, about twenty formed snowballs next to her knees. *Valiant effort, buttercup.*

But doomed to fail.

I very, very quietly removed my coat and then laid it on the ground and scooped as much snow into it as I could. Then I picked it up and used the trees for cover, moving closer and closer to her.

When I was almost directly behind her, I came out in the open and moved in swiftly as she was forming another snowball, the sound of her gloves working in the snow a mask to any noise I made. Then I raised my full jacket and dumped the whole pile of snow on her head.

She screamed and flailed, whipping around as she shook

the snow off of her. I tackled her gently and rolled her to the powdery ground as she laughed and shrieked.

"Who is the snowball-battle master?" I asked, pressing down harder into her.

She laughed harder, trying to buck me off of her.

"Who, Grace? Say it. '*You* are the snowball-battle master, Carson. The heavyweight champion of the frozen tundra. Undefeated now and forever.'"

"Okay! Okay! You, Carson, are the snowball champion of...whatever! What you said! You're the master." She shrieked again as I tickled her ribs.

"I know," I said and she laughed. I grinned back, kissed her on her lips, and jumped up and helped her to her feet. I gathered her in my arms, my smile fading as I wiped some almost-melted snow off her cheek. "I know it's not possible to entirely stop thinking about everything that's going on with Josh and that's good, because some small idea could be the thing that gives us a break. But sometimes realizations occur when you distract yourself with something else. So, let's distract ourselves today. What do you say?"

She took in a breath and nodded. "Okay."

"Okay," I repeated.

I shook my jacket out and put it back on and then I brushed Grace off and we walked to my truck. A few minutes later we were headed into town.

I took my phone out as we drove and texted the guys. I had told them that I'd text them anytime I had cell service and then they would know they could call me if they needed to.

We drove to the supermarket in town and when we got out and started walking to the store, I grinned over at Grace. I thought back to the day before, when I had run into this same supermarket for a couple items to sustain me for a few days. What a difference a day made. It was still surreal that Grace was here with me.

"What?" she asked.

"Nothing, just you," I said, grabbing her hand. "You make me happy."

She let go of my hand and grabbed me around the waist and squeezed me.

Half an hour later, our cart was loaded up with everything we'd need for the next couple of days. Christmas was two days away, so Grace insisted on buying a ham and several different side dishes and the ingredients for some dessert that was a tradition in her family's household.

As she read the back of a can of something, I asked, "Grace, your family..." I trailed off, not knowing exactly how to ask if they were okay with her missing Christmas to be with me, someone they had never even met, probably never even heard of. Someone she had gone to directly on the heels of a broken engagement.

She turned to me. "My sisters are ecstatic, Carson. They knew that Alex wasn't the one for me the first time they met him. My dad...well, that's probably a different story because he'll have more... practical concerns about whether I'm having some sort of nervous breakdown. But my sisters have tricks up their sleeves as far as handling him, and as far as making him understand. It'll be fine." She looked confident, and so as long as she felt good about it, so did I.

We walked to the deli counter and ordered several things behind the case, and I stood waiting as Grace walked a few steps away to look at something on a shelf next to the counter.

I glanced over at two young women who looked to be in their early twenties who were giggling and smiling at me. I smiled a small, polite smile and looked away as I heard one of them whisper, "He's so hot!" I had this moment of anxiety where I wondered if they would recognize me from one of my films. I braced for, *Isn't that Carson Stinger, Straight Male Performer?* I forced myself to relax, picking up a package of pita bread and pretending to read the ingredients. That description had been what was on my nametag that weekend, but no one had ever referred to me that way in the business. Sometimes though, for whatever reason, I still thought of *him,* that version of myself who had done intimate acts with strangers in front of cameras that way. A title. A product. A commodity.

The moments I felt emotionally impacted by those memories were few and far between now, but they did still happen. Maybe it would be a long, long time before I was able to figure out how to successfully merge who I'd been then, with who I was now. Or maybe the separation was good and necessary. I suppose I was still a work in progress on that front.

Grace approached and I saw her glance at the young women quickly before looking back to me. "Are you okay?" she asked. Whatever was on my face had obviously concerned her.

I smiled. "Yeah. I'm fine." I leaned down and kissed her lips.

We put our order in the cart a few minutes later and then walked over to the small pharmacy at the back of the store.

We found the condom shelves and Grace glanced around before grabbing a box and putting it in our cart under some other items.

I couldn't help laughing at her, and as I did she turned around, glared at me, and started pulling the cart. "Come on, let's go," she whispered.

"Grace, we're not robbing the place. We're buying condoms, like responsible adults."

She paused, shaking her head slightly. "I'm pretty lame, huh?" she asked. "I can speak in front of a crowded courtroom, and yet buying condoms turns me into a nervous sixteen-year-old." She reached down in the cart and brought the condom box out and then perched it proudly on top of the ham.

I laughed. "No, you're not lame. You're beautiful and amazing. Let's go put a few of those to use."

We checked out and drove back to the cabin. The snow was still falling lightly in big, fluffy flakes, casting a magical stillness and making it feel like we were in a world all our own. For now, we were.

CHAPTER 31
Grace

We brought the groceries into the cabin and started unpacking. I set ingredients for grilled cheese and tomato soup to the side so that I could make us some late lunch after everything was put away.

As I was folding up the last paper bag, Carson came up behind me and put his arms around me and whispered in my ear, "I love how you hum when you put the groceries away."

I laughed. "I do? I didn't even realize," I said, turning in his arms.

"Mm-hmm. I can't wait to learn every little thing about you," he said, looking into my eyes.

"Even the bad things?" I asked, feeling suddenly nervous at the realization that there was so much we didn't know about each other.

"Yeah, even the things you *think* are bad things," he said very seriously. He brought his lips to mine in a tender kiss that quickly heated and I moaned into his mouth. I loved the way he tasted, loved the way he kissed and the way he moved. He appealed to every single one of my senses and making love with him felt decadent, delicious. I didn't see how I'd ever get enough. What a wonderful thought.

I kept marveling at all he had revealed that afternoon. I wanted to hear the details about the operations they had carried out, but I also sensed that Carson needed a mental break. And so I wasn't going to start rapid-firing questions at him all at once. I'd let those conversations unfold naturally. It was important that we bond, and learn how to simply *be* with each other again if we were going to be the best united front we could be for whatever unfolded, not just in this case, but for our life moving forward. Another wonderful thought.

I pressed against him, a sound of satisfaction coming from my throat, almost a purr. Carson, my brave Carson. My heart burst with pride when I thought of who he had become, what he risked his safety to do for others.

And how incredibly hot he was to top it all off.

He untied the knotted sweater belt at my waist and I laughed into his mouth when his hands started traveling under the hem.

"What?" he murmured, smiling and nipping my lips.

"Nothing. You're very talented."

He rubbed his lips against mine. "No, just determined."

My smile faded as his hands reached my breasts and started rubbing my nipples through the cotton of my bra. "Ahhh," I moaned, breaking from his lips and leaning my head back.

He pressed his lips to the pulse at the base of my throat as his thumbs circled my hardened peaks slowly, lazily. I breathed harder, tingly electricity shooting to my core and my blood beginning to pulse.

I reached my hand down to rub his hardened length

through his jeans. He let out a moan and pressed against my hand. My body was coming alive beneath his touch as it always did, but there was another current running beneath my skin: joy. Joy at the knowledge that there would be much more of *this*. But even greater joy to know that from here on out I would sleep in his arms, I would be first to hear about his day, I would comfort him, and prepare meals with him, and a hundred other important and mundane things my mind was too dopey to think of at the moment as his scent surrounded me and his hands worked magic on my body. I raised my head and looked into his eyes, filled with heat, with happiness, mirroring what I was sure was on my face as well.

He leaned into my ear as he circled his hips against my hand. "I want you so much, buttercup," he said, his voice deep and slightly strained. "I've never stopped wanting you."

I moaned. I liked that. I liked that so much. "Me neither" was all I could manage.

"Tell me you're mine," he whispered.

"I'm yours. I've always been yours," I breathed out.

"I'm yours, too," he said. "Always." Then he undid my jeans and worked them down my hips as I watched him kneel in front of me.

I sucked in a breath as he put his face against the white lace of my underwear and breathed me in. I let out a small whimper. I was already wet.

He hooked his thumbs into the sides of my underwear and brought them slowly down my hips and let them drop to the floor as he looked up at me.

For a minute, he stilled and rested his cheek against my stomach, his hands gripping the backs of my thighs. I ran my fingers through his short, soft hair as I watched him. His eyes were shut and there was this expression on his face that I couldn't exactly read. It looked sort of worshipful, and partially pained. I wanted to ask him what he was thinking, but before I could form the words, I caught sight of us being reflected in the mirror over the fireplace in the open family room area. When I focused on the view of me, no pants on, and Carson kneeled before me with his head now moving lower between my thighs, the sight of it made me lose all focus, a gasp escaping my lips.

Carson urged my legs apart and I cried out when I felt his tongue dip into me from below.

"Oh God," he whispered. "The way you taste...it's like a drug."

And then he nipped my clit as I cried out with the ecstasy of it, pressing gently on his head to urge him on. "Please don't stop," I begged.

I felt his smile. "As if," he murmured. And then his tongue began circling slowly on the swollen, little bundle of nerves, and I gripped the counter behind me and pressed more firmly against his face, unabashedly seeking my own pleasure.

"Oh, Carson," I breathed as he grasped my thighs more tightly and pulled me even tighter against his face.

The pleasure built higher and higher as I watched the mirror in front of me through half-closed lids. The combination of sensory input was so overwhelming that when my orgasm hit, it was fast and hard, and I screamed out Carson's name as I pressed into his mouth.

He lingered, turning his head and kissing my thighs, and then my hipbones, his lips fluttering over my skin as I came back to reality. But then, he bent his head back and smiled, and it looked slightly wicked. I would have laughed if I'd had the wherewithal, but I didn't. All I knew was that I liked that look very much and whatever plans were behind it.

He stood and quickly stripped off his jeans, and before I could even form a coherent thought, he had lifted me onto the counter, so that I was at the very edge, grabbed a condom off the kitchen island, ripped it open, and rolled it on. He pressed into me, filling me completely. *Oh.*

I braced my hands behind me as he started pumping into me relentlessly. He took my face in his hands and kissed me, his tongue thrusting into my mouth in tandem with the thrusting of his cock.

When he pulled away from me and pressed his face into my neck, I watched the mirror behind us again, this time watching the beautiful sight of his muscular ass contracting as he moved in and out of me. It was carnal and beautiful, and I couldn't look away.

His breath hitched and he began panting into my neck, moaning my name when his orgasm hit him.

He circled his hips slowly, milking his pleasure and when he brought his head up, there was a lazy smile on his face. I liked that look too. *So beautiful.*

He kissed me again, deeply and tenderly, and then he pulled out of me and placed me back on the floor.

Fifteen minutes later, soup and sandwiches had never tasted so good.

We talked long after we had eaten, sitting at the counter as we held hands, chatting about non-specific topics: sports, entertainment, the world, why my family golden doodle continued to eat socks. We laughed so much I snorted, and then we laughed some more, and somehow in the back of my mind, I knew that our shared laughter, as much as our shared attraction, meant I had chosen well.

Carson

Later that night we made dinner together, chatting some more and just enjoying each other's company. I hadn't been this happy in… I'd *never* been this happy. There was a lot of stress waiting for us back in Vegas and so I was mindful to appreciate every moment of getting reacquainted with her and letting the feeling that we were *right* settle into my soul. I hadn't been wrong when I had thought that having her with me would make me stronger—stronger for Josh, stronger for *everything*.

I opened a bottle of wine, and we drank as we cooked, laughing and touching. I couldn't keep my hands off of her and it seemed like she felt the same way. Maybe we were making up for lost time or maybe I just needed to keep reminding myself that she was here with me. Touching her gave me comfort, grounded me to the here and now. But I also loved that we never ran out of things to say. I loved her insights and respected her opinions. She was more black and white than me on some topics and so we discussed them passionately, each persuading the other on a few points, and ending the debate with an even more passionate kiss. *This* was what life with her would look like and I couldn't fucking wait to live it.

After dinner, she got out a frying pan and told me to sit while she made a quick dessert. I drank my wine as she stirred a few ingredients together and chopped some bananas. A few minutes later when she brought it over to me, I saw what she had made and my heart squeezed. She'd remembered. "Bananas Foster," I said.

"Your granny used to make it for you. I hope mine compares."

"You remembered that all this time." I was slightly floored. We'd talked about a lot that weekend, and I thought that I recalled so much of it because I'd had hours and days where I was trudging through deserts and sitting in caves to relive it all. But it hadn't just been me.

She nodded. "I remember every part of that weekend," she said quietly.

I leaned forward and took her face in my hands and kissed her lips. "Thank you."

After dessert, we got in the hot tub again and the combination of wine and wet, naked Grace had me drunk in more ways than one.

We fell into bed a damp mess of tangled limbs. She climbed on top of me and I lost myself in her as she rode me, her head thrown back, her breasts in my face as I sucked and licked them, the sounds she made my undoing. I thrust myself up into her tight heat and came so hard I thought I might pass out.

After I got rid of the condom I had somehow remembered to put on, I pulled her body into mine and felt her smile against my chest, nuzzling into me again. Moments later, I noted that she was breathing slowly and deeply against me as I too drifted into the world of dreams.

———

"Carson, wake up, baby. You're dreaming," I heard whispered.

I shot up in bed. "Wha'?" I looked around, trying to orient myself.

"You were dreaming," Grace said again, urging me back down to the pillow.

I sank back down to the pillow and ran my hand over

my sweaty hair. *My mom. Ara.* I had been having that damn dream again.

"What was it about?" Grace whispered, pressing into my side and laying her cheek on my chest.

"My mom...then Ara. I've been having it a lot lately. I'm not sure why."

"Tell me," she said, pressing her lips to my chest and then bringing her hands up, so that her chin was propped on them.

I could just make her out in the darkness, those eyes that I knew were clear blue in the sunlight now deep, fathomless pools in the dark room.

But I felt her warmth against me, I breathed in her scent, and I heard the concern in her voice. It comforted me and made me want to share the pain that came to me in the darkness of the night.

I told her about the dream, about sneaking out of the back room, about watching my mom "perform," about her suddenly morphing into Ara.

She kissed my chest again. "Both were traumas for you, baby," she said softly.

"Yeah," I said. I knew she was right. I knew that that was the reason I combined them in my mind, why one turned into the other. I'd thought my mom was being victimized. To me, what I'd witnessed looked like violence, and even later, when I understood the context, that *feeling* of wanting to protect her but being defenseless never left me.

We were both silent for a minute. Just telling her about my dream and having her comfort me felt like a weight lifted off of my heart. "It's part of the reason I haven't been with anyone since you," I said quietly.

I felt her still. "What do you mean?"

I paused. "When I returned home from our weekend

in Vegas, I looked at everything differently. I had never experienced sex as something that wasn't just physical but emotional. It helped me define things for myself in a way I never had—or at least, begin to. It brought up a whole slew of questions that at the time, I had no answers to. That weekend changed everything for me, Grace."

She squeezed me again gently. I could tell that she was waiting for me to go on.

"It's like, with my mom, the thing that was always so confusing to me was that she'd come home from the set looking... *broken*. Every damn time. I felt so fiercely protective of her, but I was just a kid, and she was the one who was obviously in pain but kept going back for more. She did what she did at the expense of her own soul. I'm not saying it's like that for everyone. But for her, it was. I could see it and I couldn't do fuck about it. It *hurt*. And I didn't get it. And so later, I don't know, maybe I went into the sex trade myself as a way of gaining some kind of control over something that I had had no control over in the past. At the time, I told myself that it didn't matter, that it was just a way to make some easy money, but deep down, I think I knew that was a lie. Because one weekend with you and the whole house of cards I'd constructed came crashing down."

"Your ideas about sex had to be complicated, Carson," she said.

"Yeah. Yeah, they were, and I didn't even acknowledge that." I sighed. "Anyway, after you, I couldn't lie to myself about it anymore. And I realized that I didn't want to go back to the way I had been. Not just the business, but also, the nameless hookups, the one-night stands. I realized I'd approached any and all intimacy in the same way. The only difference was some of it was on camera, and some of it wasn't." It'd all been impersonal. It'd *all* been a performance. And the weekend with Grace had made it clear that that wasn't what sex was supposed to be, because despite the pain of our parting, that weekend had brought me satisfaction that I'd never known existed with a woman. She'd stripped me of all my false bravado and I was left there exposed, just *me,* and it'd made me realize I didn't know who the fuck I really was. I let out an exhale. "Anyway, then I shipped off and spent a couple years in caves in the desert which made it pretty easy to take a vow of chastity whether I had wanted to or not." But I had. I had wanted to. I'd needed time and distance to figure myself out.

Grace smiled briefly against my skin and then let her lips linger there. "What happened with Ara had to bring up some of that confusion," she said.

"Yeah," I said on a breath. "Yeah. It brought up those feelings I'd had as a kid again. It's hard to explain." It was this weird, awful twisting of sex and violence that still sometimes haunted me.

"I understand," she whispered.

And were there two words in the English language more beautiful, more comforting than those two? In that moment, I knew for sure the answer was no.

"And I think it's beautiful that you've channeled that pain into purpose," she said.

I kissed her hair and for a moment we were quiet. I could feel her heart beating steadily against my skin.

"Have you talked to your mom recently?" she asked quietly.

"No, I don't even think she knows I went into the military. Not that she'd really care. My roommate, Dylan, lived in the apartment we had shared in LA until he moved to Vegas a couple months ago, and she never contacted him there looking for me."

She nuzzled me. "She has no idea what she's missing out on." She paused for a minute. "Do you have any guesses why she might have done what she did for so long?"

"No, I don't know exactly. She mentioned an uncle once when she was strung out. I got the feeling that he had done something to her, but she didn't go into it. Maybe there *was* no reason. Maybe the drugs were the reason. I don't know." All I knew was that I hadn't been enough to convince her to change. Maybe no one could have.

She was quiet for a minute, rubbing her lips whisper-soft on my skin. I couldn't see her face, but I could tell her wheels were turning. "What are you thinking?" I asked quietly.

She was silent for a second before she leaned up on her hands again, her eyes meeting mine in the near-dark. "I was thinking about the buttercups, Carson. I was thinking that you glow as well. To me, you shine."

I let out a shaky breath of gratitude and then smiled, but I didn't say anything. I just pulled her closer and said a silent prayer of thanks that she was in my arms.

CHAPTER 32
Grace

"Wake up, sleeping buttercup," I heard whispered close to my ear.

"Grrrhmmph," I moaned and turned my head away from the annoying sound and snuggled back in to my pillow.

I heard a low, sexy chuckle and my blood started pumping just a little bit faster in response—but not enough to want to drag myself out of sleep. I was so warm, and this bed smelled so good. I turned my face into the pillow and breathed in deeply. *Carson.* That was crazy though. I hadn't seen Carson in years. I missed him. I missed his smell and his touch. And so I'd stay in this dream world just a little longer. He was here and I didn't want to leave.

An earthquake hit, shaking the bed violently and I squealed and bolted up, blinking at the room around me in terror.

"Still not much of a morning person, huh, buttercup?" Carson grinned down at me from where he was standing at the base of the bed. *Standing. On. The. Bed.*

"Were you jumping on the bed?" I asked. "That's an outrageous way to wake a person up. I thought the big one had hit," I grumped, falling back on the pillow.

"Yup. It's like waking the dead," he said, climbing down.

I snorted. "What time is it?"

"Five a.m. Come on. I want to be on the slopes by the time the sun rises and we still have to rent gear for you."

I grumbled a little more mostly on principle alone, but finally lugged myself out of bed and followed Carson into the bathroom as he started the shower for me.

I brushed my teeth and when I was done, I shooed him out so that I could pee in privacy and then convince my body to wake up under the shower spray.

"I'll make coffee," he called behind him cheerfully. Some people really were annoyingly chipper in the morning. It was hard to like people like that.

I climbed under the hot spray and began lathering my body with soap. Yes, it was difficult to like morning people. Even ones who had broad shoulders and rock-hard abs. Even ones who had smiles that made your heart skip a beat and sparks shoot down your spine. Even ones who had a beautiful little dimple right under his full bottom lip—God's last paint-brush flourish to the masterpiece that was Carson Stinger.

Even morning people who rescued women as their self-appointed job, despite the huge personal risk.

I stopped mid-lather and just stood there for a minute, letting that reality take hold. *He rescues women.* Women who were slated to exist in back-alley brothels, little girls who would end up as some sick tourist's plaything somewhere in a seedy room. I wasn't the most educated person in the world when it came to human trafficking, but I knew enough that even thinking about it made my stomach turn violently. My

God, I was still stunned when I stopped to ponder on what Carson and his friends were doing.

Okay, so it wasn't difficult at all to like some morning people. In fact, I really, really liked my morning person. He was exceptional, actually. *A hero.*

I got out of the shower and pulled a towel around my body and then returned to the bedroom and dressed quickly in a sweater and jeans.

As I was pulling on socks, Carson walked in with a steaming cup of coffee. "More awake?" he asked.

"Hmmm…" I said. I was more awake and capable of thought but not capable of too much conversation just yet. I'd need a little more caffeine for that.

I finished my coffee at the kitchen island as Carson got our stuff together, and then he came over and put my boots on me. "This is one of those bad things about me," I said. "I'm a grump in the morning."

He chuckled. "I already knew that." He winked. "And I came back for more anyway."

He put his arms around my waist and lifted me from the barstool. "Let's go watch another sunrise together, buttercup," he whispered. "One of many more to follow."

———————

I leaned back on Carson as we waited for the sun to rise from the top of the ski trail. He wrapped his arms around me and kissed the side of my neck gently, the same way he'd done when we'd watched our first sunrise together so many years ago.

I looked over my shoulder at him. If I knew that a boy in a beanie and snow goggles pushed up on his head was so damn sexy, I would have been trolling the slopes long ago.

"What are you grinning about?" he asked.

"I like this look on you. No, I love it actually. Especially the goggles."

"Oh yeah? Because I could wear them later in bed. Naked with goggles."

I burst out laughing. "Actually, that sounds kind of creepy." I tilted my head. "But also? Kind of sexy."

He laughed and pulled me closer.

A sparkle of light hit my eye, and I said, "Shh, the sun's coming up."

He leaned down close to my ear. "I'm pretty sure it will keep rising whether we whisper or not, buttercup."

I swatted him. "Ha-ha. I just meant, let's give it the proper respect it deserves."

He kissed me quickly. "Good point."

We watched the morning sun until it had broken over the horizon and the snowy hills surrounding us were glittering and bathed in yellow light. Then Carson took my hand and so began my first snowboarding lesson.

I sucked.

No, I really sucked. By the time I was competent enough to go down a hill without falling down, it was only because the pain of pushing myself back up with my arms was so utterly intolerable that I remained standing through sheer determination alone.

I didn't think I had ever laughed so hard at myself though, and Carson was patient and funny and didn't show off...too much. Although, honestly, I didn't mind. He was a thing of beauty on the slopes. He was as comfortable with his feet anchored to a board, sliding over the snow, as he was walking through a parking lot. A couple times, he brought me up a higher hill and he went up and down a couple times while I practiced staying upright, and then he finally joined up with me again to continue my lesson.

Eventually, when my body couldn't take it any longer, Carson took my hand and grinned at me and said, "You're a trooper. You did really well today."

"Well?" I groaned. "I was awful. I was on my ass more than I was on my feet."

"Everyone starts out that way. We'll try again."

"I don't think so. You're amazing at this and I would love to come back here again. But you snowboard and I'll keep the hot tub warm back at the cabin."

He laughed. "We'll see."

"Hmm. Yeah, we'll see. Hey, before we turn my gear in, I want to see you do a jump."

He raised an eyebrow. "You sure? You'll have to go down another hill."

My arms screamed out in protest. "I'll sacrifice," I said.

"Okay." He smiled. "Then let's go."

We took the lift up to an even higher run, and Carson told me to go about halfway down the mountain and watch the jump that would be to my left.

I made my way down and stopped off to the side of the ski run, watching the jump. It was after noon now, and I was starving since we had only had coffee for breakfast. But I wouldn't leave the slopes without seeing Carson perform some of the jumps he had described to me earlier when I'd asked him his favorite part of snowboarding. He had called it "catching air."

It was the day before Christmas and the slopes were practically deserted so it was easy to keep my eye on him.

After a minute, I saw him coming down the slope fast and sure as he lined himself up with the jump in front of him, and my heart started thumping loudly in my chest. *God, he is magnificent.*

I sucked in a sharp breath as he went soaring off the edge, bending his knees and doing a full rotation in the air. I squealed and unexpectedly, tears filled my eyes. It was one of those moments when a human being does something so remarkable, so unbelievably amazing, that your heart soars and a lump immediately forms in your throat at the sheer beauty of it. And in my case, the intense pride in the fact that that human was mine.

Carson landed, bending his knees and absorbing the impact perfectly, steady and sure. I could barely make out his face as he turned around at the bottom of the hill, but I could tell he was grinning.

And if I was in trouble? If I needed a rescuer? He was exactly who I would hope to show up. That man. My man.

I put my gloved hand over my heart. "And that, ladies and gentlemen, is all she wrote," I whispered to myself, knowing I was a total goner when it came to Carson Stinger. And I was perfectly fine with that.

Carson

I lathered Grace's hair and rubbed her scalp with the pads of my fingers, working the shampoo through.

"Hmmm," she moaned in front of me in the shower, making my groin throb. I ignored it though for now. My buttercup was in so much pain that she couldn't even reach her hands over her head to shampoo her own hair. Of course, I didn't mind being of service when it came to Grace naked under running water. But I did feel bad that she had worked her body so hard that she could barely move.

I turned her around and backed her up slightly so she could tip her head and I could rinse her hair out under the spray. She smiled lazily up at me.

"Better?" I asked, wondering if the combo of the Advil I'd given her and the hot water was helping her achy muscles.

She nodded, closing her eyes as the water ran over her head and down her body.

After we had left the slopes, we had gone to the restaurant in the lodge where the rental shop was and enjoyed hot soup and sandwiches.

After that, Grace had insisted that we go find a small tree. The next day was Christmas and she laughingly said that even though we were our gifts to each other and we had already been opened, we still needed a tree. I didn't care about a tree so much, but I'd do anything to make her happy, and so off we went to find one.

We asked at the restaurant we ate lunch in and were told that there was a Christmas tree lot right out of town, and so we drove there and picked from what was left, which wasn't much. But when Grace's eyes lit up at a Charlie Brown–looking thing near the gate, I laughed and told the guy working there that we'd take it.

We'd made a stop at the hardware store in town—one of the only stores that hadn't closed early—and bought a couple strings of lights. All they had were large outdoor lights, but they'd have to do as decoration. But Grace seemed satisfied with that.

By this point, the stiffness was setting in and she was moving more and more slowly, so I took her home, gave her the pain meds, and told her to go take a hot shower.

I brought the tree and lights inside and stood the tree up in the stand, and that's when I'd heard her groaning in pain. I'd gone in to see what was wrong, and she was practically crying with the effort to raise her arms above her head and wash her hair. Clearly, my services were necessary.

I wasn't going to complain too much.

Once her hair was rinsed, I turned her around again and massaged her shoulders and arms. She moaned. "Oh, God, that's like heaven," she said as she rotated her head.

With her moans and small whimpers, my cock perked up to see what was going on. But I urged him down. She was in pain, and we had all the time in the world to explore each other in any and every way. Damn, I liked that thought.

I finished helping her wash and then we got out of the shower to string the lights on our sad, little tree. In truth though, when we sat back on the couch, snuggling, with a roaring fire in the fireplace, I looked at that half-bare, leaning tree, decorated with overly large, outdoor house lights, and I didn't think I'd ever seen a more beautiful Christmas tree in my life.

I pulled Grace against me and I knew, without a doubt in my mind, that I loved her. I was in love with the woman in my arms. And the feeling of loving her was as peaceful as the snow falling gently outside the window. Maybe I had loved her for a long, long time. Maybe it didn't matter when or how or why. Maybe love was complicated and yet the simplest thing in the whole wide world.

She snuggled into me and the words hitched in my throat. After a minute, she turned to me and looked into my eyes. "Happy Christmas Eve, Carson," she whispered.

I smiled down at her. "Happy Christmas Eve, buttercup."

CHAPTER 33
Grace

I woke up to the sounds of birds outside the window, rays of sunlight streaming in around the closed shades. It was Christmas! I rolled over lazily and stretched, and then snuggled into Carson's warm back. He sighed, and I kissed the smooth skin of his shoulders, my lips lingering on his small scar, breathing him in.

"Good morning," he said, sleep still present in his voice. What a glorious sound to wake up to.

"Hi," I whispered. "So you don't *always* get up at the butt crack of dawn, huh?"

He chuckled. "No, not always. Especially not when I have a warm, soft buttercup to snuggle with."

He turned toward me and we snuggled for a few more minutes, our hands roaming as my insides warmed.

"How are your muscles this morning?" he asked.

"Good. Better." I could still feel some residual stiffness, but more like I'd done a hard workout, rather than threw myself under a moving train, like I'd felt the day before.

Carson came over me and made love to me slowly and gently, moving his hips leisurely until I groaned out in frustration, and he smiled against my shoulder and finally, finally sped up.

I cried out and Carson groaned against my neck when our orgasms hit us simultaneously, goose bumps rising on his skin.

"God, I love to hear you scream," he said, his breath hot against my ear, muffled so I could barely make out his words. He pulled out of me, rolling slightly to the side.

"I'll try to get a hold on that," I said with a soft laugh. It was so nice to let go though, so nice to get so completely lost in him.

He leaned up. "No way. We'll just buy a house way out in the countryside so we won't disturb the neighbors."

"A house?" My eyes widened. "Really?"

He studied me. "Someday, yeah, a house. I want to come home to you, Grace. I want to have Princess and Junior with you." He paused, his eyes filling with even more warmth, and a hint of vulnerability. "I love you," he said softly.

I let out a small breath. I had realized I loved him the night before, sitting in front of the fire, looking at our pathetically beautiful Christmas tree, and it was confirmed for me a million times over as I stared into his hopeful expression now. "I love you too," I said. It felt so natural, so...destined. It felt like it'd always been meant to be this way—me in his arms, whispering words of love.

The smile that took over his face was stunning and immediate. "You do?"

I nodded, my eyes filling with tears. "Yeah, I do," I said. "I really do. And I love that you remembered Princess and Junior."

"I'd never forget our kids, buttercup."

I laughed and sniffled. "Merry Christmas, Carson."

"Merry Christmas, Grace. Come on, let's get up. I have something for you."

He stood up and started to move toward the bathroom to toss the condom he'd thankfully been awake enough to grab, and I sat up too. "What? You have something for me? How?"

"Don't worry about that," he called from the hallway. "Just get up and meet me in the kitchen."

I got up and pulled on Carson's boxer shorts and one of my sweatshirts.

I stopped by the bathroom and then went out to the kitchen to find Carson making coffee. I got the ingredients out for pancakes and bacon and started preparing to cook.

He came up behind me and put his arms around my waist, whispering into my ear, "I love you, I love you, I love you." He smiled against my neck. "I love saying that."

I grinned and turned my head so that I could kiss him. "Hmmm…I love hearing it. I love *you*."

We stood that way for a few minutes and then I whispered sadly, "I wish everything back in Vegas was magically fixed and we could just stay here forever."

He sighed. "Yeah, unfortunately it doesn't work that way, buttercup. It's going to be okay though. Somehow, it is. And we're going to come back up here for Christmas next year and we're going to bring all our friends and family, and we're going to celebrate the fact that it's all behind us."

God, that sounded like a dream come true. I turned around, facing him now. "Promise?"

He nodded. "Yeah, I promise," he said, kissing me softly on my lips. "Now make me breakfast, woman."

I pushed him away and then swatted him on his ass.

"Move back, Carson Stinger. You're about to experience the best pancakes you've ever eaten."

"Yes, ma'am," he said, chuckling and going back to the coffeemaker.

We sat down at the kitchen island to eat and Carson groaned when he took the first bite of my pancakes. "Good God, woman, you know your way around a bowl of batter."

I laughed. "Damn straight. I'm the Christmas morning pancake maker in my house," I said, picking up a piece of bacon and dipping it in syrup.

Carson took a sip of coffee, studying me over the rim of his mug before lowering it. "Are you okay not being with them today?" he asked.

"I miss them. I need to call them in a little bit here. But there's nowhere I'd rather be than right here with you."

He smiled. We finished our breakfast and then brought a second cup of coffee each into the family room. There was a small present sitting under the tree. I stopped and turned to Carson. "Seriously, how'd you manage that?" I asked, tilting my head toward the gift below the tree.

"I picked something up in town when I was buying your boots and coat."

I put my hands on my hips. "Hmmm, very sneaky." I frowned. "But no fair because I don't have anything for you. And you got me something. And it's our first Christmas."

Carson took my coffee and set both our cups on the side table and then pulled me to him. "Grace, I don't think you get me very well. You broke off your engagement, changed Christmas plans with your family, ran through an airport, changed a flight, borrowed a car, drove six hours, hiked through snow, and practically got frostbite to be with me. And then when I told you I was involved in activities not exactly looked upon favorably by the legal system, a system in which you've made your career, you trusted me and accepted it without batting an eyelash. You asked how we were going to handle this when I told you about Josh, and you…well, you're pretty fantastic in bed too." He smiled and it was sort of teasing, but mostly it was tender and full of love. And though I gave him a small laugh, tears were also burning the backs of my eyes. "You've given me so many gifts that I'm overwhelmed."

"Well then," I whispered, "I guess a better question is, is that *all* you got me?"

He laughed. "Yeah. I'll try to do better next year." He let go of me to light a fire in the fireplace as I sat on the couch sipping my coffee. He brought me the small gift, and I smiled at him as I tore the paper open.

It was a jewelry store box. I glanced up at Carson and he smiled gently at me, a glint of nervousness in his eyes.

I pulled the top open and inside was a beautiful silver charm bracelet. "It's beautiful," I whispered.

"Do you have one?" he asked.

"No, I don't have a charm bracelet," I said. "Will you put it on me?" I held my wrist out.

"Wait, you didn't look at the charm," he said, turning the bracelet over.

I looked down at the small, silver coin on the other side. I stared at it for a moment, finally understanding. Tears filled my eyes and I looked up at him. "A shot for a secret," I said.

He nodded. "That's where it all started." I stood up and threw my arms around him, kissing his face—his lips, his cheeks, his eyes, his forehead. "I love it. It's the best present I've ever received."

"Good. I'm glad you like it. I can't wait to add to it," he said.

I nodded, sniffling as he fastened it around my wrist.

I kissed him one last time and then said, "I should call my family."

"Okay. We'll need to drive into town to get reception. Just pull on some warmer clothes and we'll make the call from my truck."

"Okay." I went back into the bedroom and changed into some warmer clothes and a few minutes later, we were driving into town. I took my phone out of my purse and turned it on, seeing that I had reception. I had checked it the couple times we were in town and I had texted my sisters once to let them know I'd made it to Utah. The only message on it now was a return text from Julia and a voice-mail from her number too.

Carson pulled into a parking space on the street and turned to me. "Do you want me to take a walk while you make the call?" he asked.

I smiled but shook my head no. I dialed my dad's number first and took a deep breath, bouncing my knee as I waited for him to answer.

When I heard his deep bark on the phone, I said softly, "Merry Christmas, Dad," with a forced smile in my voice.

"Grace?" his voice softened.

"Hi, Dad!" I brightened. "Are you having a nice morning?"

"Well, yeah, darlin', I am, only I'm kinda missing my oldest girl. It seems she's run off with some man and left her old dad and her sisters high and dry."

I took in a deep breath. All my life I'd worked so hard to make my dad proud, and by and large, succeeded. Even when I'd changed plans, I'd sought something socially acceptable to replace it with. But this? Well this was an entirely different beast. For the first time in my life, I'd not only changed plans, I'd done something my dad might have a hard time explaining to his friends. I'd ended my engagement suddenly and unexpectedly and went running off to be with another man.

I glanced over at Carson. He looked nervous as well, staring out the window, his jaw tense as he too bounced his knee. I stilled my own. He was worried that in choosing him, I was going to pay a price with my family. I sat up straighter, my love for him filling me with conviction. I was proud of what I'd done. I hadn't followed a plan. I'd followed my heart. And dammit, I'd do it again, a thousand times over. "No, Dad," I said, "you know I'd never leave you high and dry. But it was an emergency situation and I had to act fast. You know how you always taught me to act first and ask questions later? Well, that's what I did." Next to me, I saw Carson's knee stop bouncing too.

There was a beat of silence on the other end of the phone. "Well, I guess I can't argue with that. You love him, I suppose?"

I exhaled a whoosh of breath. "Yeah, Dad, I do, I love him. And," I said, "I think you will too." I glanced over at Carson to see him watching me, his lips tilted in a gentle smile.

"Well, if he's someone who's got your love, Gracie, I gotta figure he's okay. What happened to the one we went to dinner with in Vegas? I forget his name now."

I laughed, knowing very well he didn't forget Alex's name. Or that I was engaged to him. "We were just better off as friends."

"Well, I guess it's best that you realized that before the wedding rather than after, so good job there. You saved me a boatload of wasted money." He paused. "I love you, Gracie."

"I love you too. Merry Christmas. Did you get the package I shipped?"

"Yup. Just about to rip into it. You'll have to get your presents at Easter."

You're my gift, Dad. You always have been, all my life. "Okay."

"Okay, Gracie. Merry Christmas."

"Merry Christmas. Bye, Dad."

I hung up, sniffling and smiling at the same time. Then I texted Julia and Audrey a group text:

Merry Christmas! Miss you! Love you! Group call ASAP next week! Xxoo

I turned off my phone and smiled at Carson, scooting over and snuggling into his side. He hugged me to him.

"Everything good?" he asked quietly.

"Yeah, everything's good."

Just as he was lowering his lips to mine, his phone rang. I sat up and moved to my side of the cab so he could answer it.

"Hello?" he answered. He listened for a couple seconds. "Okay," he said, the word clipped. "We're leaving now." He turned to me and I saw the worry in his expression. "We need to get back to the cabin and pack. There's a situation at the hotel. We've gotta go."

Carson had given me a quick rundown of what was going on as we showered very quickly and packed up the cabin.

Apparently, Dylan thought he was close to pinpointing the location of the guy who had set Josh up, and they needed all the guys close by, just in case.

There was also a situation going on, on the forty-fifth floor with one of the women. She was pregnant, and although she didn't know her exact dates, the doctor who had originally

378

examined her thought she was about eight and a half months along. They all thought they could get her home before she had her baby, but she had gone into labor that morning. Likely, she was further along than they thought.

They had two doctors on the payroll that performed their services under the table, but both of them were out of town for Christmas. They would take her to the hospital if necessary, but questions might arise there. They thought a better option would be to bring Josh in, since he had been a corpsman and was plenty qualified to deliver a baby as long as no complications arose.

We had to drive back to Vegas separately, since we had two vehicles between us. That kind of sucked since I really wanted to use the time to discuss Josh's situation in more detail with Carson. However, I'd successfully put the case on the back burner as I'd enjoyed our reunion, and so now, I used the time alone to try to get things straight in my mind about the evidence against Josh and whether there were any loose threads that could potentially be used to exonerate him. I went over each piece, but I couldn't come up with anything. Unfortunately, the evidence against him was overwhelming and included plenty of DNA. Juries loved DNA—they'd come back with a guilty verdict in ten minutes. The more I thought about it, the more depressed I got. The only thing I could do was bungle the case so badly that Josh got off on a technicality. Of course, that would be career suicide. But I couldn't let an innocent man spend his life in prison. It felt like an impossible situation.

The more I pondered, the more I realized what a dangerous job Carson had taken on, full of risk not only to life and limb, but to freedom. How would I feel, sitting at home, knowing the risks he was taking every time he walked out the door on one of his "operations"?

Then again, I was already well acquainted with that scenario. I was a cop's daughter. I knew the risk my dad took every time he put his badge on, and I was fiercely proud, just like I was of Carson. I would deal with it, just like I always had with my dad, this time knowing that the man I loved was doing work that fulfilled him and made him a hero to those who truly needed one.

Carson called me when we were about two hours from Vegas and told me to follow him off the freeway so that we could find a place to eat lunch.

When I pulled Dylan's SUV up behind his truck in the parking lot of a roadside Denny's and got out, he was walking toward me, smiling. I ran the last few feet to him and jumped up, wrapping my legs around his waist. "I missed you," I said.

He was laughing. "I missed you too."

I kissed him for a minute, a gross display of PDA that I was sure was getting us plenty of "get a room" looks. Whatever. What those onlookers didn't know was that I'd waited almost five years for this and I wasn't about to apologize for taking full advantage.

We ate a quick lunch and were back on the road half an hour later.

When we pulled into the garage at Trilogy, I followed Carson to the back, where he must have used a remote in his truck to open a roll-up door that, upon first inspection, looked like a storage area.

He drove his truck in and I followed him, the door rolling closed behind me. A light blinked on and I got out and looked around at the large, mostly empty area containing two other black SUVs, and now Carson's truck and Dylan's SUV.

"What is this?" I asked as Carson approached.

"Just a more private place for us to park so no one can get in and run our license plates. Dylan doesn't usually park in here. His background wouldn't look interesting to anyone. But the rest of us do, and we keep a few extra vehicles here as well."

I nodded. Well this certainly made the fact that Carson was involved in a bona fide secret operation suddenly very real.

We walked through a door and up a back staircase that opened into a hallway. Carson grabbed my hand as we rounded the corner and waited for an elevator.

When we stepped on, Carson pulled me to him and kissed me, hard and wet. He broke away and smiled down at me as I swayed on my feet. "God, I love elevators," he said.

I laughed, grateful for the moment of lightness before we walked into what, for me, was an unknown situation.

I followed Carson through lavish hallways to what looked like an office door. He knocked and opened it before getting any response, and then took my hand as we stepped inside. Three men turned toward us. The first man, tall and muscled, with black hair, was wearing a deep frown on his face. I'd seen him before, outside Carson's office door after he'd given me an orgasm against the well. I didn't remember his name though. I'd barely remembered *mine* after that interlude. I shifted my eyes away.

I recognized Dylan, although he looked slightly more rumpled than a couple days before and like he had been running his hand repeatedly through his messy, blond hair.

I also recognized Josh Garner from his mug shot. I had

381

thought he was a good-looking guy when I first looked at the picture, but it didn't do him justice. He was…well, he was no Carson Stinger, but he was easy on the eyes, that was for sure. He had dark-brown, slightly spiky hair, a strong jaw, and, yup, dimples. I knew this because he was walking toward us smiling.

He bumped Carson and Carson took a step to the side at the impact, and then Josh stepped in, holding out his hand to me. "Hi, I'm Josh," he said, smiling what I was sure was his best panty-melting smile. *Cocky for someone facing life in prison.* Still, I could admit the smile was disarming and I gave him one in return.

Carson stepped back next to me and pulled me to him before I could reach out for Josh's hand. "Yeah, fucker, this is Grace Hamilton, the prosecutor on your case. She was on board to help you, but you just reminded me why it might be a better idea to let her do her job well."

Josh laughed, dropping his hand. "Down, boy. I was just making the lady's acquaintance." He winked at me. "Also, I think it's in my best interest to get on her good side."

"She's on *my* good side, and that's the best you should hope for," Carson said, giving Josh a searing look and moving us past him to the other guys. But I smiled at Josh again as we walked by.

"Grace, you met Dylan," Carson said, gesturing his head to where Dylan was standing.

"Your car is gassed up and parked in the garage, Dylan," I said. "Thank you." I hoped he could see the deep sincerity in my eyes. His grin as he looked back and forth between me and Carson told me he did.

Carson gestured to the taller man, "This is Leland McManus. He owns Trilogy."

"Hi, Leland. Nice to, er, see you again," I said, and he nodded, saying, "Hi Grace, nice to officially meet you." His expression held a slight bit of amusement. He had the most piercing blue eyes I'd ever seen. "It appears you both had a nice trip?" he said to me and Carson.

"Yeah, you could say that," I said, smiling up at Carson.

He smiled back, his eyes soft.

"Okay, lovebirds, we all get the picture. There wasn't a lot of skiing going on in Snowbird," Josh said, joining us and rolling his eyes as he looked around. "Let's get down to business here."

Dylan coughed, and Leland stifled a laugh. Carson furrowed his brow at Josh, but one side of his mouth quirked up.

A cell phone rang, and Leland pulled it out of his pocket. "Hello?" He looked over at Josh and tipped his chin. "Okay, he's on his way down."

He hung up the phone and looked at Josh. "Your services are required, doc."

"Okay. Anyone want to assist me here?" Josh asked.

Leland held up his hands and backed away. "I've got a hotel to run."

Dylan did the same. "I've got computer programs processing data that need monitoring…"

Josh rolled his eyes again. "Wimps. Carson?"

"I don't mind helping," Carson said. "As long as Grace is okay coming along?"

"I mean…" I'd never seen a baby born. I wasn't going to be much help when it came to the medical side of things. But there were women in that room, and I was a woman. Surely it would make them all feel more comfortable if a woman was assisting with something so intimate? "I'd be happy to. Yes. Just tell me what to do."

"Uh, guys, it sounded kind of serious down there," Leland interrupted.

We hurried out of Leland's office and Carson took my hand as we all three rushed to the elevator. Josh put a key in and then pressed forty-five and we rode down a couple floors.

There was a guard just outside the elevator and he nodded when he saw Josh and Carson. "Hey, guys. It sounds pretty intense in there."

"Intense situations are our specialty," Josh said.

The guard laughed.

We walked down a hallway and heard yelling just beyond a door to the right.

Josh took out a key and opened the door, and we all three took in the scene in front of us.

Carson

I had been in this room many times over the last couple months but I tried to imagine what Grace was thinking now as I took in Maria lying on her side on the bed, hugging a pillow for dear life, and moaning loudly. Yoselin was putting a wet cloth on her forehead and Gisella sitting on the side of the bed, rubbing her lower back.

The only other girls in the room were Deisy and Vanessa, both twelve. They were sitting huddled on the couch, watching a show on television, their eyes darting to Maria every few minutes. They were obviously scared. "Grace, do you mind sitting with them and calming their nerves?" She nodded, heading toward the girls.

All the women in the room were Venezuelan—the only

ones we hadn't been able to get back home before Christmas, due to some problems getting their paperwork. But everything was in order now for them to fly out on the twenty-seventh. It looked like there would be one extra passenger.

Josh laid the first-aid kit he had brought on the bed and went straight to the bathroom to wash up. I asked Yoselin how Maria was doing. Yoselin was the only one in the room who spoke English so she would need to translate.

"I've seen babies born, Mr. Carson. I think she's close."

"Okay. Josh is going to check in just a second."

I looked up at Maria, eyes squeezed shut tight, moaning in pain. "Maria, we're here to help you deliver your baby. Everything's going to be fine." I felt like a jackass saying that. How the hell did I know everything was going to be fine? I didn't know a damn thing about delivering babies. Yoselin translated for me, her voice soft and reassuring. Maria didn't respond, but hopefully she'd taken in the words, inadequate as they were.

I glanced over at Grace who was sitting on the couch with Deisy and Vanessa who were smiling up at her as she doled out sticks of gum from her purse. Apparently there was no language barrier when it came to kids and gum.

Josh came out of the bathroom and got to work examining Maria. I moved to the side, ready to assist Josh if necessary but not wanting to get in the way.

"She's ten," Josh said after a minute. "Baby is head down. Looks good. Let's do this. Are you with me, Maria?"

Yoselin translated and Maria nodded, still grimacing.

Yoselin and Gisella both grabbed one of Maria's legs and she started to push. I went to the bathroom and got another cool cloth and a bunch of towels.

I returned to the room, where Maria was now screaming

during every push, the women counting in Spanish. I turned to Grace, and she was leaning back on the couch, a girl in each arm, their faces pressed into her chest.

Twenty minutes later, with one final scream, the sound of a baby's cry filled the room, and Maria collapsed back on the pillow.

"It's a boy," Josh announced, tying off the umbilical cord and cutting it with a pair of small scissors. The baby gave a few more lusty yells and then was quiet, opening his eyes and looking around. "Welcome to this crazy world, little man," Josh said as he wiped the baby gently.

I looked over at Grace and she was watching Josh, her brow furrowed slightly, looking as if she was working out a puzzle. She was probably trying to figure him out—he was a smartass and a ladies' man most of the time, but he had different sides to him too, the side who put himself in harm's way for the women we rescued, and the side that had just delivered Maria's baby with skill and sensitivity. He would confuse the hell out of some woman someday. *Someday.* The word echoed in my head. Please let him get a someday that doesn't include prison bars. Please let him get a someday that doesn't include prison bars.

I caught Grace's eye, and she smiled gently at me, pulling the two girls closer to her.

Gisella and I started cleaning up while Josh finished attending to Maria, and Yoselin held the baby, wrapped in a hotel blanket. He was quiet now.

Grace, Deisy, and Vanessa came over to look at the baby. Yoselin offered him to Grace and she took him in her arms, a dreamy look on her face as she peered down at him. She ran her fingers through his full head of thick, black hair.

"He's so beautiful, Maria," she whispered.

Yoselin repeated Grace's words in Spanish and we all looked at Maria to see she was staring out the window, frowning.

"Do you want to hold your son?" Grace asked, extending the baby toward her.

Maria glanced at Grace but shook her head and looked away. She still hadn't expressed any interest in the baby.

Grace, Josh, and I all exchanged looks.

"Yoselin, will you ask her what's wrong?" I said quietly.

Yoselin went and sat next to Maria and talked to her quietly for a minute, and then looked up at all of us sadly. "She says he is the devil's spawn and she doesn't want to touch him."

Grace's eyes widened and she pulled the baby closer to her chest. "The devil's spawn…" she whispered. "Why would she say that?"

Yoselin looked at her. "Maria is only seventeen. Her family sold her to a man who came to her village in Venezuela and told them that she would be doing housework for rich families and could send some of the money back to them. Instead, he raped and tortured her. And then he brought her here to Vegas to sell her to other men so they could do the same. That is when she was rescued with the rest of us," she said, waving her hand around the room to indicate the other women and girls there.

Grace's eyes were wide with sadness as she blinked away tears. I had heard it all and worse, but it never ceased to make my guts squeeze with the sickness and depravity of it all. I'd never become desensitized to the horror of their stories. Ever.

Maria started talking and Yoselin listened, her eyes growing sadder.

"She says that her mama always told her that us women are the gatekeepers of the world. Only *we* get to decide which men become fathers, whose bloodline continues and whose does not. And we must choose wisely. She says that the boy is the spawn of an evil man, an evil bloodline."

I glanced at Grace and something fierce lit her expression. She moved to the other side of the bed and sat down next to Maria. She looked at Yoselin. "Will you translate for me?"

"Maria," she said, and Maria jerked slightly but continued to stare out the window. "I agree with your mama. But I also think that in our broken world, sometimes things happen that we don't control and cannot plan. I agree that us women should be the gatekeepers, but I also believe that this world needs strong, good men—men who are raised by mamas who have seen what weak men do. You have the ability to serve justice—by making your son everything his father was not."

Yoselin finished speaking quietly, and Maria's eyes darted quickly to Grace and then to the baby in her arms and then away.

My breath caught, and my chest felt tight, and I knew it wasn't only because I loved the woman speaking with such tenderness and conviction to a woman she didn't even know. It was also because my story began in a similar way to the unwanted boy lying in Grace's arms. A mistake. Created not in love, but by accident. And I knew Grace realized that too by the way her eyes landed on me repeatedly as she spoke, her voice soft and filled with love.

And if I hadn't known it before, I knew in that moment that there was no one better to have at my side, not just as my love and my partner, but as an extension of this team.

Maria spoke, but she sounded a little unsure now. "He is half of *him*," Yoselin translated.

"He is half of *you*," Grace countered and Yoselin repeated. Maria looked fully at Grace's face now, studying it.

"He's so precious, so beautiful," Grace said softly, her eyes falling on me. "Beauty from pain, a gift. Do you want to hold him?" she asked. "Do you want to hold your son?"

When Yoselin translated, Maria shook her head no and spoke softly. Yoselin said, "She wants to see him though."

Grace held the sleeping baby toward Maria so that she could peer down into his face. She looked at him for a minute and her face softened as she spoke. "She says he looks just like her papa," Yoselin said.

Grace smiled and held the baby toward her. After a minute, she reached out her arms and took him. She looked at him for long minutes as we watched her and then she snuggled him to her chest, a tear falling down her cheek. Grace stood and Gisella sat down on the bed, and then both she and Yoselin snuggled Maria from either side, and the little girls climbed up on the bed and sat at Maria's feet, watching the women and the baby. After a minute, Yoselin started to gently show Maria how to nurse him.

"Wrap a towel around his bottom for now," Josh said to Yoselin. "Someone will be back shortly with some diapers and clothes and other necessities." Josh moved toward the door, and I took Grace's hand.

The women looked up from the baby, smiled and nodded, and moved their gazes down to his little face again. It was clear all of them were busy falling in love. He was going to be just fine.

Once we were all three on the elevator heading back down to Leland's office, Grace looked between me and Josh and asked sadly, "How do you do it?"

I gave her a sad smile. "How can we not?"

389

Josh nodded but didn't say anything, stepping off the elevator first when the doors opened.

Dylan rushed out of his computer room, a look of sheer excitement on his face. "Suit up, boys," he said. "I got him."

CHAPTER 34
Grace

My heart was beating out of my chest as Carson rushed into Leland's office with the other guys. I stayed back, not wanting to get in the way. I knew that it all came down to this.

Leland glanced over at me, and Carson saw his movement and nodded at him, indicating it was okay to talk in front of me. My heart squeezed with love for him. He trusted me with everything.

"You gotta move, guys," Dylan said first. "Gabriel Bakos is currently in a warehouse in Henderson, but you know this guy, he doesn't stay anywhere very long. He fucked up—maybe he figured because it's Christmas, we'd be off duty."

"You got the location of the family too?" Leland asked.

"Yeah, finally. He did a decent job of hiding them. But that's how I got him too. Fucker went through the estate gates in a delivery truck. Only that particular delivery company doesn't deliver on Christmas Day. Sloppy. I knew he must be inside and so I tracked it back to Henderson.

And get this, he only has two guards with him—he must have given the other three Christmas Day off. He's quite the benevolent fellow."

All the men snorted.

"What else?" Josh asked.

"I downloaded the layout of the warehouse to your glasses."

"Okay, wait," Carson said. "We need at least three men to go in after Bakos. It takes that many of us just to clear a room properly. Any less would be too risky. That means we need you to film the family, Dylan."

"Who's gonna be the driver then?" Dylan frowned.

They all looked over at me and my eyes widened. Fear had my brain buzzing and I was working to follow along with the plan they were laying out. This was all so outside my frame of reference.

"No way," Carson gritted out. "No fucking way Grace is driving. We drive ourselves this time."

"We need a lookout, Carson," Leland said.

Carson shook his head. "We forgo a driver and a lookout just this once. I won't risk Grace's safety. I'd be no good to you if I knew she was sitting outside waiting for us," he said.

"Okay, no lookout this time," Leland said. "We capture Bakos, and Josh can go sit in the car while we question him and get what we need."

"Oh, hell no," Josh said. "If anyone gets the pleasure of talking to Bakos, it's me."

Leland paused. "Fair enough. Let's go get dressed. It's already dark out. We need to move."

Everyone nodded, starting to move toward the door. Apparently they had already made some kind of more elaborate plan and were just working out the details. At least I really hoped that was the case.

As we all walked out the office door, I noticed Leland's slight limp and recalled Carson's story of their team's ambush. It was a reminder to me that they were both lucky to be alive and caused a bolt of fear to arrow down my spine.

Carson took my hand and I followed the men down the hall to another room. Leland opened the door and he and Josh went inside. I saw lockers and showers and figured it must be where they "suited up," whatever that meant.

Carson faced me and pulled me into his arms.

"I'm scared," I said against his chest.

"Don't be, buttercup. What happened with Josh was a miscalculation. We won't make the same mistake twice. But in the meantime, you have to trust that we're good at our job and we work together well. We know what we're doing."

I nodded, squeezing him tighter. "Be careful, please?"

He tipped my chin up with his finger, looking into my eyes. "No way I'm going to find you again after all these years and not get to enjoy you for a long, long time. Years. Decades."

I smiled weakly.

"I love you, Grace," he said solemnly.

I closed my eyes for a brief second. "I love you too," I whispered.

He smiled before he said, "Now, I'm going to take you to a room where you can wait for me, maybe try to nap—"

"Nap? Are you serious? I can't *nap*. I'm not staying alone in some hotel room going crazy."

"Baby, you can't leave this hotel. I can't be worrying about you when I need to be focusing on what I'm doing."

"I'll wait with the women and girls. The baby needs

diapers anyway and some clothes." I already felt attached to them. Plus, they had survived worse situations than I could ever imagine. They'd be my reminder to be brave.

He studied me for a second. "Okay. I'll walk you down to the gift shop. It's closed, but Leland has the master key. Then you stay on the forty-fifth floor. No leaving."

Ten minutes later, I had a bag containing whatever baby products the gift shop had—diapers, wipes, five small *I heart Vegas* onesies, a pacifier, and a couple bibs.

Carson dropped me back off at the room where the women and girls were, kissed me one final time, and left.

I sank down onto the couch, but Yoselin gestured for me to join all of them, still on the bed, the baby and Maria fast asleep. Good thing it was a King.

And so that's where I waited for Carson, surrounded by those who had survived the unthinkable but were still able to give comfort when they saw another woman in need of it. And if that wasn't a thing of generous beauty, I didn't know what was.

Carson

We all pulled out of the garage together, Dylan turning in the opposite direction to go to the estate where Bakos was hiding his family. I hoped to God he'd be all right. He wasn't trained for the physical aspect of this and he'd need to get as close as possible to the residence in order to make the video we needed to pull this off. We couldn't ever afford to get complacent— especially after what had happened on our last mission.

We needed more team members. Preacher would be

joining us in the next year. He had agreed to move his family in order to work with us. And Noah would join us as well, as soon as his tour was over. It'd make the whole operation that much safer. But for now, we had to work with what we had—there wasn't much of a choice.

We followed the GPS to the location Dylan had given us and parked a couple blocks away. And then we walked the several blocks to the warehouse, sticking to the shadows of the other buildings. The area was mostly industrial and deserted due to the holiday.

Just like Dylan had said, there were no outside guards. We moved toward the building carefully and quietly, ducking behind anything we could upon our approach.

Steady. Steady. Head on a swivel. No mistakes. I'm coming home to you, buttercup.

Josh and I watched behind us as Leland picked the backdoor lock. He had the door open in roughly thirty seconds. We all put our night vision goggles down and activated the building layout Dylan had downloaded. It showed up in the upper portion of our goggles.

Thankfully our budget was such that we had the most high-tech devices available.

We had already cleared several rooms without hearing any noise when Leland halted in front of us. We all listened carefully. Was that music?

At Leland's command, we moved forward. Well, holy shit, it *was* music. Christmas music. We had showed up for a regular holiday party.

I glanced back at Josh and he gave me the thumbs–up sign, grinning.

We moved in closer and I gestured to Leland to move to the right of the door. Josh took the left. The door was old and wooden, with a cheap, builder-grade lock. Whether it was engaged or not, I wasn't worried.

I held up my fingers, counting, and when I got to three, Leland and Josh looked away as I used all my force to kick the door open. It crashed inward, splinters flying, and we moved in before it could swing back toward us.

The guard closest to the door turned, raising his gun, but Leland moved on him and had him in a choke hold, his weapon clattering to the floor, before the other two men in the room had even fully turned around. He might not be able to run as fast as he used to, but Leland McManus was still a badass.

Josh scooped up the guard's gun, stuck it in the back of his pants, and with one swift movement, brought his knee up and made contact with the other guard who'd been sitting in a chair and was just starting to stand. He fell to the floor, unconscious.

I went for the third man, who I recognized immediately by the pictures I had seen. Gabriel Bakos, evil-piece-of-shit extraordinaire. He sneered at me. "Come and get me, little boy."

Little boy? Was he joking? He was backing up across the room, going for something in the waistband of his pants. *Oh no you don't.* I rushed him and spun him around, removing the gun from his waistband and taking him in a choke hold as I held my own weapon to his side. He grunted as I pushed it into his soft flesh.

"Jesus. That was almost too easy," Josh said, not even breathing hard.

"I don't think you need to take the Lord's name in vain on his birthday," Leland offered.

Josh halted as he went toward the guard lying

unconscious on the floor. "I wasn't taking the Lord's name in vain. I was praising him. Let me rephrase. Thank you, Jesus, my lord and savior, for making that so easy!" he exclaimed, raising his arms to the sky.

I rolled my eyes. "Hey, guys, mind focusing here? We need to separate them." I gestured to the two guards and Bakos.

"I'm going to tie these jokers up in the room next door and make sure they don't move," Leland said, his gaze darting to Bakos's ankle and then away. If I'd blinked, I'd have missed it. But Leland had made sure to give me the sign when I wasn't blinking.

Bakos had a knife at his ankle just as the women who'd been unfortunate enough to make his acquaintance had told us he would. He liked to use that knife to terrorize and intimidate.

I stood up straight. Bakos was fully restrained, breathing hard, but still managing to spit out a string of epithets. I did a quick pat down of his legs for weapons, purposefully "missing" the one at his ankle and sat on the edge of the table.

"Can we cut that shit off?" Josh asked indicating the loud music. Bing Crosby was crooning about a white Christmas from a phone on a shelf in the corner.

I walked over and turned it off and pocketed the device as Leland dragged the second guard out of the room, his limp just slightly more exaggerated under the guard's weight.

I gestured to the half-empty liquor bottle sitting next to three shot glasses. I set my gun down and picked up the bottle, sniffing it. "Good stuff," I said, setting it back down. "That's one of the reasons, taking them down was like a cakewalk," I said to Josh, shaking my head. Even evil mother fuckers let their guard down once in a while. And thankfully, we'd been waiting for just such a moment.

Josh turned to Bakos. "I'm disappointed, old man. I expected more from a real-life super villain."

Bakos narrowed his eyes, looking at Josh with disgust. This man's disgust was a compliment. I itched to obliterate his face. He'd caused so much pain. He'd torn families apart and victimized the weak and the innocent. *Keep calm, Stinger. Don't let your emotions get the best of you. That's when you slip up.* I pulled in a deep breath, picturing Grace's face momentarily. It gave me peace. And purpose. A reason to stay steady.

I watched from the corner of my eye as Bakos's hand moved incrementally toward the weapon at his ankle, and I signaled to Josh the same way Leland had signaled to me. Josh's gaze hung on mine an extra beat, letting me know he got it.

Josh sat down on the edge of the table where I had been a minute before, placing his firearm next to him and crossing his arms, pausing as he studied the fat man with the graying mustache tied to a chair in front of him. "So, Bakos, turns out this probably won't be a very merry Christmas for you. In fact, it's probably gonna be real shitty."

Bakos remained silent, his eyes moving back and forth between us, that hand inching down every time we shifted or glanced away even for a second.

"Here's how it's gonna go, jackass," Josh said. "I'm gonna press record on this little device here and you're going to tell the story about framing me for a murder that I didn't commit."

Bakos laughed. "Why would I do that?" he asked. "I won't talk. I'd rather die knowing you'll spend the rest of your miserable life in prison for trying to ruin my business."

"Your *business*?" Josh asked, narrowing his eyes.

"Yes, my business. Where there is money, there is business."

"You're a piece of human garbage, you know—"

"Josh," I warned, "don't waste your breath on him. Let's just get what we need."

Josh looked back at Bakos, studying him. "We didn't figure you'd talk to save your own sorry ass, but maybe this will convince you," Josh said, taking his cell phone out of his pocket.

Come on, Dylan, I thought. If he had been successful, there'd be a live video streaming to Josh's phone right now. As Josh pressed a few buttons on his phone, I turned my head just enough to give Bakos the opportunity to slide the knife from his ankle. Both of our guns were just out of our reach. If Bakos was quick, he'd take us by surprise, unarmed. But I was almost positive he hadn't gotten free just yet.

Josh held his phone up in front of Bakos. Bakos's face paled.

And I knew we had been right. Even a sick fuck like Bakos, who sold human beings for a living, would try to protect his own family. We were bluffing, but by the look on his face, it was working. We'd also left him a weapon though. And that would give him an extra reason to share the truth and distract us as he worked to get free and then attack.

Josh continued. "Recognize her? Cute, isn't she? See that little red dot that moves wherever she does? That's our sniper's gun. Start talking or he takes her out right now. The guard you have posted in the next room won't even be able to blink before we take them *all* out."

Bakos narrowed his eyes, a look of hatred on his face. Josh clicked on the tape recorder and after a long pause,

Bakos started talking. I couldn't even tell he was sawing at his rope bindings. The man was good at multi-tasking, I'd give him that. The adrenalin must have sobered him up.

"I was in that warehouse the night you came in," Bakos said. "My men and I were going over plans to ship the merchandise out in the morning. While you were taking my guards down, I was able to make it to a hidden room with a trapdoor, with one of the girls as a hostage. The bitch cried and I heard you coming toward the room, so I watched out the peephole until you turned around, and then I opened it and hit you over the head with a rock I found on the floor. Simple. I dragged you inside, gagged the girl and waited until your men left. Then I executed the bitch with your gun, put some of her blood on your clothes, and left the rock in her hand. I had you dropped off in an abandoned house. Easy. I barely broke a sweat." Bakos went silent. And utterly still. A coiled snake, waiting.

Josh clicked off the recorder, his eyes never moving from Bakos. He sent the file to Dylan, and his phone dinged a second later saying Dylan had gotten it and that the file was good. I saw Bakos's thigh muscles tense very subtly and before he could spring up, I lunged forward, wrapping my arms around him and pinning his arms next to his body. Bakos bellowed, fighting me, surprisingly strong for an old, fat man and Josh moved like lightning to the back of the chair. Bakos screamed and I barely heard the crack of his wrist breaking under the shrill sound. And then Josh was next to me, the knife in his hand and his gun at Bakos's temple.

I let go, stepping back quickly as Bakos breathed harshly, bringing his untied wrist around his body and cradling it as a storm of rage moved through his eyes.

I took the knife from Josh and tossed it on the table. As I

was beginning to move around Bakos to re-tie his bindings, I glanced down to Josh's hand and I saw it fist, but I didn't stop him. Once again, Josh moved forward like lightning and punched him in the face, Bakos's head whipping back and blood flying out of his nose. His head lolled on his neck, the arm with the broken wrist dropping down by his side— he was out cold.

Josh turned around, his jaw clenching as he shook his hand out. "Holy shit. Hidden rooms with trapdoors? He got me with some *Scooby-Doo* shit." He ran his hand through his hair, letting out a small, humorless laugh.

I shook my head. I was sure he was affected by hearing how the girl we had come to rescue had ended up shot in the head. So was I. I clapped him lightly on his shoulder. "Let's go, Shaggy. I believe we have a delivery for the head prosecutor on your case. Call the police and give 'em the address where they can find this waste of space." I nodded back toward an unconscious Bakos. "Let's move," I said quietly.

Ten minutes later, we were pulling around the corner as we heard the sirens moving in the direction of the warehouse.

CHAPTER 35
Grace

Two weeks later

I pulled the straps of my dress over my shoulders and smiled into the mirror. The last two weeks had gone by in a whirlwind. A happy whirlwind but an intense one.

After presenting the videotape evidence to Larry, we took it to the judge and the murder case against Josh was dismissed a couple days later. Bakos had attempted to recant what he'd said on tape, claiming it was taken under duress and he had lied to save the lives of his family, but the evidence found in the warehouse and the phones that had been confiscated was far too overwhelming. The murder he had framed Josh for was only one of the charges filed against him.

Larry, my boss, the DA, had come to me the next day and asked me if I would trust him to present an idea to his contacts and good friends, higher-ups in the police department.

And so on a cold, drizzly Sunday in the beginning of

January, Carson, Josh, Leland, and Dylan had sat behind closed doors for three hours, while I chewed my nails to the quick and jumped every time my cell phone rang.

Finally, when I was so wound up, I didn't think I could wait a second longer, there was a knock on my door and when I pulled it open, Carson was standing in my doorway, grinning.

I had squealed and jumped into his arms, kissing his face again and again. "They agreed?"

"Yup. You're looking at not just a member but also the leader of the Vegas PD Sexual Trafficking Task Force. First of its kind."

I sucked in a breath and tears sprung to my eyes. Larry had listened to my story about how I had come by the tape and although I didn't say that I knew the names of the group members other than Josh, he didn't ask. A couple days later, he had asked me if I thought I could contact them with an opportunity. People he trusted wanted to talk to them.

It turned out that the police department didn't have a budget for their own task force, but they were very interested in getting behind one that took care of its own training and budget. They wanted to do more in the world of trafficking but their hands were tied. And so Carson and the guys now had the full support of law enforcement behind them, without having to strictly work within the guidelines of the police department. That last part may not have been spelled out exactly, but it was understood.

Carson's team would still focus on rescuing the victims, and they would still put them up at the hotel while their transport home was being arranged. But now they could also focus more energy and effort on tracking the location of the people in charge of the crime and turning them over to the police without raising questions. It was still a dangerous job, but I would rest easier knowing that it was a legitimate operation, and although there were plenty of risks, a possible prison sentence wasn't one of them.

Trafficking crime in Vegas was already lower because of their team. Word had gotten around that Vegas wasn't the best place to do business if human beings were your commodity. But unfortunately, it would never stop completely. It was a sad truth that where there was money to be made, there would always be someone to sell their soul to the devil.

But my heart belonged to one of the *good guys*, and his heart belonged to me.

Work had picked up for me too. I was given the case of prosecuting Gabriel Bakos, my first actual murder trial, or at least the first one that would end up going to court. Once the trafficking charges came to light, the case was suddenly thrust into the limelight, both on a local level and also on a national level. I didn't necessarily love being involved in something high profile, but I was glad that human trafficking was being discussed. People needed to know the reality of it if they were going to be inspired to help the cause.

Alex had decided to take the job in San Francisco after all. We had sat down and talked, and he had assured me that it wasn't solely because of our breakup but that he thought it would be a good thing for both of us anyway. I wished him nothing but happiness. He was a good man—he just wasn't the man for me.

I took a deep breath and finished my hair and makeup. As I was putting on my charm bracelet, I heard a knock at my door.

I opened it and there he was, standing before me in all his masculine beauty. I leaned my head to the side and rested it against the open door as I held it steady. I sighed in appreciation as I took him in: gray suit pants, black dress shoes, and a light blue dress shirt.

He grinned. "You look beautiful, buttercup."

I smiled back. "Thank you, Agent Stinger," I said, opening the door wider for him to pass through.

He gathered me in his arms and kissed me as I brought my hands up to his hair, a little longer now, more like it had been the first time we met. I felt its silky texture under my fingers and thought about the first time he had kissed me, on that elevator a million years ago.

I pulled my lips away from his and gazed up into those hazel eyes, thinking about who he had been and what he had become, a fierce pride swelling in my heart.

"What?" he asked, his eyes moving over my face.

"You," I said, my smile fading. "You're stunning. On the outside, but even more so on the inside. The world is a better place with you in it, Carson Stinger."

"I'm better by your side," he told me. "It turns out the world needed us after all, buttercup." He paused, rubbing his nose against mine. "I love you, Grace Hamilton."

"I love you too."

"Ready to go celebrate?"

"You have no idea."

Twenty minutes later, we were walking into the bar at the Bellagio where I had walked away from Carson Stinger, Straight Male Performer, all those years ago. What a crazy, unexpected ride from that moment to this one.

Josh was there, busy hitting on a pair of blonds sitting at the bar, and Leland and Dylan were sitting at a table, chatting.

We approached the table and the men turned and smiled, greeting me and Carson, Dylan saying, , "Hey, Prosecutor!"

When the first round of drinks came, Leland raised his glass first and looked around at the guys. "To Ara," he said. "Always."

"To Ara," they said in unison. And we raised our glasses and toasted in memory to the girl whose life and death inspired a group of good men to go to radical lengths to save others like her. It was her legacy, her last gift to the world. And it meant that she hadn't died in vain.

We laughed and talked and celebrated that night. Celebrated all they had accomplished, all they had overcome, and all that they would always work to vindicate.

As Dylan was in the middle of telling a story, I caught Carson's eye and I smiled. As he smiled back, his eyes warm and happy, I thought back to our first exchange in this very bar, and how I had thought I hated him. I looked at the same man in front of me now, the man I knew I never wanted to live without. And I thought to myself, *Life is wild.*

Carson

I hung up the phone and sat at my desk thinking about the call I had just been on. I had spoken with the Houston chief of police. He wanted us to organize a similar task force in their city, as human trafficking was a growing crime, and they simply didn't have the resources to address it.

I'd have to talk to Leland, but I thought it was a good possibility that we could get something going there, maybe not just in Houston but in other cities as well. He had a lot of contacts—wealthy contacts—that would have the means to fund an operation like ours.

Leland was out today, and so I opened my computer and started composing an email that he would see tomorrow morning, outlining all my thoughts on the proposal, making sure I wrote it all down while it was still fresh in my mind.

Just as I was finishing up, I heard a soft knock on my door and called, "Come in."

Grace peeked inside and smiled. "Hey, baby, this is a nice surprise," I said.

"I brought lunch," she said, holding up a couple of takeout bags. "Hot dogs."

I laughed. "God, that sounds good. How'd you know I love hot dogs?" I asked teasingly as she placed the bags down and walked around my desk to sit on my lap.

"Oh, I know everything about you, Carson Stinger," she said, a glint in her eye.

"You think so, do you?" I asked, smiling and kissing her neck.

She laughed as I tickled her ear with my tongue. "Mm-hmm," she said. "But." She paused. "You don't know everything about me."

"Oh really?"

She shook her head. "No. I have a secret."

"A secret? Ah, well, how about we play a little game then? A shot for a secret?"

She paused. "Well, okay." She leaned forward and took the pens out of the cup on my desk and moved it to the far edge. Then she reached into her purse, next to the takeout bags, and pulled out a dime.

I took it from her hand. "Last time I won your secret, my whole life changed."

She just smiled, tilting her head in the direction of the cup.

What was she up to, exactly? I lined up my shot and threw the dime. Perfect shot. Yup, still had it. "Give it up, buttercup," I said.

She took in a big breath and blew it out. "So, as it turns out, your boys are really good swimmers too," she said quietly.

"My boys?" I asked, confused.

She just kept staring at me.

And then I suddenly understood and my whole body froze. "You're pregnant?"

She nodded, still watching me nervously.

"You're pregnant," I repeated, letting it sink in. "We're having a baby."

"Yes," she confirmed.

I couldn't help the grin that spread over my face.

"You're happy?" she whispered, relief dancing across her features.

"Yes, buttercup, I'm happy." I smiled. "Very happy."

She laughed, but it sounded like there was a small sob beneath it.

"Did you think I wouldn't be?"

She shook her head. "I thought you'd be happy, but I wasn't sure... The timing... I know you have a lot going on and we're..."

"Grace," I said, looking into her eyes. "I'm happy," I repeated, letting her see in my face that it was true.

When she nodded, tears appearing in her eyes, I said, "Marry me, Grace. Marry me today. Let's go to one of those chapels on the Strip. We're already practically living together. Let's make it official."

She laughed through her tears. "I don't want you to marry me because I'm pregnant."

"Marry you because… Grace, I've been waiting to marry you for five years now. Maybe I didn't exactly know it, but it's true."

She laughed and then leaned in and kissed me softly before replying, "Okay, I'll marry you. But not in a chapel on the Strip. I want our friends and family there."

"Okay, whatever you want, buttercup."

After a minute, I pulled away from Grace, frowning as something occurred to me.

"What?" she asked.

I put my hand on her belly. "I think this needs to be a boy. I don't know if I can handle having a daughter."

She smiled a gentle smile at me, understanding my reasons for that. "If I remember my biology lessons correctly, the man is in charge of the baby's sex."

I breathed out. "Okay, then it's in the bag," I said. I bent down and whispered to her belly, "Hey, Junior."

She grinned and kissed me, for the second time giving me a secret and changing my life.

EPILOGUE
Grace

One year later

"That is the saddest tree I've ever seen," Audrey muttered, tilting her head to look at it.

I laughed, stepping back and admiring the half-bare, leaning tree, weighed down by the heavy strands of outdoor lights, standing—for now anyway—in the middle of our cabin.

"I love it," I sighed. "Anyway, it's our first tradition. Don't knock it."

Audrey continued to look at the tree with a disapproving expression. I swatted her playfully on her ass.

She let out a shriek and jumped away from me, laughing. "Fine, fine. Maybe I'll learn to love it too." She looked at the tree and tilted her head again.

I grinned, shaking my head. I started to turn toward the kitchen, where I was in charge of basting the twenty-pound Christmas Eve turkey we had in the oven, when the door burst open and all the men came crashing loudly into the cabin.

"We're back, ladies," Josh yelled. "Who's in for naked hot-tubbing?"

I laughed and Audrey rolled her eyes. I saw her look around Josh, her eyes landing on Dylan. He caught sight of her and stilled, adjusting his glasses. *Interesting.* I'd have to ask her about that later. I'd noticed more than a few heated looks going on between those two this week.

Just as Carson had promised me a year ago, we had come back to Snowbird for Christmas. Only this time, our family and friends were with us and instead of lots to worry about, we had much to celebrate.

Unfortunately, there was one person who hadn't been able to join us and that was Abby. But she had a really good reason—she was almost nine months pregnant and not able to fly. Her little boy, Kyle, and the new baby would only be thirteen months apart, but as Abby said, that's what happens when you drink three margaritas on your first night out postpartum. A warning to us all. Truthfully, her and Brian were thrilled.

We had rented a big, ten bedroom "cabin" and had spent the week skiing, snowboarding, and playing in the snow, with me strictly doing the latter. My muscles still remembered last year's lesson and weren't interested in signing up for more. Everyone had at least one gift. Snowboarding was not mine.

"Carson missed an epic afternoon on the slopes," Leland said, hanging his jacket up.

"I was busy doing something way better," Carson said, coming out of the bedroom, our daughter curled up on his chest. "I was cuddling in front of the fire with my girls." He grinned. "And decorating our tree." All the men looked over at the tree Carson was referring to and tilted their heads as a unit. I huffed out a breath as Carson walked up to me and put one arm around my shoulders, kissing my head.

"Oh God, he's choosing cuddling and decorating over sports," Josh muttered. "Time to hand in your man card, Carson." Josh shook his head, feigning deep sadness.

Carson raised his brows. "Yeah, your day is coming, my man. Mark my words. And when it does, payback is a bitch."

"Hey, watch your mouth. My girls are in this room," my dad said, coming out of his room where he had been napping.

Carson looked appropriately repentant as he said, "Sorry, sir," but a corner of his lip quirked up as my dad walked by and punched his shoulder lightly.

The truth was, my dad and Carson couldn't have been any closer. My dad loved both his sons-in-law, but he and Carson had a special bond. Maybe it was because Carson had never had a dad of his own and my dad got the "man's man" he always wanted in a son, maybe he just saw how well Carson loved us, but whatever it was, they loved and respected each other. It reminded me that I had never been meant to be everything for my father, and that that had been a losing battle. But in following my heart, I'd ended up bringing another person into my family's life who helped fill the hole my brother had left. Funny how fate worked that way. It warmed my heart and had me constantly fighting back tears when I watched them together.

We had invited my mom to come for the weekend too, but she had declined, even when my sisters and I suggested renting two cabins. I wished we were closer, especially now that I had a daughter of my own, but I couldn't do all the work in our relationship. Maybe someday she'd realize that she had responded to loss by creating more loss, and she'd seek to repair it. I hoped that would be the case, but I thought more likely that too much time had already passed. It was one of my biggest heartbreaks, but I vowed every day that it was going to inspire me to pull people closer, not push them away.

Carson had written his own mother a letter and sent her a picture of our daughter, Ella, when she was born—an olive branch that he extended to the woman who had given him life but simply hadn't been capable of giving him much more than that when he was a boy.

She had written him back and they were corresponding with letters and pictures. He still seemed cautious, but it was a start.

I smiled up at my husband, and then I turned my eyes to our baby and kissed her on her blond head. "Hey, little miss," I said. "How come you're not sleeping?"

"We're working on it," Carson said. Then he leaned in and whispered, "I was telling her this really good story about a girl I fell in love with once upon a time between the twenty-first and twenty-second floor."

"Ah," I said, looking at our daughter, "no wonder you wanted to stay up for that one. That's a really great story. Some angst, some heartbreak, some really unexpected twists, but the most wonderful HEA." I touched her nose with my index finger gently and she gave me a gummy smile, her hazel eyes lighting up at the attention, that small dimple that I loved so much popping out to the left of her lower lip. Carson smiled too, showing that twin dimple. Double whammy.

"It really is a great story," he agreed.

"I hope it was the PG version, however," I said.

He chuckled softly, his eyes warm.

"Hey, Sis, are you helping in here or what?" Julia called from the kitchen. She and Evan were on mashed potato duty and as I listened to the bangs and soft swears coming from the kitchen, I stifled a laugh. "Sounds like it's getting serious in there. I better go. Sleep well, baby girl," I said, kissing her again and smiling at Carson as he turned to take her back to the room where we had a portable crib set up.

As I walked toward the kitchen, I turned my head to watch them move away. My husband and our daughter. There are many soul-stirring sights in this world, but not many as profound as watching the beautiful man you love holding the baby you created together. No, not many.

Carson

I held my baby daughter in my arms, rocking her in the big, upholstered rocking chair in the guest room, loving her so intensely that it felt like a tangible thing. I put my nose to her head and breathed in the sweet smell of her. I would do anything to protect her, to keep her safe, to make sure she always felt loved.

I had made it my life's work to rescue women from suffering, and most of the time, I felt steady and competent in the part I played in that endeavor. But when it came to the lifelong job of protecting the one small girl in my arms, I felt a tremble of fear inside. I supposed that was as it should be.

As Ella snuggled into me, and her eyes started to flutter closed, I let my mind wander to the first little girl who had set a fire alight in my gut that burned for justice. *Ara*. Once upon a time, someone had held her in their arms like this. Once upon a time, someone had held each little girl just like this. And if they didn't, they should have. I closed my eyes, rocking, rocking, my daughter exhaling her sweet baby breath, her tiny, chubby hand fisting my T-shirt.

I wanted her to be proud of me. I wanted her to see how I loved and worshipped her mother and want nothing less than that for herself one day. To be loved completely, body, heart, and soul. To be understood. To be *known*.

Someday, I would have to have a very difficult conversation with her about the choices I had made before I knew better. I cringed with the thought, but the fact of the matter was, the internet is forever, and it would be better that she hear it from me.

I thought about who I was when I first met Grace, all the ways in which I defined myself back then. Sometimes, you don't even realize anything is wrong until someone comes along and changes you and makes you want more. In my case, it was a beautiful girl with a plan who shattered the world I thought I knew. And when I put the pieces back together, they were all rearranged, different—and so was I. Until her, I had never even considered the possibilities.

In life, there are those who save us, both in big ways and in small. Sometimes that means being set free from a dark, windowless room or being pulled out of a burning building. More often, it means being saved from yourself and made to finally believe that letting someone love you isn't just a big lie that you're unwilling to tell.

Grace had saved me by calling my bluff and then listening to the secrets I believed made me unlovable, with acceptance in her eyes. The gift she gave me was her glow—and it shined for me so brightly that my own darkness disappeared.

I kissed our daughter again, now sleeping peacefully on my chest, lost in her own world of dreams, safe and loved in my arms.

Author's Note

This story is a work of fiction, but human trafficking (also known as modern-day slavery) is very real. Today, 50 million people are being trafficked. Modern-day slavery disproportionately affects women and girls, who make up 71% of total victims. For more information and ways you can help, visit:

www.ourrescue.org
www.polarisproject.org
www.fbi.gov/investigate/violent-crime/human-trafficking

Acknowledgments

Special, special thanks from the bottom of my heart, once again, to my Executive Editing Committee, Angela Smith and Larissa Kahle. This time around, I was also lucky enough to have an amazing group of beta readers who were not only tough but were thoughtful and connected to Grace and Carson's story, and gave invaluable advice and commentary: Elena Eckmeyer, Karleigh Lewis-Brewster, Kim Parr, Nikki Larazo, and Stacey Price—endless love and thanks! Gratitude, as always, to my family for putting up with me through this process, and to my amazing husband for picking up the slack around our house with an endless amount of patience. I am so lucky to have you.

An add on huge thank you to the editors at Bloom for your time and patience with this story: the second one I ever told and filled with all that I didn't know. Thank you for helping me shine it up, add needed depth, and bring it into present day.

About the Author

Mia Sheridan is a *New York Times*, *USA Today*, and *Wall Street Journal* bestselling author. Her passion is weaving true love stories about people destined to be together. Mia lives in Cincinnati, Ohio, with her husband. They have four children here on earth and one in heaven.

Mia can be found online at:

MiaSheridan.com
Twitter, @MSheridanAuthor
Instagram, @MiaSheridanAuthor
Facebook.com/MiaSheridanAuthor